Mother Goose Refigured

SERIES IN FAIRY-TALE STUDIES

General Editor
Donald Haase, Wayne State University

Advisory Editors
Cristina Bacchilega, University of Hawai'i, Mānoa
Stephen Benson, University of East Anglia
Nancy L. Canepa, Dartmouth College
Anne E. Duggan, Wayne State University
Pauline Greenhill, University of Winnipeg
Christine A. Jones, University of Utah
Janet Langlois, Wayne State University
Ulrich Marzolph, University of Göttingen
Carolina Fernández Rodríguez, University of Oviedo
Maria Tatar, Harvard University
Jack Zipes, University of Minnesota

A complete listing of the books in this series
can be found online at wsupress.wayne.edu

Mother Goose Refigured

A Critical Translation of Charles Perrault's Fairy Tales

Christine A. Jones

Wayne State University Press
Detroit

ISBN 978-0-8143-3892-6 (paper) | ISBN 978-0-8143-3893-3 (e-book)
Library of Congress Control Number: 2016937228

Published with the assistance of a fund established by Thelma Gray James of Wayne
State University for the publication of folklore and English studies.

Designed and typeset by Charles Sutherland, E.T. Lowe Publishing Co.
Composed in Minion Pro

Wayne State University Press
Leonard N. Simons Building
4809 Woodward Avenue
Detroit, Michigan 48201-1309

Visit us online at wsupress.wayne.edu

For my godchildren,

Paul Robert Ryan

James O'Connell

Lindy O'Connell

Contents

Acknowledgments

Insights about how mature and playful the Mother Goose fairy tales look in seventeenth-century French began making sense for me over the course of two years, roughly 2007–9. At that time, I was asked to translate authorial prefaces to the seventeenth-century editions of Charles Perrault's *Histoires ou Contes du temps passé* for the volume *Fairy Tales Framed*, edited by Ruth B. Bottigheimer (Albany: SUNY Press, 2013). During this first experience wielding the pen of the translator, I found myself amazed again and again by how witty, strangely vernacular, and sometimes snarky the language felt. Jokes of the slapstick variety I associate with Molière poke fun at the lifestyle of the very men and women to whom Perrault dedicates the volume; narrators speak in multiple voices, presenting an unstable moral universe; the stated morals of the tales hardly serve to make their lessons clearer, especially when there are two that deliver quite different ideas. I thank Ruth Bottigheimer for commissioning these translations and encouraging my interest in their complex poetics and modern sense of humor. In 2010, when my collaborator Jennifer Schacker and I began gathering translations of Perrault's tales for *Marvelous Transformations* (Peterborough, ON: Broadview, 2012), we realized that none satisfied our interest in making it easier to teach Perrault as a funny, ironic writer. And so it was that I did new translations of three fairy tales. Eventually my cherished colleague convinced me to translate the collection. I owe her a great debt for sharing and encouraging my enthusiasm.

Several scholars, some known to me and others unknown, read the manuscript with an eye to improving it. To all of them I am grateful. My University of Utah colleague Eric Laursen saw more versions of this book than I care to admit and always steered me back to the best version of my voice. The anonymous readers consulted by Wayne State University Press gave me a spectacular range of comments and a host of titles to consult that taught me how better to tailor these arguments for a wide academic and public audience. Of those readers whose names are known to me, I owe special thanks to Annie Martin and Donald Haase, who not only read and appreciated the project but went to bat for it. Discussions with Anne

Duggan about how Perrault and feminism do or do not intersect were an invaluable source of insight. I thank all other members of the WSUP Series in Fairy-Tale Studies editorial board, who also had a hand in moving the book to final contract, and Robin DuBlanc for expertly copyediting the manuscript. She became an interlocutor in ways I did not expect, found great solutions to pesky problems, and helped me make user-friendly formatting decisions. As for the book's design, I am grateful to Matt Saunders for granting me the right to use his beautiful art and to Bryce Schimanski for creating an eye-catching cover around it.

Three generous grants made research for this book possible. A University of Utah Great Ideas in the Humanities grant allowed me to do research at the Osborne Collection of Early Children's Books in Toronto, the Pierpont Morgan Library in New York, and the Cotsen Children's Library at Princeton University to piece together the translation history that became a crucial backdrop for this book. A National Endowment for the Humanities Summer Stipend funded the first months of work on the translations. Thanks to the support of a Publishing Grant awarded by the Textbook and Academic Author Association, I was able to add the images from the *Mercure galant* and hire Robert Swanson, whom I trust, to index the book.

Finally, a word of thanks to my parents, who have by now read more fairy tales than they ever knew were written, and my sister, whose website womenyoushouldknow.net has been an important public forum for me to try out alternative theories of how to read fairy tales. And a personal note of gratitude to my partner Muriel, as always, for living through this publishing adventure with me. This book is dedicated to three extraordinary people by whom I have the pleasure of being called godmother.

Author's Note

The image captions in the Introduction, the footnotes throughout the book, and the Annotated Bibliography preserve historical capitalization when possible and the original orthography. However, capitalization of titles has been standardized in the body of the Introduction for ease of reading.

All translations from period dictionaries are the author's own.

Introduction

Mother Goose and Charles Perrault

Charles Perrault (1628–1703) published the *Histoires ou Contes du temps passé* (Stories or Tales of the Past) in French in 1697 during what scholars call the first "vogue" of such tales produced by learned writers in France.[1] The genre that we now know so well was then new, an uncommon kind of literature in the epic world of Louis XIV's court. A little volume with big impact, Perrault's inaugural collection of French fairy tales featured characters that soon, over the course of the eighteenth century, became icons of social history in France and abroad. Today they are no less a part of our cultural fabric in North America:

> "La Belle au bois dormant" (Sleeping Beauty)[2]
> "Le Petit chaperon rouge" (Little Red Riding Hood)
> "La Barbe bleue" (Blue Beard)
> "Le Maître chat; ou, Le Chat botté" (The Master Cat; or, Puss in Boots)
> "Les Fées" (The Fairies)
> "Cendrillon; ou, La Petite pantoufle de verre" (Cinderella; or, The Little Glass Slipper)
> "Riquet à la houppe" (Ricky with the Tuft)
> "Le Petit poucet" (Hop o' My Thumb)

The eight delightful tales of the *Histoires ou Contes du temps passé* were inaugural in the sense that, in the 1690s, Perrault was one of only a handful of writers who tried their hands at the new genre. They did not simply "write" fairy tales, they invented the form as we know it today. Older genres,

---

[1] Mary Elizabeth Storer uses the term vogue (*mode*) in the early twentieth century to describe the sudden appearance of the form, the participation of a dozen authors, and the immense output of several of them during the last decade of the seventeenth century. *Un Episode littéraire de la fin du XVIIe siècle: La Mode des contes de fées (1685–1700)* (Paris: Champion, 1928).

[2] These are the English titles by which the tales are most commonly known, which are used throughout the introductory parts of the book for clarity.

such as the folktale (*conte*), Italian literary tale (*fabula*), and the fable (*fable*) had a rich history before 1690, but when learned French writers tailored them to the courtly world of Louis XIV's France, they gathered together the marvelous features that we now associate with fairy tales: sumptuous balls, ogres, sophisticated animals, vengeful and well-dressed fairies, and the like. And none of the 112 French fairy tales penned by writers over the course of fifteen years, 1690–1715, enjoyed the enduring popularity of Perrault's *Histoires ou Contes du temps passé*.[3] Other writers of the day, Marie-Catherine d'Aulnoy, for example, who coined the term "fairy tale," enjoyed significant fame in the eighteenth century.[4] Still, her longer, more complex stories— save one or two—did not have the same widespread appeal as what Perrault called *les contes de ma Mère l'Oye*, "the Mother Goose tales." Although he was an author with a long life in court service and writing, Perrault's legacy in literary and cultural history rests on the fame of these brief, pithy tales. And these stories, in turn, owe their legacy as much to their many translations—begun in 1729—as to Perrault's French.

Petit chaperon rouge, Belle au bois dormant, Cendrillon, Maître chat— the characters as they were created in French in 1697—are generally not as recognizable to English speakers today as are Little Red Riding Hood, Sleeping Beauty, Cinderella, and Puss in Boots. While that may be an inevitable, even desirable, effect of the tales' translation into English, it has a consequence taken up by this study: these seemingly timeless and fixed names in English mask the rich historical and linguistic environment of seventeenth-century French out of which these fairy-tale castles, magic, and opulent balls emerged. The same might be said of the author, Charles Perrault, whose name no longer readily attaches, as it once did, to the royal personalities of the French characters, as they have become naturalized in English. Other authorities, notably the nursery rhyming Mother Goose and the Walt Disney Studios, have lent their names and identities to many popular versions of these fairy tales today. More than French heritage, rhymes and animated films are the lenses through which generations of North Americans view fairy-tale history. Those lenses prove thickly layered because ideas about these fairy tales—and particularly their female characters—spread quickly in translation, with

---

[3]Henceforth, the French title appears shortened to *Histoires ou Contes*.

[4]In Marie-Catherine d'Aulnoy's *Histoire d'Hypolite, Comte de Duglas* (1690) a character tells a tale, "L'Isle de la félicité" (The Island of Happiness), which made it the first fairy tale published in France. Eight years later, in 1698, d'Aulnoy published her own multivolume collection under the title *Les Contes des fées* (Tales of the Fairies), which became "fairy tales" in English by the end of the eighteenth century. Two collections had appeared before hers, Perrault's in 1697 and Marie-Jeanne Lhéritier de Villandon's *Les Oeuvres meslées* (Diverse Works) in 1696.

long-lived and wide-reaching impact in the English-speaking world, where they have achieved the status of cultural lore.

Translating the 1697 *Histoires ou Contes* means grappling not only with the strangeness of seventeenth-century French but also with the ubiquity and familiarity of plots and heroines in their famous English versions. From the very first British translation by Robert Samber in 1729, traditions and characteristics of enduring recognition were established. This dependable identification, although it ensured transhistorical fame for these seventeenth-century princes and princesses, makes innovative translation a challenge. For example, can Perrault's invented name Cendrillon be retranslated into something other than Cinderella? And what would happen to our understanding of the tale if it were? Is it possible to sidestep the anglophone tradition and view the seventeenth-century French anew? Such questions inspired the translations in this volume, which aim to regenerate critical interest in heroines and heroes that seem frozen in time.

But why not leave Cinderella alone, as she is deeply engrained in cultural lore and beloved the way she is? A first answer to that question is concern about the modern sense of her integrity as a cultural icon, which is misleading. Cinderella is not singular but plural, not a stable identity but a constantly shifting one. She is made of so many different versions of identity layered up in printed, oral, and visual media that she might be called a "palimpsest."[5] Second, each iteration of the heroine has many facets that we cannot see on the surface. To get at what exploring these facets could offer readers, in this introduction and the following "Notes on Editions, Translations, and Interpretations" I lay out and challenge various cultural and academic perspectives that are operative in how we encounter the Mother Goose fairy tales today. Although the full tapestry of the history of these tales, whose fame is worldwide and which have been recast in dozens of media, cannot be contained in a single genre history or study of a national tradition (much less in an introduction), a good start will be to put North

---

[5]Martine Hennard coins this term to talk about a quality in the relationship between the French text and other previous and subsequent versions of Perrault's tales that emerges in Angela Carter's translation: "The palimpsest-like quality of the modern fairy tale becomes noticeable in the translation, coloured as it is by memories of Grimm's 'Rotkäppchen': in the opening sentence, Perrault's *petite fille de village* is conveyed by *deep in the heart of the country, there lived a pretty little girl . . .* , which immediately evokes the imagery and *folk* setting of Grimm's tales." Martine Hennard Dutheil de la Rochère, "Updating the Politics of Experience: Angela Carter's Translation of Charles Perrault's 'Le Petit chaperon rouge,'" *Palimpsestes* 22 (2009): 189.

American presuppositions into dialogue with early modern French cultural history (Introduction) and the volume's translation past (Notes).

Each section of this introduction reviews and explores inherited wisdom about the plots and characters in the *Histoires ou Contes* with a view to interrogating common and sometimes cherished interpretations of the tales. The first three sections each take up a key figure in that cultural history: Princess Elisabeth Charlotte and Mother Goose, Cinderella as a case study in North America, and the biography of Charles Perrault as an author. The next two parts pick up from the biography of Perrault to highlight key texts in his bibliography as anchors for beginning to rethink the textual strategies that emerge in the fairy tales of the *Histoires ou Contes*.

A Princess and a Goose

Perrault chose the now-legendary name *Contes de ma Mère l'Oye* (Tales of Mother Goose) for the title of the very first incarnation of his volume of fairy tales: a handwritten manuscript decorated with brightly hand-colored gouache illustrations. The manuscript was dedicated and presented to Elisabeth Charlotte de Bourbon d'Orléans, first princess of France and niece of Louis XIV, and she would remain its dedicatee in the 1697 publication of the book version as well. The book's frontispiece—the image that precedes the title page—depicts the eponymous character Mother Goose as an older woman holding a distaff (as though spinning in suspended animation) and speaking to a group of youthful aristocrats before a fireplace (see figure 1). As Jacques Barchilon and Henry Pettit, and many critics since have noted, the metaphor of a maternal goose and the weighty humanity of the figure in the image evoke aged female wisdom, matronly tasks, and peasant stories.[6]

In English-speaking cultures, parents and children may associate Mother Goose with the voice behind children's stories and nursery rhymes. As early as the late eighteenth century, parents could purchase scores for nursery rhymes entitled *Mother Goose's Melody*.[7] Maurice Ravel also used the title for children's music in his *Ma Mère l'Oye* (Mother Goose)

---

[6]Jacques Barchilon and Henry Pettit, introduction to *The Authentic Mother Goose Fairy Tales and Nursery Rhymes*, ed. Jacques Barchilon and Henry Pettit (Denver: Alan Swallow, 1960), 8–10.

[7]Barchilon and Pettit report that the Newbery publishing house, then under the direction of John Newbery (d. 1767), hatched the plan to publish well-known rhymes under this title in the 1750s, although the only extant edition, which they reproduce in the volume, dates from the 1790s. Ibid., 11.

Figure 1. Frontispiece of Charles Perrault's 1695 manuscript, "*Contes de ma Mère l'Oye*." (The Pierpont Morgan Library, New York.)

suite—"five juvenile pieces for piano, duet"—in 1908. And the expression itself proves far older than that. Indeed, the language of *ma Mère l'Oye* already had a juvenile connotation in Perrault's day. The *Dictionnaire de l'Académie française* identifies the title with "the tales told to amuse children."[8] Barchilon has traced the possible origins of the expression to the historic practice of tending geese in a village, a task entrusted to older women.[9]

Certainly, the clash in register signaled by the clothing of the subjects in the picture lends itself to the idea that the seated woman is of a lower social class than the smaller figures around her. The room too looks simple and bare. It is as though aristocrats have been transported into a world quite different from their own to enjoy Mother Goose's stories. This space and the teller look unsophisticated on a first glance, belonging to a world of hard work and traditional values. Nonetheless, the image is simultaneously highly allegorical. The woman reaches for the yarn she is spinning at the top of her distaff and draws it down to her spindle, at once miming the act of spinning and demonstrating—her mouth open—its metaphorical association with storytelling. The frontispiece offers our first glimpse into the complex web of registers in which the volume works.[10]

One way to consider the allegorical impact of this image is to read it as a composite—not as a scene that occurred but as a story about tales and who appreciates them. Each figure could then represent a different element of the story: the teller recalls a long tradition of women figured as storytellers, the seated young man with hair reminiscent of Louis XIV's wig could be Perrault himself, and the younger boy perhaps his son Pierre, whose relationship to the volume is taken up below.[11] The young woman with plaited hair and a muff—a telltale sign of her elevated rank—could be Princess Elisabeth Charlotte, the collection's dedicatee. The image of an older, simply dressed woman talking to a well-heeled audience personifies the same kind of confrontation—old/young, low/high, popular/worldly, common/elite—that we see in the book's simple, rural title read against the sumptuous, colorful artistry of its contents.

---

[8]"*Contes de ma mère l'oye,* Les contes dont on amuse les enfans." "Oye," *Dictionnaire de l'Académie française* (1694), artfl-project.uchicago.edu/content/dictionnaires-dautrefois. All subsequent definitions are from this edition unless otherwise noted.

[9]Barchilon and Pettit, introduction, 10.

[10]Louis Marin considered Perrault's frontispiece emblematic of the role such images play in printed books. He identified it as strategic, first emphasizing its ostensible orality, then demonstrating that the writing on the placard had a relationship to the book's title page, which it faces, and instead showed Perrault dialoguing with the print tradition. See "Préface-Image: Le frontispice des *Contes* de Perrault," *Europe* 739–40 (1990): 116; and "Les Enjeux d'un frontispice," *Esprit créateur* 27, no. 3 (1987): 53.

[11]On the tradition of the woman teller, see Marina Warner, *From the Beast to the Blonde: On Fairy Tales and Their Tellers* (New York: Farrar, Straus & Giroux, 1996).

Figure 2. Pierre Gobert, *Elisabeth Charlotte d'Orléans, duchesse de Lorraine* (1676–1744). (Photo by Jean Popovitch. Châteaux de Versailles et de Trianon, Versailles. © RMN-Grand Palais / Art Resource, NY.)

Critics tend to privilege the figure of Mother Goose and read those attributes into the stories themselves, but if the young woman in the image is an avatar of the manuscript's royal dedicatee, then Elisabeth Charlotte d'Orléans, also both mentioned and pictured, is equally as important as Mother Goose. Louis XIV's niece, who was nineteen in 1695, was the highest-ranking bachelorette in the kingdom. Known as a *petite-fille de France* (granddaughter of France) and by the name Mademoiselle at court, Elisabeth was a princess of the blood twice removed from the main royal line. She was daughter to Louis XIV's brother, Monsieur, so the daughter of a *fils de France* (son of France) who would have been next in line for the throne after the king's own sons. Mademoiselle's pedigree says something of the place these stories enjoyed at the French court. Although it was commonplace for writers to dedicate "up," by association with Mademoiselle, Perrault's stories traveled right to the very top of the royal bloodline. Thus, while the teller shown in the frontispiece has her source in the legend of goose women, the aristocrats pictured with her come to life in the learned mind and fashionable body of the first princess of France.[12]

The dedication casts her as a perspicacious reader sure to find more in the tales than meets the eye: "Mademoiselle, whatever difference there may be between the childish simplicity of these stories [*récits*] and the extraordinary constellations of knowledge that nature and education have brought together in you, I am not as worthy of blame as I may at first appear if you consider that these tales almost always contain a very wise lesson, which becomes more or less apparent according to the sharpness of the listener's perception."[13] The experiences of both listening and reading are pictured in the frontispiece, with the scene of telling complemented by writing on the wall. But the dedication adds a second consideration to this binary. The act of taking in the story—in either register—changes that story, making elements "more or less apparent." Whether one listens or reads, it matters *how* and with what mental interest; the posture of the listener/reader changes how a text is understood.

The doubling of reception modes in the frontispiece teaches a lesson in the history of the tale, which has both oral and written forms, neither of which lacks artistry and strategy. Mademoiselle's perspicacity—an effect of education tailoring natural curiosity—models how to be the volume's ideal listener/reader. The dedication invites her to engage with the superficially simple plots of the fairy tales thoughtfully with her mind. By virtue of the echo between the action of the frontispiece and the acumen attributed to

---

[12] A 2010 master's thesis by Sarah Lebasch catalogues a long list of sketches of Elisabeth Charlotte as a fashion plate wearing haute couture of the day. "Elisabeth Charlotte d'Orléans (1676–1744), une femme à la mode?" (MA thesis, Université de Nancy II, 2010), 16–104, www.masterscontributions.fr/content/elisabeth-charlotte-d-orleans-1676–1744-une-femme-a-la-mode-1.

[13] "Dedicatory Letter to Mademoiselle (1695)," in *Fairy Tales Framed: Early Forewords, Afterwords, and Critical Words,* ed. Ruth B. Bottigheimer (Stony Brook: State University of New York Press, 2013), 126. For the French, see *Perrault's Tales of Mother Goose. The Dedication Manuscript of 1695 reproduced in Collotype Facsimile with introduction and critical text,* vol. 2, ed. Jacques Barchilon (New York: The Pierpont Morgan Library, 1956), 113–15.

Figure 3: Mademoiselle featured prominently in the fashion plates of her day, modeling the latest in couture for the high court. Her hair plaiting and bodice bear some resemblance to the style worn by the standing figure in the 1695 frontispiece of Perrault's "*Contes de ma Mère l'Oye*." *Elisabeth-Charlotte de Bourbon, Mademoiselle de Chartres*, seventeenth century. (Photo by Hervé Lewandowski. Châteaux de Versailles et de Trianon, Versailles. © RMN-Grand Palais / Art Resource, NY.)

the dedicatee, Mademoiselle, the image of a clever adult reader eclipses the figure of Mother Goose as the volume's ethos. The frontispiece now announces a set of writings whose subtleties must be teased out and meanings made whole through the act of reading.

History has shown that Mademoiselle applauded the association of fairy tales with her name, as the manuscript dedication remained (edited for style) when the tales appeared in a print edition in 1697, the year she prepared to marry the Duke of Lorraine. In 1695, the princess's Mother Goose tales consisted of five fairy tales: "La Belle au bois dormant" (Sleeping Beauty), "Le Petit chaperon rouge" (Little Red Riding Hood), "La Barbe bleue" (Blue Beard), "Le Maître chat; ou, Le Chat botté" (The Master Cat; or, Puss in Boots), and "Les Fées" (The Fairies). When the handwritten pages turned into a printed book, two changes suggest that the print volume was destined for readers even older than Mademoiselle: the title was made more sophisticated and the number of stories increased by three. To make the private manuscript a public document, reference to the goose in the title was removed but did not disappear altogether; it still hung, as it did in the 1695 manuscript, on the door of the frontispiece illustration. But having lost its prominent position on the cover, it lost some of its semantic influence over the volume as a whole. The book's new title, *Histoires ou Contes*, further displaced emphasis from the teller and onto the matter told and its reception. Because the book was designed with Elisabeth d'Orléans in mind as its first reader, the print edition announces itself as a modern collection with high-class appeal.[14]

The three stories that were added to round out the collection for publication, "Cendrillon; ou, La Petite pantoufle de verre" (Cinderella; or, The Little Glass Slipper), "Riquet à la houppe" (Ricky with the Tuft), and "Le Petit poucet" (Hop o' My Thumb), have a trackable relationship to a prior print history.[15] "Cinderella" has a distant Italian relative in Giambattista Basile's

---

[14]As Marin notes, in the printed book the word *listener* was replaced by *reader*, highlighting further that the volume was for independent readers, not young listeners ("Enjeux," 53).

[15]Literary studies and folklore studies have long debated the relationship between print and oral transmission in the history of the fairy tale. Poles of the debate are currently occupied by Ruth B. Bottigheimer, *Fairy Tales: A New History* (Albany: SUNY Press, 2009), who has argued for thinking about print and orality as creating separate traditions and for the "flimsy foundation" upon which we have built the folk past (2), and Jack Zipes, *The Irresistible Fairy Tale* (Princeton: Princeton University Press, 2012), who uses a theory of memetics to argue for oral tradition as the fairy tale's "vital progenitor" (3). Many scholars find the middle ground in a theory of cross-pollination. Mine is not an argument about exclusive genealogy or known paths of transmission, as orality/performance and print go hand in hand, but rather about how the lengthy stories have a traceable print history. Recent scholarship by Christelle Bahier-Porte and Jennifer Schacker (whose work is discussed below), reminds us too that early modern media such as public plays and comedy ballets contributed significantly to that cross-pollination, creating a triple helix of influence.

"La Gatta cenerentola" (The Cinderella Cat), which first appeared in 1634 in his bawdy collection *Lo Cunto de li cunti* (*The Tale of Tales*), considered a seminal collection of literary tales in Europe.[16] The title character and plot of Perrault's "Riquet à la houppe" appeared in a story published one year earlier in a collection of fairy tales by Catherine Bernard, who frequented the same circles as Perrault.[17] Finally, the brief adventures of "Le Petit poucet" telescope the extensive trials and tribulations of Richard Johnson's 1621 "The History of Tom Thumbe."[18] Thus the three additions reference stories that a learned reader such as Mademoiselle could have encountered in print.[19] Ute Heidmann refers to this intertextual nourishment as the "dialogic poetics" of the fairy tale.[20] The designations *histoires* and *contes*, in other words, do not simply mean tales passed down orally by old women who tend geese (or children); it refers also to the rich and vibrant way in which modern authors

---

[16]Giambattista Basile, "La Gatta cenerentola," in *Lo Cunto de li cunti*, De Gian Alessio Abbattutis (Naples: Ottavio Baltano, 1634). "The Cinderella Cat," in *Giambattista Basile's The Tale of Tales, or Entertainment for Little Ones*, trans. Nancy Canepa (Detroit: Wayne State University Press, 2007), 83–89. The title of Basile's tale in English uses the conventional translation for Perrault's "Cendrillon," Cinderella, to translate the nickname of its cat-heroine Zezolla, Cenerentola, literally, "little ashes." The Neapolitan could be the source of Perrault's inventive name, also a diminutive of *cendres* (ashes) in French.

[17]Catherine Bernard's "Riquet à la houppe" is a story told by a character in her novel *Inès de Cordoue* (1696). On Bernard and the debate around this tale, see "Catherine Bernard: Introduction," in *Enchanted Eloquence: Fairy Tales by Seventeenth-Century Women Writers*, ed. Lewis Seifert and Domna C. Stanton (Toronto: Centre for Reformation and Renaissance Studies, 2010), 47–50.

[18]Richard Johnson (R.I.), *The History of Tom Thumbe, the Little, for his small stature surnamed, King Arthur's Dwarfe* (London: Thomas Langley, 1621). Part legend, part marvelous tale, Tom's story borrows both from the cycle of King Arthur stories and early British fairy lore.

[19]Where scholars of folklore classify tales according to shared tropes chronologically and synchronically, scholars of literary print history often work chronologically to find linear echoes from antecedent traditions: Basile's collection features details that appear in both "Sleeping Beauty" and "Puss in Boots." The central trope in Perrault's "The Fairies"—gemstones falling out of the good daughter's mouth—links that tale to Giovanni Francesco Straparola's 1550s collection, *Le Piacevoli notti* (*The Facetious Nights of Straparola*), wherein Biancabella's hair drops gems and a peasant girl weeps pearls ("The Snake"). In *Le Conte populaire français* (Paris: Maisonneuve et Larose, 1957–85), Paul Delarue published a version of the Little Red Riding Hood story—"Le Conte de la mère-grand" (The Grandmother's Tale)—collected by Achille Millien (1838–1927) in the Nivervais region of France circa 1870, and suggested it as an oral antecedent to Perrault's print version, though it was documented two hundred years afterward. The character of *Barbe bleue* remains enigmatic in antecedent print or projected oral history.

[20]Heidmann, who documents networks (rather than linear echoes) of influence across print history, cites Perrault's tales as the moment when the fairy tale emerged in its fully dialogic form: "Cette poétique fondamentalement dialogique des contes conçus en réponse intertextuelle et intergénérique aux ouvrages latins, italiens et français existants se met en place dès le premier recueil de Perrault." Ute Heidmann and Jean-Michel Adam, *Textualité et intertextualité des contes* (Paris: Classique Garnier, 2010), 40.

in the seventeenth century found, translated, edited, and creatively adapted books—particularly literature—of the past.

The coupling of Mother Goose and Mademoiselle, or the plain woman teller and the young *mondain* (worldly wise) royal, epitomizes a paradox in the style of the tales that scholarship has long attempted to reconcile. Are the stories primitive or modern? Are they courteous or canny? Oral tradition or literary history? As I have argued above, the collection exhibits a fundamental hybridity that can feel odd, sometimes dissonant, manifesting what linguists call "code-switching" between different registers of language: learned and popular, serious and humorous, proper and bawdy. Contradictory styles are spread across different types of characters in the collection, pointing the reader to their personalities through the way they use language. Such contradictions also inhabit the same character, who is capable of switching back and forth depending on the situation, demonstrating a level of depth and ingenuity we do not often credit to fairy-tale dwellers.

Mother Goose and the princess together framed the 1697 collection as a testament to oral history and literary poetics, both of which underwent extraordinary innovation at the hands of fairy-tale writers in the seventeenth century. This linguistic ambiguity and depth of character can be difficult to see in the twenty-first century, even reading the French, because history has provided enduring interpretations of the Mother Goose tales—"Cinderella" the most famous among them—that relieve the modern reader of the responsibility of following the model of Mademoiselle and reading carefully for subtlety. To a very great extent, twenty-first-century English-language readers come to the collection with the weight of three centuries of ideas on their shoulders. As an artifact of literary history, the *Histoires ou Contes* is not merely a book within culture; it has generated international subcultures since 1729.

The many spin-offs and adaptations these stories continue to inspire have ensured that there are not many corners of popular culture, particularly in North America, into which one or more of Perrault's heroines have not crept in their anglophone personae. Already by the late nineteenth century, Perrault's heroines had turned into cultural metaphors—symbols of a habit or disposition—and circulated culturally from the street to the most rarified intellectual work. Walter Benjamin invoked Sleeping Beauty in the title of a short essay he wrote in 1911 in which she represents the blissfully ignorant slumber of youth who do not engage with the political world around them: "Youth, however, is the Sleeping Beauty who slumbers and has no inkling of the prince who approaches to set her free."[21] In Benjamin's metaphor, he himself is the prince who will wake her with a new academic journal, following in a long line of princes who have awakened humanity to philosophical ideas. Benjamin's 1911 maiden metaphor took its cue from many late nineteenth- and early twentieth-century Sleeping Beauty characters who began to populate literature as inert objects of affection; this formal association of the character with comatose repose endures to the present. Characters thus became metaphors. Today, those metaphors have also become merchandise, with none more ubiquitously visible or sellable than Cinderella. Even more than the other characters in her coterie whose presence persists, Cinderella symbolizes how heroines act, what princesses wear, and where fairy-tale plots end.

Cinderella in North America

A search for "Cinderella" on Amazon.com reveals about fifty-five thousand items—books, dolls, movies, figurines, soundtracks, bedspreads, tiaras, costumes, "Decopacs," and even Cinderella pumpkin seeds (?!)—that keep her alive and well in the cultural imaginary. According to the shorthand by which the characters are now known, Sleeping Beauty is a helpless, innocent young woman who must be saved from herself, and Cinderella is a princess created through an arsenal of finery (merchandise). These descriptions of the heroines—which are representative of the way they appear across a spectrum of media—are the aggregate of ideas about them that have turned into folklore. Perrault did not write these characters as such, but their rich ambiguity in 1697 made them pliable enough to survive outside their French context as transcultural mythologies.

Many of Amazon's Cinderellas, which appeal to a very modern vision of the heroine, were inspired not directly by Perrault but via the Walt Disney Studios' animated film adaptation of the 1697 story, *Cinderella* (1950). Among the watershed interpretations of Perrault over the course of the twentieth century, none proved as definitive as those presented by Disney.

---

[21]Walter Benjamin, "Sleeping Beauty," in *Early Writings, 1910–1917: Walter Benjamin*, trans. Howard Eiland et al. (Cambridge, MA: Harvard University Press / Belknap, 2011), 26. The essay appeared on the occasion of the launch of a journal that Benjamin hoped to publish to inspire students to become involved in political debate on the eve of the First World War. In it he lists Schiller, Goethe, Nietzsche, Shakespeare, and Tasso among the "princes" who awoke previous generations and whose ranks he hoped to join.

Perhaps because these versions are visual and found an audience larger than that of any earlier edition of the tales, they have become woven into the social fabric thoroughly enough that they heavily influence the way we think not only about Perrault but about fairy tales in general. Jack Zipes calls that effect "Disneyfication": "Our contemporary concept and image of a fairy tale has been shaped and standardized by Disney so efficiently through the mechanisms of the culture industry that our notions of happiness and utopia are and continue to be filtered through a Disney lens even if it is myopic."[22]

Indeed, the twentieth century witnessed the convergence of a number of influences, including animation film, folkloric classification, and critical methodologies such as psychoanalysis, that still guide how modern readers read fairy tales. In addition to Disney, several important trends in critical theory impacted the public perception of the fairy tale in the twentieth century. *The Types of the Folktale: A Classification and Bibliography*, a catalogue by plot features of the world's folktales known as the ATU index, was begun by Antii Aarne (A) in the late nineteenth century, amplified and translated by Stith Thompson (T), and recently (2004) updated by Hans-Jörg Uther (U). It created a taxonomy of world folktales, emphasizing the structural and thematic elements they shared rather than their idiosyncratic nuances, thereby creating the illusion that many plots were universal.[23] Vladimir Propp's *Morphology of the Folktale* (1928) developed a structural model (morphology) for the basic plot of a wonder tale (Tales of Magic, ATU 300–749).[24] Bruno Bettelheim's popular *Uses of Enchantment* (1976) found in fairy tales the seeds of modern psychology, exploring them as road maps to adulthood that placed particular emphasis on adolescent changes and fears. In one of his more enduring interpretations, he identifies "Little Red Riding Hood" with sexual maturation and dismisses Perrault's tale as useless to children because the character is "stupid" or wanting "to be seduced."[25]

---

[22]Jack Zipes, *The Enchanted Screen: The Unknown History of Fairy-Tale Films* (London: Routledge, 2011), 17.

[23]Hans-Jörg Uther, *The Types of International Folktales: A Classification and Bibliography, Based on the System of Antti Aarne and Stith Thompson*, FF Communications no. 284–86 (Helsinki: Suomalainen Tiedeakatemia, 2004).

[24]Vladímir Propp, *The Morphology of the Folktale* [first published in Russian in 1928], trans. Laurence Scott, rev. Louis A. Wagner (Austin: University of Texas Press, 1968). Propp's morphology was based on his analysis of the Russian folktales collected by Aleksandr Afanás'ev and consists of a set of thirty-one functions or actions in sequence which, combined in a pattern, form the backbone and meaning of a wonder tale's plot.

[25]Bruno Bettelheim, *The Uses of Enchantment* (New York: Knopf, 1989), 169.

The classification of the French "Cendrillon" with dozens of others under the moniker Cinderella, coupled in the 1970s with the idea that fairy tales encode archetypal problems children face through puberty, worked together to de-emphasize the specificity of each iteration of the tale. These widely influential theories converged with Disney's seductive interpretations on movie screens—for example, Cinderella's "timeless love story"—linking tropes across fairy-tale history so that certain plots seemed universal and the particularities of each version of the lost slipper became less salient. Although they would be better described as adaptations, the Disney films pitch themselves as filmic translations "based on" the tales of Charles Perrault. As Zipes suggests, the overlay of visual imagery, such as a baby-blue dress, onto Cinderella imposed it on the long tradition behind her until its train appeared to stretch back as far as 1697.

Although any interpretation can be regarded as the standard for how to understand a literary text, a translation can achieve the status of "original" for its culture. André Lefevere describes the enormous power translation can acquire over a subject within a culture that prizes it: "It happens not infrequently that a certain translation, the first translation of such a classic to be made into a certain language, remains an authoritative text, even lives on as an authoritative text in its own right long after it has ceased to function as a translation."[26] Disney's authority as a translator looms over Perrault's stories and has created weighty expectations that make the rediscovery of Perrault's 1697 texts a challenge. Undoing those trappings to encounter and interpret older heroines in their unique cultural outfits—to read the words of the story as they are written without a prefabricated image in our heads—is not an easy task, but it is a worthwhile one. An artifact from contemporary American culture will demonstrate how historical layering accrues, why it impacts interpretation, and what value there might be in working around it.

The game Trivial Pursuit tests a player's knowledge of lore that people growing up in the United States would typically have learned. The questions target white middle-class associations and practices, the kinds of ideas treated over time by the media and reflected in school books that encapsulate history from this perspective. Rendered as a subject of trivia, then, Cinderella takes her place among the icons of mainstream American life. Classified under the category "Art & Literature," she also enjoys an elevated status as something respected by that culture and worthy of preservation. Judge your Cinderella savvy by taking the quiz.

---

[26]André Lefevere, *Translating Literature: Practice and Theory in a Comparative Literature Context* (New York: Modern Language Association of America, 1992), 121.

Question 1: "What fairy tale character has two ugly stepsisters?" If you guessed Cinderella, give yourself a point. (If you got the answer by reading down to the next question, give yourself two points for cleverness, but take away two for cheating.)

Question 2: "When is Cinderella required to leave the ball?" The witching hour, of course: midnight.

Question 3: "What does the fairy godmother transform into a coach for Cinderella?" The fairy makes her a coach with a pumpkin harvested from the garden.

Most players should now have three points. The first questions invoked a generic Cinderella figure about which one is expected to possess basic cultural knowledge. But question number 4 takes a bit of a leap: "What name did the meaner of Cinderella's stepsisters call her in the story by Charles Perrault?" This question raises the stakes of the contest, requesting specific textual information about a version of Cinderella written by one Charles Perrault in French in 1697. As the game implies by referencing him, the seventeenth-century version of the heroine's trials and tribulations left a significant mark on the tale's history. The question as it is written further implies that the generic plotline of the story as we now know it in North America has some relationship to the seventeenth-century tale, a connection that triviaholics are expected to understand.

Do you know the answer to the fourth question? A player who has studied some French and has had the pleasure of reading these fairy tales in that language might guess "Cucendron"—the name in the 1697 French edition. But Trivial Pursuit offers "Cinderwench" as the answer, a name that has its source neither in seventeenth-century French nor in Disney's movie. The moniker *wench* has its source in nineteenth-century Britain. The writers of this brainteaser reference Andrew Lang's very famous 1889 English translation of the older, meaner sister's made-up name for the ash-heroine and attribute it directly to Charles Perrault.[27] They neither identify it as a translation nor present it as a name embedded in Victorian history. That may be because

---

[27] Andrew Lang, "Cinderella," in *The Blue Fairy Book* (London: Longmans, Green, ca. 1889), 78–87. In his final volume of the the Rainbow Fairy Books series, *The Lilac Book*, Lang gave his wife, Leonora Blanche Lang, credit for much of the collecting and editing of the tales he published. Although he stands as the default name to which these volumes are attributed, she usually warrants a note of acknowledgment in discussion of his work, as here in the Folio Society's biography of Lang: "Whilst Lang also worked as the editor for his work and is often credited as its sole creator, the support of his wife, who transcribed and organised the translation of the text, was essential to the work's success." www.foliosociety.com/author/andrew-lang. See also Gillian Lathey's discussion of the women in Lang's life who did most of the translating in *The Role of Translators in Children's Literature: Invisible Storytellers* (New York: Routledge, 2010), 104.

of Lang's enduring legacy; indeed, many sources that refer to the heroine in English use "Cinderwench" as the default translation.[28] The card relies on the fact that anglophone readers have derived their knowledge of Cinderella from standard translations, even if they credit the plot to Charles Perrault.

Questions 5 and 6 work together to bring Disney to the fore as the vehicle that introduced Cinderella—that name and the aesthetics of a blue ball gown and blond bun—into the hearts and minds of Americans:

"What was the name of the devilish cat in Walt Disney's *Cinderella*?"

"What was Cinderella's real name?"

The devilish cat—Lucifer—belongs to the family of characters, along with mice, invented by Disney animators to paint Cinderella's visual social world. Animals create the plot twist many have come to love, which pits the cat against an army of helpful worker mice in a struggle for emancipation that parallels and amplifies the heroine's own plight. The word *real* in the sixth question makes it a zinger. Perrault never did give his heroine a proper name prior to the one she famously acquired from her stepsister. The first English translation of Perrault, by Robert Samber in 1729, dubbed her "Cinderilla," a spelling with a Spanish ending that was anglicized at the turn of the nineteenth century to the now-standard Cinderella.[29] But it was Disney that created the name "Ella" for the heroine to make the moniker Cinderella logical: Ella + cinder = Cinderella. Once they confect this name, the mean stepsisters turn it into an infuriating taunt, repeating it again and again in the high-pitched tones of their mocking song about the heroine. As the question is phrased, Disney gave Cinderella her real name, circa 1950.

Would you have won this round of Trivial Pursuit? Much of that depends on where you tend to get your Cinderella intel: if from children's stories in English and Disney, you would score high; if from French history

---

[28]See the annotated bibliography for earlier nineteenth-century editions that pioneered this translation, which identifies the heroine with the work of a chimney sweep. Lang's edition was followed by another in 1901 by Charles Welsh (*The Tales of Mother Goose, as first collected by Charles Perrault in 1696* [Boston: D.C. Heath, 1901]), who repeated the name Cinderwench and helped to cement its reputation. It is not uncommon for contemporary anglophone versions of the story to default to Lang for the "French Cinderella": sites.google.com/site/whichistherealcinderella/french-cinderwench.

[29]Robert Samber, trans., *Histories, or tales of past times. . . . With morals. By M. Perrault* (London: J. Pote and R. Montagu, 1729). The spelling of this name was altered at the end of the eighteenth century from Samber's Cinderilla to Cinderella. Benjamin Tabart published a single-tale edition of Samber's translation in 1804 under the title *Cinderella, or, The little glass slipper: a tale for the nursery* (London: Tabart and Co. at the Juvenile and School Library, 1804). It appears to be the first print edition with the new spelling. As Tabart's audience consisted of parents and young readers in London, there may have been an attempt in the spelling change to eliminate the Spanish flair that Samber's invented name had bestowed upon the heroine.

and scholarship, you would score low. The card makes two moves that help show how the American lore about the heroine took root. First, it presumes that the Cinderella story exists in time, but erases all historical markers in the way it casts knowledge about her. One type of erasure is linguistic: Perrault's mean sisters could not have called her Cinderwench because they were French. Another is historical: because no dates are given anywhere, all of this could have happened around the time of Disney or even after Disney. There is no interest here in showing that heroines and characters might look a certain way because of when they were born onto the page or screen.

Second, due to these erasures, Cinderella is made to operate like Johnny Appleseed or Santa Claus, a folk character whose story accrues so much cultural importance that it detaches from the time and place of its making (and remakings). Taking away the depth of her history and conflating the languages in which she has been written does something with this heroine that typifies how we have come to see her in North America: it conflates seventeenth-century French, nineteenth-century British, and twentieth-century Hollywood versions of the story. Once that happens, the story looks "timeless" and unchanging, as though the heroine has always been known as Cinderella and has always had a cat named Lucifer.

To be sure, there may be excellent reasons to consider her this way. There are, for example, innumerable versions of the Cinderella story for adults and children in English, and the same is true in other languages.[30] It becomes convenient to call all these heroines "Cinderella"—the late eighteenth-century British translation attached to Perrault's seventeenth-century French heroine—to highlight the similarities among the plots and to acknowledge that Perrault's famous print version exists alongside many others, although it dominates them in general celebrity.[31] The many instantiations of the plot indeed draw on a common transcultural thread of ideas to bring about their own Cinderellas. Similarly, as a way of testing trivia knowledge, talking about all the versions as an amalgam makes good sense.

As a way of approaching historical versions of the story, which a scholarly volume such as this one will do by highlighting a culturally specific print version, an ahistorical account of the heroine has serious drawbacks.

---

[30]For a bibliography and discussion of the collections devoted to the Cinderella plot, see Alan Dundes's introduction to *Cinderella: A Casebook*, ed. Alan Dundes (1982; repr., Madison: University of Wisconsin Press, 1988), vii.

[31]"If one were to select the single most popular version out of all the hundreds of texts of Cinderella that have been reported, that version would almost certainly be the tale told by Charles Perrault" (ibid., 14).

A recent conference and exhibit in Rome, *Cinderella as a Text of Culture*, made this case poignantly with talks on the many incarnations of Cinderella as products "related to a given geo-cultural, historical and literary and mediatic ec(h)o-system."[32] Though from the vantage point of twenty-first-century America there exist innumerable Cinderellas (and slumbering beauties and pusses that wear boots), each one of them is uniquely designed or repackaged, even when she looks as much like Disney's 1950s animation as possible. As much as retellings borrow from the past, they also reinvent the story. Every time another teller, writer, or cinematographer reimagines her tale, it benefits from creative insight—they are all "translators," that is to say, writers of the tale.

Beyond identifying us as a Disneyfied culture, Zipes has further argued that none of the present obsession with princesses like Cinderella is an accident. Disney, he finds, positioned itself through a concerted effort in branding as the primary source of fairy-tale lore for North America. Its stories are designed to be addictive and are marketed, like Coca-Cola, to be available for consumption everywhere: "If the Disney fairy-tale films constrain the utopic imaginary and fix our image of utopia through hallucinatory images, they have done this through the systematic dissemination of images in books, advertising, toys, clothing, houseware articles, posters, postcards, radio, and other artifacts that have mesmerized us into believing that the 'genuine' fairy tale is the Disney fairy tale."[33]

But why should any of this matter? The public cheats itself of the fullness of Cinderella's tale history when it sees all Cinderellas in a blond bun. Feminists, for example, have rewritten politically charged and often hilariously upside-down versions of the tale over the last fifty years, intending to challenge the Disney vision and imagine Cinderella otherwise. I am suggesting that if we look back into history, we also find many iterations that do not correspond to the popular ideas anglophone readers, especially those residing in North America, bring to these tales today. Perrault's are among those that do not, except in the most superficial ways, look like Disneyfied versions; translation can help denaturalize the stories. When historical

---

[32] *Cinderella as a Text of Culture,* "Sapienza" University of Rome, November 8-10, 2012, cinderellaroma2012eng.wordpress.com/. The conference and exhibit were published under the title *Cinderella across Cultures: New Directions and Interdisciplinary Perspectives,* ed. Martine Hennard Dutheil de la Rochère, Gillian Lathey, and Monika Woźniak (Detroit: Wayne State University Press, 2016).

[33] Jack Zipes, "De-Disneyfying Disney: Notes on the Development of the Fairy-Tale Film," (paper presented at the University of Hawaii Manoa International Symposium "Folktales and Fairy Tales: Translation, Colonialism, and Cinema," Honolulu, September 23–26, 2008), 14–15, scholarspace.manoa.hawaii.edu/handle/10125/16447.

translations aim to challenge convention, as the ones in this volume do, part of the task involves exploring how ideas about these particular stories grew into lore and what value there might be in questioning it.

Attributing Lang's 1889 translation and Disney's visual choices to Perrault delivers to Trivial Pursuit players a universal Cinderella who operates like Santa Claus: she appears to be a myth without a traceable print or performance history. There are also more pressing and political reasons to revisit the long, messy series of transformations that brought Perrault's and other classic characters down to us in the twenty-first century. Disney heroines in particular have deeply influenced aspects of American life. Trivia is not trivial in the sense that it speaks to ideas the culture takes for granted and does not interrogate. Commercial vendors and buyers alike continue to promote the Disney Cinderella, with all of her race, gender, and class issues, as an American dream. Centuries after their cultural moment and filtered especially through Disney's lens, Perrault's heroines still influence—some say afflict—us in the way they mythologize norms. Fairy-tale women in particular can look like hapless victims of fate, whether it be a happy fate like Sleeping Beauty's waking by the prince or a sad one like Little Red Riding Hood's absurd death by wolf.

Scholars have dubbed female characters in that predicament "innocent persecuted heroines."[34] They are innocent because they are young, have not yet done anything, and, when they try to, prove ineffective in acting on their own behalf; they are persecuted because they are treated badly and need help. Logically, perhaps, it is difficult to think about them as "heroines" in the conventional sense of that term. A gender divide brought to life in Technicolor by Disney thus became associated with Perrault's tales, wherein helpless young women suffered and brave young men saved them. Since the 1960s, two generations of feminist scholars, led by Marcia Lieberman, Karen Rowe, Allison Lurie, and others, have questioned the effects of fairy tales on culture and particularly on women's self-definition.[35] They called for reinterpretation of the tales to break

---

[34]The term was coined by Aleksandr Isaakovich Nikiforov as early as 1927 when he identified persecution as one of two primary activities by women in fairy tales (the other being "winning" a prince in marriage). It lived on as a subgenre in which folklorists classify the Sleeping Beauty and Cinderella stories. See the special issue dedicated to a typology of the genre and interpretations of particular stories classified in it: "Perspectives on the Innocent Persecuted Heroine in Fairy Tales," ed. Cristina Bacchilega and Steven Swann Jones, special issue, *Western Folklore* 52, no. 1 (1993).

[35]For a thorough overview of feminist scholarship on the tale, see Donald Haase, "Feminist Fairy Tale Scholarship," in *Fairy Tales and Feminism: New Approaches*, ed. Donald Haase (Detroit: Wayne State University Press, 2004), 1–36.

the damaging spell they had cast on women in North American culture. In the 1980s and 1990s, Jack Zipes, Lewis Seifert, and Patricia Hannon, working in the French tradition, identified Perrault's stories as a source of that damaging spell.[36] Since then, a host of excellent studies, several of which will be discussed below, have echoed this idea. More recently, according to a 2012 BBC report, many parents also question reading the ever-popular but now deemed politically incorrect plots of "Cinderella" and "Sleeping Beauty" to a new generation of children.[37] They register concern about modeling, or worse yet glorifying, social rules of behavior that teach children to operate according to social norms we have spent the better part of a century stripping away.

Late twentieth- and early twenty-first-century readers are right to be increasingly suspicious of the traditional Prince Charming story line and anxious about how it works to reinforce damaging stereotypes about women, people of nonstandard size or capacity, racial identity, and more—including, perhaps most glaringly, the heteronormative marriage requirement. In the case of Perrault's fairy tales, all of these preoccupations are remnants of a political and social environment in which oppressive power was in the hands of a very few—a male few—and not appearing different was a great advantage; it was, in fact, a social and political requirement to conform. Within that environment, stories like Perrault's and those of the other authors of the 1690s took the risk of interrogating classical behaviors at the absolutist court of Louis XIV by bringing disadvantaged characters into their plots and letting them star in the adventure. That the silly and dead Petit chaperon rouge should be a radical character choice in the literature of 1697 is certainly hard to perceive now from the vantage point of modern gender politics. Surprisingly, then, Charles Perrault's Cendrillon and Belle au bois dormant who, along with the hapless hooded girl, are held up as bastions of heteronormative values today, were unprecedented starlets of literature in 1690s France.

---

[36]Both Seifert and Hannon compare Perrault's tales to those of the women writers of the 1690s with considerable nuance, although they find, with Zipes, that the tensions in his narratives nonetheless reinforce patriarchal values. Lewis Seifert, *Fairy Tales, Sexuality, and Gender in France, 1690–1715: Nostalgic Utopias* (Cambridge: Cambridge University Press, 1996), 52–64. For Hannon, "Perrault's tales appear to subscribe to the view of human sexuality offered by the literature on women: identified and confined to the female body, sexuality is circumvented through codes of propriety entrusted to women." Patricia Hannon, *Fabulous Identities: Women's Fairy Tales in Seventeenth-Century France* (Amsterdam: Rodopi, 1998), 47.

[37]Reproduced under license from BBC News © 2012 BBC, www.bbc.com/news/entertainment-arts-17024101.

Imagine a world in which these characters were not the tiresome and cloying icons that inspire questionable Halloween costumes but the exception to the social rule, not a centuries-old ideal but a new way of thinking about how to navigate politics. That is the challenge of reading French fairy tales as cultural documents. Here is what that might look like:

In the seventeenth century, when Perrault wrote the story of Cendrillon, kings ruled all of Europe, an absolute monarch ruled France, and women had limited social and scant political influence. Stories of girls and their princes were not fantasy, they were the inexorable fate of any high-ranking member of society. In that world, writers of fairy tales did not so much project a dream about larger-than-life success—the way we tend to read these plots today—as draw on the material conditions of court life in France. (The myriad details in the stories that have cultural significance in the period are noted in the translations in this volume.) Monarchy accorded evident advantages to the privileged and none to the rest of society. Yet it also imposed inviolable strictures—properly fashionable attire not the least of them—on courtiers, whose lives depended upon conformity. This was especially the case for women and any man who could not or would not play by the rules. Unmarried women could end up in convents or exiled and unruly men could find themselves imprisoned.[38]

Madame de Lafayette's *La Princesse de Clèves* (1678), a landmark novel by a woman writer in France and the first psychological account of the pressures of court life, tells the story of a young woman embroiled in a love triangle at court who ends her life in a convent. The novel takes up and denounces a practice that was also the fate of women whose families could not provide a dowry or who could or would not marry for other reasons. Read in this context, at its cultural core, Perrault's "Cendrillon" looks less like a rags-to-riches tale and more like a story of how to recover from social death: find someone to lend you rank-appropriate clothing and shoes so you can move back into society and make your way to a good life.

Under an absolutist monarchy, when a Cinderella had fallen from grace, she would have to claw her way back to the top by hook or by crook and would probably fail. Failing would likely mean exile or death. Appealing to

---

[38]Further details from the novel will be discussed below. In the historical world of Louis XIV's court, fairy-tale writers Marie Catherine d'Aulnoy and Henriette-Julie de Murat both spent time in exile, d'Aulnoy for the mysterious and unresolved death of her husband and Murat for rumored transgressions that range from insulting royalty to debauchery. I list the many sources of these anecdotes in my dissertation, "Noble Impropriety: The Maiden Warrior and the Seventeenth-Century *conte de fées*" (PhD diss., Princeton University, 2002). At the beginning of Louis XIV's reign, Nicolas Fouquet, superintendent of finances from 1653 to 1661, inadvertently erred by displaying his wealth for the king's pleasure—which greatly displeased the king—and found himself jailed for life.

a fairy—should one alight in your bedroom—does not seem like an entirely foolish strategy in that situation. Dressing the part so that people take you seriously as a way to draw attention to yourself when you would otherwise go unnoticed, again, sounds logical. Finally, wanting to attend the ball where everyone in power would be in attendance and no one outside the walls would stand a chance of success makes the heroine clever and enterprising, not shallow and needy. On its merits, the story of *why* a young girl with no power would focus her mental energy on fashion savvy and marital prospects as a way back to a life of enjoyment rather than degradation is neither particularly oppressive nor out of step with seventeenth-century social sense. In several tales by women writers of the decade in which Perrault wrote, clever girls take to cross-dressing to break out of proper channels of success and eventually secure a worthwhile royal marriage.[39] Fashion and power mutually enhance each other in the fairy tales of the 1690s.[40]

This anecdotal story of seventeenth-century French society, which the rest of this introduction will elaborate in more historic terms, offers a different set of cultural tools than those readily available to the modern public for reading Perrault's 1697 fairy tales. By rehistoricizing their plots and, as we will see, their language, I intend to make the tales foreign again to counter what can seem like overwhelming evidence that American fairy-tale icons hail from a long line of gentle, naïve characters just like Disney's. The productions of the Walt Disney Studios, for that matter, which have served as a foil up to this point in the discussion, would also open up to new interpretations read in the context of gender, economy, and power in 1950s America. Historicizing any version of a fairy tale illuminates political and social strands of its narrative that are not apparent out of context.

The act of revisiting the historical past to mine new ideas from a seventeenth-century text necessarily yields the best results if it works

---

[39]These tales include Marie-Jeanne Lhéritier de Villandon, "Marmoisan, ou l'innocente tromperie" (Marmoisan; or, The Innocent Trick), 1695; Marie-Catherine d'Aulnoy, "Belle-Belle, ou le chevalier Fortuné" (Belle-Belle; or, The Knight Fortuné), 1698; and Henriette-Julie de Murat, "Le Sauvage" (The Savage), 1699. My dissertation work concerned these tales, which Catherine Velay-Vallentin grouped under the title "la fille en garçon," girl as boy tales, in *La Fille en garçon* (Carcassonne: Garae/Hésiode, 1992). The women writers will be discussed below.

[40]I have explored the relationship between heroines in Perrault and their cross-dressed counterparts in d'Aulnoy on a spectrum of "heroism" in "Thoughts on 'Heroism' in French Fairy Tales," *Marvels & Tales* 27, no. 1 (2012): 15-33. On fairy-tale fashion and power at Louis XIV's court, see Joan DeJean, *The Essence of Style: How the French Invented High Fashion, Fine Food, Chic Cafés, Style, Sophistication, and Glamour* (2005; repr., New York: Free Press, 2007), especially chapter 4 on shoes; and the recent thesis by Katherine Kasten on the appearance of lace in the fairy tales of the 1690s: "Writing Luxury: Mirrors, Silk, Lace, and Writing Desks in French Literature, 1660-1715" (PhD diss., University of Pennsylvania, 2013).

around the Disney spell. Even if we cannot unlearn what we know or step fully out of our cultural and intellectual comfort zone, as readers we can relieve history of the obligation to meet our expectations. Once we do that, the act of reading takes the form of discovery and surprise—as well as, perhaps, some productive confusion. By peeling away layers of what we expect, we are in a position to interact again with these vintage fairy tales and their cultural contexts on new terms. Refiguring the Mother Goose tales through their cultural context begins with a discussion of Charles Perrault. Because Perrault's identity, like his fairy tales, has accrued several centuries of meaning, his life and times are legends well worth investigation.

Charles Perrault (1628–1703)

Charles Perrault, a highly visible figure in the political landscape of his day, is a most elusive character when it comes to the authorship of the *Histoires ou Contes*. His name does not appear on an edition of the tales in France until 1707, four years after his death. Perrault's biography and the history of his writing thus feature a rather significant hole where the story of how and when he wrote the Mother Goose tales should be. When it comes to how Perrault's personal biography intersects with the tales, then, anecdote is the order of the day.

The *Mercure galant*, Paris's first journal with a mission to run "true stories and everything that happened" in the high world of court fashion and literature, featured a single, unattributed short story called "La Belle au bois dormant" in 1696.[41] The journal's founder and editor, Donneau de Visé, identified the author of the story as "the same person who wrote *L'Histoire de la petite Marquise*." That allusion might have been helpful except for the fact that the *Marquise* was also published anonymously.[42] The following

---

[41]"histoires véritables et tout ce qui s'est passé." This is the extended subtitle on the title page of the first issue of the *Mercure galant* printed in 1672.

[42]This novella about a cross-dressed courtier (male to female transvestite) could not readily be attributed to any major author of the 1690s. Two centuries of scholarly debate have led finally to the conclusion that it was likely coauthored by Perrault, his niece Marie-Jeanne Lhéritier de Villandon, and Francois-Timoleon de Choisy. Choisy, both an abbot and an occasional cross-dresser at Louis XIV's court, left memoirs that share details with the fictionalized narrative, such as the fact that he was dressed as a girl by his mother for years during his childhood. Recent modern editions credit him as lead author of the novella. See both the French and English editions published by the MLA: *Histoire de la Marquise-Marquis de Banneville*, ed. Joan DeJean; and *The Story of the Marquise-Marquis de Banneville*, trans. Steven Rendall (New York: Modern Language Association of America, 2004). In the introduction, Joan DeJean presents the various theories of authorship.

year, 1697, when "Belle au bois dormant" was published with seven other stories in the now-famous volume entitled *Histoires ou Contes du temps passé*, publisher Claude Barbin similarly left the author's name off the publication. Yet Barbin's edition contained a dedication to Her Royal Highness, Elisabeth Charlotte d'Orléans, Louis XIV's niece, signed with the name P. Darmancour: Perrault's youngest son, Pierre. Furthermore, Pierre Perrault Darmancour opens the dedication by stating that "a child took pleasure in composing the tales in this collection." Designed to meet the princess at eye level, young man to young woman, the dedicatory text makes no reference to Charles Perrault or his generation. Later that year, an announcement published in the *Mercure* identified the author of two new books—both published under the name Charles Perrault—as the same man who had written "La Belle au bois dormant" and the recently pubished *Histoires ou Contes*.[43] With printed evidence of two authorities behind the stories, publishers had to make choices.[44]

Throughout the first quarter of the eighteenth century, roughly half the editions attribute the collection's authorship to *le fils de M. Perrault* (the son of M. Perrault) and roughly half to *Monsieur Perrault* himself. As early as 1697, the year of the first Paris edition, Amsterdam publisher Jaques Desbordes attributed his pirated copy to *le fils*.[45] Paris publishers—Barbin as of 1707, a few years after Perrault's death, and Nicolas Gosselin in 1724—list M. Perrault as author. In 1721, the Desbordes family publishing house in Amsterdam removed "le fils de." Robert Samber's 1729 translation published in London, the first English translation of Perrault's tales, also credits Perrault. Subsequent eighteenth-century British editions follow his lead. By 1725 the word *fils* had fallen off title pages and the dedication was removed.[46] Thanks to editorial decisions made long after his death, Perrault lived on as the collection's sole author. For our purposes here, it will also be expedient to think about authorship in two ways. On the one hand, appointing Pierre

[43]The announcement appears in Ruth B. Bottigheimer's *Fairy Tales Framed*, 165-66.

[44]For a full rendering of the mentions of authorship in the work of other authors and personal correspondence, see Jean-Pierre Collinet, preface to *Perrault, Contes*, ed. Jean-Pierre Collinet (Paris: Folio Classique, 1981), 25–30; and in English, see Jacques Barchilon and Peter Flinders, introduction to *Charles Perrault* (Boston: Twayne, 1981). I will add that Perrault makes no mention of composing fairy tales in his *Mémoires*, written around 1700 and published posthumously.

[45]The Amsterdam edition is an unauthorized copy of the Barbin Paris edition.

[46]Estienne Roger published one of the rare editions after 1721 that still attributed the work to *le fils*. *Histoires ou contes du tems passé, avec les moralitez par le fils de Monsieur Perrault de l'Académie Françoise* (Amsterdam: Estienne Roger, 1725). Several opt for "de la Mère l'Oye" or "by Mother Goose." See the bibliography in this volume for a list of French and British editions of the *Histoires ou Contes* published in the eighteenth century.

dedicator of the volume makes good sense in terms of what I will describe below as the generational politics of the *Histoires ou Contes.* On the other, the sophistication of the collection's poetics point toward someone with experience and skill in the literary styles of the day. Again, the combination of these identities, a youthful ingenue and a learned man, complement the feminine identities of the princess and the woman teller. Perhaps, in short, the confusion was not accidental but strategic, designed to frame the volume as an inheritance. Offered by one generation (Perrault and the woman teller) to the next (Pierre and Elisabeth Charlotte), this wisdom belongs to the young, to share and to interrogate among themselves. We will return to that point in the next section below.

As the historical record stands, the oddity about the fairy tales for which Charles Perrault became so famous is that he never claimed responsibility for writing them. Equally oddly, thanks to a series of editorial decisions in the eighteenth century that put the question to rest, his authorship has not since encountered significant debate. Scholars and translators have drawn one of two conclusions about the tales, each of which justifies publishing them under Perrault's name: the son wrote versions that the father edited, or the father authored them alone.[47] The print history offers another vantage point from which to judge the authorship that is in line with the strategic reading of the frame devices offered above: whoever penned the stories in the 1690s, Charles Perrault has come down through history as the intellectual weight and the authority attached to the stories. With this inheritance comes the idea that Perrault's posthumous editorial history created his legacy as a fairy-tale writer and created a legacy for the fairy tale through his name. Michel Foucault called this mutually sustaining effect, whereby authors' names are created through their work and, at the same time, the identity of the work is bound up with the author, a text's *fonction-auteur* (author-function).[48] The effect can be particularly strong when writing achieves worldwide recognition.

In that sense, Perrault himself is no less a text constructed over time and by various publishing forces than his fairy tales. One reason Perrault's

---

[47] See Gilbert Rouger, *Contes de Perrault* (Paris: Garnier, 1967); Marc Soriano, *Les Contes de Perrault, culture savant et traditions populaires* (Paris: Gallimard, 1968); and Barchilon and Flinders, *Charles Perrault*, 24.

[48] "[T]he author does not precede the works; he is a certain functional principle by which, in our culture, one limits, excludes, and chooses. . . .The author is therefore the ideological figure by which one marks the manner in which we fear the proliferation of meaning." Michel Foucault, "What Is an Author?" trans. Josué Harari, in *Aesthetics, Method, and Epistemology*, ed. James D. Faubion (New York: New Press, 1998), 221-22.

reconstructed identities are important to the scholarly record is that they are often written with a view to explaining why he wrote fairy tales. This apparent anomaly in his official public profile has caused certain ideas about his life to come to the fore and, through them, generated theories about his motivations. Although my ultimate goal will be, as I put it above, to relieve the stories of the burden of meeting our expectations about their author, nonetheless his image has been a crucial companion to the tales throughout their history. In this biography, I lay out the most salient identities that have attached to Perrault as a fairy-tale author over the last hundred years, the first of which is intellectual fortitude.

The study of the biography of Charles Perrault began in the nineteenth century with his own testimony about his life until about 1670. Perrault left an autobiography written for his adult children, *Mémoires de ma vie* (Memoires of My Life), which was published posthumously for the first time in 1769.[49] In it he details his life as a scholarly young man—always "top of his class"—the intellectual life of the court and its newly formed academies (in which he would take part), the extensive feats of architecture at Versailles achieved under the reign of Louis XIV, and his important work as historiographer to the king. His memoirs are slim on details about his family and heritage, leaving scholars to sift through records of birth, baptism, and marriage as well as private correspondence to map his family life.[50] On the other hand, they are thick with poignant flourishes about his intellect, as one might expect from an academician. As far as fairy-tale scholarship is concerned, one spectacular detail Perrault tells about his education defines him as a freethinker, the kind of writer who, in 1695 at the age of sixty-seven, might write fairy tales: he quit school at the age of about twelve to pursue his own intellectual path.[51]

As Perrault records it, in the mid-seventeenth century, the study of ancient philosophy crowned a young gentleman's education in his last year of

---

[49]Charles Perrault, "Mémoires de ma vie," in *Mémoires de ma vie par Charles Perrault et Voyage à Bordeaux (1669) par Pierre Perrault*, ed. Paul Bonnefon (Paris: Renouard, 1909), 19–137. *Mémoires* was reissued in two editions in the nineteenth century, 1826 and 1878, before Bonnefon's definitive modern edition of 1909.

[50]Jacques Barchilon, Perrault's first biographer and scholarly ambassador in English, mined letters, registers, and various publications from the late nineteenth and early twentieth century to reconstruct the chronology and cultural environment of Perrault's private and early public life. He had recourse, too, to precursors Marc Soriano, who wrote the first extensive study of Perrault in French in the 1960s, and Andrew Lang, nineteenth-century folklorist and translator of Perrault (Barchilon and Flinders, *Charles Perrault*, 19–23). Both Soriano and Lang will be discussed below.

[51]This episode corresponds to the period in his life when Perrault first began writing his burlesque verse adaptation of Virgil's *Aeneid*, circa 1650.

school; he excelled so well at it that his tutor hoped he would write a thesis. His parents, who had funded his education up to that point, declined to pay for it. The tutor took his disappointment out on Perrault, refusing to let him engage with the work of the other students at their own thesis defenses. At one particular defense, the tutor publicly forbade Perrault to contribute to the conversation. Silenced once by his parents and then again by the tutor, Perrault had had enough: "[S]ince he no longer let me do my lessons . . . , no one challenged me, and I was forbidden to challenge others, there was no reason for me to come to class."[52] He bowed in the fashion of the court and walked out. With a friend called Beaurain, who was the object of his classmates' disdain and therefore also in need of an out, he spent the next three years reading the classics—the Bible, Tertullian, Virgil, and Horace—at home.[53] Together they read, translated, and discussed intellectual history. Each day at 5:00 p.m., when they put their dutiful pens down, they walked in the Luxembourg Gardens, musing about their study and ideas.[54]

Paul Bonnefon, editor of the only modern French edition of the *Mémoires*, counseled caution about taking this anecdotal evidence at face value: "Was his education indeed as unorthodox as he says it was? Perhaps he exaggerated to spice up his story, but today we have no way of correcting these very personal details."[55] That the anecdote could not be verified only made it more inviting as a personal mythology, and many scholars, translators, and historians who have profiled Perrault as a writer of fairy tales invoke the episode as evidence of his genius and iconoclasm. Andrew Lang's 1888 biography used the story of the jilted tutor to depict Perrault as a free spirit from an early age: "a truant from school, a deserter of the Bar, an architect without professional training, a man of letters by inclination, a rebel against the tyranny of the classics, and immortal by a kind of accident."[56]

Thomas Bodkin similarly emphasized his precocious rejection of the tutor's instruction as a sign of Perrault's native independence of spirit. Bodkin believed he refused the tutor's approach to classical education—an

---

[52]"[P]uisqu'il me faisoit plus dire ma leçon . . . qu'on ne disputoit plus contre moi, et qu'il m'étoit défendu de disputer contre les autres, je n'avois plus que faire de venir en classe" (Perrault, *Mémoires de ma vie*, 20–21).

[53]The one French author Perrault lists, the most likely French candidate for the honor of standing among the great writers of antiquity in the 1630s, is Pierre Corneille.

[54]Charles Perrault, *Charles Perrault, Memoires of My Life*, ed. and trans. Jeanne Morgan Zarucchi (Columbia: University of Missouri Press, 1989), 29–30.

[55]"Son éducation fut-elle aussi originale qu'il le dit ? Peut-être a-t-il un peu exagéré, pour rendre son récit plus piquant, mais rien ne nous permet maintenant de rectifier ces fait si personnels." Paul Bonnefon, "Introduction: Charles et Pierre Perrault," in Perrault, *Mémoires de ma vie*, 6. The English translation is mine.

[56]Andrew Lang, *Perrault's Popular Tales* (Oxford: Clarendon, 1888), vii–xvi.

education in the best ideas of antiquity—altogether and instead schooled himself in very modern thought. As Bodkin concludes, this anecdotal stunt would have "certainly prevented Perrault from being a thorough scholar, though it made him a man of taste, a sincere independent, and an undaunted amateur."[57] Angela Carter lyrically cast the intellectual adventure as a Rousseauian utopia; Perrault and his intellectual ally Beaurain retreated to the Luxembourg Gardens to read on their own and indulge their love of modern writing (though they read the canonical classics).[58] This rebel indeed seems like the kind of man who would flaunt literary convention to take up a new genre in the 1690s, and this episode in his autobiography went far for translators and scholars toward explaining why a male writer who grew up in the clutch of high classicism would find himself writing about fairies.

When this image of Perrault prevailed, as it did for Angela Carter in her 1977 translations of the *Histoires ou Contes*, the tales themselves looked similarly daring. Carter no doubt cited this anecdote of his early life because it corresponded to something she saw in his writing: "What an unexpected treat to find that in this great Ur-collection—whence sprang Sleeping Beauty, Puss in Boots, Little Red Riding Hood, Cinderella, Tom Thumb, all the heroes of pantomime—all these nursery tales are purposely dressed up as fables of the politics of experience. . . . Cut the crap about richly nurturing the imagination. This world is all that is to the point."[59] Lang and Bodkin, too, had an interest in identifying Perrault with deep intellectual engagement in the debates of his day. Carter's more radical maneuver to address so bluntly the "crap," takes on the popular idea of fairy tales in the wake of Disney as escapist and divorced from lived existence. She cites the "politics of experience," on the contrary, as the very concern that motivates tale writing in the first place. Her Perrault is "a man who wanted to make of Paris a modern Rome, a visible capital of sweet reason, and his fairy tales are in a style . . . marked by precision of language; irony; and realism."[60] Early biography, much of it based on Perrault's own description of his native genius, set the stage for the adult writer to make a mark on history.

---

[57]Thomas Bodkin, introduction to *The Fairy Tales of Charles Perrault*, trans. Robert Samber, translation revised and corrected by J. E. Mansion (London: George G. Harrap, 1922), 11.

[58]Angela Carter, *Little Red Riding Hood, Cinderella, and Other Classic Fairy Tales of Charles Perrault* (New York: Penguin Books, 1977), 71.

[59]Quoted in Martine Hennard Dutheil de la Rochère, "Cinderella's Metamorphoses: A Comparative Study of Two English Translations of Perrault's Tales," *Przekładaniec: A Journal of Literary Translation* 22–23 (2009-10): 256.

[60]Angela Carter, afterword to *Little Red Riding Hood, Cinderella, and Other Classic Fairy Tales of Charles Perrault*, 76.

Figure 4. Perrault at the beginning of his artistic direction of monuments at Versailles under the superintendent of buildings and finance, Jean-Baptiste Colbert. Etienne Baudet after Charles Le Brun, *Charles Perrault, conseiller du roy, controlleur des bastimens de sa majesté*, 1665. (Photo by Gérard Blot. Châteaux de Versailles et de Trianon, Versailles. © RMN-Grand Palais / Art Resource, NY.)

Nonetheless, few intellectuals after her shared Carter's exuberant sense that the older rebellious Perrault was as iconoclastic as his younger self. Jeanne Morgan Zarucchi, who did the only translation of the *Mémoires* into English, epitomizes a tendency to turn childhood rebellion into mature behavior by refining the act of defiance into an expression of honesty. She concludes from the truancy that Perrault's writing reveals "the force of his character, driven by a persuasive intelligence and an underlying sincerity that is impossible to falsify. Perrault wants us to believe him, and ultimately we do." Casting young Perrault as an intellectual of integrity, a rebel against old-world rules with a righteous cause, honesty and by extension earnestness became a formal lens through which to interpret the writer's adult intellectual life. That character naturally bled over into his writing: "For Perrault . . . , the tales served a serious and legitimate purpose." [61] The arc of his life between quitting school and writing fairy tales follows a trajectory toward legitimacy. Now rebellion occurs within the strictures of government and the official writing circles of men, which inevitably dulls its edge.

When we pick up the thread of Perrault's work life circa 1671, where his memoirs and subsequent discussions of his life jump next, we find him fully embedded in court life and academic circles, serving an absolute monarchy in the position of *historiographe du roi* (historiographer to the king)—a sincere purpose, indeed. Inducted into the Académie française, France's high council on arts and letters, in 1671, Perrault took part in his century's most important cultural agendas. Court-appointed intellectuals were charged with nothing less than developing new representational and propagandist strategies for the Sun King; memorializing the reign by documenting all its major military, social, and architectural exploits (the role in which Perrault is pictured in figure 4); and standardizing French by writing dictionaries. Successful writers of the 1670–90s like Perrault had a hand in defining genre, defining language, and regulating meaning for the court and kingdom. His reading at the Académie of a panegyric celebrating literary achievement under Louis XIV, "Le Siècle de Louis le grand" (The Century of Louis the Great, 1687), sparked heated debate, and a verse tract, *Apologie des femmes* (Defense of Women, 1694), punctuated it as Perrault's direct and final response to a vehement intellectual adversary and fellow academician, Nicolas Boileau. (This text and Perrault's debate with Boileau will be discussed below.) During the period of his most prolific time at the Académie, he led the editorial team on the first official French dictionary

---

[61] Jeanne Morgan Zarucchi, introduction to Perrault, *Charles Perrault, Memoires of My Life*, 24, 18.

(1694) and also produced his magnum opus on the great literary debates of his age, *Le Parallèle des Anciens et des Modernes* (Parallel of the Ancients and Moderns, 1688–97).

Le Parallèle and *Apologie des femmes* played a role in the great debates that were touchstones for this period of official nation building in France: the *Querelle des Anciens et des Modernes* (Quarrel of the Ancients and the Moderns), about literature and genre, and the older but recently reinvigorated *Querelle des femmes* (debate about women or the woman question), about the nature and political subjectivity of women.[62] In the first, "Ancients" faced off against "Moderns" regarding the role that the literature of antiquity should play in the intellectual life of modern France and the status of contemporary French writing in comparison with authoritative canonical works in Greek and Latin. Both sides promoted the French language as a literary medium but they proposed very different formal prescriptions. Ancients held that antiquity had produced the best literary and linguistic models possible in Greek and Latin texts and that French authors should imitate classical genres to raise French to the standard of the ancient languages. Moderns staked a claim for innovation in French, which they thought could supersede in quality and impact the ancient languages, whose genres were designed for a pre-Christian mentality. The former lamented the fall of greatness after antiquity in premodern Europe and sought to recapture it for modernity with French poets exercising their wit in ancient forms. The latter heralded the possibilities that awaited poetry if it threw off its old forms and blossomed anew through the particular grammatical and syntactical beauty of French. Perrault's writing exemplified and in some ways created the Modern position.

His official work at the Académie and participation at the highest levels of publishing secured Perrault's fame among intellectuals of his day. Portraiture, though no simple reflection of history, nonetheless provides relevant images of where Perrault fit within the pantheon at the court of Louis XIV. Circa 1665, figure 4 shows him entering a government post, and figure 5, dated 1694, depicts how he looked the year he published the *Apologie*.

---

[62]For a telescopic view of this explosive moment in French literary history that focuses on Perrault's role in the debate, see Robert J. Nelson, "1687: The Quarrel of the Ancients and Moderns," in *A New History of French Literature* (New Haven: Yale University Press, 1989), 364–69. Nelson uses warring definitions of humanism to contrast the Ancient and Modern positions: "humanism with an authoritarian and, largely, aristocratic face" versus "humanism with a libertarian and, potentially, democratic face" (365). For a broad sketch of the historical debate about the status of women, see "Querelle des Femmes," in *Women's Studies Encyclopedia*, ed. Helen Tierney (Greenwood, 2002), www.gem.greenwood.com.

Figure 5. The academician the year he published the *Apologie des femmes*. Gérard Edelink after Jean Tortebas, *Charles Perrault de l'Académie française (1628–1703)*, 1694. (Photo by Gérard Blot. Châteaux de Versailles et de Trianon, Versailles. © RMN-Grand Palais / Art Resource, NY.)

In the first he sits as a newly appointed *contrôleur général des bâtiments du roi*, or comptroller general of the king's estate, second in command to the superintendent in charge of designing and executing—not simply documenting—architectural planning, installations memorializing the reign, and court celebrations. In the second he sits as a seasoned academician who has not only influenced building and ceremony but has played a significant role in publishing the dictionary and ushering in a new way of writing and speaking his language that will live on beyond some of those buildings as standardized modern French.[63] The second portrait, showing an older man with wig, flowing academic mantle, and books, illustrates how far Perrault had penetrated into the inner circles of the court—and how the fashion of looking the part had blossomed under Louis XIV. This Perrault corresponds to Zarucchi's writer for whom even a fairy tale would have to serve "a serious and legitimate purpose." For much of the formative era of modern fairy-tale criticism, just about the period between Carter's work (1977) and Zarucchi's (1989), this vision of the man was brought to bear upon interpretation of the tales, which were folded into the image of a great intellectual. This overlay had the effect of giving Mother Goose a place in learned cultural history that she had not been granted before and, to the benefit of the genre, made fairy tales appear as important as their author was construed to be.

Three major scholars ascribed to Perrault motivations for writing fairy tales that line up well with the idea that he brought the earnest agenda of his intellectual life to this rebellious genre. Perrault's first scholarly biographer, Marc Soriano (1968), inducted Perrault into the canon of French literature partially by outlining a series of justifications for finding in the tales the sincerity and firmness of purpose that scholarship had long recognized in his other intellectual work. In this case, the purpose was preservationist. Soriano took both a psychological and sociocultural approach to Perrault's stories, finding in Mother Goose an allegory not simply of women tellers or nursemaids but of a whole class of people—the largest swath of the population by far in the seventeenth century—whose lives were agrarian and who transmitted their beliefs through stories: *le peuple* (the common people, the folk).

Under this guise, Perrault takes on the allure of a great intellect of the scientific revolution who watched in dismay as progress marched into

---

[63]"Perrault avait eu une part importante dans la réalisation du *Dictionnaire*, car Colbert dont les domaines d'activités étaient très vastes . . . avait demandé à Perrault qui était alors son commis d'entrer à l'Académie pour accélérer la production de l'ouvrage." Gérard Gélinas, *Enquête sur les contes de Perrault* (Paris: Imago, 2010), 87.

France, across fields and through villages, threatening the extinction of the kingdom's lore, which peasants carried in their beliefs about the world.

> Perrault well knew, deep down, that the progress of science would one day dispel popular superstition. And he presented us with a volume of just these superstitions, these reveries, captured in their historical becoming at the very moment when they existed still as they had and were about to become something else. Now towards completion, now towards annihilation, these apparently contradictory elements blend, culminate in a work that remains deeply popular. A learned artist, as though in spite of himself, devoted his science to the cause of 'naïve' tales.[64]

At stake in the survival of what peasants thought, Soriano shows, was not really an ethnographic impulse to help them thrive as a culture but rather an attempt to preserve their prerational knowledge for the increasingly rationalist patrimony. Their "superstitions" formed the bedrock of French history—or rather prehistory—from which science would help it emerge and grow into modernity. From Soriano's vantage point in the twentieth century, Perrault's unique blend of sophistication and empathy for that which lacked intellectual rigor made him an ideal candidate for the job of preservationist. Why save the peasantry? Because the modern world looked upon its youthful, prerational self as its ancestry and the roots of its current questions. Superstitions gave early answers that revealed the very questions science was now rising to tackle.

Perrault's unique contribution to his scientific age was thus to realize the threat to prehistory (when no one else did) and set its lore down on paper. Perrault broke molds, threw off courtly habits, and flouted rules of decorum to write tales, to keep for the Enlightenment what the Enlightenment itself would have cleared away (as Soriano puts it, *dissiper*, to dispel) with its erudition. For folk wisdom to survive in the light of reason, Soriano's Perrault knew, it had to be preserved as bedtime stories but be relieved of its dullness by sophisticated poetics. Eloquence and sophistication adorned and also

---

[64]"Perrault savait bien, au fond de lui-même, que la Science, dans son progrès, dissiperait un jour les superstitions populaires. Et il nous offre un recueil de ces superstitions, de ces rêveries, saisies dans le devenir historique, à l'instant même où elles sont encore elles-mêmes et où elles vont devenir autres. Tantôt se complétant et tantôt s'annulant, ces données apparemment contradictoires se combinent, aboutissent à une œuvre qui, elle, est profondément populaire. Un artiste savant, presque malgré lui, met sa science au service des contes 'naïfs'" (Soriano, *Les Contes de Perrault,* 490).

elevated peasant stories, giving them a place in intellectual history.[65] In that sense, Soriano gave Perrault a purpose for which he had not yet been given credit: fairy tales were a ligature he affixed across the widening gap between the past and the future of France.

Jacques Barchilon (1960, 1975, and 1981) formulated an explanation of Perrault's tales that placed them within the history of literature rather than folklore. He showed that because they constituted a confluence of fables and mythologies in print history with the stylish writing of the court, fairy tales were poised to influence folklore: "It seems he influenced popular tradition far more than he was influenced by it."[66] Perrault at once participated in an old tradition of telling and also updated it stylistically, as the Mother Goose of the frontispiece and the Mademoiselle of the dedication together suggest. As such, Barchilon dubbed him the "Classical Teller" (*Le Conteur classique*).[67] In Perrault's hands, Sleeping Beauty, for example, looks formally neoclassical (the reigning style of Louis XIV's France) in contrast with the older German, Italian, and French material identified as Perrault's sources for the story.

> The impressive difference between these stories and that of Perrault consists in his treatment of Sleeping Beauty's discovery by the prince. In each of these previous versions, the enchanted princess is raped during her sleep by her discoverer, becomes pregnant. . . . We find none of this in Perrault. . . . He would "clean it up" according to the French classical tradition of *bienséance* ("decorum"). . . . The censoring, editing, and pen of the author are everywhere present in *The Tales of Mother Goose.*[68]

Viewed within a transcultural history of myth and folklore, Perrault's writing stands out. For Barchilon, it does more than elevate folklore to a literary

---

[65]Another facet of Soriano's work on Perrault is his research and reliance on the author's life in his assessment of the writing, particularly a detail he digs up about a dead twin brother. In his review of Soriano's book, Barchilon takes it to task for displacing emphasis from the narrative material to Perrault as the "subject" of his study. He cites particularly Soriano's fascination with Perrault as the pathological brother of a twin who died in infancy. "Les Contes de Perrault, culture savante et traditions populaires," *French Review* 43, no. 1 (1969): 188–89. Nicole Belmont finds the psychologizing most powerful in Soriano's identification of the author's loss with the figure of the underdog hero. "Les Contes de Perrault: Culture savante et traditions populaires by Marc Soriano," *L'Homme* 11, no. 1 (1971): 124–25.

[66]Barchilon and Pettit, introduction, 9.

[67]This is the title of Barchilon's chapter on Perrault in *Le Conte merveilleux* (Paris: Honoré Champion, 1975).

[68]Jacques Barchilon and Peter Flinders, "Perrault's Fairy Tales as Literature," in Barchilon and Flinders, *Charles Perrault,* 93.

idiom. It bears the distinct mark of the grammatical sophistication and courtly values—*bienséance*—characteristic of Louis XIV's reign. In fact, following Barchilon's assessment, Perrault would become known as the first writer who consistently censored the bawdy folk traditions from which he borrowed.

Jack Zipes (1983) took up the question of Perrault's style, interrogating its relationship to French court culture and teasing out the implications of writing *bienséance* (court civility and its attendant values) into fairy tales. Part of the novelty of this approach lay in its interest in what happened *after* the stories were published and achieved widespread popularity. With the aid of the theory put forth by Norbert Elias in *The Civilizing Process*—that the history of the West follows a consistent pattern of increased restraint on natural human habits that peaked in European court life—Zipes argued that Perrault's tales reinforced "the standards of the civilizing process set by upper-class French society" by "endowing it with an earnest and moral purpose to influence the behavior of adults and children in a tasteful way."[69] And because these social standards took the form of relatively simple and entertaining stories, they spread quickly and broadly, leading Zipes to credit and, more pointedly, charge Perrault with disseminating French monarchic values to the masses.

The theory of what Zipes called the "bourgeoisification" of folklore—glorifying gender paradigms of the ancien régime—demonstrated that contemporary Western ideology owes a debt, and perhaps its current structure, to the infectious appeal of Perrault's heroines:

> There is a direct line from the Perrault fairy tale of court society to the Walt Disney cinematic fairy tale of the culture industry. Obviously, many samples of the French fairy-tale vogue have not survived the test of time and have been replaced by more adequate modern-day equivalents. But, for the most part, Perrault and his associates stamped the very unreflective and uncritical manner in which we read and receive fairy tales to the present.[70]

Zipes credited Perrault with being the premier literary stylist of his day,[71] but took him to task for promoting oppressive elements of Western culture,

---

[69]Jack Zipes, *Fairy Tales and the Art of Subversion* (1983; repr., New York: Routledge, 2012), 42.
[70]Ibid., 42, 34. More recently, Zipes has used the concept of the "infectious" meme to explain how some stories "stick" and flourish over the course of time. For a summary of the memetic theory see especially 17–20 in *The Irresistible Fairy Tale*.
[71]Jack Zipes, ed. and trans., *The Great Fairy Tale Tradition: From Straparola and Basile to the Brothers Grimm* (New York: Norton, 2001), 840. Norbert Elias, *The Civilizing Process: Sociogenetic and Psychogenetic Investigations*, rev. ed. (Hoboken, NJ: Blackwell, 2000).

especially the heteronormative paternalism that, many years later, took shape as Prince Charming in the *Cinderella* and *Sleeping Beauty* of the Walt Disney Studios. The standards of childhood development that most concerned Zipes are the stringent gender norms that molded people into elite social creatures under Louis XIV, especially at his court: "The task confronted by the model female is to show reserve and patience. . . . The male acts, the female waits."[72] Through Perrault, Zipes suggested, tenets of sociability under the ancien régime found a way to far outlast the monarchy of Louis XIV under which they flourished—so far and with such tenacity that they are still visible in Disney animation.

The merging of biography and bibliography, as it occurred when major scholars attempted to read the fairy tale through Perrault's celebrity as a Modern, has had the welcome effect of putting a highly influential Perrault and his fairy tales onto the academic map.[73] One of its less productive features was the cementing of a reading of the fairy tales that made them suspicious for a generation of feminist scholars. Another yardstick they used to judge Perrault's agenda about women in the fairy tale is how he took up the defense of women in his earlier writing. A crucial text for this assessment in French studies is the *Apologie des femmes* (Defense of Women, 1694). As we saw above, few issues divided French academicians more than the question of genre, and the way it was framed in the 1690s catalyzed intellectual inquiry into the status of women, placing the textual depiction of women squarely at the crossroads of these debates. The Ancient position was embodied by Nicolas Boileau, Perrault's virulent adversary, who promoted the virtuosity of the Greek and Roman writers. His own masterful imitations of classical forms became legendary. They include his *Art poétique* (Art of Poetry, 1674), a rule book for poetry written in verse in homage to Horace's *Ars poetica* as well as a series of ten satires, *Satires*, in imitation of Juvenal's most important work, *Satirae*, a collection of invectives on a wide variety of subjects concerning social and political life. Of the sixteen satires Juvenal wrote, "Satire VI," the longest in the series, is on the subject of women. Boileau's imitation of this, his own "Satire X" published in 1694, was the last one in the series and the satire for which he is still best remembered. Boileau's work pays homage to Roman poetics by taking up the violent verbal weapons Juvenal used on the women of Rome and turning them onto the women of Paris.

---

[72]Zipes, *Fairy Tales and the Art of Subversion*, 41.

[73]For a bibliography of the first significant wave of criticism on the *Histoires ou Contes*, see Claire-Lise Malarte, *Perrault à travers la critique depuis 1960: Bibliographie annotée* (Paris: Papers on French Seventeenth-Century Literature, 1989).

Boileau's "Satire X" is designed, as the genre suggests, to rail in its depiction of women based on ancient models of abjection: caricatures of female excess in the coquette and the zealot. As a writer firmly on the side of the Moderns, Perrault famously denounced the reliance on exempla espoused by Boileau, which he believed should be superseded. His *Apologie des femmes* was read as a response, albeit a temporally co-incident one, to Boileau's work and a formal rejection of Juvenal's pre-ferred genre: satire. In the place of these old and enduring models of the female problem—the whore and the saint—the *Apologie,* popularly translated *A Vindication of Wives* (not women in general), presents the modern French woman in a home environment capable of managing her everyday domestic affairs. The stylistic parallel he makes with the poetic arts to attack Boileau on aesthetic as well as thematic grounds is not without interest: some women overpaint their faces, some men overblow their poetry, neither makes for a very attractive sight, and both are remnants of Roman excess. Perrault attacks Boileau's rant against women by ranting against his use of "slutty" rhetoric as a weapon of oppression.

Put another way, writing that berates women and swells their carica-ture to mythic proportions fails to depict women in any productive way and proves dangerous to them socially. This seemingly obvious tenet was nonetheless one of the pillars of the quarrel because fictional women served artistically to represent a commentary on the nature of woman. Socially speaking, women are what they are depicted to be, and in 1690, those de-pictions were not in their hands. Perrault reduces the issues in Boileau's rant to conquerable proportions—a tactic he used often in his writing, as we will see below—adapting language from a religious lexicon and applying it to social character. Behaviors Boileau attacks as indicative of the base nature of women Perrault identifies instead as a sort of "infidelity" to decorum and notes that while such a depiction may represent one type of female behavior, it in no way implicates the nature of women, which corresponds instead to living "faithfully":

> Go into the rooms of families of favor,
> And watch the mothers and daughters labor,
> Focused only on their tasks and on receiving
> Their father or husband when they come back in the evening.[74]

---

[74]*A Vindication of Wives* (Emmaus, PA: Rodale Books, 1954), 3, 7.

Locating women in the home, working faithfully for men, suggests a tone and a language with which to record women stylistically that does not exploit ancient stereotypes about their uncontrollable urges and outlandish self-presentation. Paramount in this rescripting of women's impulses, metaphorized here by their work, is the socially productive way they use their energies for something other than sexual arousal or false devotion (Boileau's vision). In Perrault's Christianized scene, domestic work looks virtuous, in opposition to social exhibitionism. Yet, keeping in mind that Perrault is also talking about French aesthetics and pitting them against Roman literary style, particularly as those modes impact the image of women, we can note too that these women do not give up taste and charm because they are depicted in the home; they simply swear off satirical excess. They are not plain and simple for being domestic and French. Like the modern French writer, women in "families of favor" express themselves with "refinement, subtle affect, good taste, and fine manners" and encourage the same in men or, according to the metaphor of the piece, male writers.[75]

Critics have tended to agree, nonetheless, that this "defense" of women does little to advance their political cause in practical terms unless it can be read as a parody of domesticity, which my reading above would preclude.[76] Even were parody the work's modus operandi, Anne Duggan argues, it does not sufficiently reject the negative premises of "Satire X," many of which are precisely caught up with keeping women out of the public sphere. Significantly, too, for feminist scholarship, Perrault's is a notable but not unique response to "Satire X" and perhaps the weakest in terms of social critique.[77] Duggan has eloquently enumerated its shortcomings, among which the most salient are: (1) the poem does not address women's equality, only their difference from men; and (2) it reduces their contribution to society to ensuring that men act civilly in their domestic lives.[78]

I do not disagree with these insightful concerns. Perrault's defense of women as people who deserve to be depicted as productive members of

---

[75]Ibid., 7.

[76]For a helpful overview of its failure to refute Boileau, see Anne Duggan, *Salonnières, Furies, and Fairies: The Politics of Gender and Cultural Change in Absolutist France* (Newark: University of Delaware Press, 2005), 146–47.

[77]Ibid., 141. Perrault was not the only Modern who had a formal response to Boileau's infamous satire. See chapter 4, especially 137–39, of *Salonnières* for an overview of the work of other writers inspired by Perrault's *Apologie* whose critiques of Boileau's "Satire X," Duggan compellingly argues, build a stronger defense of women in public life.

[78]Anne Duggan, "Women Subdued: The Abjectification and Purification of Female Characters in Perrault's Tales," *Romanic Review* 99, no. 2 (2008): 211–26. This argument leans especially on "Blue Beard," often read as a prescription of Taming-of-the-Shrew-like discipline of women, both publicly and in their domestic spaces.

society leans heavily on the idea that men do the doing and women make sure they can. My own work, in fact, participated in the period of feminist scholarship that read Perrault's tales through texts such as the *Apologie* and concluded that they were conservative in their values and their poetics. Below I will argue instead that this poem does not present the most productive lens through which to read the fairy tales, which depart from it stylistically and thematically. First I will spend a moment contextualizing the important feminist critiques inspired by the *Apologie*.

In the early 1990s, scholars including Zipes and Barchilon, who had helped forge fairy-tale studies through their work on Perrault, strongly advocated studying the woefully neglected tales of women writers of the 1690s. Of the 112 tales produced during that first French vogue (mentioned at the very beginning of this introduction), women's stories had lost ground to Perrault's in history and therefore had not received the full critical attention they deserved. As Lewis Seifert would put it in 1996, "Since the mid-nineteenth century, the notoriety of a single fairy-tale writer, Charles Perrault (1628–1703) has eclipsed that of all the others."[79] Scholars such as Raymonde Robert and Catherine Velay-Vallantin in France, and Gabrielle Verdier along with Zipes in the United States, answered the call for historical recovery and theorized the major contribution of women tale writers (*conteuses*), beginning with Marie-Catherine d'Aulnoy, Marie-Jeanne Lhéritier de Villandon, and Henriette-Julie de Murat.[80]

Ensuing feminist attention to the complex literary scene of the 1690s proves pertinent to this discussion of Perrault because work on his life and stories necessarily slowed in France and the United States as a generation of scholars of the genre—Lewis Seifert, Patricia Hannon, Elizabeth Wanning Harries, Sophie Raynard, and Anne Duggan, among others—focused book-length studies on the *conteuses* to explore what in 1983 Zipes had dubbed the genre's subversive strategies.[81] The work of feminists has been

---

[79]Seifert, *Fairy Tales, Sexuality, and Gender in France,* 5.
[80]For an excellent overview of how feminism grew up in the French tradition, see Lewis Seifert, "On Fairy Tales, Subversion, and Ambiguity: Feminist Approaches to Seventeenth-Century *Contes de fées,*" in Haase, *Fairy Tales and Feminism,* 53–71.
[81]Sophie Raynard-Leroy, *La seconde préciosité: Floraison des conteuses de 1690 à 1756* (Tübingen: Gunter Narr, Biblio 17, 2001); Duggan, *Salonnières*; and Allison Stedman, *Rococo Fiction in France (1600–1715): Seditious Frivolity* (Lewisburg, PA: Bucknell University Press, 2012). My 2002 dissertation worked within this feminist tradition and its core argument appeared in condensed form as "The Poetics of Enchantment: 1690–1715," *Marvels & Tales* 17, no. 1 (2003): 55–74. For many of us working on gender in fairy-tale studies today, the language of Zipes's inaugural study, *Fairy Tales and the Art of Subversion,* continues to generate productive ideas about genre and innovation.

critical in fleshing out fairy-tale history and establishing gender balance in scholarship. This is especially important when we consider that within France, Perrault and the few other male writers of his generation continue to be held up, as they were before the 1980s, as more sincere—in this case, "less defiant"—than the women writers: "less verbose and less affected than the *conteuses*, less defiant towards the folkloric roots of the genre, they appropriated the fairy tale innovatively, usurpers of literary territory considered essentially feminine."[82] In other words, Perrault's project in writing tales was construed as fundamentally different from that of the women: where he preserved, they innovated, where he wrote simply by virtue of his intellectual sophistication, they embellished by virtue of their prolixity.

Few scholars on this side of the Atlantic continue to pit the gender camps against each other on strict stylistic grounds, but the residual appearance as recently as 2005 of the above statement suggests that such judgments about gender and writing persist. Yet, positively assessing the style of women's tales—on average, long and rich in detail—has indeed relied on the image of Perrault's authorship as Soriano, Barchilon, and Zipes laid it out: he was indebted to the folkloric past, a translator of mythic story into classical prose, and a progenitor of bourgeois values who promoted patriarchal heteronormativity. His biography, as we have seen, tends to support this assessment, and vice versa. Hitching the fairy tales to Perrault's illustrious court literature may not have done him a disservice (on the contrary), but I will argue below that it may have done his tales a disservice.

Scholars have, for decades, also argued that the tales of the *Histoires ou Contes*—that *all* fairy tales, by virtue of the genre's mutability—are slippery. Many scholars, several quoted above, have elaborated theories of the "subversive" tendencies of the genre.[83] Jennifer Schacker has encapsulated this

---

[82]"moins prolixes et moins précieux que les conteuses, moins rétifs envers les origines folkloriques du genre, ils s'approprient le conte de fées d'une façon originale et, en usurpateurs d'un territoire littéraire tenu pour essentiellement féminin." This statement comes from the online description of a volume on male fairy-tale writers including Perrault, part of a recent multivolume collection of tales from the seventeenth and eighteenth centuries published in France. *Bibliothèque des génies et des fées: Perrault, Fenelon, Mailly, Préchac, Choisy et autres anonymes*, vol. 4, ed. Tony Gheereart (Paris: Honoré Champion, 2005), www.honorechampion.com/fr/champion/6612-book-08531307–9782745313072.html. The English translation is mine.

[83]Marc Soriano and Jeanne Morgan Zarucchi have argued that far from stabilizing meaning or providing "the moral of the story," the poetic morals at the end of Perrault's tales, which are sometimes doubled and always enigmatic, undermine attempts to fix the story's meaning. See Soriano, *Les Contes de Perrault*, 341; and Zarucchi, *Mimesis and Metatextuality in the Neo-classical Text* (Geneva: Droz, 1991), 141, 150–51. Lewis Seifert's argument about the *merveilleux* (the marvelous) in French fairy tales hinges on irony as a way of understanding how authors deploy childish naïveté to comment on adult sociability, "mimicking a discourse so as to subvert it" (*Fairy Tales, Sexuality, and Gender in France*, 44).

awareness in terms of what it means to read French fairy tales: "These tales imply a reader ready, willing, and able to find pleasure in the subversion of generic convention—ready, willing, and able to find pleasure in complicity with a subversive narrator."[84] Her point resonates with the invitation extended to Elisabeth Charlottte d'Orléans by Pierre Darmancour in the dedication of 1695 to engage in reading that penetrates beneath the surface of the story. In effect, the *Histoires ou Contes* suggests that we read the tales against themselves. Indeed, recent trends in criticism have brought to the fore ironies in the prose and in the relationship between the tales and the morals that continue to make the Sleeping Beauty and Cinderella characters worthy of interrogation. For example, Gérard Gélinas has argued for a stylistic shift from Perrault's earlier writing to the prose tales: "The tales are a departure from ideals of civility that Perrault used to condemn the Ancients and proclaim the superiority of the Moderns."[85] And as a reader of Angela Carter, Martine Hennard builds a theory of Perrault out of Carter's engagement with the tales, which highlights their ambiguity and playfulness: "Carter perceived the emancipating potential of Perrault's *contes*" and went so far as to "use [them] against the cultural stereotype of Cinderella."[86]

While these critical insights have germinated in scholarship and innovative rereadings of Perrault's tales occur in college classrooms, the most recent critical trends have not had significant impact on translation practice or public perception. I hope to bring this recent scholarship to greater prominence by presenting in this introduction and the next section on the history of translation an alternative analysis of the *Histoires ou Contes* suggested by the critical trends, and by translating the tales in the spirit of their ironic tendencies. Unhitching the language of the stories from the biography and bibliography that have forged the image we now have of the man and his politics opens the reader to the slipperiness of the fairy tales. But reading for irony, as many critics have demonstrated, presupposes a backdrop of cultural ideology against which to perceive

---

[84]Jennifer Schacker, "Unruly Tales: Ideology, Anxiety, and the Regulation of Genre," *Journal of American Folklore* 120, no. 478 (2007): 387.

[85]"Les contes sont bien éloignés des idéaux de civilité dont se sert Perrault pour condamner les Anciens et clamer la supériorité des Modernes" (Gélinas, *Enquête sur les contes de Perrault*, 87; my translation). Gélinas cites the "hypocrisy," which I will call the strategy, of the wife of Blue Beard, who claims to want to pray, as an example of how ideals of civility are violated so that characters can make their way to the happy ending (86).

[86]Martine Hennard Dutheil de la Rochère, *Reading, Translating, Rewriting: Angela Carter's Translational Poetics* (Detroit: Wayne State University Press, 2013), 40, 269. This study is, in fact, designed to refute the theory that to appreciate Perrault, the feminist in Carter had to "misinterpret" him (13).

certain tropes or articulations as subversive. As I lay that ideology out below, the dutiful domestic women of the *Apologie* do not become the protagonists of the fairy tales. Each heroine, like the heroes, leaves home to make her way. In lieu of the *Apologie*, whose orientation toward the past and toward Boileau grounds the author-function in traditionalism and retrograde gender politics, I offer alternative ideological anchors that help illuminate the qualities of the heroines that populate the *Histoires ou Contes*. One is Perrault's professional historiography for the court, where he refines his writing in compelling ways to deliver cautionary lessons on the nature of power. The other is a new interpretation of a verse tale, whose form (poetry) and source (a Roman story) seem as traditional as the *Apologie* but which features a rare younger character worthy of our attention.

Court Historiography (1671 and 1677)

The life of Perrault coincides with that of Louis XIV (1638–1715) with only a ten-year difference, which means that he grew up, matured, and aged alongside the king under whose reign France confronted modern science, fashionable art, and global commerce. Not long after Louis XIV began his personal reign, developing the autocratic style of absolute monarchy, he appointed chief advisors, most important among them Jean-Baptiste Colbert, who set out to found or reform institutional branches of government designed to engineer the rapid expansion of the cultural life of France. Image building laid a foundation for a new national identity that could rise into this world of exploration and change. That is to say, under Louis XIV and Colbert's direction, poetry and other arts would be subsumed under councils, the aforementioned academies, so that politics could take full advantage of poetics.[87] Perrault not only watched this happen, as we have seen, he was employed to lead the effort by which linguistic sophistication, pageantry, and fantasy became political tools.

During this initial phase of political rejuvenation, Colbert offered Perrault the post of secretary in the newly created Petite académie, the

---

[87]On the formal integration of scholarship and state building under Louis XIV and Jean-Baptiste Colbert, see especially 4–7 in Jacob Soll, "Jean-Baptiste Colbert's Republic of Letters," *Republics of Letters: A Journal for the Study of Knowledge, Politics, and the Arts* 1, no. 1 (2009), arcade.stanford.edu/rofl_issue/volume-1-issue-1.

government council charged with engineering the public image of Louis XIV.[88] From the beginning of this long, important reign, Perrault played a key role in what has become known as the Sun King's propaganda "machine."[89] The job description of his position was simple and crucial to the representation of absolutism: to oversee projects related to promoting and preserving life at the court of Louis XIV. Perrault's position in the Petite académie then bore a certain resemblance to the role of a public relations officer today: managing the court image for the present and for posterity meant forging a consistent vision of its splendor and finding innovative ways to spread it far and wide.

Activities—everything from battles to outdoor spectacles—were preserved by talented writers in the form of written and visual chronicles that told the continuous story of Louis XIV's reign as it happened. To create this seamless mythology, the king's advisors conscripted legions of workers who devoted their energy (and sometimes their lives) to building a playhouse of luxury for his court at Versailles and marshaled the realm's most talented subjects into the service of the king to orchestrate his glory in word and image. All court events held in Paris and then at Versailles look and sound spectacular in the historical record. Writing such a vision of the present for posterity demanded the skills of the poet. Literature and politics were not distinct enterprises in the mid-seventeenth century; on the contrary, the literati supplied the eloquence necessary to depict France's glory.

As a young academician, Perrault spearheaded a number of projects dedicated to the king's and France's edification. Each of the two books discussed here, *Courses de testes et de bague* (Running of the Heads and the Ring, 1670) and *Le Labyrinthe de Versailles* (Versailles's Labyrinth, 1677), was commissioned by the king to commemorate an event: the Grand Carrousel held at the Louvre and the building of the large-scale walkable labyrinth in the gardens of Versailles, respectively. In each case, Perrault both oversaw the event and preserved it in print. Writing things down in a style intended to memorialize them for posterity guaranteed first that events would be remembered, and second that their official memory would be shaped by those in service to the king. The events

---

[88]The Petite académie evolved in 1663 into the more politically efficient Académie des inscriptions et belle-lettres during Perrault's tenure. See Peter Burke, *The Fabrication of Louis XIV* (New Haven: Yale University Press, 1994), 61–83.

[89]Jean-Marie Apostolidès called Louis XIV the "king-machine" in his study of how Louis XIV's advisors helped him turn his body into a commanding theatrical personification of the state, and in the end how the image exceeded his control. *Le Roi-Machine, spectacle et politique au temps de Louis XIV* (Paris: Editions Minuit, 1981).

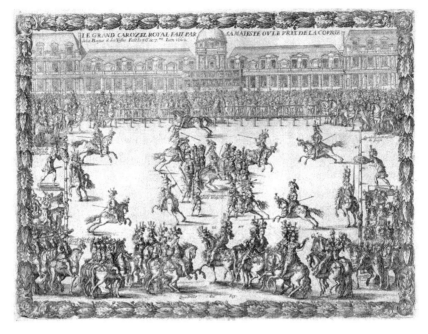

Figure 6. The Roman quadrille surrounds Louis XIV in the center of the image. *Le Grand Carozel Royal fait par sa majesté; ou, Le Prix de la course de la Bague et des Testes*, 1662. (Bibliothèque de l'Arsenal, Bibliothèque nationale de France, Paris.)

were feats of material pageantry and the books had to depict those feats in poetic language and sumptuous imagery appropriate to the splendor guests would have witnessed. Both of these commissions gave Perrault a lesson in mythmaking.

One of the first events he chronicled as secretary set a precedent for grandeur in court spectacle. In the year after Louis XIV's assumption of personal power at his majority in 1661, the Petite académie staged an epic battle known as the Grand Carrousel.[90] This type of mock tournament involving the high aristocracy brought fantasies of medieval knighthood to

---

[90] "Sorte de feste qui consiste en courses de testes & de bagues entre plusieurs personnes, divisées par Quadrilles distinguées par couleurs & livrées, & différents habits magnifiques" (Type of festival that consists of competition in the running at the heads and at the rings by groups of people divided into quadrilles that are differentiated by color and by livery and by their different magnificent outfits). "Carrousel," *Dictionnaire de l'Académie française*. Running at the head was also known in French as *la course du faquin* for the wooden model used as the target. Claude-François Ménestrier wrote a history of court games in which he outlined the rules of the *course de testes*. He references the Grand Carrousel of 1662 in his section on the function of quadrilles. See *Traité des tournois, joustes, carrousels, et autres spectacles publics* (Lyon: Jacques Muguet, 1669), 112, 126.

life in the courtyards of France's palaces. Carousels (the modern spelling) were not new to European courts, but this one was Louis XIV's first event of great significance and splendor as ruler of France and was designed to commemorate the birth of his first son and heir to his throne, the Dauphin.[91] The tournaments of 1662 included *courses de têtes et de bague*—"running at the heads" and "running at the ring," or tilting at the ring, as it is known in English—events for which the commemorative book about the carousel would be officially named. During the two-day celebration, members of the court divided up into five quadrilles (teams) and mounted on horseback as *cavaliers* and *cavalières* or *dames* (women participated as well). Dressed to represent five "famous nations"—Rome, Persia, Turkey, Asia (nations of "the Indies"), and the Americas—each team was led by a prince, in descending order of importance: the king was the Roman leader, his brother Monsieur head of the Persians, and so on.[92]

Ostensibly, then, the teams fought against one another in the competitions, although in reality the contests were little more than a vehicle for the king's inevitable triumph. In the "heads" contest, knights sped toward a *faquin*, a human shape made from the trunk of a tree, to simulate plunging a lance into a resistant body. For the "ring," contestants put their lances through a ring, vying for accuracy of aim. Reminiscent of combat but without the negative consequences, carousels staged power as an elaborate pageant that asked players to demonstrate their skills before the king. Significantly, they also brought the battlefield into France's backyard and staged it for ten to fifteen thousand spectators to see. In that sense, and minus the casualties, the carousel proved to be a brilliant power-building exercise for the young king. Furthermore, the logic of the world map predetermined the carousel's finale, with Rome—immediate precursor to European culture and model for Louis XIV's omnipotence—claiming victory.

As secretary of the Petite académie, Perrault would spend the next eight years after the event heading the team of writers and artists that produced the commemorative book, *Courses de testes et de bague*, which was published in 1670 at the Imprimerie royale, the king's official publisher.[93] Perrault's contribution as director of the project included writing the story of the event, choosing a series of images to commission and include, and

---

[91]Louis succeeded to the throne at the age of four upon his father Louis XIII's death in 1643. His mother, Queen Anne of Austria, acted as regent until he reached his majority in 1661, when he was twenty-three.

[92]Ménestrier, *Traité des tournois*, 126.

[93]Charles Perrault, *Courses de Testes et de Bague Faittes Par Le Roy et par Les Princes et Seigneurs de sa Cour En l'Année 1662* (Paris: Imprimerie royale, 1670).

MARESCHAL DE CAMP ROMAIN.

L E Cafque étoit d'argent brodé d'or avec des plumes, couleur de la livrée.

Le corps de cuiraffe & les lambrequins étoient de brocart d'argent brodé d'or, & orné de bandes de pierreries.

Les manches tant celles de deffus que celles de deffous, & le faye étoient de fatin blanc brodé d'or.

Les brodequins étoient de brocart d'argent brodé d'or.

Le caparaçon étoit de fatin couleur de feu brodé d'or & d'argent ; & dans les lambrequins des mufles de Lion en broderie.

V

Figure 7. *Courses de testes et de bague faites par le roy et par les princes et seigneurs en l'année 1662,* 1670. Perrault wrote this work, Henri Gissey was the artist, and François Chauveau did the engraving. (Bibliothèque nationale de France, Paris.)

writing the dedication to the Dauphin, then eight years old.[94] That the king's young son was the dedicatee illustrated one of the book's explicit goals: to demonstrate for the uninitiated prince the political use of spectacle as a display of power. Perrault dedicates the book in direct speech, addressing the Dauphin in the second person. On intimate terms with the embodiment of France's future, the dedication performs a welcome of the young boy onto the political stage as its heir—heir to the glory made concrete in 1662 by the event commemorated in the book. Beyond this apparent audience of one lay both the French and British nobility, who had attended the event and received copies of the book. They bear witness in this dedication to the instruction of the Dauphin in the ways of absolute monarchy—another form of publicity for the endurance and cultural reach of Louis XIV's policies.

There is more to say about the dedication as a political charm, but the concern of the present volume is the way it broadcasts Perrault's proximity to the core of the kingdom's power and, more importantly still, the high art of persuasion that it practiced. Rhetorically, in order to serve as the dedicator of the Grand Carrousel's memorial, Perrault claimed the event—or at least unique understanding of its purpose—as his own masterpiece and offered it to the future king, the kingdom, and the European nobility on behalf of Louis XIV. By speaking publicly to the Dauphin in this important historical document, Perrault established his role as a crafter of royal knowledge and a purveyor of royal pedagogy. Its dedication also makes apparent that in appearing to speak to a child, the book nonetheless addresses an adult audience, guiding subjects and foreigners alike toward the future under Louis XIV, and teaching them how to orient themselves to it. With his earliest court work, then, Perrault began to forge an identity of intimacy with monarchic pageantry and a strong pedagogical voice: ostensibly writing for young people, he subtly targeted adults who did not yet fully understand the lessons in power that the new regime wanted them to learn. This was a technique he would use again in his fairy tales.

His second major project for the court involved designing Versailles's labyrinth—a maze constructed in the gardens of the château. Like the Grand Carrousel and the commemorative book about it, Perrault conceived the labyrinth as another lesson, this one sculptural, for the Dauphin. The physical maze was originally designed by André Le Nôtre, chief painter to the

---

[94]The description of the Grand Carrousel was one among a series of visual and verbal documents commissioned by the king and featuring buildings, garden innovations, and events at Versailles, as well as military campaigns, to create a retrospective of the triumphs during the first decade of Louis XIV's reign. As secretary of the Petite académie, Perrault served as head of the whole massive visual art enterprise.

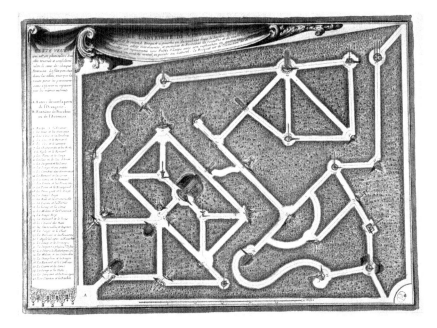

Figure 8. Map of the labyrinth's fountains designed by Perrault with the text of the thirty-nine quatrains, written by Isaac de Benserade, carved into them. *Le Labyrinte de Versailles,* 1680. Gabriel Perelle did the engraving. (Photo credit: Kharbine Tapabor, The Art Archive at Art Resource, NY.)

king and head of artistic planning, as a hedge ornament for the grounds. Perrault proposed adding to it art that offered—again—lessons in power and governance. He chose to commission sculptures depicting Aesop's fables, which "each contain a gallant moral" or a lesson in courtly sociability. Court poet Isaac de Benserade wrote verses about each fable that were carved into the base of the sculptures. Three hundred and thirty-three animals participated in this walkable tutorial: an entire book of fables come to life. Here were animals helping men, as they would in "Maître chat; ou, Le Chat botté."

As all labyrinths do, the living maze mapped the idea of navigating "a significant problem, a significant complication of affairs."[95] More important, this one also represented power relations as Aesop described them by positioning the animal fountainheads against each other. The animals' mouths served as spouts and water was their language of communication, such that

---

[95]"Un grand embarras, un grand embroüillement d'affaires." "Labyrinthe," *Dictionnaire de l'Académie française.*

when the fountains flowed they appeared to be sharing their "passion and ideas" with all who looked upon them. According to Perrault's account in *Le Labyrinthe de Versailles,* the commemorative publication of 1677, the garden maze was the work of Cupid, who declared, "I am myself a labyrinth where you can easily lose your way" and sought to help lovers with "maxims" from allegories.[96] Navigating labyrinths, learning from tales with talking animals, love as the reigning metaphor of sociability . . . in spirit, if not in letter, such lessons in understanding power and its coded representation are ones that Cendrillon will need to learn and Petit chaperon rouge will fail to comprehend in the *Histoires ou Contes* decades later.

At the Grand Carrousel festival, walking Versailles's labyrinth, and later reading fairy tales, people learned a modern creed particular to the reign of Louis XIV: manners of the court take shape around specific forms of display that communicate the nature of power and hierarchy, which all courtiers would do well to know. In the fairy tales, there will be one crucial difference: the tales tell the dystopian side of the power game. When deployed strategically as Louis XIV did, pageants were pedagogical tools used to instruct people in how the world should be ordered and who should be on top. These lessons in power ensured success at Versailles. Written into fairy tales, as Perrault would do in the 1690s, power looked more explicitly dangerous—like the *fâcheux* (nasty) labyrinths of legend—and its navigation became a treacherous game indeed, one young people could win only with marvelous help and through their wiles.[97]

As a writer and an intellectual, Perrault came of age at a time when French politicians and learned men—who generated the vast body of printed ideas known as the Republic of Letters—took up what it meant for a nation to have an officially codified way of expressing its cultural values and aspirations.[98] In the 1670s and 1680s, when Perrault was in the prime of his public life, the meaning of just about everything wordy, and especially literary, was up for hot debate in Paris. In the twenty years that elapsed between the

---

[96]Charles Perrault, *Le Labyrinthe de Versailles* (Paris: Imprimerie royale, 1677), n.p.

[97]*Fâcheux* is Amour/Love's description of what he does to mortals on a quest for romance (Perrault, *Labyrinthe*).

[98]"[T]he Republic of Letters is a historiographical tool to refer to networks of scholars organized around academic institutions, learned journals, informal gatherings and epistolary exchanges; on the other hand, it is the normative ideal of a community of scholars and writers who have egalitarian and personal relationships, autonomous from political power, from religious solidarities and from national identities." Antoine Lilti, "The Kingdom of Politesse: Salons and the Republic of Letters in Eighteenth-Century Paris," *Republics of Letters: A Journal for the Study of Knowledge, Politics, and the Arts* 1, no. 1 (2001): 2, arcade.stanford.edu/rofl_issue/volume-1-issue-1.

publication of the *Labyrinthe de Versailles* and the *Histoires ou Contes*, Perrault transitioned from historiography to full engagement with the formal oversight of creative writing in the kingdom. Starting public life as a propagandist and growing into an intellectual during the decades of the creation of the first major unofficial (1690) and then first official (1694) modern French dictionaries, Perrault trafficked in words—what they can do and how to use them. The 1690s were a decade that celebrated the French language and the ways it could change writing and ideas themselves. As an academician, again, Perrault managed the editorial team that oversaw the publication of the official dictionary and, as a writer, he took part concretely in the celebration of language. Additionally, the question of genres—which were best suited to French, which were best suited to the century of Louis XIV, and their power to change the way history was memorialized—recurs throughout his writing.

The term for the method of seventeenth-century historiography, or how writers memorialized current events, is *vraisemblance*, whose strict translation in modern English would be verisimilitude but which can be better understood as idealized realism: depicting life not in its material detail but rather as the age hoped to be remembered. In the 1690s, most writing, from panegyric to satire to political writing above all, spoke not to "reality" but to "ideality," the world the way it could or should be perceived. As we have seen, while Ancients remained faithful to the idealism of pagan antiquity, Moderns sought out new ideals to promote in modern Christian France. Genres such as Christian epic, of which Perrault was a firm advocate, the Platonic philosophy of René Descartes, and advances in astronomy were appropriately modern ways of rethinking ancient ideas. But so was the mockery of the burlesque, perhaps the most poetic way to deflate the power of tradition. Out of this highly inventive Republic of Letters, composed of a literati convinced that fiction would help craft the tenets of French nationalism in its own language and faith, also came the ironic—in the language of the period, burlesque—fairy tale. Unsurprisingly, perhaps, most of them were written by learned women barred by tradition from exercising their skills in older genres.

By 1697, when he published the *Histoires ou Contes*, Perrault had been hearing and reading fairy tales written by a cohort of smart, talented women (including his niece, Marie-Jeanne Lhéritier, and Marie-Catherine d'Aulnoy) and men considerably younger than he for at least eight years.[99]

---

[99]The women writers include Henriette-Julie de Murat, one of the exiles mentioned in the notes above, Catherine Bernard, Charlotte-Rose de Caumont de la Force, and Jean de Préchac. For translations of these less commonly treated women writers, see Seifert and Stanton, *Enchanted Eloquence*.

At the age of nearly seventy, he was the only academician in France deciding to write fairy tales about young heroines and heroes. Yet, that choice
coincides chronologically with the publication of the last installment of his
intellectual magnum opus, *Parallèle des Anciens et des Modernes*, a philosophical conversation at Versailles among an abbot and a young knight,
who represent forms of knowledge espoused by Moderns, and a provincial
president (presiding court-appointed official), who argues the side of the
Ancients. Pitting the first two characters against the third, the dialogue allows Platonic reason and current courtly knowledge to overcome the angry
and weak voice of past knowledge. Here the wise abbot and his bright young
charge, the knight (Perrault and the Dauphin of the labyrinth?), herald a
way of thinking that privileges ideas of the present.

On the surface, philosophical dialogue and fairy fiction draw from different ends of the intellectual spectrum. In Perrault's writing, they have in
common a focus on young people living and navigating in the moment. The
idea of relations among generations indeed joins the question of women
among the norms of sociability considered by the *Histoires ou Contes*.[100]
The philosophical theme of generation forms the backbone of a poetic tale
Perrault published at the same time as the *Apologie des femmes* and the
Parallèle in the thick of the debates about women. Written in the traditional
genre of the verse tale and long perceived as Perrault's most misogynist
piece, "La Marquise de Salusses; ou, La Patience de Griselidis" (The Marquise of Salusses; or, The Patience of Griselidis) sets out a plot that takes the
reader from one generation to the next in a family drama about marriage. In
the last few pages of this introduction, I reconsider "Griselidis" against the
Apologie as the writer's testing ground for new young fairy-tale characters.

Generation and Genre (1694)

First printed in book form in 1694, "Griselidis" made its intellectual debut
a few years earlier. Read aloud at a meeting of the Académie française in
1691, it appeared in print later that year in the *Mercure galant*, Paris's literary and cultural journal, and then again in 1694 with two other verse

---

[100]R. J. Howells has argued that the dialogic form of the *Parallèle* serves the Modern cause by virtue of its many voices and deft balance of the sides of Perrault's position, namely, that the Modern is "a Catholic yet an enthusiast for the new science, anti-pagan yet syncretist, a proponent of
material progress yet a Platonist, a reductive rationalist and a mystic." "Dialogue and Speakers
in the *Parallèle des Anciens et des Modernes*," *Modern Language Review* 78, no. 4 (1983): 795.

tales under the title *Contes en vers*.[101] Thus, "Griselidis" was the first tale Perrault made public in the 1690s, and it can be considered his first major contribution to the debates of the Ancients and Moderns on the subject of women. The printing of 1694 coincides by a matter of months with the first printing of the *Apologie*, Perrault's more philosophical tract about women, and indeed, with their similar emphases on domesticity, they read as companion pieces.[102]

"Griselidis" recounts the life of a beautiful young farming woman from the moment she captures the heart of a prince who has lost his way in the woods to the celebration of their daughter's wedding. Although the story is named for the woman, the narrator speaks from the perspective of the prince, sovereign ruler of a provincial territory at the southern base of the Alps where the Po River flows. The backstory of this prince is that in spite of all heaven's gifts "of the body and the soul," he has adamantly declared himself uninterested in women. To the horror of his subjects, who hope for an heir, he cites a litany of offenses visited by wives upon husbands they intend to dominate, and vows never to wed until he finds "another Lucretia." That heroine in ancient Roman legend famously resisted the adulterous advances of a prince of Rome, suffered rape at his hands, and committed suicide to spare her family the dishonor. She served as a paragon in Roman history and surfaces here, in the prince's threat, as the kind of mythic woman whose sterling virtue cannot be found in the modern world.

Perrault's plot unfolds with the prince on a hunt one day in the woods by his castle. He finds himself irresistibly drawn to a remote clearing beyond the edge of the trees and comes upon Griselidis working her fields. She appears to him "the most delightful, delicate, and lovable object that was ever seen under heaven."[103] Griselidis, a shepherdess tucked away beyond the woods who spins as she tends her flock, displays the peasant work ethic and ignorance of courtly sophistication that fit the moral profile of a Lucretia. The prince brings her back to the palace and marries her. He then begins with

---

[101]For the first printing, the poem's full title was "La Marquise de Salusses; ou, La Patience de Griselidis," in *Recueil de plusieurs pièces d'éloquence et de poésie présentés à l'Académie française pour le prix de l'année 1691* (Paris: Coignard, 1691). When it was published with two other tales in Perrault's first short collection, it appeared under the heroine's name: *Griselidis, Nouvelle, avec le conte de Peau d'Ane et celui des Souhaits ridicules* (Paris: Coignard, 1694).

[102]Shawn C. Jarvis links the story's roots in folklore and the medieval tradition to its role in the querelle, arguing that Modern thinkers staked a claim in the historical patrimony of France through their interest in folk material and also early vernacular literature. "Salon," in *The Greenwood Encyclopedia of Folktales and Fairy Tales: Q-Z*, ed. Donald Haase and Anne Duggan (Westport, CT: Greenwood, 2016), 3:883.

[103]"Griselidis, Nouvelle," in Collinet, *Perrault, Contes*, 64; my translation.

unrelenting cruelty to test her character and resolve. Griselidis suffers constant psychological and emotional torment from her husband for nearly the entire length of the story. As per the title, she "patiently" endures all of it. The tale ends when the prince has a conversion of sorts, declaring that Griselidis has suffered enough, proven herself worthy of him, and that he will forevermore be a loving husband. As the traditional interpretation of the story goes, Griselidis is Perrault's modern model of the perfect woman whose silent submission tames the beast in man. Feminists have found the tale of Griselidis intractable, not unlike the *Apologie*, unless it can be read as a parody.[104]

The Italian source for the plot is Giovanni Boccaccio's *Decameron* (circa 1350), the tenth tale on the tenth day told by Dioneo about the Marquis of Saluzzo.[105] Christopher Betts suggests that the story appears "rather untypical" of the *Decameron*, "a work known for comic bawdiness," but critics find the story of a penitent woman perfectly at home in Perrault's bibliography, especially as a companion piece to the *Apologie*.[106] Patricia Hannon links the two texts in a genealogy such that "the subjugated female sensuality embodied by the heroine [of "Griselidis"] will evolve into a subdued and perhaps more 'modern' version of the serene housewife of Perrault's later *Apologie des femmes*."[107] Given that, as Perrault claimed, the conception of the *Apologie* preceded that of the tale, we might also argue that the *Apologie* scenario, in which women save boorish men, can be said to furnish the premise of the plot in "Griselidis."

The centrality of the boorish man, which dictates a secondary and sacrificial role for the woman, does seem to link the texts. The verse tale of "Griselidis" has a tragic edge in that the heroine is viciously abused and her extreme modesty is larger than life. Indeed, the prince expresses his requirements in a marriage partner in language reminiscent of Perrault's obedient wife in the *Apologie*:

> For there to be a chance of married bliss,
> Authority must not be shared by both.

---

[104]Yvette Saupé accepts the tale as a parody, arguing that the figure of Griselidis cannot be taken seriously as a model. See *Les Contes de Perrault et la mythologie: Rapprochements et influences* (Seattle: PFSCL, 1997), 120–30.

[105]Giovanni Boccaccio, *The Decameron*, rev. ed., trans. Wayne A. Rebhorn (New York: Norton, 2013), 839–50. Saluzzo is a region at the base of the Alps in the far west corner of northern Italy not far from the Po. Perrault resists naming the city in his version.

[106]Christopher Betts, introduction to *Charles Perrault: The Complete Fairy Tales*, trans. Christopher Betts (Oxford: Oxford University Press, 2009), xiii.

[107]Hannon, *Fabulous Identities*, 46. For important feminist critiques of the tale, see especially Holly Tucker and Melanie Siemens, "Perrault's Preface to Griselda and Murat's 'To Modern Fairies,'" *Marvels & Tales* 19, no. 1 (2005): 126–30; and Duggan, *Salonnières*, 139–47.

> If therefore what you want to see
> Is that I take the marriage oath,
> Find me a woman who has never shown
> The slightest disobedience: she must be
> Of proven patience, modest, lacking pride,
> And free from any wishes of her own.
> When she is found, I'll take her for my bride.[108]

Once he discovers Griselidis, whose beauty, the narrator interjects, "could have pacified / The angriest of men,"[109] he plans the wedding before ever introducing himself to her, and then goes back to the woods to announce that she will marry him. She agrees readily, pledging full obedience to his will. When his interest in her wanes after marriage, her continued submission tortures him. Finding her greatest love directed toward their newborn daughter, he takes the child from her and then, a few days later, announces that she is dead. Years later, he informs Griselidis that he must leave her and take another wife, a ruse he sweetens for his own sadistic pleasure by bringing his own daughter, now fully grown, back as the lovely young stranger he will wed.

Griselidis's purity in the face of her husband's cruelty assumes proportions of saintly dimensions. She welcomes the young woman into their home and tends to her needs. Indeed, Perrault's personal faith, Catholicism, and his writings on explicitly Christian themes (for example, *Les Pensées chrétiennes*) have been brought to bear on reading this story as an endorsement of women's suffering.[110] As long as the critical focus remains trained on the eponymous character Griselidis, anchored as she is in Roman and Renaissance Italian patriarchal lore, the moral needle of the story indeed points toward exemplary self-sacrifice. Reading the whole sordid scenario ironically presents an appealing option, but there are few textual details that support it because the narrator/prince's perspective drives the plot; we rarely hear Griselidis's voice.

---

[108]"Or je suis convaincu que dans le mariage / On ne peut jamais vivre heureux, / Quand on y commande tous deux; / Si donc vous souhaitez qu'à l'hymen je m'engage, / Cherchez une jeune beauté / Sans orgueil et sans vanité, / D'une obéissance achevée, / D'une patience éprouvée, / Et qui n'ait point de volonté, / Je la prendrai quand vous l'aurez trouvé." Collinet, "Griselidis, Nouvelle," 62–63. All French passages are taken from this edition. This and subsequent English translations are by Christopher Betts, who has produced the only verse translation of the tale. "The History of Griselda," in *Charles Perrault: The Complete Fairy Tales*, 14.

[109]Betts, "The History of Griselda," 15. "Elle aurait pu dompter les coeurs les plus sauvages" (Collinet, "Griselidis, Nouvelle," 64).

[110]See Duggan's thorough and compelling use of the *Pensées* to set up an argument about disorder and wifely misconduct in "Griselidis" and "Blue Beard" (*Salonnières*, 144–45, 155–64).

Nevertheless, adopting the stance of the ironic reader here invites the practice of rethinking what we think we know about the eponymous character. The place to begin that sort of reading is in the quiet but present voice of the heroine herself. Since she says very little, those words have weight and expose a fissure in the character's submissive and pious façade. When her husband arrives home with his new wife-to-be, Griselidis does not present herself as an example for the wife to follow but as a singular exception, and a lamentable one at that. That is to say, far from thinking *herself* a model, although the prince, the narrator, and even the reader might at this point in the narrative, Griselidis does not believe any other woman could or should endure what she has:

> Permit me sir to make a plea
> In favour of the maiden you will wed,
> For she was tenderly brought up, and bred
> To live in luxury and splendour, free
> From any cruelty; she could not bear
> The trials you impose on me:
> She would not live through treatment so severe.
>
> Of lowly birth and poor, I was inured
> To toil and hardship; married, I endured
> All kinds of misery and pain;
> It did not vex me, nor did I complain,
> But she has never suffered grief or woe.
> The slightest hardship that you show
> Will kill her; angry words, a look, no more,
> Would be to her a mortal blow,
> Alas! Sir, treat her kindly, I implore.[111]

As the eponymous character upon whom eyes focus with awe (or horror), Griselidis earns the right to be heard by the reader, if not by her husband.

---

[111]Betts, "The History of Griselda," 36–37. "Souffrez, Seigneur, que je vous représente / Que cette Princesse charmante, / Dont vous allez être l'Epoux, / Dans l'aise, dans l'éclat, dans la pourpre nourrie, / Ne pourra supporter, sans en perdre la vie, / Les mêmes traitements que j'ai reçus de vous. Le besoin, ma naissance obscure, / M'avaient endurcie aux travaux, / Et je pouvais souffrir toutes sortes de maux / Sans peine et même sans murmure; / Mais elle qui jamais n'a connu la douleur, / Elle mourra dès la moindre rigueur, / Dès la moindre parole un peu sèche, un peu dure. / Hélas! seigneur, je vous conjure, / De la traiter avec douceur" (Collinet, "Griselidis, Nouvelle," 85).

Here she casts the comparison with the other woman as one of rustic versus privileged life. The privileged woman, unlike the woman reared on the land, cannot withstand abuse. On the surface the argument looks banal: toughened mother versus coddled daughter. But thinking textually about why she would want to spare her daughter the suffering opens up other possibilities.

Figuratively, the positions of farmwoman and noblewoman also correspond to modes of existence: poor/rich, country/courtly, past/present. Allegorically, we might further read the contrast as one between the ancient world, where Roman women were portrayed through victimization or fury, and the modern, where French women are portrayed as noble and worthy of a good marriage. Through these lenses, it is possible to see Griselidis as the facilitator of a future moment in which both she and her husband's master/servant dynamic will collapse in obsolescence and new stories about marriage will be told. A future that is different from Griselidis's life thus appears on the narrative horizon in the figure of the woman—unbeknownst to her, the daughter—she tries to protect.

The daughter has been read as a pawn in the relationship between husband and wife: her removal from the home the ultimate atrocity to commit against a mother, and her return the sign of the prince's conversion. But there is more to her than that. Offstage, she has grown into a woman capable of falling in love of her own accord with a man who loves her and choosing him as her husband; this is a model of behavior completely unlike that of the mother figure. Furthermore, she serves a narrative purpose for Griselidis, who changes when she witnesses the potential embodied in her now adult daughter; though it is subtler, Griselidis's transformation is no less powerful in the narrative than the prince's. Faced with the prospect of her husband taking a new wife and imagining this young woman forced to walk in her shoes, Griselidis reacts, making demands on her husband for the first time: Do not do to her what you have done to me; she will not survive it. Even the woman who endures everything cannot stay silent at this threat to another woman. In fact, this expression of her anxiety (very uncommon in the poem, though in keeping with her selflessness) brings the full weight of her self-awareness into the story: she perceives herself as different from other women, especially urban women, inviting the reader to do the same.

With a plea to her husband to leave other women alone—to let the young woman go off and grow into a softer, better, and less tortured wife— she critiques her own idealism. Griselidis lives the life of a relic, a thing of the past, something a charming, determined young woman hoping to experience a new courtly narrative of her own will simply fail to approximate. In anticipatory fairy-tale fashion, Perrault writes the daughter into a marriage that does not look at all like the one her mother has endured. More important, Griselidis's supplication applies equally—and persuasively—to the poetic arts if here she speaks in the voice of the Moderns: idolizing the old will stifle and suffocate the new. Let modern French words and grammar and themes have a new narrative of their own.

In that sense, the future plot of the daughter's happy marriage is crucial to the story's success, as Perrault tells it. Critically, her character has sustained very little inquiry, but there are textual cues to suggest that she is the endpoint of narrative struggle.[112] A dedicatory letter to Monsieur, Louis XIV's brother, which served as an afterword to the poem in 1695 (its second edition) makes this case, too. In this odd piece, written in the form of a debate among half a dozen people who sound like academicians, Perrault responds to his critics in the voice of the letter's narrator. Although printed as a dedicatory letter to a royal prince, the text has exceptionally fictional qualities, such as entire conversations recorded as though verbatim. Potentially no more historical than Griselidis herself, the letter strategically serves the narrative both as a justification of its modern style and, importantly for our purposes, an argument for the literary role of the marriage plot. Perrault's voice says, in particular, that there were too many opinions about the first draft of his story. Early in the letter, one critic objects to nearly everything in the poem, finally targeting the "side story" of the prince and the daughter, which he finds superfluous. Perrault argues with him that without it the story's ending remains "unhappy":

[Critic 1:] I would also cut the episode of the young lord who is only there to marry the princess. It makes the poem too long.

[Narrator:] But, I argued, the story has an unhappy ending without the marriage.

[Critic 1:] I don't know what to tell you, he answered, but I would not hesitate to take it out.[113]

---

[112]Marie-Dominique Leclerc has explored Griselidis as a *thème littéraire* (literary theme) that was reborn in France with Perrault's version of the story. The daughter appears and warrants mention in the discussions of the later adaptations she covers, but never becomes the focus of inquiry. "Renaissance d'un thème littéraire au XVIIe et XVIIIe siècles: La Patience de Grisélidis," *Revue d'histoire littéraire de la France* 91, no. 2 (1991): 147-76.

[113]"'Griselda' Letter to Monsieur," trans. Christine A. Jones, in Bottigheimer, *Fairy Tales Framed*, 119. Neither Appelbaum nor Betts includes the afterword in their translation volumes.

Here Perrault argues for the public's interest in the marriage and the way it ends what would otherwise be an unhappy story—identifying the older versions of Griselda with tragedy—on a positive note.

Later in the letter, critics again find the marriage plot a distraction. Readers must see, they argue, the work of God in the heroine's behavior; that is, see Griselidis as the moral ideal in the story. This time the dialogue ends in the voice of a different critic in favor of the marriage ending:

> [Narrator:] Others also criticized, I insisted, the episode of the lord who marries the princess.
>
> [Critic 2:] They're wrong, he answered. Since your piece is a poem, although you call it a *nouvelle* [novella], its ending must leave nothing to be desired. If the young Princess returned to the convent instead of entering into the marriage she expected, she wouldn't be happy and neither would the reader.[114]

In his support of the marriage, critic 2 expresses concern about the young female character, the same one Griselidis expresses—"angry words . . . a mortal blow"—and suggests the reader's enjoyment of this story at the end of the seventeenth century depends upon the daughter's happiness. While none of these voices can be said fully to embody the authorial figure of Perrault, critic 2 does end several pages of debate with the argument for the popularity of secular happiness in modern literature. In that sense, at the end of the dedication, the vote swings in favor of the balanced marriage plot. Indeed, in the end, the narrator tells us, he followed none of the advice and published it as he had written it with the princess's romance intact.

How might this detail illuminate a new way to read the verse tale? We know that the bachelor prince in "Griselidis" suffers from the same dark and angry attitude as Boileau in Perrault's *Apologie*. When his advisors beseech him to marry and secure his succession with an heir, he rails against the prospect of marriage, citing the following concerns:

> She of the gloomy sort, refusing fun,
> Decides to be exceedingly devout;
> She looks for things to make a fuss about,
> And scolds us constantly; another one
> Becomes a fully fledged coquette

---

[114]Ibid., 120.

With all the would-be lovers she can get,
But only chats and gossips all the time;
Another ardently takes part
In keen debates on books and art,
Lays down the law on prose and rhyme,
Another tells our authors where they err;
She thinks she is a connoisseur. [115]

So close are the prince's descriptions of the ills of womanhood to those attributed to Boileau in the *Apologie* that it is possible to see "Griselidis" not only as the story of a patient woman but also as the story of a traditional misogynist's conversion to modern gender ideals. Patricia Hannon linked the prince to Boileau in her chapter entitled "Corps cadavres" (Cadaver Bodies) in *Fabulous Identities*.[116] Jean-Pierre Collinet has suggested, too, that Perrault's source for the attitude of the prince has a precedent in Jean de La Bruyère's tract against the excesses of Parisian women in "Des femmes" (On Women).[117] La Bruyère, one of the seventeenth century's more vocal moralists on the subject of gender, similarly categorizes Parisian women and condemns them all squarely for falsehood. This comparison suggests that the prince is reacting to the excess of women; yet, there is no narrative evidence at all in the story that women are ever excessive; only the prince's stereotypes of them are excessive. I am suggesting that if the comparison with Boileau holds it is because the prince, like Boileau, is not the denouncer of excess but the *source* of excess in the story.

The prince's boiling wrath does not stop at Griselidis; it spills over onto his daughter as he wrenches her out of the arms of the man she has chosen to marry and orchestrates the last trick he plays on his wife. He even rationalizes this cruelty as a prerequisite to love: "in order for their love to grow more firm and content, they must undergo a harsh ordeal of fear and dread."[118] This is a man Griselidis comes to believe must be stopped, and indeed he is transformed in the course of the narrative. But a wholly different ethos governs the princess's marriage in that it does not involve a saintly woman curing a brutal man. Whatever else it can be taken to be, "Griselidis" is the story of a satirist of women (Boileau) who is converted to the cause of the Moderns when he meets the ancient ideal of womanhood and *she* explains that her

---

[115]Betts, "The History of Griselda," 13.
[116]"Indeed the misogynist frame that defines the melancholic hero's perception of *le sexe* [in "Griselidis"] is nearly identical to the scathing antifeminism expressed in Boileau's 1694 *Satire X*" (Hannon, *Fabulous Identities*, 48).
[117]Collinet, *Perrault, Contes*, 13.
[118]Betts, "The History of Griselda," 32.

own narrative has no place in the future. Perrault's poem ends with the prince giving his daughter in marriage to a "noble youth who loves her heart and soul" and about whom "she feels the same" at a sumptuous wedding party.[119] The daughter's right to leave the old master/servant world behind occasions a rebirth of genre in the form of a new plotline for balanced gender relations.

In the intense wish Griselidis expresses to love and protect her daughter and in the ability of the daughter to choose, Perrault's verse tale models, for the next generation, a forward-thinking approach to marriage that breaks with a patriarchal vision of women as objects of exchange or prizes for hunting men. Marrying for love is the lifeline Perrault gives the daughter of "Patient Griselda," one not afforded her in Boccaccio's tale, which is focused wholly on a married woman and her punishing fate.[120] In the Italian Renaissance version of the tale, the daughter is very young (twelve years old) and married by her father to a nobleman of his choice; the plot is incidental. In the modern French version, because she was not raised with her mother in the oppressive environment of the prince/Boileau, Perrault's young woman operates with new instincts that are perhaps risky—can marriage for love work in a courtly world?—but they are not naïve. She can be said to represent the spirit of the Moderns in the debate, younger but wiser than their ancient counterparts who, for their part, appear quite juvenile in their behaviors by comparison.[121] Next to the prince's antics and Griselidis's self-sacrifice, the young couple is the picture of balance.

"Griselidis" suggests literary strategy quite unlike the "blunt terseness" for which Perrault would come to be known.[122] In fact, the very next year, 1695,

---

[119]Ibid., 38. "à ce jeune Seigneur / Qui l'aime d'un amour extrême / Et dont il est aimé de même" (Collinet, "Griselidis, Nouvelle," 87).

[120]Marga Cottino-Jones made the case that Boccaccio's version of Griselda, the likely source of Perrault's knowledge of the tale, represents an allegory of religious devotion embodied in the suffering Jesus's acceptance of God's inexorable will. "Fabula vs. Figura: Another Interpretation of the Griselda Story," in The Decameron, ed. and trans. Mark Musa and Peter E. Bondanella (New York: Norton, 1977), 295–305.

[121]In The Shock of the Ancient: Literature & History in Early Modern France (Chicago: University of Chicago Press, 2011), Larry Norman proposes a new way of thinking about the Ancient and Modern positions in contradistinction to their inherited titles. He characterizes the terms of Moderns in the quarrel as a "radical reversal of the traditional analogy between the lifespan of collective humanity and the lifespan of the individual" (64). Rather than revere the ancients as fonts of time-honored wisdom, they suggest instead that antiquity was an intellectual childhood that has matured into modern France.

[122]Elizabeth Harries used this language to describe how writers like Walter Benjamin characterized the fairy tale in the early part of the twentieth century and notes in parentheses that Perrault approximates this model, whereas the conteuses of the 1690s do not. Elizabeth Wanning Harries, Twice upon a Time: Women Writers and the History of the Fairy Tale (Princeton: Princeton University Press, 2001), 17.

he and his son dedicated a volume written in the entirely new literary genre that would come to be known as the fairy tale to the first princess of France. She represents the first generation of young royals and aristocrats who could grow up reading fairy tales in French. The volume's dedication invites her to approach the volume as what Jennifer Schacker called an ironic reader. A new genre for a new generation, the fairy tale arose from older genres, of which "Griselidis" is an example. Perrault carved space already in that ancient tale to make room for the modern redemption of a young heroine in love. He would fill his next volume with stories about adolescent women and men who find their way out of twisted plots and away from oppressive adults. They do not come from the woods but go into the woods, and they do not quietly suffer abuse like Griselidis but, like her daughter, claim their future through a loving marriage plot and/or financial gain.

Armed with fairies and clever cats as their guides in the *Histoires ou Contes*, that next generation, the young people of fairy land, learn to navigate the behavioral strictures of the courtly world, notably the unequal male/female and have/have not dynamics of the seventeenth-century courtship ritual. I have suggested in this introduction that the designation "of the past" in Perrault's title does not date the ideas in a time gone by but announces a Modern project: to update inherited wisdom and make it pleasing and meaningful to perspicacious young courtiers such as Elisabeth d'Orléans and the fictional Griselidis's daughter.

As this introduction has shown, Disney's portrayals, scholarly assumptions about Perrault's gender politics, and intellectual anchors such as "Griselidis," make it harder to see the young women of the French fairy-tale in their own right.

The next section, "Notes on Editions, Translations, and Interpretations," locates the Mother Goose tales within the collection's translation history and argues for ways to bring that context to bear upon how the stories and particularly the fairy-tale characters look in English. Translation, like Disney, has traditionally operated as a stabilizing force in the collection's meaning but can instead generate new twenty-first-century appreciation for Perrault's three-hundred-year-old heroines and heroes.

Notes on Editions, Translations, and Interpretations

Early Editions with Lasting Impact

Claude Barbin

French-language editions of Charles Perrault's *Histoires ou Contes du temps passé* abound in the first decade after its initial publication, even in the first year, 1697. The very first French edition, issued by publisher Claude Barbin, was official; that is to say, it bore the royal imprimatur—official permission to print stated on the title page—of King Louis XIV, which guaranteed Barbin exclusive rights to publish the book for a period of time in France.[1] What must have been a rapid pipeline to press resulted in the first printing being issued with typographical errors. A few months later Barbin updated and reissued the volume, calling it "corrected." This corrected copy of the official edition, now known as the Barbin second state printing, was the basis for my translations. It was also the source for the five French-language editions produced by other publishers over the next twenty years in France and Holland (see "Early Francophone Editions" in the bibliography), who issued their books with the notice "suivant la copie de Paris" (based on the Paris edition).

All such French-language editions printed during the duration of the Barbin privilege, renewed until 1709, are considered pirated, as they violated copyright. Beyond the privilege, many presses reissued the Barbin edition with minimal changes for most of the century, even copying the woodcut illustrations—albeit in reverse—with remarkable precision. In the matter of the book's form, however, the Barbin table of contents did not traverse history well. Most French editions of the eighteenth and nineteenth centuries printed the tales in another order. That trend began at the Dutch publishing house of the family Desbordes, which had been printing pirated copies since at least 1700.

---

[1] The words *avec permission du roi* or *avec privilège du roi* appear at the bottom of the title page. Often early editions printed the privilege at the back of the book, as is the case with this edition.

Jaques Desbordes

Very early on in the publication history of the French-language editions, an editor exchanged the positions of two of the eight stories in the *Histoires ou Contes*. This small change had substantial implications for what a literary fairy tale looked like to its eighteenth-century audience. In the early French editions until about 1720, readers of the collection first encountered "Belle au bois dormant" / Sleeping Beauty, the longest tale in the volume at anywhere from thirty-five to forty-five pages in early print editions.

Violent as it is long, the story centers not on the courtship of the couple, which happens quickly, but on their married life. Owing to the tale's length, however, the plot has time to resolve the many problems it sets up, notably the family homocide perpetrated by the ogress stepmother, who orders that her grandchildren and the princess be cooked for dinner and then savors the flesh when she thinks they have been served to her bathed in a *sauce Robert*. Clearly a cultured woman, in that she asks for this labor-intensive staple of French cuisine, she nonetheless ends her days in a vat of vipers and snakes.

Readers progressed past this dysfunctional family drama to encounter a young red-clad heroine and old woman, eaten alive within five pages, followed by Perrault's bloodiest tale of marital woe, "Barbe bleue" / Blue Beard. Each of the first three tales in its own way has the heroine cross paths with a murderer. Twice she marries into a homicidal household: a very adult theme.

Around 1721, a major publisher in Amsterdam, the family Desbordes, changed the order of the texts: "Petit chaperon rouge" / Little Red Riding Hood was placed first, followed by "Les Fées" / The Fairies.[2] These, the shortest tales in the corpus, balance each other out with dystopian and utopian endings: young girl dies by talking to a wolf versus young girl lives by talking to a fairy. This order eases the reader into the idea of a tale with two short ones, tempering the red-clad child's death with a story of gemstones and happiness. Only then does the collection plunge into the world of marital homicide with "Barbe bleue" / Blue Beard followed by "Belle au bois dormant" / Sleeping Beauty. At the least, this alteration foregrounds brevity

---

[2]Jaques Desbordes printed 1697, 1700, 1708, and 1714 editions of the French 1697 version, all marked "after the edition of Paris." When he died, his widow took over the press. She published the 1721 edition, still called "after the edition of Paris," but changed the table of contents. See "Early Francophone Editions" in the bibliography.

and moves the heft of longer stories to a central place in the collection. Beyond that, it changed the headlining character from one of the oldest to one of the youngest.

All but one series of publications out of France and Holland followed the Desbordes edition, including a fine 1777 edition with a black and red print title page by Jean-François Bassompierre and an extraordinary 1781 printing on velum by Pierre-Michel Lamy for Marie Thérèse Charlotte, oldest child of Louis XVI and Marie Antoinette.[3] Even the landmark 1862 *Contes de Perrault* featuring illustrations by Gustave Doré similarly placed "Petit chaperon rouge" / Little Red Riding Hood first, followed by the other "little" hero, "Le Petit poucet" / Hop o' My Thumb, then "Belle au bois dormant" / Sleeping Beauty, and relegated the bloody tale of "Barbe bleue" / Blue Beard to last place.

Among the extant copies housed in major libraries in the United States and Europe, only chapbooks, editions produced inexpensively and with no images, produced in Paris at the house of Nicholas Gosselin (1724) and in the city of Troyes by Pierre Garnier (1737) and Jean Oudot (1756), seem to have returned to the 1697 order.[4] While this anomaly does not illuminate why the order was changed, it does point to a curiosity—namely, the preeminence of the shorter tales as a model for what a fairy tale looks and sounds like—that endured for much of the print tradition. Because Robert Samber followed the Dutch edition of 1721 when he made the first English translation, Desbordes's choices influenced two centuries of the print tradition in English.

Robert Samber

The translation history of the *Histoires ou Contes du temps passé* began with Robert Samber's 1729 *Histories, or Tales of Past Times*. Perrault's collection has been consistently republished in English since then. For most of the eighteenth century, Samber's translation choices for the tales were not significantly altered. Martine Hennard's reminder that Samber's English quickly became the standard for the eighteenth and nineteenth century is a point laid bare by the extensive bibliography of translations that

---

[3]For more information on this edition, see "Early Francophone Editions" in the bibliography.
[4]Roger Chartier and Henri-Jean Martin identify the Troyes editions as a group, but do not offer an explanation of why the 1697 order would have started circulating again in chapbook (*bibliothèque bleue*) edition. *Histoire de l'édition française: Le Livre triumphant, 1660–1830* (1984; repr., Paris: Fayard, 1990), 661.

accompanies the present volume.[5] Nearly all English translations from 1729 to 1804 refer back to Samber the way Dutch publishers referred to Barbin, the editions numbered with reference to his first edition. Editions well into the twentieth century still mention Samber as their source, with translators sometimes working from Samber alongside or in lieu of the French.[6]

Thus, from 1729 to the early nineteenth century, via Samber, British editions copied the Desbordes's change to the table of contents, with "Petit chaperon rouge" / Little Red Riding Hood first and "Belle au bois dormant" / Sleeping Beauty in the middle.[7] Because editors tended to reprint and tweak the earlier translations by Samber and another credited to Guy Miège rather than start from scratch, it was already very difficult by 1750 to flout this convention.[8] Preservation of style had its analogue in illustrations, which were redrawn constantly from the plates reproduced by Antoine Clouzier that had adorned the 1697 edition and Samber's 1729 translation. The Desbordes edition reversed the Clouzier images, Samber used them as models, and thus most English-language printings of the century also include the reversed images.

Again, only one extant English edition returned to the 1697 order, and it broke with the style of standard editions in other ways as well.[9] An exception such as this one proves a rule: early English-language editors accepted the authority of changes produced decades after 1697. Tracing this parallel history in French and English shows that the Barbin edition had less formal impact on the long tradition of republication of the volume than those

---

[5]She cites Lang, who still refers back to Samber: "This first translation became the standard, and Andrew Lang's beloved *Blue Fairy Book* (1889) confirmed its reputation as a classic in English. In the short preface to the first volume of his famous collection, Lang mentions that 'the tales of Perrault are printed from the old English version of the eighteenth century.'" Hennard, "Cinderella's Metamorphoses," 255.

[6]This is the case notably for J. E. Mansion's translations in *The Fairy Tales of Charles Perrault* (1922), in which he "revised and corrected" Samber's original translation.

[7]Samber, *Histories, or tales of past times.*

[8]*Histories or Tales of Passed Times, Told by Mother Goose. Englished by G.M. Gent* (Salisbury: Benjamin C. Collins / London: William Bristow / Devizes: Mrs. Maynard, 1763) appears to be the earliest extant reference to the initials G.M., later identified as Guy Miège. An edition from the Opie Collection entitled *Tales of passed times by Mother Goose with morals, Englished by R.S.* (London: S. van den Berg, 1764), also credits Miège with the translation in spite of the R.S. in the edition's title. An 1802 edition in the British Library, which identifies itself as the eleventh using G.M.'s translations, and another from 1810 at the Osborne Collection of Early Children's Books in Toronto attest to its reprinting through at least the early nineteenth century. See both entries in the "Early Translations" in the bibliography for a discussion of the controversy surrounding this name.

[9]*Old Mother Goose's Interesting Stories of Past Times* (London: S. Fischer and T. Hurst, 1803). See the bibliography.

produced in the 1720s in both languages. One likely effect of repeating the Desbordes/Samber choices over more than a century is that they helped forge the image of the Perraultian corpus. As the three verse tales of 1694, including "Griselidis," were rarely produced in the same edition as the eight tales of the *Histories or Tales of Past Times*, they did not serve as a point of comparison for readers, allowing the latter to forge their own identity in the context of other publications and arts of the fairy tale in the eighteenth century.[10] Before addressing the methodology behind the present translations, the next section fleshes out some key ways in which the repetition of illustration and translation choices helped brand the collection ideologically.[11]

Enduring Choices

The British persona of Mother Goose, which Samber introduced in his translation of *Ma Mère l'Oye*, had a history before he used it but gained in popularity because of frequent reprinting of his translations over the next few generations. At midcentury, the figure and name Mother Goose took on another association, for which she would forevermore be known. John Newbery's *The Original Mother Goose's Melody; or, Sonnets for the Cradle* (circa 1760) contained nursery rhymes, not fairy tales.[12] Newbery's introduction identifies the human tellers behind the metaphorical goose as "old British nurses" and their audience, as per the title, as children in the cradle. Each rhyme is followed by a one-line "maxim" that draws out the lesson from the poem into truisms such as "If we do not govern our passions, our passions will govern us" and "All work and no play makes Jack a dull boy." Part 2 of the collection pairs the fifty-one short rhymes in the first

---

[10]Lamy's 1781 edition may be the first to contain the verse tales: *Contes des fées, par Charles Perrault de l'Académie Françoise*, 3 vols. (Paris: Pierre-Michel Lamy, 1781). They were not often printed together with the prose tales until the twentieth century.

[11]Jean-Michel Adam's extensive stylistic analysis of the volume leads him to conclude that the stories in the *Histoires ou Contes du temps passé* are formally linked through such varied poetic strategies as capitalization, conjunctions, onomastics, and even parenthesis. This network of echoes across the tales "transform[s] the collection formally into a literary text and not a succession of eight tales" (transforment le recueil en un véritable texte littéraire composé et non en une suite arbitraire de huit textes). Heidman and Adam, *Textualité et intertextualité des contes*, 234.

[12]The earliest extant copy of this book was printed for Francis Powers (noted on the title page as Newbery's grandson) in 1791. *Mother Goose's melody, or, Sonnets for the cradle*, Lilly Library Digital Collections, www.indiana.edu/~liblilly/digital/collections/items/show/87. Jacques Barchilon and Peter Flinders identify a lost 1781 copy as the first issue (*Charles Perrault*, 166n23). Barchilon and Pettit produced the 1791 edition in facsimile under the title *The Authentic Mother Goose Fairy Tales and Nursery Rhymes*.

with fourteen sonnets, called lullabies, by "that sweet Songster and Nurse of wit, Master William Shakespeare."[13] This concretely British goose figure who knows Shakespeare's "Spring" and "Winter" and teaches *Poor Richard's Almanack*-style lessons from stock nursery rhymes bears little resemblance to the Perraultian voice. French Mother Goose retooled old stories and attached to them long-winded ironic morals that undo rather than reinforce the meanings of the tales.

Conflating fairy tales and nursery rhymes by association with the same stock British figure helped reshape the convention about what a fairy tale did and for whom it was written for the latter part of the eighteenth century. But the result was not simply or plainly infantilized versions of the stories. Rather, when the idea of the fairy-tale Mother Goose began to look more like her British embodiment, the stories began to show their age. By 1785 (although the change began as early as the 1740s), the woman in the frontispiece of both French- and English-language editions looked considerably older than her 1697 counterpart—as though she had aged in real time—and she performed for younger children who appear mesmerized by her words (see figure 9). This late-eighteenth-century trend presented fairy tales as nursery rhymes: entertainments for rapt and eager learners.

As the tales started to show their age in the frontispiece and short tales such as "Petit chaperon rouge" / Little Red Riding Hood could be compared to rhymes and lullabies by "nurses of wit," the door opened to rethinking the adult stories as ideal children's reading. Additionally, there are economic reasons why, by the end of the eighteenth century, editors sought to produce shorter, more didactic versions of these and other French tales, not the least of which was the desire, circa 1800, to reach a wider (and thus more lucrative) readership by targeting parents who read to children. Stories such as "Belle au bois dormant" / Sleeping Beauty and "Cendrillon" / Cinderella were shortened to more closely resemble "Petit chaperon rouge" / Little Red Riding Hood. Benjamin Tabart's 1804 "Sleeping Beauty" presents one of the first examples in English of significant plot reorientation for a wider reading public. Tabart ended the tale at the marriage, shifting its emphasis from the conjugal life that occupied most of the French tale to courtship. Not only was the result significantly shorter, it also featured a dialogue unknown during the eighteenth century that amplified the character of the prince and the romance of the courtship ritual.

---

[13]Subtitle of part 2 of *Mother Goose's melody* on the title page (reprinted in Barchilon and Pettit, *The Authentic Mother Goose Fairy Tales and Nursery Rhymes*).

Figure 9. Simon Fokke, frontispiece of *The Histories of passed times; or, The Tales of Mother Goose, with Morals* (London: B. Le Francq, 1785). (Courtesy Lilly Library, Indiana University, Bloomington.)

While truncating the tale halfway through its plot was a new idea, the dialogue included in this edition was not. Tabart shrewdly lifted it from a French volume printed under the First French Republic in 1799.[14] In point of fact, this chatty prince was not a revolutionary invention either. The prince first gave this speech in the 1695 manuscript of the *Contes de ma Mère l'Oye*, which is also the version printed in the 1696 issue of the *Mercure galant*. Once it was edited out for the volume Barbin published in 1697, it never appeared again until the post-French Revolution editors rediscovered it. While we may never have a historical explanation for why they chose to reprint it a century after it was removed, the gesture speaks to cultural context. The time had come for a revolutionary prince to transform the power dynamic of old classical French "Belle au bois dormant" / Sleeping Beauty; ironically, that new personality was a classical reject.

The new/old scene occurs after the prince and princess have talked for four hours, "not saying half of what they had to tell each other" in 1697. Now the prince launches into the following speech:

"Could it be, beautiful princess," the prince said to her with eyes that said a thousand times more than his words, "could it be that the fates gave me life to serve you? Those beautiful eyes opened only for me? And that all the kings of the world, with all their might, could not have done what I did with my love?"

Quoi, belle Princesse, lui disait le Prince, en la regardant avec des yeux qui en disaient mille fois plus que ces paroles, quoi, les destins m'ont fait naître pour vous servir? Ces beaux yeux ne se sont ouverts que pour moi, & que tous les rois de la terre, avec toute leur puissance, n'auraient pu faire, ce que j'ai fait avec mon amour?[15]

Once it appeared in French, the speech quickly passed into English through Benjamin Tabart's Juvenile Library bookshop for young consumers of literature. As part of the initial offerings for his store in 1804, he published a new translation, *Sleeping Beauty in the Wood*—shortened and with the heroic speech added—first as a chapbook and then in part 2 of his *Popular Stories for the Nursery*. M. O. Grenby notes that these translations, not credited on Tabart's title page, were done by William or Mary Jane Godwin of the family

---

[14]*Contes des fées. Par Charles Perrault de l'Académie française* (Paris: André, An huitième [1799]). See "Early Francophone Editions" in the bibliography for details about this rare extant revolutionary edition.

[15]Ibid., 43–44. The English is my translation.

and circle of the younger William Godwin, Mary Shelley—of *Frankenstein* fame—and their friend and collaborator the poet Lord Byron.[16]

In the hands of these illustrious writers of early Romanticism, the prince was reborn from the French in the Gothic style and became a romantic hero: "'What happiness, beautiful princess!' said the prince, looking at her with the greatest tenderness imaginable, 'what happiness to be able to do you such a service, to see you smile so sweetly, and to be thus rewarded by your love! To think that the most powerful princes upon the earth could not have performed what I have done, in breaking the cruel enchantment that condemned you to sleep so long!'"[17] In the Godwin monologue, the prince again claims dominion over the princess by listing his heroic and superlative accomplishment. Yet, instead of enumerating his exploits in a series of rhetorical questions as he did in 1799, here he exclaims his heroism directly. Fate turns into his own power as he claims responsibility for breaking the "cruel enchantment" that condemned the princess. The scene is no longer about the princess; she has turned into his just reward.

Romanticism thus found its properly swashbuckling prince. Changes like these and their rapid market success in English translation opened the collection to the already seasoned audience for sentimental, child-friendly fairy tales. Sentiment and nostalgia can also be seen in the choice of late-century French, British, and Dutch editors to emphasize the antiquity of the stories, by then over one hundred years old, by aging the title just as the mid-century had aged the image into Old Mother or Grandmother Goose (see figure 9).[18] As a crone, she was written into pantomime plots for the stage where, along with bawdy costuming, she acquired a nose that prefigures one of her later avatars, the pointed-hat-wearing, broom-bearing witch.[19] Rendering her comical and popular, pantomime plots set the stage for a Mother

---

[16]M. O. Grenby, *The Child Reader, 1700-1840* (Cambridge: Cambridge University Press, 2011), 151. William Godwin and his first wife, Mary Wollstonecraft, are the parents of Mary (Shelley). Mary Jane, Godwin's second wife, was the mother of his only son, William.

[17]*The Sleeping Beauty in the Wood* (London: Tabart and Co. at the Juvenile and School Library, 1804), 30.

[18]*Old Mother Goose's Interesting Stories of Past Times* (London: S. Fisher and T. Hurst, 1803); and *Winter Avond Vertillingen van Grootmoeder de Gans* [Winter Tales of Grandmother Goose] (Amsterdam: G. Roos, 1803).

[19]Famed pantomime actor Joseph Grimaldi made his character Clown famous in *Harlequin and Mother Goose; or, The Golden Egg*, circa 1806. The character of Mother Goose, played by Samuel Simmons, was cross-dressed. The cast list appeared in the *European Magazine* (1807), available online, and the image of Simmons drawn by George Cruikshank for *Fairburn's Description of the Popular and Comic New Pantomime, called Harlequin and Mother Goose* (1806) is in the public domain and was reproduced by Richard Vogler in *Graphic Works by George Cruikshank* (New York: Dover, 1979), 26–27. See also Marina Warner's description of the evolution of Mother Goose before and at the turn of the nineteenth century in *From the Beast to the Blonde*, 155–56.

Goose associated with the folk. Jennifer Schacker has argued in fact that theatrical traditions such as pantomime, as much as or more than the print tradition, encouraged the British reception of French fairy tales.[20]

In the course of the nineteenth century, both the Grimms' landmark collection *Kinder- und Hausmärchen* (Children's and Household Tales, 1812) and Gustave Doré's legendary 1862 illustrations (see figure 10, from the Hood 1866 edition) drew similarly on the patriotic nostalgia by then associated with folklore to market the Mother Goose tales as folk classics of the genre, in spite of their courtly origins. According to the preface to volume 1 of 1812, the Grimms collected the folktales "from oral traditions in Hesse and Main and in the Kinzig regions of the Duchy of Hanau, where we grew up."[21] Scholarship, beginning with the work of Maria Tatar, has taken full account of the poetic transformations for which the Grimms and others can be credited in the published versions of their stories. Nonetheless, their claim to collection and transcription based on oral tradition can be read as a clever strategy in a century of growing folkloric awareness and appreciation.

That strategy bled through the Grimms' stories to Perrault's and impacted the reception of his collection as well: "His merit consists in his decision not to add anything to the tales and to leave the tales unchanged, discounting some small details. His style of depiction deserves only praise for being as simple as possible."[22] Not only do they claim Perrault as a predecessor, they forge behind him a legend of oral tradition that can never be recovered but became and remains a commonplace assumption in criticism on fairy tales of the 1690s. Among other ideals they attached to the *Histoires ou Contes*, the principles of aged wisdom and simplicity impacted translation methods of the period and fueled marketing to children.

---

[20]"Fairy Gold: The Economics and Erotics of Fairy-Tale Pantomime," *Marvels & Tales* 26, no. 2 (2012): 153–77. An 1826 scholarly edition of Perrault's collected works with "remarks" on each tale references plays from the eighteenth century inspired by the tales, such as Anseaume's 1759 *Cendrillon* and Sedaine's 1789 Orientalized *Raoul Barbe-Bleue*. *Oeuvres choisies de Ch. Perrault*, ed. Collin de Plancy (Paris: Brissot-Thivars et cie, 1826), 42, 79. Eighteenth- and nineteenth-century comic operas and other dramatic forms inspired by fairy tales were the subject of a special issue of *Féeries*. Especially worthy of note are Isabelle Degauque's presentation of Marignier's 1730 Orientalized play about a "glass slipper" ("Des contes des mille et une nuits à la pantoufle de Marignier," 117–30) and a list at the back by Christelle Bahier-Porte, editor of the special issue, of all the plays mentioned. *Féeries* 4 (2007), ed. Jean-François Perrin, feeries. revues.org/195.
[21]Jacob Grimm and Wilhelm Grimm, "Preface to Volume I" [1812], in *The Original Folk and Fairy Tales of the Brothers Grimm*, trans. Jack Zipes (Princeton: Princeton University Press, 2014), 4.
[22]Ibid., 8.

FRONTISPIECE.

Figure 10. Gustave Doré's frontispiece reprinted in *Fairy Realm: A Collection of the Favourite Old Tales* (London: Ward, Lock & Tyler, 1866). (Courtesy UCLA, Los Angeles.)

Doré's frontispiece, for its part, turns *Ma Mère l'Oye* from a crone into a grandmother, with three generations pictured around her. In fact, reference to the goose entirely disappears in the absence of a placard. Surrounded by a brood of children that appear to be her progeny and not simply her educational charges, she more closely resembles *La Mère Gigogne*, a Mother

Hubbard character in French vaudeville of the period whose lineage as a theater persona extends back to the early seventeenth century. Gigogne has been long understood as a deformation of *cigogne,* or stork.[23] In her vaudeville incarnation, attested as early as 1602 in French puppet theater in Paris (Théâtre des marionettes), she had the stock feature of a skirt out of which came many children. Her primary attribute both sexualized the fecund figure by overemphasizing her seemingly endless capacity for maternity and made children the focus.[24]

Characters from Doré's frontispiece make their way into the stories as well. Doré's "Belle au bois dormant" / Sleeping Beauty illustration of the princess pricking herself, which was not illustrated in any Clouzier/Samber editions, depicts the spinner in the story with the same attributes (wrinkled face, glasses, a bonnet) and age as the teller in the frontispiece. In his depiction of "Petit chaperon rouge" / Little Red Riding Hood sleeping with the wolf, today the best-known illustration from the volume, Riding Hood bears a striking resemblance to the young girl standing to the right in the frontispiece. Doré's characters thus move out of the frame of the frontispiece and into the tale narratives to color them with the familial patina of the grandmother. Turning the goose into a matriarch and allowing visual cues to seep from the frontispiece into the pages of the stories themselves proved a visually striking way to transform Perrault's social lessons for 1690s France into time-honored life lessons for audiences living a century and a half later.

Tabart, the Grimms, and Doré illustrate in a helpful way the magic aging process that editors, artists, and anglophone translators performed on the stories until the early twentieth century. In spite of intriguing differences

---

[23]"Paraît être une déformation de *cigogne*, oiseau connu pour son amour maternel, d'où le sens fam. de 'mère extrêmement tendre'" (Appears to be a deformation of *stork*, a bird known for its maternal love, giving the colloquial meaning "very affectionate mother"). Nancy Université: Centre National des Ressources textuelles et lexicales, Lexicographie, www.cnrtl.fr/definition/gigogne. "Madame Gigogne ou la mère Gigogne, nom d'un personnage de théâtre d'enfants; elle est entourée d'un grand nombre de petits enfants qui sortent de dessous ses jupons" (Madame Gigogne or Mother Gigogne, name of a character in children's theater; she is surrounded by a large number of small children who come out from under her skirts). Émile Littré, *Dictionnaire de la langue française* (1873–77), University of Chicago: ARTFL Project, Dictionnaire d'autrefois, artfl-project.uchicago.edu/content/dictionnaires-dautrefois.

[24]While I draw a heuristic distinction here between Mother Goose and "Mother Stork" to make sense of the aging and potential sexualizing of the frontispiece figure, Jennifer Schacker has demonstrated that the figures of Mother Goose, Mother Bunch, and Mother Hubbard overlap in complex ways in the nineteenth century. Goose and Bunch predate Perrault (and d'Aulnoy, the subject of her study) and are redeployed consistently in British theater as bawdy figures. See "Fluid Identities: Madame d'Aulnoy, Mother Bunch, and Fairy-Tale History," in *The Individual and Tradition: Folkloristic Perspectives*, ed. Ray Cashman, Tom Mould, and Pravina Shukla (Bloomington: Indiana University Press, 2011), especially 256–59.

among them that can be traced to their place and time, as I have done only rapidly here, the aggregate of the work done on Perrault to deliver the antique stories to new audiences over the eighteenth and nineteenth centuries comes down to a vision of classicism. If for different reasons, most hands that tinkered with the older French volume after 1730 let its age suggest moralism. Frequently it was exaggerated—as in the crone and rapt young listeners of 1785, Doré's grandmother, and Tabart's prince—into romanticized didacticism. Translators both popular and scholarly continued to return to Samber's English and updated it with matter-of-fact choices in line with recovering Perrault as a moralist.

Andrew Lang's 1889 versions of Perrault's tales (he included all but "Riquet à la houppe"), published in *The Blue Fairy Book*, are one significant example. His preference for those of Samber's creative choices that had endured in the anglophone tradition include custards for *galettes* (a flat bread or cake) in "Little Red Riding-Hood," the spelling of that title, the name Sleeping Beauty, the name of her dog Mopsey, and the name Cinderella. Lang tends, however, to familiarize the language, changing "Cinderbreech" to "Cinderwench."[25] Passages in Samber that present vivid or cultural description are attenuated:

> Samber: One day, her mother having made some custards, said to her, Go my Biddy, for her Christian name was Biddy, go and see how your grandmother does. ("Little Red Riding-Hood")

> Lang: One day her mother, having made some custards, said to her, Go my dear, and see how thy grandmamma does. ("Little Red Riding Hood")[26]

> Samber: As she was going through the wood, she met up with Gossop Wolfe. ("Little Red Riding-Hood")

> Lang: As she was going through the woods, she met Gaffer Wolf. ("Little Red Riding Hood")[27]

> Samber: [S]he likewise touch'd all the horses that were in the stables, as well pads as others, the great dogs in the outward court, and

---

[25]Lang, "Cinderella," *The Blue Fairy Book*, 79.
[26]Samber, "Little Red Riding-Hood," in *The Classic Fairy Tales*, ed. Iona Opie and Peter Opie (Oxford: Oxford University Press, 1974), 123; Lang, "Little Red Riding Hood," in *The Blue Fairy Book*, 62.
[27]Samber, "Little Red Riding-Hood," 62; Lang, "Little Red Riding Hood," 123.

pretty little Mopsey too the Princess's little Spaniel bitch that lay by her on the bed. ("Sleeping Beauty")

> Lang: [S]he likewise touched all the horses that were in the stables, pads as well as others, the great dogs in the outward court, and pretty little Mopsey, too, the Princess's little spaniel, which lay by her on the bed. ("Sleeping Beauty")[28]

In an echo of this tendency, D. J. Munro made illustrations after Doré for the new American translations by Charles Welsh, published in 1901 as *The Tales of Mother Goose, as First Collected by Charles Perrault*. His passages from "Little Red Riding-Hood" and "Sleeping Beauty in the Woods" read very much like Lang's:

> Go, my dear, and see how your grandmother does, for I hear she has been very ill; carry her a custard and this little pot of butter.

> [S]he likewise touched all the horses which were in the stables, the cart horses, the hunters and the saddle horses, the grooms, the great dogs in the outward court, and little Mopsey, too, the Princess's spaniel, which was lying on the bed.[29]

Like Lang, Welsh also pared down the use of adjectives in description and changed cultural references to make them more accessible, sometimes borrowing from Lang, as he does with Cendrillon's name, "Cinderwench." While full-length variations of the 1697 version never disappeared, translations like Welsh's sustained a relationship to much younger readers or listeners. Children's or all-age editions were a common feature of the early twentieth-century pushlishing scene. Alongside that relatively new tradition, bawdy British pantomimes and early animation, such as Walt Disney's 1922 *Cinderella*, which features Cinderella as a flapper, and Lotte Reiniger's papercut masterpieces of the 1930s, kept adults interested.[30] Indeed, these and other media made fairy tales available to an ever wider cross-section of society in Britain and the United States until dissemination reached its zenith with the iconic adaptations of *Cinderella* (1950) and *Sleeping Beauty* (1959) by

---

[28] Samber, "Sleeping Beauty in the Wood," in Opie and Opie, *The Classic Fairy Tales*, 110; Lang, "Sleeping Beauty in the Wood," in *The Blue Fairy Book*, 69.

[29] Welsh, *The Tales of Mother Goose*, 80, 18.

[30] The 1922 short from Walt Disney's first studio, Laugh-O-Grams, and several of Reiniger's fairy-tale animations can be viewed on YouTube.

the Walt Disney Studios. The *Histoires ou Contes* existed in the busy fairy-tale market of the twentieth century under many guises, all looking quite different from how they had looked in the seventeenth century.

In the latter half of the twentieth century, translation theory did shift away from reproducing a new version of Samber in favor of reinterpreting the French, which yielded some insightful changes (discussed below). What translators did not challenge nevertheless are the titles of the best-known tales or the idea, built up over centuries, that the tales targeted youthful audiences to educate them in the ways of bourgeois society. Angela Carter and Christopher Betts, representing the popular and scholarly British traditions, respectively, work from the premise that the tales are classics and were, as Betts puts it, "mostly intended for quite young children."[31] "Little Red Riding Hood," the shortest and most apparently folkloric of Perrault's tales, proves especially moldable to this interpretation of the volume's purpose. Carter's "Your granny is sick; you must go and visit her" infantilizes the character, and her ending verb "gobbled her up" for *la mangea* gives the wolf the texture of a beast in a children's tale.[32] Bett's "Go and see how your grandmama is, because I've heard she is not well" locates the story in the nineteenth-century world of Doré's illustrations, which he reprints to promote the connection visually. His ending phrase "and ate her up" employs deliberately childish phrasing.[33] Both of these strategies add playfulness to the story, helping children to see themselves in the role of the protagonist.

On the American side, Stanley Appelbaum and Jack Zipes have produced popular and scholarly editions, respectively. Appelbaum attempts literal accuracy, wherein "not a word has been basically altered, or omitted." This methodology, along with his hope to render the tales "democratic" and "about and for children of all social classes," involves one-to-one substitutions such as the translation "hood" in "Little Red Hood" for the culturally complex word *chaperon*.[34] Similarly, the mother's "Go see how your grandmother is feeling, because I've been told she was ill" turns the reflexive third-person present conjugation *se porte* into the present progressive "is feeling," and "because" fills the space of *car* in French.[35] Zipes's translation

---

[31]Betts acknowledges nonetheless that the tales were likely read by adults and the morals were "separately addressed to grown-ups." Introduction, xxiii.

[32]Carter, "Little Red Riding Hood," in *Little Red Riding Hood, Cinderella, and Other Classic Fairy Tales of Charles Perrault*, 1, 3.

[33]Betts, "Little Red Riding-Hood," in *Charles Perrault: The Complete Fairy Tales*, 103.

[34]Stanley Appelbaum, introduction to *The Complete Fairy Tales in Verse and Prose: A Dual-Language Book*, ed. and trans. Stanley Appelbaum (Mineola, NY: Dover, 2002), xxi, vi.

[35]Appelbaum, "Little Red Hood," in *The Complete Fairy Tales in Verse and Prose*, 133.

of the same depicts the moment when a "naïve bourgeois girl pays for her stupidity" and employs appropriately dry diction. The mother tells the child in clear spoken grammar, "Go see how your grandmother's feeling. I've heard that she's sick." The wolf arrives at "the grandmother's house."[36] These strategies simplify diction for the modern reader and especially for the younger one.

To a very great extent Robert Samber's translation of 1729 stands as one of the least reverent of the tradition sketched out above, perhaps because he was the last person to produce a significant translation of Perrault before anyone knew his tales would become "classics." Recent translations, such as the ones discussed above, labor under the weight of that celebrity, which all but set titles and character personae in stone. What would the stories look like if they were relieved of the great responsibility to be classics? The translations in this volume challenge the assumptions of a three-hundred-year old history that progressively aged the tales into didactic literature for young readers. I have instead rendered the tales in a modern English idiom, the result of reading their French as new, sophisticated, and playful in the 1690s; their texts as innovative literature set against the sober tones of genres favored by the ancients, such as tragedy and satire; and their style as ironic, set against Perrault's own verse tales of 1694. *Histoires ou Contes* struggles with the dominant ideologies of the 1690s and thereby tests the fairy tale's skill in addressing those questions with an adult audience (as I have outlined in the introduction). Accordingly, my translations are designed to emphasize how the tales interrogate adult issues that feel socially engaged and wry, and that stand to appeal to a twenty-first-century audience as innovative relics. In this approach, I lean on translators of other national traditions who have returned to fairy tales of old to read them as innovations of their day.

Translation Theory and Practice

Over the past twenty-five years, there has been a move among people working in literary studies and folklore to rediscover the way classical fairy tales looked before they were classics. Exploring anew the linguistic and cultural tenor of older European stories has proved exciting for scholars in a world of Disneyfication. Upon inspection, the most traditional fairy tales teem

---

[36]Zipes, "Little Red Riding Hood," in *The Great Fairy Tale Tradition*, 744, 745.

with raw cruelty and raunchy humor unmediated by the dreamy colors of animated celluloid. Within the then nascent field of literary fairy-tale studies in the United States, Maria Tatar cracked open the discussion of the ugly, the disgusting, and the violent in traditional fairy tales. Her early work on the tales of the Brothers Grimm, appropriately named *The Hard Facts*, brought out a dark side of tale history, one that may seem obvious today in the wake of the long-running Stephen Sondheim musical *Into the Woods* (1986) and, more recently, the NBC television series *Grimm* (2011).[37] At the time, Tatar's identification of the tales' "hard core"—the central episodes of sex and violence that anchor so many plots—challenged North American stereotypes about how fairy tales operate and what kind of message they deliver.

As Tatar pointed out, those stereotypes are often traceable to Disney. While Tatar concedes that the Grimms did sanitize socially taboo ideas, such as pregnancy and incest, in tales they collected, the overall effect of that sanitation is to highlight the violence that remains.[38] Elisabeth Panttaja made a similarly bold critical move when she argued that reading bourgeois politics back into the Grimms' tales—letting Disney's omissions overshadow history's texts—eschews our own contemporary discomfort with the sexual power women wield even in texts like "Aschenputtel" (the Grimms' Cinderella story). "In so doing," she cautions, we "camouflage exactly what is most troubling—and true—about the story, its depiction of class ambitions and class violence."[39] As much as critics help us peel back layers of time and rediscover the past on different terms, translation can, too. Recently, translators in several fairy-tale traditions have followed this critical lead to revise dated language, local idiom, and other ideological choices that characterize translations done in the early to mid-twentieth century. As the present ideals and values change, how we read the past changes, too. These shifts in sensibility can radically alter the way translators interpret language of the past. Through discovery and rereading, new eyes on the past tend to ask of it different questions and, consequently, see new answers.

---

[37] Maria Tatar, *The Hard Facts of the Grimms' Fairy Tales*, 2nd ed. (Princeton: Princeton University Press, 2003).

[38] Ibid., 7–10. Indeed, one of Tatar's purposes in exposing the violent episodes is to contrast them to the sanitizing effect the Grimms' alterations had on plot details perceived to offend decorum.

[39] See her reading of the mother and daughter's political ambitions in "Going Up in the World: Class in 'Cinderella,'" in Bacchilega and Jones, "Perspectives on the Innocent Persecuted Heroine in Fairy Tales," 103.

Tiina Nunnally's translations have been hailed for the way they bring out the previously unacknowledged choppy wit of Hans Christian Andersen's style.[40] Andersen, author of "The Princess and the Pea," "The Ugly Duckling," and "The Little Mermaid," has been the subject of biographies and his works have appeared in countless editions for adults and children. His tales began rolling off the press for a Danish audience in the 1830s and in translation by the 1840s. In her introduction to Nunnally's 2004 translations, Jackie Wullschlager (Andersen's biographer) explains the necessity of producing new English versions even of stories so well known and so widely translated: "The earliest Andersen versions in English are a particularly acute example of how translations are made through the prism of their times, for the very revolutionary language that so shocked yet enticed Danish readers was filtered out by the sentimental Victorians." Nunnally, she explains, instead works from a "feel for Andersen's slightly eccentric yet beautifully fluent and easy use of language."[41]

Nancy Canepa's translations of the lesser-known tales of Giambattista Basile produced a similar effect. She both introduced the seventeenth-century Neapolitan writer to a millennial anglophone readership and rescued the bawdy, sometimes raunchy language in the tales from early-century linguistic patterns. Canepa calls Norman Penzer's 1932 English translation of Basile "readable" and "elegant" but replete with "deficiencies."[42] Deficient for two reasons: first, it is a translation from Benedetto Croce's Italian translation (so at least once removed), and second, it "domesticates," as she puts it, prose that would simply have sounded too bawdy in English in 1932. Add to this that Croce had already done some domesticating himself, and Penzer's is a brand-new text nostalgically claiming to be a precise translation.

Taken together, these explanations make a strong case for promoting new translations of old fairy tales. In the case of Charles Perrault, much hard work—some of it documented above—has already been done to make the 1697 French versions available to twenty-first-century readers. The present volume cannot claim to respond to the entrapment of English translation in Victorianism (as Nunnally could) or to tackle a subject that has been avoided in English-language criticism (like Basile's bawdiness). On the contrary, this volume's bibliography shows that, unlike Basile and Andersen, Perrault has never wanted for translators and commentators invested in

---

[40]Tiina Nunnally, trans., *Hans Christian Andersen: Fairy Tales* (2004; repr., New York: Penguin, 2006).

[41]Jackie Wullschlager, introduction to Nunnally, *Hans Christian Andersen*, xlii, xliii.

[42]Nancy L. Canepa, trans., *Giambattista Basile's The Tale of Tales, or Entertainment for Little Ones* (Detroit: Wayne State University Press, 2007), 28.

finding inventive ways to render the faraway language of the 1690s present and marketable. What we learn from the corpus of English Perraults, as Maria Tatar put it, is that "just as there is no definitive version of 'Little Red Riding Hood', there is also no definitive interpretation of her story."[43]

Appelbaum, furthermore, produced the first complete English-language volume of Perrault's tales including the morals and the dedication in the first edition, which was frequently removed from translations after the early eighteenth century.[44] Betts, for his part, presents the morals—which, in contrast to the tales, were published in verse in 1697—translated into English verse for the first time.[45] Indeed, most translators, Appelbaum included, opt for prose to avoid the thorny problems presented by translating the passage from French, in which declension allows the rhyming of verbs and adjectives, to English, where repetitive endings are less regular.[46] Their efforts helped to historicize the stories, as I do here first by reproducing the collection's 1697 elements. Like Appelbaum, I have included the dedication and like Betts, I have rendered the morals in verse.

Furthermore, this translation advances the effort to draw new and unexpected meanings from these vintage stories by highlighting the difficulty in translating them. Perrault's tales have never been printed with significant lexical annotation. Yet, Claire-Lise Malarte-Feldman long ago flagged the problem of proper names and culinary terms in Perrault, which anchor the text in cultural history and thus do not travel well. They must be exchanged or creatively explained.[47] Annotation serves two purposes in this edition. First, I note the many places where vocabulary in the stories carries cultural freight, has multiple definitions, or both. Using this notation, readers can weigh my choices against the many others that are possible. In this sense, language in Perrault the way I have worked with it is never simply vocabulary and often cannot be merely broken down by word. My work illustrates the idea that "translators do not just translate words; they also translate a universe of discourse, a

---

[43]Maria Tatar, introduction to *The Classic Fairy Tales*, ed. and trans. Maria Tatar (New York: Norton, 1999), xiv.

[44]Appelbaum, introduction, xxi.

[45]Betts, introduction, xxxviii.

[46]See ibid., xl-xlii for a thoughtful summary of some general challenges posed by French to English.

[47]She cites the regional bread galette in "Petit chaperon rouge" / Little Red Riding Hood, which has yielded translations as different as custard and biscuit to reflect what she calls the target society's "cultural practice," and proper names such as Cucendron, a neologism that produced a wild range of names discussed below. Claire-Lise Malarte-Feldman, "The Challenges of Translating Perrault's 'Contes' into English," *Marvels & Tales* 13, no. 2 (1999): 187.

poetics, and an ideology."[48] Written in a decade obsessed with how to use language—their composition coinciding with the publication of the first official French dictionary in 1694—Perrault's stories are also full of odd and playful word choices, including neologism. They occasionally twist well-known idioms in ways the modern reader can only guess at understanding. And I make many educated guesses, a practice always identified in an annotation.

Take the wolf in "Le Petit chaperon rouge" / Little Red Riding Hood, for example. He has been called the dark moon to her bright sun, the figment of her infantile rape fantasy, and the "deceptive male seducer" to her "pretty defenseless girl."[49] In Perrault's story, when first introducing the character, the narrator gives him an epithet: *compère le loup*. *Compère* has many meanings in seventeenth-century French, ranging from family friend and godfather to accomplice or one in a close bond between men. I chose "the neighborhood wolf" for its ambiguity because, like *compère*, that identity could make him friend or foe, caring or complicit, and either way, it emphasizes his familiarness and local standing, which would explain why Little Red Riding Hood speaks to him without fear.

Second, annotations are a reminder that older tales belong to a lost sociocultural environment to which we can hopefully relate but with which we may not—and need not—be entirely comfortable. Making stories that have become very familiar seem strange again has the advantage of inviting the reader to stop, think, compare, and appreciate the words on the page. The boots in "Maître chat" / Puss in Boots, for example, have distinctive meaning in the seventeenth century. Although there are other stories about cats and other stories about boots, Perrault is the first to put the footwear on a cat. Furthermore, Perrault and his day had a veritable obsession with fashion and footwear.[50] Boots were a mark of status and quite concretely give the cat a particular social identity, something the modern reader might not see in the details of the plot if it was not mentioned explicitly in a note. It will not be lost on the reader that it is also supremely ironic for Perrault to bestow such status on a talking animal. Like the familiar and fearsome wolf,

---

[48]Lefevere, *Translating Literature*, 94.

[49]Pierre St. Yves [Emile Nourry], "Little Red Riding Hood; or, The Little May Queen," in Alan Dundes, ed., *Little Red Riding Hood: A Casebook* (Madison: University of Wisconsin Press, 1989), 79; Alan Dundes, "Interpreting 'Little Red Riding Hood' Psychoanalytically," in Dundes, *Little Red Riding Hood: A Casebook*, 225; Jack Zipes, *The Trials and Tribulations of Red Riding Hood* (New York: Routledge, 1993), 78, 26.

[50]See Joan DeJean's chapter on footwear and fairy tales, "Cinderella's Slipper and the King's Boots," in *The Essence of Style*, 83–103.

the boot-wearing cat opens up fascinating questions of how characters, particularly humanoid avatars (animals, ogres), operate in these tales.

Gillian Lathey has focused attention on translators—the "invisible" force driving textual history—as significant generators and conveyors of meaning.[51] Beyond lexical complexity, Perrault's tales indeed carry so much traditional meaning from the many hands that have touched them that it can feel irreverent to violate those precepts. Recent theorists of translation such as André Levefere (quoted above), Laurence Venuti, and Sandra Bermann offer useful ways of considering texts steeped in history. For Venuti, every translation must balance three concerns: autonomy ("the textual features and strategies that distinguish it from the foreign text and from texts initially written in the translating language"), equivalence, or the translation's relationship with the foreign-language text, and function, the role of the new text in the target language. He notes that the practice of translation, as prescriptive as it may sound, remains a deeply embedded practice tied to the time, place, and condition of the translator as well as to the local appraisal of the foreign language text he or she takes up.[52] The translator's own positionality and also the newly created translation itself exist in dynamic tension. In other words, the translations in this volume do not faithfully render the 1697 fairy tales in a void. Instead, they represent a particular scholarly interpretation of Perrault's words and their seventeenth-century context: the work of a feminist scholar in 2016. Which cultural markers a translator chooses to highlight, which definitions she chooses from the possibilities in context and the choice of whether to reproduce meaning or syntax—all of these deliberations make a translation peculiar and culturally rich in its own right.

Sandra Bermann has further cautioned modern translators about what is at stake when they interact with a text across time, culture, and language, especially when it is done for publication (in this case, at a major university press). "[T]ranslation has itself become an important border concept in the humanities, affecting some of the most salient intellectual and ethical issues of our time. It requires attention to cultural values, to economic and political inequalities, to individual choices and, perhaps most obviously to otherness

---

[51]"[T]ranslators were more or less invisible agents in the recycling process" of carrying ideas from one language into another. Lathey, *The Role of Translators in Children's Literature,* 49. See also the variety of approaches to literary translation in *The Translation of Children's Literature: A Reader,* ed. Gillian Lathey, Topics in Translation 31 (Cleveland: Multilingual Matters, 2006).

[52]Lawrence Venuti, introduction to *The Translation Studies Reader*, ed. Lawrence Venuti, 2nd ed. (New York: Routledge, 2004), 5–6.

in its linguistic and cultural forms."[53] The culture with which I have aligned my vision of these stories has as much to do with our own—in need of what Zipes calls de-Disneyfication—as with Louis XIV's academic French milieu.

I make a political choice in opting to translate Perrault—a white male author who has never been ignored—rather than other authors of his day, many of them women and some lesser-known men. That choice stems from how much press the Mother Goose characters attract in our culture and how badly they are in need of rethinking and reinterpretation. The provocative art by Matt Saunders on the cover of this volume, a drawing that one gallery dubbed his "fractured fairy-tale" art, makes concrete how the familiar becomes newly intriguing when we take it apart.

As the bibliography below and the discussion of translation history above suggest, disrupting the conventions of the *Histoires ou Contes* must tackle the names by which these fairy tales have been known throughout most of their anglophone existence.

Titles and Names

For many translators, the names of Perrault's characters are too culturally ingrained to be interrogated.[54] While "Barbe bleue" / Blue Beard and "Les Fées" / The Fairies raise few questions (although the latter story has but one fairy), "Riquet à la houppe" and "Petit poucet" have both standard and unconventional translations. Riquet is sometimes translated Ricky, and the *houppe* can be metonymic (Betts, "Ricky the Tuft") or an attribute (Zipes, "Riquet with the Tuft"). *Poucet* can be left in its French form (Samber, "Little Poucet"), translated "Little Thumbling" (Appelbaum), or metaphorized in the folk expression "Hop o' My Thumb" (Carter, Betts, Zipes). Those names are not difficult to alter. As for the other names, each one iconic, they have remained nearly unchanged since Robert Samber's inaugural translation of 1729: Little Red Riding Hood, Sleeping Beauty, Cinderella, and Puss in Boots.[55] Repeated translations, discussed above, that aged the stories into classics and then into folk types—as well as Disney's famous reprisal of two

---

[53]Sandra Bermann, introduction to *Nation, Language, and the Ethics of Translation*, ed. Sandra Bermann (Princeton: Princeton University Press, 2005), 5.

[54]For Betts, the names and catch phrases "have been settled long ago and it is simply a matter of fine tuning" (introduction, xliii). He, Zipes, and Carter adopt Samber's titles, and even Appelbaum, who opts more literally for "Beauty in the Sleeping Forest" and "Little Red Hood," reproduces "Cinderella."

[55]On the altered spelling of Samber's "Cinderilla" at the turn of the nineteenth century, see the introduction.

of them—make these characters ubiquitous. As cultural fixtures, the names seem inviolable even though they are all highly inventive on Samber's part, as they were in French on Perrault's. As the name has much to do with how readers perceive character identity, viewing the protagonists in a new way begins with reinterpreting Perrault's highly inventive names.

The name Cendrillon (as she is known in the French story) and its naughty companion Cucendron (the first name the crueler stepsister gives the heroine) are both formed from the root word *cendre* (ash). Samber's Cinderilla looks and sounds close to the French because he opted for the homophone cinder instead of using ash and mimicked the "illa," later changed to "ella," in the suffix. But for the nastier name, where cinder is paired in French with *cul*, ass, Samber opted to change the body part to the garment that covers it, breech: Cinderbreech. Perhaps because the name continued to seem out of step with seventeenth-century court culture, most translators took their cue from Samber and opted for less overtly offensive monikers: "Cinderwench" (Lang, 1889), "Cinderbritches" (Carter, 1977), and "Cindertail" (Zipes, 2001). A few have tried out a colloquialism closer to Perrault's language—"Cinderbottom" (Brereton, 1957), "Cinderbutt" (Philip and Simborowski, 1993), "Cinder-ass" (Appelbaum, 2002), and "Cinderbum" (Betts, 2009)—but only Stanley Appelbaum opted for the word *ass*.[56]

Consistently, too, Samber's homophone stuck. *Cendres* yields *ashes* in English—the powder left after wood has burned—whereas *cinders*, burning embers, are *braises* in French. While cinder can be a synonym of ash in English, the latter is by far the less volatile description of the chimney matter in which the heroine sat at the hearth. A play on the words *ash* and *ass* could produce "Ashyass," "Ashcan," or my translation, "Ashwipe." Fully indulging the adolescent inventiveness of the insult in French and at the same time pointing to the drudgery to which her rank in the household condemns her, I opted to make the cruel humor of the sister more vivid. To be consistent with the aural echo between the names, Cendrillon became Ashkins, which captures the diminutive *-on* as *-kins*, as in "babykins."

Other name choices follow the same pattern. Grammatically closer than "Sleeping Beauty," the "Beauty in the Sleeping Woods" or, as I have

---

[56]Geoffrey Brereton, "Cinderella," in *Charles Perrault: Fairy Tales,* ed. and trans. Geoffrey Brereton (New York: Penguin Classics, 1957), 54; Neil Philip and Nicoletta Simborowski, "Cinderella," in *The Complete Fairy Tales of Charles Perrault*, ed. and trans. Neil Philip and Nicoletta Simborowski (New York: Clarion Books, 1993), 61. See also popular translations, such as Anne Carter's "Cinderpuss" (1967) and A.E. Johnson's daring "Cinder-slut" (1969), in the list provided by Claire-Lise Malarte-Feldman (188).

called her, "the Beauty in the Slumbering Woodland," has the added advantage of removing sleep as a quality of the heroine, instead attaching dormancy to the rest of the landscape and opening the possibility of reading her as a character who is awake and active for most of the tale. In "Riquet the Tufted," Riquet retains his French flair, as this word operates as a proper name in the story, and the tuft becomes his hallmark, as in Peter the Great. Rather than a riding hood or hood of any kind, I clothed the heroine in a "tippet," which in point of fact names the scarf portion of the Renaissance headgear known as a *chaperon*, a bonnet/scarf ensemble that frames the face with fabric.

Hazarding new translations of standardized character names speaks to my desire to make these stories strange for audiences, to shake them loose from inherited patterns. Readers can encounter them as fresh faces, as though they did not carry on their small backs three hundred years of normalized meaning. This type of linguistic modernization rubs off the patina of age, such that readers may find the diction surprising as they get to know these new characters. This balancing act between retaining historical markers and also capturing the innovation of the French in modern English idiom—rendering the tales foreign and familiar at the same time—is a technique that carried over into formal elements of the writing, namely, formatting and voice. Here, too, choices reflect whether an element felt like standard practice of the day, in which case I rendered it that way in modern English, or highly idiosyncratic, in which case I reproduced idiosyncrasy.

Structure

Elements of Barbin's 1697 edition require alteration for a modern readership. In the late seventeenth century, printed pages in books still resembled the block text of handwritten medieval manuscripts. Text formatted for print had very occasional paragraphing, and the margins were justified on both sides. In the 1690s, that standard early modern page layout would not have been remarkable, but today it could cause the modern reader undue hardship. Consequently, most modern editions and translations of the *Histoires ou Contes* paragraph the tales.[57] I have followed this practice of updating basic formatting for the twenty-first-century reader. On the other hand, I have not updated the formatting of the morals at the end of each tale.

---

[57]A notable exception is Jean-Pierre Collinet's critical edition, *Perrault, Contes*, based on the 1697 second state Barbin edition, which adds quotation marks to direct speech but respects seventeenth-century page layout.

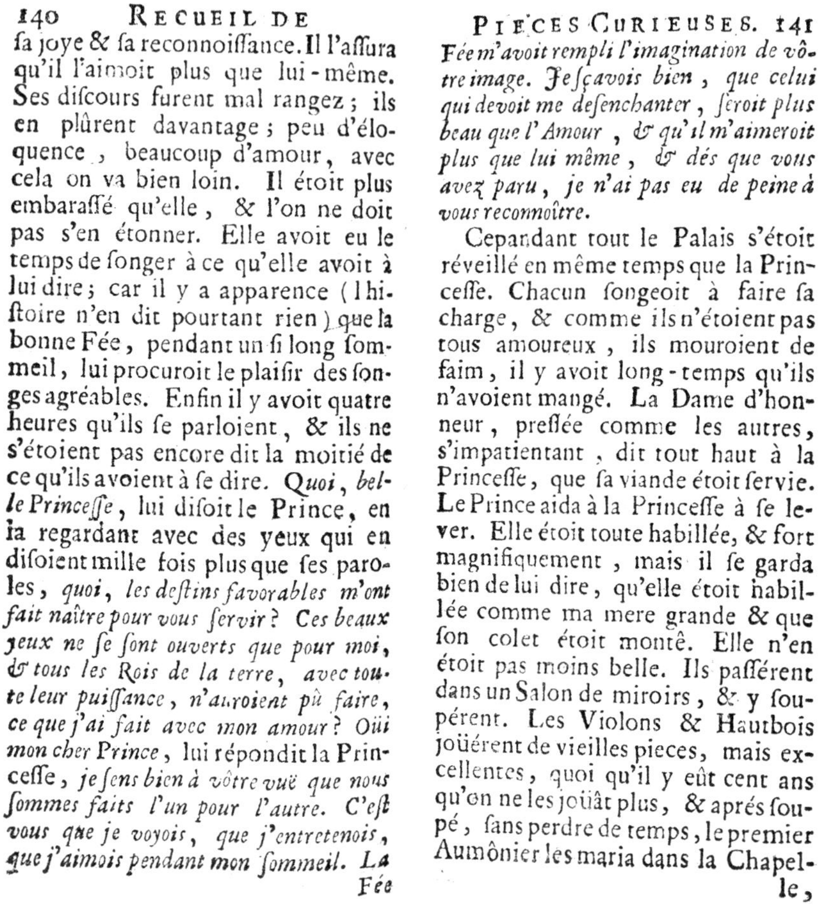

140   RECUEIL DE

fa joye & fa reconnoiffance. Il l'affura qu'il l'aimoit plus que lui-même. Ses difcours furent mal rangez ; ils en plûrent davantage ; peu d'éloquence , beaucoup d'amour, avec cela on va bien loin. Il étoit plus embaraffé qu'elle , & l'on ne doit pas s'en étonner. Elle avoit eu le temps de fonger à ce qu'elle avoit à lui dire ; car il y a apparence (l'hiftoire n'en dit pourtant rien) que la bonne Fée, pendant un fi long fommeil, lui procuroit le plaifir des fonges agréables. Enfin il y avoit quatre heures qu'ils fe parloient , & ils ne s'étoient pas encore dit la moitié de ce qu'ils avoient à fe dire. *Quoi, belle Princeffe*, lui difoit le Prince, en la regardant avec des yeux qui en difoient mille fois plus que fes paroles , *quoi, les deftins favorables m'ont fait naître pour vous fervir ? Ces beaux yeux ne fe font ouverts que pour moi, & tous les Rois de la terre, avec toute leur puiffance, n'auroient pû faire, ce que j'ai fait avec mon amour?* Oüi mon cher Prince, lui répondit la Princeffe, *je fens bien à vôtre vuë que nous fommes faits l'un pour l'autre. C'eft vous que je voyois, que j'entretenois, que j'aimois pendant mon fommeil.* La

Fée

PIECES CURIEUSES. 141

Fée m'avoit rempli l'imagination de vôtre image. Je fçavois bien , que celui qui devoit me defenchanter , feroit plus beau que l'Amour , & qu'il m'aimeroit plus que lui même , & dés que vous avez paru, je n'ai pas eu de peine à vous reconnoître.

Cependant tout le Palais s'étoit réveillé en même temps que la Princeffe. Chacun fongeoit à faire fa charge, & comme ils n'étoient pas tous amoureux , ils mouroient de faim, il y avoit long-temps qu'ils n'avoient mangé. La Dame d'honneur, preffée comme les autres, s'impatientant , dit tout haut à la Princeffe, que fa viande étoit fervie. Le Prince aida à la Princeffe à fe lever. Elle étoit toute habillée, & fort magnifiquement , mais il fe garda bien de lui dire, qu'elle étoit habillée comme ma mere grande & que fon colet étoit monté. Elle n'en étoit pas moins belle. Ils pafférent dans un Salon de miroirs, & y foupérent. Les Violons & Hautbois joüérent de vieilles pieces, mais excellentes , quoi qu'il y eût cent ans qu'on ne les joüât plus, & aprés foupé , fans perdre de temps, le premier Aumônier les maria dans la Chapelle ,

Figure 11. Pages from Moetjen's reprint of the Mercure galant "Belle au bois dormant" containing the prince's heroic speech. *Pièces curieuses et nouvelles, tant qu'en prose qu'en vers,* ed. Adrian Moetjens (The Hague, 1696), 140–41. (Bibliothèque nationale de France, Paris.)

Beginning with the Barbin edition and all the way up to the most recent translations, the rhymed morals were separated out from the prose block on the page and printed as poetry.

Additionally, there is every indication that early modern fairy tales were printed to be read aloud among adults. As public reading is less common in modern adulthood, I have indicated with punctuation, line returns, and indentation those elements—for example, when focus moves from one character to another (usually followed by direct speech) and shifts in the plot—that a teller might emphasize with body and voice in the telling. Finally, I have adapted another commonplace in French and British literature of the late seventeenth century, the capitalization of nouns, as it is not particular to Perrault, although scholars have remarked and recently theorized about capitalization in Perrault's titles.[58] Poetry and lyrical prose of the period tended to capitalize names, titles, and significant nouns, but the practice was inconsistent. Thus I have eliminated the standard nominal capitalizations in the prose of the stories except in the case of proper names. One idiosyncratic element of the 1697 "Petit chaperon rouge" presented the opposite case: within the tale the name petit chaperon rouge remains lowercased. In other words, it never looks on the page like a proper name the way Barbe bleue and Cendrillon do. As this choice bears upon how the narrative creates the identity of the little girl and how the reader receives her as a character, I left the words "little red tippet" lowercased throughout the tale.

Voice

The register of the tales' French can sound higher to the modern ear than it would have in a court environment built upon formal interaction, where the equivalent of the Queen's English would be standard comfortable fare. An example today might be the language of *Downton Abbey*, where characters live their daily lives in their comfortable aristocratic register, wielding it for comedy, tragedy, love and hate. Nothing about the diction used by fairies or main characters in the stories would have sounded stilted in the world of Louis XIV's court. We can occasionally hear pretension in the exaggerated dignity of the nasty stepsisters and self-conscious ogres that populate the volume, but they are exceptions that stand out against the rule of colloquial aristocratic speech.

Plot pacing of the *Histoires ou Contes* is analogously quick, and narrative style tends frequently toward humor. Narrators, for their part, make numerous intrusions into the tales to judge a character, signal a gap in the plot, and offer general commentary on such things as fairy work habits. Perrault's self-reflexive narrative voices are reminiscent of the narrator

---

[58]See most recently Jean-Michel Adam's analysis of capitalization in the 1697 Barbin edition: "Quand les majuscules font sens," on in-text capitalization, and "Systématique des titres des contes," on the titles, in Heideman and Adam, *Textualité et intertextualité des contes*, 174–80, 206–10. Of particular interest is his analysis of the word-objects in "Les Fées," where the first girl's gemstones are capitalized and the second girl's reptiles are not (176).

pioneered by Cervantes in *Don Quixote*, who also appeared in the 1690s in the novels of Marie-Catherine d'Aulnoy.[59] In order to give the English the same colloquial edge and pace as the French, I frequently took advantage of contractions, following Jack Zipes's translations in *Great Fairy Tale Tradition* (2001), both in direct speech and in the voice of the narrator in the case of address to the reader.

Perrault's tales are always about power dynamics, which emerge semantically in several ways that are hard to reproduce in modern English. First, he allows characters to code-switch (change the social register of their language) in the course of a tale. This means that characters can have multiple voices. Cendrillon, for example, famously reacts to her condition with childlike sadness and whining, but there are moments when she exhibits annoyance and when she learns to manipulate conversations. I chose colloquial phrasing (for example, "I really don't need that") to indicate an unformed identity, which develops with her command of language in the tale. The princess of "Belle au bois dormant" / Beauty in the Slumbering Woodland reacts in childish surprise to the spinner, with thick sexual innuendo to the prince, and with dignity when her executioner comes to take her. In these cases, I have allowed the voice of a character to evolve. Barbe bleue engages in a clever power play with his wife when he shifts from the respectful *vous* form of address to *tu*, the informal second-person singular, as he hunts her down to kill her. As this precise shift is not possible in modern English, I have opted to intensify his tone and degenerate behavior by choosing strong verbs, such as the idiom "scream at the top of his lungs" for *crier de toute sa force* and "Now you die" for *il faut mourir*.

Miscellaneous Effects

French has an affinity for what in English we would call a "run-on sentence" (many clauses separated by commas) and Perrault had a talent for writing sentences with multiple clauses. Often the clauses have similar weight in the sentence and offer a series of statements in a particular order, as though the narrator keeps remembering more details that delay the end of the sentence. With identical punctuation and syntax in English, the sentence would lose the poetry of the repetition. Multiple clauses strung together, though they may be balanced in weight, can become choppy. Frequently, I made use of

---

[59]D'Aulnoy's early novels borrow from the picaresque tradition but fill those plots with sillier, often absurd characters (for example, Monsieur de La Dandinardière in *Le Nouveau gentilhomme bourgeois*, also a spoof on Molière), which provide ample fodder for the narrator's mockery.

semicolons to support the weight of the clauses, and occasionally moved a clause to facilitate flow in English.

Perrault shifts to the present tense for a line or two in several of the tales, though no translation of which I am aware has reproduced this. I have translated those few sentences into the present tense in English. This jarring effect occurs consistently enough across the tales to be significant and also appears occasionally in seventeenth-century fairy tales by other authors (compare Catherine Bernard's "Riquet à la Houppe," 1696). The use of the present tense usually marks a significant moment in the plot and indeed halts the narrative flow to plunge the reader into the action, as though we bear witness to it. This usage suggests the expectation of performance (reading the tale aloud) and may constitute what Elizabeth Harries has aptly called a simulation of orality (writing that simulates polite conversation).[60] Stage directions also come to mind, whereby we are learning how the character gets from one place or posture to the next. The intrusion of the present has the effect of providing a flash of visual movement, as though the narrator is a radio sportscaster.

French versification of the variety Perrault practices in the morals was common in the seventeenth century. These are relatively loose rhymes built for humor and an ironic punch line. What's more, their form and wit helps trouble rather than stabilize the meaning of the tale. For this reason, I accepted the challenge of rendering them in verse. Often terminal rhymes or ending words are semantically rich, but they are also exceedingly difficult to keep in that formal position in the line. Both meaning and humor created by the French rhymes took precedence over language and syntax, even when that meant sacrificing important word pairings. To take one example, the second moral to "Cendrillon" ends, importantly, on the word *marraine* (godmother). It rhymes with *vaine* (vain), creating a fine struggle in the rhyme between the bad (in vain) and the good (the godmother's help). The end position of the word *marraine* allows her to carry the day.

There are a variety of feminine words with the *-aine* ending in French—a Google search pulls up 174 words with the masculine ending *-ain*, of which approximately 12 have feminine counterparts, including *vain/e, certain/e,* and *humain/e.* In English, the word *godmother* does not rhyme well with anything that does not contain the root *other.*[61] Moments such as these

[60]Elizabeth Wanning Harries, "Simulating Oralities: French Fairy Tales of the 1690s," *College Literature* 23, no. 2 (1996): 100–115.

[61]Word Hippo lists only words with the root *other* as potential rhyming mates. www.wordhippo. com/what-is/words-that-rhyme-with-mother.html.

must be transformed to translate well. To avoid a heavy-handed rhyme with *godmother,* the idea of the line had to take precedence over the word itself. That choice produced a rhythm and metaphorical meaning close to the 1697 French moral but at the expense of the bad/good struggle of the ending rhyme. Instead the word *vain* is hidden within the line, *godmother* in the third line of the quatrain, and *might/light* create something closer to a good/better parallel:

> But in you they will come to nothing
> Bloom in vain, try as you might,
> If you have not godfather or godmother
> To bring their worth to light.[62]

This is a case where manipulating syntax opened the possibility of writing the whole quatrain around the godfather and godmother, and casting doubt on the power of anyone in the closed system of absolutism to survive without help. In the concluding section below, I elaborate on the way I interpreted the stories. From this point on, the titles given in the text reflect the translation choices in this volume.

Interpretative Strategies

Venuti and Bermann, discussed above, developed translation theory around how thoroughly the translator's own political and social identities affect how he or she reads, interprets, and translates. André Lefevere calls the result of that interaction "the image of the source text a translator consciously or unconsciously sets out to develop."[63] The translator's *image* of the text's words—rather than fidelity to an original and fixed meaning said to reside in the text's words—is what emerges on paper when a translation is done. The late Umberto Eco similarly encouraged translating for what he called the "deep" story based on interpretation. His example is a passage from his own novel *The Island of the Day Before,* in which a character describes the colors of a coral reef. Translators must choose between following the particular list of colors (surface story) or mimicking the rich diversity

---

[62]"Mais vous aurez beau les avoir, / Pour votre avancement ce seront choses vaines, / Si vous n'avez, pour les faire valoir. / Ou des parrains ou des marraines" (Collinet, *Perrault, Contes,* 178).
[63]This line appears in chapter 4, "The Function of Translation in a Culture," in which Lefevere explores the power translation has over cultural and literary history. *Translating Literature,* 115.

of the adjectives in the passage (deep story). Producing a string of similarly compelling adjectives in English necessarily involves sacrificing the literal correspondence of color terms. He concludes that "it is on the basis of interpretive decisions of this kind that the translator plays the game of faithfulness."[64]

More than rendering the surface of Perrault's words in English, I made choices of language and grammar that spoke to deeper implications based on interpretation, such as the tone of descriptions and the attitude of characters in dialogue. As for my interpretive strategies, I have relied on the richness of the poetry in the stories and on recent critical trends in the discipline. In 1993, Elisabeth Panttaja suggested that then current critical perspectives—namely, psychoanalytic scholars such as Bettelheim who considered fairy tales developmental tools, and neo-Marxist and feminist criticism that overemphasized the tale as a bourgeois tool of socialization—"limit our appreciation of the heroine's cultural presence and political function."[65] A number of scholars working in or on the French tradition have over the last twenty years revisited Perrault to rediscover in the Mother Goose tales some of the semantic complexity and instability that they agree are inherent to the genre itself.[66]

Lewis Seifert has suggested that both the language and the morals of Perrault's tales present ironies that invite reading the stories against themselves: "To read the seventeenth-century fairy tale is to read ironically, to read the irony of the marvelous . . . to subject oneself to irony."[67] Patricia Hannon finds fissures in the political instability of the tale universe: "The modernist world of the *Contes* is plagued by mismatched couples and shifting conjugal hierarchies. . . . [T]he foundations of household authority are now undermined and the state is consequently unsteady."[68] Jennifer Schacker and others quoted in the introduction remind us that, in Schacker's words, fairy tales "imply a reader ready, willing, and able to find pleasure in the subversion of generic convention."[69] Contemporary criticism

---

[64]Umberto Eco, *Experiences in Translation*, trans. Alastair McEwan (Buffalo: University of Toronto Press, 2008), 39.

[65]Panttaja, "Going Up in the World," 86.

[66]I have drawn inspiration from Martine Hennard Dutheil de la Rochère's reading of the Perraultian heroine through Angela Carter's engagement with the tales. See *Reading, Translating, Rewriting*, quoted above, and "But Marriage Itself Is No Party: Angela Carter's Translation of Charles Perrault, 'La Belle au bois dormant'; or, Pitting the Politics of Experience against the Sleeping Beauty Myth," *Marvels & Tales* 24, no. 1 (2010): 131–51.

[67]Seifert, *Fairy Tales, Sexuality, and Gender in France*, 59.

[68]Hannon, *Fabulous Identities*, 50.

[69]Schacker, "Unruly Tales," 387.

thus opened the door to highlighting the many ironies in Perrault's tales. Translation offers a unique opportunity for current scholarly ideas about the period and its power dynamics to emerge in the language of the stories themselves. Reading for the instability of meaning and for contradiction brings out unexpected strength and humor in characters' personalities, particularly around the identity of heroes and heroines.

Take the word *pauvre* as an example. The simple and common translation for this word, which appears all over fairy tales, is "poor." The poor girl, the poor woman. Few question that choice. I found that translation helpful in many instances, with a few notable exceptions. At one point in "The Blue Beard" the narrator refers to the wife as *la pauvre femme*. While "the poor wife" would keep the translation consistent with the usage of the word in other tales, not to mention most of fairy-tale history, it rings untrue according to the pathos of this scene. In this moment the woman's life is on the line. She has violated one of her husband's precepts and has been caught. "Poor" seemed a halfhearted way to describe such a condition. Working through the semantic range of the word *pauvre* in the seventeenth century, from lacking in what is necessary to being worthy of compassion, I chose to emphasize the depth of her lack and need for compassion at that moment in the tale with "miserable." Now a different way of thinking about this character opens up—she is not just another suffering fairy-tale character but a woman suffering to the point of death at the hands of an abuser, yet she finds a way to survive.

Similarly, unlike most transformations in fairy tales, the two featured in "The Fairies" are considered shocking even within the narrative. This idiosyncrasy brings to the fore the fact that although it is scarcely longer than "The Little Red Tippet," about half the narrative is dialogue that consists of a string of exclamations. As exclamations are often idiomatic and deeply historical, they help determine the setting of the story and the character's personality. There are six in just over two pages, the last of which is *hélas*. Anyone familiar with French literature of the period knows that exclamation well, and it remains part of standard spoken French today. The register in French does not sound particularly old, but "alas," the literal translation, does sound dated. It resonates with such excessive emotion in American usage particularly that it is more likely to be used in jest. But certainly in the seventeenth century and even today in French, *hélas* need not sound romanticized; it is a mark of disappointment/despair, frustration, or resignation, but not necessarily of helplessness. My decision to talk out the sentiment in the phrase "It's terrible" credits the heroine with a touch of annoyance not audible in "alas."

If these translations are the result of close literary analysis, they also invite close reading, a strategy suggested by the tales themselves. On the surface, Perrault's heroes and heroines live up to the stereotypes that have been spun around them. Yet, when we expect charm from fairy-tale princes, we are likely to overlook how much bumbling and confusion narrators attribute to them. If we believe they exist to save the day, we will overlook their struggles, which are significant. Finally, if we give male characters the power of heroism without critically reading them, we may inadvertently offer them more benefit of the doubt than they merit from the narrator, and deny that benefit to heroines. Interrogating the identity of hero throws suspicion on the binaries strong/weak, valiant/suffering, wise/innocent, and savior/saved that typically graft onto hero/princess.

Each of Perrault's three princes fails the test of heroism, both according to the dictionary definition of the French *héros* of 1690 and the modern English definition.[70] They are neither particularly courageous nor "extraordinary" and "noble" in the actions they take on behalf of their princesses. The prince in "The Fairies" does nothing but come upon the princess spewing gems at the end of the tale and marry her. The celebrity princes of "Beauty in the Slumbering Woodland" and "Ashkins," in spite of the roles Disney gave them, are also two-dimensional. In the case of "Beauty in the Slumbering Woodland," the prince does muster the courage to cross a forest and petrified staff of servants to arrive at the room where she sleeps. Yet until the moment he meets her and for several pages after that, the prince does not act so much as find himself acted upon. He goes out on a hunt not far from the sleeping woods just before the midpoint of the narrative. His first tasks are to ask about the towers in the trees, listen to a series of responses, not know what to think, be told by a farmer that a girl is asleep in the castle, and feel "all hot and bothered" by that news. Pushed "by love and glory," he goes toward the trees, they open to let him pass (which "did unsettle him a bit"), and he advances into the castle. Thus far, he has done nothing but react. Even as he encounters the beauty in her bed, the language that characterizes his movement and his reactions rings with panic more than courage: he approaches "trembling and admiring" and falls to his knees before her. Then, as we will discuss below, she does all the talking. Once married to the beauty and crowned king upon his father's death, he takes her to his castle and goes off to war, leaving her at the mercy of his ogress mother, the dowager queen. Finally,

---

[70]"Héros," in *Dictionnaire de l'Académie française*; "Hero," in *OED Online*.

he inadvertently saves his wife and children from his mother when he comes home early from the war and catches the queen in the act of killing them. Upon seeing him—stunned and wondering what is going on—the queen throws herself to her death. Twice this prince does little more than arrive on the scene; narrative fate, not heroism, saves the day.

Ashkins's prince, who, more than most, embodies Prince Charming today in the popular imaginary, ranks among the least interesting characters in Perrault's cast. When he sees Ashkins for the first time he falls into a rapture and forgets to eat. He loses track of her after that first ball and is "just sick about it" and "would give everything in the world" to discover her identity. At the second ball, he trails her and showers her with compliments until the stroke of midnight, when she flees and proves too fast for him: "he followed her but could not catch her." Gingerly picking up the slipper she has dropped, he spends the rest of the ball staring at it, "deeply in love" with the woman who wore it. In the end, although he trumpets the news that he will marry the woman whose foot fits the slipper, he sends his gentleman to do the actual searching around the kingdom.

Princes do and say very little in this collection. The rest of the cosmos is populated by nonroyal humans who, not unlike their princely counterparts, act in a manner that could be described as unheroic. The men in "The Blue Beard" and "Cat-in-the-Boots" prove brutal in the first case and docile in the second. The Blue Beard traps women with money, then kills them and hangs them in a spare room. He ranks as the lone sociopathic character in the *Histoires ou Contes*—the only other murderers are ogres who eat flesh by nature—and yet his powerless young wife outwits him and survives. The miller's son who inherits the famous Cat-in-the-Boots expects to die of hunger once he has eaten it. With no ideas or imagination of his own, he puts his faith in the conspiring cat. Listening carefully and executing the cat's commands are his only skills; never does he learn to confect ruses and solutions on his own. He ultimately weds because the princess thinks he is "just her type" and falls "madly in love" with him after he glances at her two or three times. Like the beauty's prince, he simply shows up—the princess does the rest. And like Ashkins, the prince inspires ardent lust once he dresses up in finery to become an object worthy of royal affection, but he has done even less than she to earn that recognition. In "Cat-in-the-Boots," the cat makes the effort expected of the hero, turning the prince-to-be into his *compère*, rather than the other way around.

Male human heroes in Perrault's fairy tales exhibit a passivity—they are swept along by fate, overwhelmed, or speechless—similar to the helplessness traditionally associated with the creature known critically as "the innocent persecuted heroine," or IPH, of which the woodland beauty and Ashkins are primary examples.[71] They do not usually "dispatch their adversaries personally," as a Disney viewer might expect, and thus do not exist in "direct contrast" to heroines who need help.[72] Overall, the male characters of Mother Goose are not heroic swashbuckling forces of nature but rather all-too-human men who fall in love and find themselves overwhelmed (or mad with homicidal tendencies, as in the case of the Blue Beard).[73] Significantly, while the relative ineffectualness of male princes and upstarts might make them appear tailored to their innocent persecuted princesses, such a characterization does not fit the coterie of heroines in the tales. Once the hero loses his cultural luster, the heroine stands to recover a bit more bite than popular images such as Disney's afford her. Their identities come out especially in their voices, and while some of them do not say much, their sometimes singular speech acts are significant. Donald Haase has highlighted the especially poignant "role of speech and storytelling as driving forces in the narrative" of the woodland beauty, who indeed speaks only three key lines in the tale.[74]

To take one as an example, the following line is the first the heroine speaks when she wakes in the tale. It is a focal point for her identity and a grammatically challenging one: "Est-ce vous, mon Prince? lui dit-elle, vous vous êtes bien fait attendre."[75] The verb compound in the French *se faire attendre*, which loosely means to be made to wait but also implies unexpected delay, adds a layer of complexity to the tone of the heroine's words: "Is that you, prince? You certainly took your time." Dreaming about this prince day and night in her restless state, this beauty might be said to be stewing instead of sleeping, all the while screaming an internal monologue of "Get me out of here!" and "Where is that prince?!" When in the next line she leers at the prince in a way that Perrault cautions is not entirely appropriate, we

---

[71]Created as a subgenre in 1927 and associated with ATU 510, the title evokes a dominant personality trait shared by this type of female character: they suffer. For a landmark overview of this critical category, see the special issue of *Western Folklore* "Perspectives on the Innocent Persecuted Heroine in Fairy Tales," ed. Bacchilega and Jones.

[72]Steven Swann Jones, "The Innocent Persecuted Heroine Genre," in Bacchilega and Jones, "Perspectives on the Innocent Persecuted Heroine in Fairy Tales," 25.

[73]The singular exception to this rule is Little Thumbling, who vanquishes an ogre and saves his brothers. And animals such as the wolf and the cat, for their part, embody a particular variety of craftiness; they talk their way to success.

[74]Donald Haase, "Kiss and Tell: Orality, Narrative, and the Power of Words in 'Sleeping Beauty,'" *Etudes de lettres* 289, nos. 3-4 (2011): 283.

[75]Collinet, *Perrault, Contes*, 136.

Figure 12. Anna Nilssen, "Disney Princesses," *What if? Comics*, 2011. (Reproduced with the artist's permission.)

can feel her channeling that frustration into ardent desire. Each subtlety changes the way we think about the heroine's personality and also the gender dynamic in the scene. Choosing a colloquialism with bite—which is audible in the French—gives her a strong personality, so that even through her time in the sleeping woodland, she remains the same boisterous girl who excitedly pricked her finger.

A very recent fantasy on the *What if? Comics* website lamented that Disney would not likely create strong heroines "before Hell Freezes Over" and imagined its own twist on the plot (see figure 12). While the writers of the cartoon acknowledge that the expletive packs a certain offensiveness lacking in the French, the rage of the language and the princesses' scowls characterize the power dynamic in an interesting way. Comedy turns the energy of the heroines' grammar into anger, which seems honest and funny. The translation I offer here makes the line a hallmark of her strength in the scene, as though their brief exchange of words and winks would be followed by her throwing off the covers, grabbing the prince, and getting down to business with him—which is exactly what happens. They retreat to her bed for four hours to chat and amuse themselves while the castle staff, who have also been asleep for a century and just woken up, impatiently suffer their hunger.

Each tale has a series of key moments in which characters acquire another contour of the personality they need for the narrative to move forward and conclude. Deciding which scenes are the most important is as much an act of interpretation as deciding on the tone of a phrase. Much of what has become iconic about the Cinderella story centers on her interactions with the fairy in the story—she whines and cries and waits to be finely dressed. If this is not the most formative moment in the story, it nevertheless plays that role in critical history. Yet, the language of her interactions with her sisters, rarely emphasized in critical work on the tale, is equally formative for her development as a character. The scene in which she tries on the slipper may be the most important of these key moments as it shows us the depth to her character. Here is the rendering featured in this volume:

> They brought it to the sisters, who tried everything in their power to get their foot into the slipper but did not succeed. Ashkins was watching, recognized the slipper, and *chuckled*, saying, "I should see if it fits me!"
>
> Her sisters cracked up and made fun of her. The gentleman trying the slipper, who had looked carefully at her and found her very attractive, said that this seemed fair and that he had been ordered to try it on every girl. He directed Ashkins to the seat and, drawing the slipper to her foot, saw that it went in easily and that it fit like a hand in a glove. (My emphasis) [76]

Quoted in full, these lines paint a scene that Ashkins interrupts with her unexpected speech. How she says this line can alter the way we read it. Against the general trend in past translations and even against the way I translate that word elsewhere in the story, I chose "chuckled" instead of "laughed" for *rire*. This episode in the story might be called an elaborately staged plot; one orchestrated not by the prince or his valet but by Ashkins. This reading becomes possible if it builds from Ashkins's earlier interactions: she had been toying with her sisters in the story, pretending not to be the beauty they saw at the ball so that she could hear them talk about her. She also saved the slipper that did not fall off, a detail we do not know until this penultimate episode. Waiting with the slipper in her pocket for this spectacular occasion, Ashkins patiently anticipated the moment when

---

[76]Ibid., 176. "On l'apporta chez les deux sœurs, qui firent tout leur possible pour faire entrer leur pied dans la pantoufle, mais elles ne purent en venir à bout. Cendrillon qui les regardait, et qui reconnut la pantoufle, dit en riant. Que je voie si elle ne me serait pas bonne! Ses sœurs se mirent à rire et à se moquer d'elle. Le Gentilhomme qui faisait l'essai de la pantoufle, ayant regardé attentivement Cendrillon, et la trouvant fort belle, dit que cela était juste, et qu'il avait ordre de l'essayer à toutes les filles. Il fit asseoir Cendrillon, et approchant la pantoufle de son petit pied, il vit qu'elle y entrait sans peine, et qu'elle était juste comme de cire."

she could steal the fire, the plot, and the prince right out from under her sisters.

In Perrault's corpus, the dictum "[W]hile male protagonists are sometimes cast in the role of unpromising hero in folktales, their female counterparts much more frequently fulfill that function" meets a healthy challenge.[77] For the Mother Goose tales, the ratio is about fifty-fifty. Furthermore, heroines generally say more than their male counterparts, and in that singular feature of their personae have something unexpected in common with crafty animals. Although the traditional Sleeping Beauty and Cinderella—along with Snow White and Rapunzel in the tales of the Grimms—form the critical category "innocent persecuted heroine," that language masks the proactive ways in which they respond to the forces that persecute them.

To be sure, scholars have noted that occasionally heroines of the Cinderella plot, known through folkloric classification as ATU 510, "gain all the time in determination and strength" through their suffering and "begin to lose their tag of unpromise and start shaping their lives and futures, at times, not without a little deception."[78] We can now go further and argue that the tag of unpromise is false and deception is not accidental but part of a social learning curve. In fact, neither the tag nor the deception need define the heroines. By lifting the moniker, I do not mean to suggest that Perrrault's heroines do not suffer; rather, I want to emphasize that they are not necessarily innocent in the sense of naïve and artless. Heroines do many things besides suffer and, as such, have a hand in alleviating their own misery.

As Steven Swann Jones points out in his definition of the official innocent persecuted heroine (IPH) genre, gender bias in tales, while it exists, is often far from absolute and, indeed, "the encouragement to rely on social justice [or help from others] is ethically admirable on the whole."[79] Female characters must grow into their pluck, but this commonplace in tales makes more of a social statement than an anthropological one. They are often held down by social forces that trap them in frustrating or deadly situations; so are a few male characters who also need help ("Cat-in-the-Boots" and "Little Thumblette"). When heroines do enlist or simply enjoy the help of fairies or friends ("Ashkins," "Fairies," "The Blue Beard"), they profit aggressively from those gifts to make their way to higher social status. Only Ashkins and the first daughter in "Fairies" deal with actual fairies; other heroines

---

[77] W. F. H. Nicholaisen, "Why Tell Stories about Innocent Persecuted Heroines?" in Bacchilega and Jones, "Perspectives on the Innocent Persecuted Heroine in Fairy Tales," 62.
[78] Ibid., 67.
[79] Jones, "The Innocent Persecuted Heroine Genre," 34.

suffering persecution are left to their own devices or the good graces of animal and human people around them who respect them. Men may represent riches the heroines seek, but they do not aid the heroines in acquiring them.

In only one case—"Beauty in the Slumbering Woodland"—does a heroine undergo rescue that is not the result of her actions; and in this case, her real savior is not the prince, who wakes her accidentally, but the butler, who likes her too much to betray her by cooking her for dinner. In other words, those that relieve the persecution of the innocent in Perrault are figures whose personal relationship with the heroine/hero—brother, servant, pet—gives them a particular stake in her/his survival. Indeed, even the homicidal wolf in "Little Red Tippet" begins the story as her *compère*—the role played by the cat in "Cat-in-the-Boots." Helpers are socially relevant because vicious figures in the *Stories or Tales of the Past* are social power mongers who destroy women and poorer men.

Rethinking the hero as a social creature pulls a thread out of the weave that changes the look of the entire tapestry. Elisabeth Panttaja suggested as much when she argued for setting aside psychoanalytic developmental theories of the IPH because they are based upon the "privatization of female struggle in literary criticism," and thus fail to take note of the larger sociopolitical stakes in her struggle.[80] "Ashkins" and "The Beauty in the Slumbering Woodland" are not the same tales if their hero and heroine are not pitted against each other as opposites but regarded as literary types that, upon inspection, bleed readily into each other. If they begin with different abilities to move in the world and different social expectations imposed upon them, nonetheless heroines and heroes can become active or passive, heroic or awed, strong or weak, depending upon the scene. Read this way, and through the ambiguity of the tales' morals, the Mother Goose tales force a reconsideration of power—particularly male and generational—in society. Hermann Rebel has recently credited Perrault's stories with an urgent social rather than moral mission: they "point to the ogres doing what they wanted with people behind castle walls, to the apparently civilized, to the 'falsely sweet' or 'smooth' wolves (*ces loups douceureux*) who populated the courtly social world."[81] Gendered behavior need not be read as a biological inevitability but as an unfortunate social prescription handed down by patriarchy, and the measures heroines take to navigate the politics of gender can then be understood as tactical.

---

[80]Panttaja, "Going up in the World," 87.
[81]Hermann Rebel, *When Women Held the Dragon's Tongue, and Other Essays in Human Anthropology* (Brooklyn: Berghahn, 2010), 166.

Ruth Bottigheimer has called the inaugural 1550s print tales by Giovanni Francesco Straparola "rise tales" because they follow a general plot development from rags through magic and marriage to riches.[82] A more proactive term for Perrault's stories about young women and men might be "climb tales" to highlight how heroines and poor heroes learn what it takes to succeed socially in spite of generational power that thwarts their progress. If these fairy tales set up a fantastical universe designed to seduce and entrap young women and men, they also demonstrate that knowing how to read and deploy deceit and wit can get you out of a lamentable situation and/or into an enviable one. Not possessing those skills, in the example of the little red tippet and the ineloquent sister in "The Fairies," can kill you.[83] If Perrault's is a classical frame of reference, it nonetheless champions the benefits of modern young adults reading the paternalistic world carefully and, when they can, turning expectations of them—courtship, marriage, beauty—to their own advantage. To be sure, Perrault's characters learn to walk through courtly seventeenth-century plots, but part of their appeal is that they face obstacles with their eyes open. The translations that follow show them wide-eyed and resourceful as they grab hold of the future.

---

[82]Ruth B. Bottigheimer, *Fairy Godfather: Straparola, Venice, and the Fairy Tale Tradition* (Philadelphia: University of Pennsylvania Press, 2002), 5.

[83]Rebel registers how differently the tale reads if its point is not the child's innocence, "insufficiently inhibited to be considered civilized," but concern about her socially inadequate education, or "concern for the nurtured ignorance of the girl and her resulting illusion of being in control in the midst of a murderous deception" (*When Women Held the Dragon's Tongue*, 166).

Stories or Tales of the Past

Dedication (1697)

Mademoiselle,

You will not find it strange that a child took pleasure in composing the tales in this collection, but you might wonder that he dared to offer them to you.[1] Nevertheless, Mademoiselle, whatever difference there may be between the simplicity of these stories and the brightness of your knowledge, I am not as worthy of blame as I may at first appear. They all contain a very wise lesson, which becomes more or less apparent according to the depth of the reader's perception. And as nothing indicates the vast expanse of an intellect better than the ability both to raise itself to the greatest things and lower itself to the simplest, it is not surprising that the same princess for whom nature and education have made the lofty familiar would not refuse the pleasure of such bagatelles. It is true that these tales give a sense of what happens in the humblest homes; there the worthy haste to teach children inspires the invention of nonsensical stories appropriate for these children who have not yet developed sense. But who better to understand how the common people live than the persons chosen by heaven to chaperone[2] them? The desire for this understanding has driven heroes, and heroes of your race, into huts and cabins to see up close and for themselves the most peculiar happenings; which seemed a necessary part of a complete education. In any case, Mademoiselle,

---

[1] The wording of the 1695 dedication, quoted in translation in the introduction, was altered for the 1697 publication.

[2] The verb in French is *conduire*, to lead or guide. My translation draws out the relationship between the verb in the dedication and the clothing worn by le petit chaperon rouge / the little red tippet. For a definition of *chaperon* see footnote 2 to that tale. All references to the French in the notes to the tales are taken from Jean-Pierre Collinet's critical edition of the *Histoires ou Contes du temps passé*, which modernizes orthography and accents. Because of the large number of words referenced, no page numbers are provided. The collection appears over pages 125–200 in *Perrault, Contes*.

Could I have chosen a better person to make sense of fairytale
    nonsense?
Never did a fairy in days of yore
Give to a young creature
Greater gifts and more
Than nature has seen fit in you to feature.

I remain with profound respect,
Mademoiselle,
Of Your Royal Highness,

    The most humble and very devoted servant,
    P. Darmancour.

The Beauty in the Slumbering Woodland

Once upon a time a king and a queen were so upset about not having any children, so upset that there are no words to describe it. They tried thermal baths all over the world, wishes, pilgrimages, everyday prayers; they spared no effort and nothing worked. But eventually the queen got pregnant and gave birth to a girl. They gave her a fitting baptism and made all the fairies to be found in the kingdom (they found seven) godmothers so that each one of them might grant her a blessing, as fairies customarily did in those days. Thus, the princess was endowed with every exceptional talent imaginable.[1]

After the baptismal rites, everyone went back to the king's palace where he hosted a sumptuous banquet for the fairies. Set before each one of them was a magnificent service in a solid gold box; it contained a spoon, a fork, and a diamond- and ruby-encrusted knife made of pure gold. But as they took their places at the table, in walked an old fairy whom no one had thought to invite because it had been fifty years since she left her tower and everyone assumed she was dead or under a spell. The king had a place set for her but could not give her the solid gold box he had given the others because he had had only seven made for the seven fairies. The old fairy took it as an insult and grumbled some threatening remarks.[2] One of the young fairies close by heard her and, sensing that she might grant the tiny princess a sinister blessing, went immediately when they left the table to hide behind a wall tapestry; she wanted to speak last and be able to remedy as best she could any harm the old fairy might do.

---

[1] This detail seems premature since the next two paragraphs describe the scene in which the princess receives her blessings. We can take the second and third paragraphs as explanations of this introductory remark about the fairies' contributions. In Perrault, the transaction between a fairy and her charge results in a *don*, conventionally translated "gift" or "blessing," as it appears below, since she offers it without warning to those who manifest social graces or simply need help. In this instance and in the same context in "The Fairies," I have instead chosen the word *talent* to capture the social (rather than moral) efficacy of the gifts, which endow the heroine with culturally required skills that meet the expectations of a court environment. The heroine receives these capacities at birth, suggesting that she can spend her childhood doing things besides working to acquire virtuosity, such as amusing herself with spindles (knowledge of which is not part of traditionally noble acculturation).

[2] An older English equivalent of the French expression "grommeler entre ses dents" is "muttered through one's teeth," a metaphor captured also by the verb "to grumble."

Meanwhile, the fairies began granting the princess blessings. The youngest declared that she would be the most charming person in the world; the next that she would have the mind of an angel; the third that she would do everything with exemplary grace; the fourth that she would be a fine dancer; the fifth that would sing like a nightingale, and the sixth that she would play an assortment of instruments to the highest perfection. When it was the old fairy's turn she said, with her head shaking more out of spite than old age, that the princess would puncture her own hand with a spindle and die from it. This ghastly blessing sent shivers through the assembly and no one could hold back the tears. Just then the young fairy came out from behind the tapestry and spoke these words out loud: "Take heart, king and queen, your daughter will not die. I'm afraid my limited powers cannot completely undo what my superior has done. The princess will have to puncture her own hand with a spindle. But instead of dying, she will only fall into a deep sleep for one hundred years, and when they have elapsed, the son of a king will arrive to wake her up."

In an attempt to escape the misfortune pronounced by the old fairy, the king issued an edict forbidding anyone to spin yarn on a spindle or even to have spindles around the house under penalty of death. Fifteen or sixteen years later, the king and queen having traveled to their country estate, it happened one day that the young princess, running in the castle and climbing to room after room, went all the way up to the small room at the top where an aged woman was alone spinning at her distaff. This old girl had not heard a word about the king's prohibition against spinning.

"What are you doing, old woman?"

"I'm spinning, sweet thing," she replied, not recognizing the princess.

"Wow! That's really something,"[3] said the princess in response. "How do you do it? Let me try to see if I can do it as well as you."

The minute she grabbed the spindle (she was very energetic and a bit impulsive, and besides, the Fairies' Decree[4] mandated it), she punctured

---

[3] *Ah! que cela est joli.* Literally, "Ah, how pretty that is." I opted to capture the exuberance of the French grammar in the expression "wow." As her surprise refers to the action of spinning, "pretty" seemed an odd choice of words in English.

[4] *Arrêt des Fées* (Fairies' Decree) appears capitalized in the 1697 text. While other important nouns are also capitalized, here the combination creates what looks like a title and I have retained it. The word *arrêt* refers generally to a binding decision made by an authority figure and, specifically in the jurisprudence of 1690, to decrees published by Louis XIV's court that expressed his law in final legal decisions. It suggests that like kings, fairies have a binding authority. Since this reads like a title it seems furthermore that these laws are disseminated officially through print or public announcement. Calling the enunciation an *arrêt* raises the fairy's baptismal blessing to a political act. It is further contrasted in the text with the word *edit* (edict), or proclamation, which is what the king issues to stop the practice of spinning in the kingdom. In political terms, the *arrêt* expresses a final ruling, whereas the *edit* issues an order.

her own hand and passed out. The old girl was at a loss and called for help. They come from every direction, throw water on the princess's face, untie her corset, slap her hands, massage her temples with the magical water that preserved the queen of Hungary[5]—but nothing brought her back.

In the meantime, the king, who had followed the noise up the stairs, remembered the fairies' prophesy. He deemed the incident inevitable because fairies called for it and had the princess set up in the most elegant apartment in the palace on a bed cover embroidered with gold and silver. You would have taken her for an angel, she looked so beautiful. Fainting had not drained her face of its warm color. She had rosy cheeks and lips like coral. She did have her eyes shut, but her gentle audible breathing proved she was not dead.

The king instructed everyone to let her sleep in peace until it was time for her to wake up. At the moment of the princess's mishap the good fairy who had saved her by condemning her to sleep for a hundred years was twelve thousand leagues[6] away in the kingdom of Mataquin. But she learned of it instantly from a little dwarf wearing seven-league boots (those were boots that moved you seven leagues with every step). The fairy left as soon as possible and arrived within the hour in a blazing chariot pulled by dragons. The king extended his hand as she stepped down from the carriage. She approved everything he had done, but her gift of incredible foresight made her realize that the princess would be lost waking up all alone in this old château. So here is what she did. She tapped everything in the château (besides the king and queen) with her wand: governesses, maids of honor, ladies-in-waiting, courtiers, the king's attendants, butlers, chefs, the kitchen help, security guards, gatekeepers, pages, and footmen.[7] She also tapped all the horses in the stable with their grooms, the guard dogs, and little Puff,

---

[5]*L'eau de la reine d'Hongrie*: curative astringent and perfume made from macerated rosemary. It was named for Elisabeth of Poland, queen consort of Hungary from 1320 to 1342, who credited its rejuvenating properties with preserving her beauty and strength throughout her life. She lived to be seventy-five. Important women at the court of Louis XIV, the writer Madame de Sévigné among them, used it as perfume.

[6]The classic Roman measurement of the overland league is the distance a man can walk in one hour, or 3–4 miles, which would make 12,000 leagues about 40,000 miles. France had an official standard calculated for grain transport in the late seventeenth century known as the "league of Paris" (*lieue de Paris*) at 3,898 kilometers, or about 2,400 miles. The second measurement yields epic distances that would involve circling the globe multiple times. Presumably the boots are calculated on the Roman scale.

[7]Note that in noble houses, the number of hired help attached to a prince could be staggering. Louis XIV had fifteen people concerned with his meals alone. And lest these positions appear menial, many were jobs of privilege. The managerial positions were held by nobility, with a prince of the blood (*grand maître*) overseeing the whole operation.

the princess's pet dog that was with her on the bed. As she tapped them, they all fell asleep, to wake up only when their mistress did and be ready to tend to her needs. Even the spits over the fire pit, heavy with partridges and pheasants, fell asleep. The fire, too. All of it happened in an instant. Fairies did not waste time.

Then the king and queen kissed their precious child without waking her up, left the château, and had prohibitions issued preventing anyone from coming near it. These prohibitions proved unnecessary because fifteen minutes later such an impressive number of big trees and small, and brambles and thorns, wove themselves in and around the château grounds that neither beast nor man could get through; you could only see the top of the château's towers, and for that matter only from very far away. No one doubted that the fairy had once again worked her art[8] to ensure that while the princess slumbered, she was safe from inquiring minds that wanted to know.[9] At the end of the hundred years, the son of the reigning king, from a different family than the slumbering princess, was out that way for a hunt. He asked about two towers he could see above a tall, thick forest. Each person told him the story he had heard. Some said it was a castle haunted by spirits, others that all the wizards of the land gathered there for their midnight Sabbath. Popular opinion had it that the château belonged to an ogre who brought all the children he could catch there to eat them at his leisure where no one could follow him because he alone had the cunning to forge a path through the woodland. The prince did not know what to think, but then an old farmer spoke up and told him: "Your Highness, more than fifty years ago I heard someone tell my father that in this château lay the most beautiful princess in the world, that she would be woken up by the son of a prince, and that she was promised to him."

---

[8]The expression *tour de son métier*, which I have rendered "worked her art," does not appear in dictionaries until the word *métier* does in the eighteenth century. According to the figurative meaning of *tour* in the seventeenth century, it ranged from how a friend might lend a hand (*tour d'ami*) to the way a charlatan fooled a crowd with a sleight of hand (*tour de main*). The ambiguous phrasing "tour de son métier" suggests that the fairy outdid herself with this performance of magic, while the context of the sentence identifies the gesture as a benevolent charm rather than the kind of clever maneuver one could play if one were skilled in the abuse of power or taking advantage of others.

[9]The word *curieux* in the seventeenth century referred to a disposition among the elite: to be curious was to be fashionably interested in the exotic. The *curieux* was a gentleman who sought out novelty and was probably a collector. If it sounds negative in this context, as though the public has prying eyes, it is because the trait was unsavory in everyone besides the gallant nobleman—namely, women and townspeople who would be prone to curiosity out of inappropriate or prurient desire. The colloquial turn of phrase I've used here refers to such a nosy personality. On the feminine manifestation of curiosity as a dangerous desire, see footnote 10 to "The Blue Beard."

The prince felt all hot and bothered[10] after this speech and knew without a second thought that he would be the one to conclude this marvelous adventure. Impelled by love and glory, he resolved right then and there to see about it. Barely had he stepped toward the woodland when all the big trees and brambles and thorns moved aside on their own to let him pass. He walked toward the château at the end of the long majestic avenue that led to it. It did unsettle him a bit to see that none of his men had been able to follow him because the trees wove themselves back together as soon as he came through. He continued on his path all the same—a young prince in love is always brave. He came to a grand courtyard and everything he saw there could make the blood run cold. The silence was terrible, visions of death everywhere, and it was strewn with bodies of men and animals that looked lifeless. But he could tell from the pimpled nose and ruddy cheeks of the porters that they were just sleeping, and the remaining drops of wine at the bottom of their glasses were proof enough that they had nodded off mid-drink.

He crosses a marble courtyard, climbs a staircase, and walks into the guards' quarters where they were all lined up in formation, rifles on their shoulders and snoring like champions. He crosses several bedrooms full of sleeping courtiers and ladies, some standing, some sitting. He enters a gilded room—and there on the bed, curtains drawn on every side, was the most exquisite vision he had ever seen: a princess who was probably about fifteen or sixteen years old, of a radiant splendor that had a sort of luminous and divine glow. Trembling and in awe, he dropped to his knees before her. Since the end of the enchantment had come, the princess woke up. She looked at him with more feeling in her eyes than is really appropriate for a first encounter and said: "Is that you, prince? You certainly took your time."

Enchanted by these words and even more by the manner in which she expressed them, the prince was at a loss to communicate his joy and thanks. He swore that he loved her more than he loved himself. His language was clumsy, but all the more charming for it—little eloquence, much love. He

---

[10]The expression in the French is *tout de feu*, the same one used to describe the fairy's dragon-drawn chariot earlier in the tale. It has a range of meanings from literally aflame or blazing to intellectually vivacious or zealous. Paired with the verb *sentir* (to feel) the context suggests the more metaphorical idea of emotional charge. Eugène Fasnacht's *Contes de fées*, produced as a primer with vocabulary and grammar explanations, offers "his heart was kindled." *Contes de Fées par Charles Perrault* (1884; repr., London: Macmillan, 1898), 100. I opted for the modern idiom "to be hot and bothered" because it connotes both anxious excitement and sexual arousal. The prince's sudden, unthinking resolve also has a humorous edge, as his rush is partially the result of his inexperience.

was more flustered than the princess, which should be no surprise since she had had time to think about what she wanted to say to him, since it seems (although this detail is missing from the story) that during such a long slumber the good fairy allowed her to have pleasant dreams. After talking together for four hours, they still had not said half of what they wanted to say to each other.

In the meantime, the whole palace had woken up with the princess. Everyone readied themselves to work, but as they had not fallen in love, they were dying of hunger. The maid of honor, no less affected by it than the others, lost patience and loudly told the princess that the meal[11] was ready. The prince helped the princess get up—she was fully and sumptuously dressed—but he kept silent on the subject of her high collar, which made her look like my grandmother.[12] It did not make her less attractive. They came into a hall of mirrors and ate a meal served by the queen's attendants. Violins and oboes played old tunes; they were excellent even though it had been a hundred years since anyone played them. Right after dinner and without delay, the family chaplain married them in the chapel of the château and the maid of honor opened the bed curtains.[13] They hardly slept. The princess didn't really need it and the prince left bright and early to return to the village and his father, who was no doubt concerned about him. The prince told him that while he was out hunting, he got lost in the forest and slept the night at the cabin of a coal maker who fed him black bread and cheese. His father the king, who was good-natured, believed it, but his mother did not find the story compelling. He hunted almost every day and always had an excuse ready. Once when he slept two or three nights away from home, she became convinced that he was having an illicit love affair. In truth, he lived that way with the princess for two full years and had two children with her: the first a daughter named Aurora and the second a son named Daylight because he was even lovelier than his sister.

Several times the queen attempted to get an explanation out of her son, telling him that he should be satisfied with the life he had, but he never could trust her with his secret. She descended from ogres and the king had

---

[11]The word *viande* (meat) has the broader meaning of *repas* (meal) in the seventeenth century. Frédéric Dillaye gives this explanation in *Les Contes de Perrault* (Paris: Alphonse Lemirre, 1880), 234.

[12]The use of the possessive here is puzzling. On the one hand, it sounds like the narrator commenting on the passage. On the other hand, there is a "ma mère-grand" in the collection: petit chaperon rouge's grandmother.

[13]Pulling the curtains on a poster bed in the seventeenth century would be the equivalent today of turning down the sheets. In other words, she prepared the bed for them.

only married her for her vast fortune. People at court even declared under their breath that she had an ogre's desires and when she saw little children walk by it was all she could do not to throw herself at them. So the prince never said anything. Now, when the king died, which happened two years later, and the prince found himself sovereign of the realm, he publicly announced his marriage and, with great pomp and circumstance, brought his wife and children to the château. A spectacular ceremony attended his entrance into the capital city flanked by his children. Some time later, the king left to make war on Emperor Catalabutte. He designated his mother the queen regent and entrusted his wife and children to her care. The war was to last all summer and as soon as he left the Queen Mother sent her daughter-in-law and the children to a country house in the woods to be able more easily to sate her violent desire. She visited there a few days later and one night told the butler: "I want to eat young Aurora for lunch tomorrow."

"No, Madame!"

"I want to," said the queen—and she said it in the drawl of an ogre hankering for young flesh—"and I want her in a *Robert* sauce."[14]

Seeing very well that it does not pay to fool with an ogress, the poor man grabbed his knife and went up to young Aurora's room. She was four years old then and, jumping gleefully, she threw her arms around his neck and begged for candy. He began to cry, the knife fell from his hand, and he went down to the barnyard to kill a young lamb instead. The sauce he made was so good that his mistress swore she had never eaten anything so delicious. At the same time, he had taken young Aurora to his wife with instructions to hide her in the little room they occupied at the back of the barnyard. Eight days later the evil queen said to the butler: "I want to eat young Daylight for dinner."

He did not respond, resolved to trick her as he had before. He went to look for young Daylight and found him with a miniature foil in his hand playing at fencing with a large monkey. He was only three. The butler brought him to his wife, who hid him with young Aurora. In his place, he prepared a small and tender young goat that the ogress found absolutely

---

[14]*La Sauce Robert* dates from the birth of modern French culinary techniques in the seventeenth century and is one of only a few recipes from that era that remain among French cuisine's classic sauces for meat, especially lamb and beef. A basic roux (browned butter with flour) combines with onion and spices and simmers in a demi-glace, a veal-based wine reduction. The preparation of demi-glace alone takes hours, which makes this rich sauce time consuming to make. The ogress's desire for meat *à la sauce Robert* attests to her conventional noble taste in spite of her monstrous birth, but her sudden demand for French gastronomy as though it were fast food betrays her savagery and would tax even a seasoned chef.

delicious. Things had gone smoothly so far, but one evening the horrible queen told the butler: "I want to eat the queen in the same sauce you made for her children."

At that point, the butler despaired of tricking her again. The young queen was over twenty, to say nothing of the hundred years she had been asleep: her skin was a bit tough, even if smooth and white, and who could find an animal as tough-skinned as that in the menagerie? He resolved to save his own life by taking the life of the young queen and went up to her room intent on doing it once and doing it right.[15] He worked himself into a fury and burst, knife drawn, into the young queen's room. And yet, he did not want to catch her off guard, so he conveyed with utmost respect the order he had received from the Queen Mother.

"Do what you have to do," she told him, offering him her neck. "Execute the order you were given. I will go to my children, my poor babies, that I loved so much." She believed they were dead since they had disappeared without explanation.

"No. No, Madame," responded the weary butler. "You will not die and you will go to your precious children, but at my home where I hid them. I will trick the Queen Mother again and serve her a young doe in your place."

He showed her to his room where she could embrace and cry with her children, and went to prepare a doe. The queen ate it for dinner, savoring it as though it were the young queen. She was very pleased with her cruelty and was prepared to tell the king upon his return that rabid wolves in the area had eaten his wife and his two children.

One evening as she paced the courtyards and barnyard to sniff out fresh meat, which she did routinely, she heard the sound of young Daylight crying coming from a room below—because his mother the queen wanted him whipped since he had been bad—and she also heard young Aurora plead for mercy on her brother's behalf. The ogress recognized the voices of the queen and her children and, furious that she had been tricked, she demands first thing the next day—in a dreadful voice that terrified everyone—that they bring a big tub to the center of the courtyard so that she can have it filled it with toads, vipers, water snakes, and serpents and have the queen and her children, the butler, his wife, and her maid thrown in. She had given orders that they be brought to her with their hands tied behind their backs. There they stood with the executioners poised to throw them

---

[15]"De ne pas en faire à deux fois." Curiously, the ogre in "The Little Thumblette" has the same thought on his way to kill the young boys. This reflection gives two very different characters something in common.

into the tub when the king trotted in on horseback. He had arrived home earlier than expected and, in total shock, demanded that someone explain this horrible spectacle. No one seemed willing to apprise him of the situation, when suddenly the ogress, enraged by this turn of events, threw herself headfirst into the tub and was devoured by the vile creatures she had put there. The king could not help but be vexed by the scene—she was his mother—but he soon took comfort in his beautiful wife and his children.

Moral

Waiting a time for a husband to find
Rich, dashing, elegant, and kind
That's the traditional way.
But wait a hundred years for him . . . asleep?

You won't find a female today
Whose slumber is so deep.
The fable also tries to make us see
That a strong marriage bond
May be differed, long postponed
And not for that reason be less happy.

But the fair sex does so require
The promise of conjugal heaven
That I've neither the strength nor the desire
To force upon them this lesson.

The Little Red Tippet

Once upon a time there was a young country girl, the prettiest you ever did see. Her mother was crazy about her and her grandmother[1] crazier still. The older woman had made-to-fit for her a tufted red bonnet and tippet.[2] It suited her so well that everyone called her the little red tippet.[3]

One day after baking and making galettes,[4] her mother told her, "I would like you to go see how your grandma[5] is doing because I heard she was sick. Take her a galette and this small jar of butter."

---

[1]Perrault writes *mère-grand*, not *grand-mère*, as it is usually written in French. The Perraultian word appears in the dictionary today as an old form of "grandmother," with "Petit chaperon rouge" as its textual example (see *Le Petit Robert*).

[2]I have opted for a name quite different from the classic hood or cap monikers traditionally associated with this heroine because the word in French, *chaperon,* denotes a specific type of fashionable headgear from the Renaissance, which has no desirable one-word equivalent in English today. I have opted to use the name of part of that gear, the scarf, in the word *tippet*. The word *chaperon* in English is the precise term for the style of tufted hat and scarf combination worn in the Renaissance (to which the French word refers), but could be confusing to modern readers, who might hear in it only the modern definition, a guardian of young charges. A drawback of the translation is that it suppresses a relevant secondary definition: "an older woman who accompanies young women to social gatherings" (une femme d'âge qui accompagne les jeunes filles dans les companies). *Dictionnaire de l'Académie française*. That both of those definitions—related to caretaking and to fashion—are operative in the seventeenth-century French suggests that having the bonnet and tippet made for the girl is a way for the grandmother to send her out protected; yet, its loud color belies that strategy, as the story goes on to reveal.

[3]Like "The Blue Beard," this title is a metonymy. I have kept the article in the title and in the text (as Perrault does) when it becomes her identifying feature and left the words lowercased because it is never capitalized in the 1697 edition. That is to say, unlike the name la Barbe bleue or Cendrillon, "le petit chaperon rouge" is not identified textually as her proper name in the usual way. Even when the girl takes the name of the garment she remains grammatically nameless. While it is not uncommon for characters in French fairy tales to be called only by their title or salient feature (Princess, Father, Queen, Beauty, Beast, Ogress, Woodsman, and so on), it is rare that a heroine should have a descriptor that is not capitalized. This omission is particularly striking in the literary style of poetry and prose in the seventeenth century, which permits any noun to be capitalized for emphasis.

[4]A *galette* is a flat cake that one makes when baking bread. Today the word is used in France to designate a buckwheat crêpe, which is served savory, not sweet like a dessert crêpe.

[5]When the mother speaks to the little red tippet and when the little red tippet addresses the wolf at the end of the tale, the usually capitalized word *Mère-grand* takes a lowercase *m*, which I have rendered here in the more familiar "grandma."

The little red tippet left right away for her grandmother's house, where she lived in another village. While she was crossing the woods, she ran into the neighborhood wolf,[6] who very much wanted to eat her but did not dare because of the woodsmen in the forest. He asked her where she was going. The poor girl, who did not know that it is dangerous to stop and listen to wolves, told him: "I'm going to see my grandmother and bring her a galette with a small jar of butter from my mother."

"Does she live far?" said the wolf.

"Oh, yes," said the little red tippet, "it's further than that mill you see way over there. There, the first house in the village."

"You know what?" said the wolf, "I would like to go see her, too. I'll set out on this path and you take that one. We'll see who gets there faster."

The wolf raced down the short path, while the young girl set out on the long one, happily picking hazelnuts, running after butterflies, and making bouquets with tiny flowers she found.

It did not take the wolf long to arrive at the grandmother's house. He knocked: knock, knock.

"Who's there?"

"It's your granddaughter, the little red tippet,"[7] said the wolf, imitating her voice, "with a galette and a small jar of butter from my mother."

The old grandmother, who stayed in her bed[8] because she did not feel well, called out:

"Pull the pin, loose the latch."

The wolf pulled the pin and the door opened. He threw himself at the old woman and devoured her in a flash because he had not eaten for three days. Next he closed the door and lay down in the grandmother's bed to wait for the little red tippet. A little while later, she came knocking at the door: knock, knock.

"Who's there?"

The little red tippet heard the wolf's gruff voice and was afraid at first, but she figured her grandmother must have gotten the flu and answered, "It's your granddaughter, the little red tippet, with a galette and a small jar of butter from my mother."

---

[6]See the Notes (83) for a discussion of the word *compère*, the unlikely title of familiarity the narrator uses to introduce the wolf in the story.

[7]Note that the wolf knows the little red tippet's name.

[8]Although most critics translate this "had stayed in bed," the tense in Perrault matches the rest of the sentence, which could mean that she does not get up to open the door *this time*, although she normally would.

Softening his voice a little, the wolf called out, "Pull the pin, loose the latch."

The little red tippet pulled the pin and the door opened. Watching from under the covers as she entered, the wolf said to her, "Put the galette and small jar of butter on the hutch and come lie down with me."

The little red tippet takes off her clothes and goes to get into bed . . . where she was shocked to see how her grandmother looked undressed.[9]

She said to her:

"Grandma, you have such big arms!" "That's to hug you better, my dear."
"Grandma, you have such big legs!" "That's to run better, my dear."
"Grandma, you have such big ears!" "That's to hear better, my dear."
"Grandma, you have such big eyes!" "That's to see better, my dear."
"Grandma, you have such big teeth!" "That's to eat you."[10]

And with those words, that miscreant[11] wolf threw himself at the little red tippet and ate her.

Moral

Here we see that children so young,
Especially young girls,
Beautiful, striking pearls,
Fare very badly when they listen to just anyone.[12]

---

[9] The expression "en son déshabillé" refers to the clothes one wears to stay home or sleep, as opposed to those one wears to go out. I have opted for "undressed" here because of the substantial difference it would make in the seventeenth century to see someone without her public clothes (which covered the whole body), perhaps for the first time. According to the wording of the text, the effect of this *déshabillé* is that the little red tippet can see parts of her grandmother's body. As the body in question belongs to the wolf, she registers particularly strong shock.

[10] The 1695 illuminated manuscript of the tales features an accessory to the text that was rarely reprinted with this story: there is an asterisk after the word *manger* in "c'est pour te manger" (that's to eat you). The commentary reads: "[O]n pronounce ces mots d'une voix forte pour faire peur à l'enfant comme si le loup l'alloit manger" (Say these words in a loud voice to frighten the child as if the wolf were going to eat him). This detail has particularly striking humor if we imagine that it would have been read by adults enjoying a salon evening or by a princess in her chambers. This form of stage direction does not so much offer advice to parents (again, it dropped out of subsequent editions, even those targeting young children) as create the illusion of the fireside performance in the frontispiece of the 1695 and 1697 versions. Adults reading the book in a chair could enjoy imagining it scaring children. Thus, the tale that seems most earnest may be the most finely theatrical.

[11] The word in French is *méchant*, which since Samber has often been translated "wicked" in English. I opted for a word that captures how this *compère* becomes an outsider, even a villain, by acting out of character.

[12] The line "toute sorte de gens" could be rendered with the words "many types," "all types," or "several types." My choice of "just anyone" emphasizes the ambiguity of how many.

And that it's no surprise
If the wolf takes many a prize.
I say the wolf because not all wolves are the same.
There are those of courteous fame,
No noise or bile or rage,
But reserved, compliant, and sage,
Who will trail a girl well bred
All the way home, into her bed.[13]
Ah! But as everyone knows, it's the saccharine[14] tongues,
Of all the wolves, who are the most dangerous ones.

[13]The word here, *ruelle*, which I translated "bed," was loaded with cultural significance in the seventeenth century. It refers specifically to the area of an aristocratic bedroom between the bed and the wall where one might place seating and receive guests (even ones of the opposite sex). It can also mean an intellectual salon. Perrault's wolves lurk openly in society and even find themselves invited into women's bedrooms.

[14]*Doucereux*: "Sweet without being agreeable. Used figuratively for people . . . who appear too sweet and too affected. We say, 'To be saccharine with a woman' to mean 'Act so as to make her believe that you are in love with her'" (Qui est doux sans estre agreable. . . . Il se dit fig. des personnes . . . Qui paroist trop doux & trop affecté. On dit, *Faire le doucereux auprés d'une femme*, pour dire, Affecter par ses façons de luy faire croire que l'on est amoureux d'elle). *Dictionnaire de l'Académie française*.

The Blue Beard

Once upon a time a man had magnificent townhomes and country estates, serving ware in gold and silver, embroidered upholstery, and richly gilded carriages. By some terrible misfortune, the man's beard was blue, which gave him such an improper,[1] shocking appearance that women and girls fled at the sight of him. One of his neighbors, a noblewoman, had two daughters who were the perfection of beauty. He asked the woman for the hand of one of her daughters in marriage and let her decide which one she would offer him. They wanted no part of it, and each sent him back to the other, neither one able to commit to marrying a blue-bearded man. What sickened them even more was the fact that he had already married several women and it was unclear what had become of them.

To get to know them, the Blue Beard[2] invited them along with their mother, three or four of their best girlfriends, and some young neighbors to one of his country estates, where they stayed for eight long days.[3] The visit was filled with strolling, hunting and fishing, dancing and feasting, afternoon tea; they stayed up all night playing pranks on each other and, in the end, it was all so enjoyable that the younger sister began to think that the

---

[1] The word *laid*, ugly, had a range of connotations in the seventeenth century as the antonym of beautiful. Beauty was construed first and foremost as the fulfillment of aesthetic expectation. What was ugly failed to meet those expectations, which had to do with proportion and color. Its first definition, *difforme*, means out of proportion or disfigured. The narrator emphasizes the beard's color, which would "disfigure" him in that his look was not in accordance with propriety. *Dictionnaire de l'Académie française.*

[2] Like "The Little Red Tippet," this title and the eponymous character it names are metonymies, a habit that seems particular to Perrault in the French fairy-tale corpus. "Ashkins"'s subtitle, "The Little Slipper of Glass," arguably functions in a similar way. Since Perrault uses the article in French to highlight the part of the man that represents his identity in the story, as though he is reducible to his beard (which he does not do for Ashkins, for example), I have retained it in translation.

[3] The last clause of the French reads: "où on demeura huit jours entier." The verb *demeurer* in French marks the length of a stay, as though it were extended. I have displaced this sense of time stretched onto the adjective "entier" and rendered it "eight long days" instead of "eight whole days." While that expression could also mean a week (as in the present French habit of saying *quinze jours*, fifteen days, for two weeks), I have retained the day count for emphasis.

man's beard was not all that blue and that he was a very courtly gentleman. Upon their return to the city, they decided to marry.[4]

A month had passed when the Blue Beard told his wife that he had important business that required a trip to the provinces that would take him at least six weeks; that he hoped she would amuse herself in his absence; that she should invite her friends; that she should take them to the country if she wanted to; and everywhere show her guests a good time.[5] He told her: "Here are the keys to the two furniture attics, here are the keys to the buffet with the gold and silver services not for everyday use, keys to the safes with my bouillon and silver coin, keys to the boxes where I keep my jewels, and here is the master key to all the apartments. Now, this little key is the key to the office[6] at the end of the great hall of the downstairs apartment. Open everything, go everywhere, but as far as the little office goes, you may not go in there—and I am so serious about this that if you do end up opening it, my anger will know no bounds."

She promised to follow all the directives he had just given her and after he kissed her—he gets in his carriage and leaves for his trip. The neighbors and good friends did not wait for an invitation to visit the young wife, so badly did they want to see the splendor of her home and so unwilling to visit while the husband was around because his blue beard scared them. There they were, right away making their way through the bedrooms, offices, and dressing rooms, one more splendid and sumptuous than the next. After that, they climbed to the furniture attics, where they could not believe the number of beautiful tapestries, beds, day beds,[7]

---

[4]In French "le marriage se conclut" employs the verb *conclure*, to conclude, which might appear to suggest accomplishment, as though the marriage took place, but in fact has the same meaning here as in the expression *marché conclu*—which marks agreement on the terms of a transaction. Thus, upon their return to town, the couple agreed and arranged to be married.

[5]*Faire bonne chère* refers etymologically to putting on a good face (a warm welcome), but the expression had evolved by the seventeenth century into something closer to a general sense of entertaining guests. Today it refers to a good time at the table, eating well or preparing a good meal.

[6]The word *cabinet* (office), which refers generally in the seventeenth century to any room in the house where one retreats to work and where one keeps important documents and books, has a secondary meaning that seems pertinent here: "*Cabinet* also refers to the most closely guarded secrets and mysteries of the court" (*Cabinet,* veut dire aussi, les secrets, les mystères les plus cachés de la Cour). *Dictionnaire de l'Académie française.*

[7]The first seventeenth-century definition of sofas identifies them as Turkish benches covered in rugs that would have been used by prime ministers of the Ottoman Empire when they gave audience. The more likely meaning here applies to a relatively new type of furniture in the 1690s. "We also call a *sofa* a kind of two-sided day bed, which has recently come into use in France" (On appelle aussi, Sofa, Une espèce de lit de repos à deux dossiers, dont on se sert depuis peu en France). *Dictionnaire de l'Académie française.*

curios,[8] pedestal tables, dressing tables and mirrors—mirrors long enough to reflect them from head to toe[9] and with the most magnificent decorative edging you have ever seen, some in crystal and others in silver or gold plate. They went on and on with their exaggeration and envy of their friend's happiness. She, for her part, took no pleasure in seeing all that splendor because she was eager to go and open the office in the downstairs apartment.

Her curiosity[10] was so acute that without even considering how rude it was to leave her guests, she hurried down a private staircase, moving so fast that two or three times she nearly broke her neck. She stood before the door for a while thinking about the restrictions her husband had placed on her and considering the misery that could befall her for disobeying, but the temptation proved so strong that she could not overcome it. So she took out the little key and, shaking, opened the door to the office. At first she could not see anything because the shutters were closed. Moments later, she began to see that the floor was covered with congealed blood wherein the corpses of several women that had been hung along the walls could forever see their reflection[11]—all the women the Blue Beard had married and slit at the throat one after the other. She nearly died of fright and dropped the little key that she had just pulled out of the lock.

When her wits came back to her, she picked up the key, locked the door, and went up to her room to rest a little. But she could not relax for being

---

[8]"Curios" is my translation for another use of *cabinet* here, which could refer to a piece of furniture in which one kept papers and also curiosities: exotica and other expensive objects such as porcelain in which one would invest to demonstrate one's fashionability. Cabinets of this sort could also be entire rooms, especially at royal palaces.

[9]Mirrors were a new technology based on glassmaking in Italy in the early seventeenth century, which Louis XIV promoted and significantly advanced during his reign. Full-length mirrors were exceedingly difficult to make and prohibitively expensive. Louis XIV had the technology stretched, as it were, to produce mirrors long enough for his famed gallery at Versailles, the Hall of Mirrors. The seemingly gratuitous detail about the girls seeing their whole bodies in the mirror in fact makes these objects a symbol of the Blue Beard's immense wealth.

[10]Curiosity has multiple implications here because of the way men and women were made to relate to knowledge. In men, curiosity was a virtue linked to intelligence and an expansive mind. The *curieux* was a man about town who would indulge in exotic objects and novelties. In women it tended more toward insatiable desire. Significantly, at the time that Perrault writes, women are playing a much larger role in the cultural commerce of knowledge, both as writers and as consumers in their own right. Given that the heroine in this story is both overly desirous and cunning about acquisition, which makes her both feminine and masculine, the word is appropriately ambiguous.

[11]The verb for what is happening in the blood in this passage is *se mirer*, literally to see oneself reflected—that is, to watch or contemplate oneself. The reflexivity of the verb suggests more active meaning in the passage than the transitive verb to reflect. That is to say, Perrault gives the corpses agency of a sort—they "see" themselves in the blood—which I have attempted to capture with the idea that they are condemned to look at their bloody forms.

so disturbed. She saw that the key was spotted with blood and tried two or three times to rub it off, but the blood would not budge. She washed to no avail, and even when she rubbed it with a scouring abrasive and with sandstone the blood was still there. You see, the key was enchanted and there was no way to clean it thoroughly. When you got rid of the blood on one side, it appeared on the other.

That very night the Blue Beard came back from his trip saying that he had received word en route to the effect that the business for which he had set out had been resolved in his favor. His wife made every effort to appear thrilled by his sudden return. The next day he asked for the keys back and she gave them to him, but her hand shook so much that he readily guessed what had happened.

"What happened," he said to her, "that the key to the office is not with the other ones?"

"I must have left it upstairs on my dressing table."

"Be sure to give it to me soon."

When he had asked several times, she had to deliver the key. After looking it over, the Blue Beard said to her, "Why is there blood on this key?"

"I know nothing about that," replied the miserable[12] wife, pale as death.

"You know nothing about that," repeated the Blue Beard. "I know all about it: you wanted to get into the office! Alright, Madame, you shall go in and shall take your place among the ladies you've seen there."

Wailing and begging for forgiveness, she threw herself at her husband's feet—all signs of sincere remorse for her failure to obey. Her beauty and pain would have melted[13] even stone, but the Blue Beard's heart was harder than stone.

"You are going to die, Madame, and right now."

Her eyes wet with tears, she replied, "Since I am going to die, give me some time to pray."

---

[12]This is the first of several references to the wife as "la pauvre femme." The simple translation of *pauvre* in fairy tales is typically "poor"—the poor wife. But the character's pitiful gestures of remorse have all been feigned—once her wits return to her after the terrible vision, they never leave her. She acts not out of weakness but out of disgust, an attitude I have rendered in the word *miserable*. The use of "la pauvre femme" may well be ironic here.

[13]The verb in French is "to soften (*attendrir*) stone," which may be a play on the expression "soften the heart" (*attendrir le coeur*) but also refers to a process used in mining in lieu of explosives, *attendrir la roche*, whereby the rock is heated with the caustic vapors of burning wood so that it can more easily be broken (*Encyclopédie; ou, Dictionnaire raisonné des sciences, des arts et des métiers*, ed. Denis Diderot and Jean le Rond d'Alembert, s.v. "Mine," encyclopedie.uchicago.edu/). Although we have a similar expression in English, "to have a heart of stone," the common verb used to describe touching someone emotionally is *to melt* the heart and I have used that to mix the metaphor.

"You can have half of fifteen minutes," the Blue Beard shot back, "and not one minute more."

When she was alone, she called to her sister and told her, "Anne, sister Anne" (that was her name), "please climb to the top of the tower to see if my brothers are not on their way. They promised to come see me today. If you spot them, signal to them to hurry."

Sister Anne climbed to the top of the tower and the miserable wretch cried out to her now and then, "Anne, sister Anne, is there nothing in sight?"

And sister Anne would[14] reply, "I see nothing but the sun dusting and the grass greening."[15]

In the meantime, the Blue Beard gripped a wide blade in his hand and would scream at the top of his lungs to his wife, "Get down here or I'll come up there!"[16]

"Just a moment, please,"[17] his wife would answer and quickly call out in a whisper to her sister, "Anne, sister Anne, is there nothing in sight?"

And sister Anne would answer, "I see nothing but the sun dusting and the grass greening."

"You get down here," the Blue Bead would scream, "or I'll come up there!"

"I am on my way!" his wife would say and call out, "Anne, my sister Anne, is there nothing in sight?"

Then sister Anne said, "I see a thick spray of dust approaching from one side."

"Is it my brothers?"

"I'm afraid not, sister, it's a herd of sheep."

---

[14]At this point in the story and throughout the dialogue, the narrator switches from the simple past to the imperfect tense, a tense typically reserved in French for the description of an emotional or physical state, or a repeated action. Used to describe a back-and-forth dialogue, as it is here, the imperfect is an odd choice. It implies that phrases may have been repeated (and not all reported by the narrator?), which suggested to me the choices of "would + infinitive," also indicative of repetition. With the implication of a drawn-out verbal fight, the narrator sets us up for the Blue Beard's explosion.

[15]In French, Perrault gives agency to the sun and grass, which *poudroie* (makes the dust visible) and *verdoie* (grows green), respectively, and I have reproduced that anthropomorphization.

[16]The Blue Beard suddenly switches to the informal *tu* in French with his wife, which establishes his power over her. We can also see in this shift from "Madame" to informal address that his anger is unhinged and establishes a certain perverse intimacy between them because of the physical act he is about to commit. The blade he holds is a cutlass: a compact, wide, single-edged sword used at the time by sailors. Because of its size, it would have been convenient to the task at hand, but it (and he) will prove weak against the soldier's sword at the end of the story.

[17]In this, her last direct address to him ("please"), the wife continues to use the formal *vous* with her husband, confirming her subordinate position. But as the dialogue unfolds, we can see that modesty as part of her elaborate plan to stall him.

"Are you coming down?" the Blue Beard would scream.

"Just a moment," his wife would answer and then call out, "Anne, sister Anne, is there nothing in sight?"

Then she said, "I see two cavalry soldiers arriving from this side but they are still very far away . . . Thank God! It's my brothers. I'm signaling as well as I can to tell them that they should hurry."

The Blue Beard started screaming so loudly that the house shook. His miserable wife came down looking distraught and a mess, and was about to throw herself at his feet when he said: "That won't work. Now you die."[18]

Then he grabbed her by the hair with one hand and raised the blade with the other, ready to slash her throat. His miserable wife turned to him with cold, dead eyes and requested a brief moment to collect herself.

"No, no," he said. "Commend your soul to God."

Just then, there was pounding at the door so loud that the Blue Beard froze. It opened and in came two cavalry soldiers drawing swords and running straight for the Blue Beard. He knew they were his wife's brothers, one a dragoon and one a musketeer,[19] which made him run for his life; but the two brothers followed him so closely that they overtook him before he could get out the door. They drove their swords through his body and left him for dead. The miserable wife was almost as dead as her husband and could not find the strength to get up and hug her brothers.

As it was, the Blue Beard had no heirs and thus his wife retained possession of his entire fortune. She spent some of it on the marriage of her sister Anne to a young nobleman who had been in love with her for a long time and some more buying the title of captain for her two brothers. The rest she used to marry a very courtly gentleman who helped her forget the bad times she had had with the Blue Beard.

---

[18]In the final moments of this scene, the Blue Beard uses his wife's feigned piety against her. He repeats "Il faut mourir," the same statement he makes when he first discovers the blood on the key, where it is followed by "tout à l'heure" ("You are going to die . . . right now"). The impersonal expression "il faut mourir" can be seen both in sermons of the period as the inevitable fate of all sinners—we must die to be reborn—and in romances such as Madeleine de Scudéry's *Artamène; ou, Le Grand Cyrus* (Paris: Augustin Courbé, 1654), 170, in which the title character chooses death over living without seeing his mistress again: "Madame, il faut mourir, j'y consens" (Madame, I accept death as my fate). The perversity in this scene is that the Blue Beard has chosen death for her and accelerated its arrival, a temporal experience that I have incorporated into the translation of the phrase in this instance.

[19]Dragoons fought on horseback and on foot, riding in and then acting as first responders. In the period, they were armed with weaponry appropriate to this task: an arquebus, a portable gun that could be propped on a tripod for a better shot. Musketeers, who carried muskets instead of arquebuses, would have served as the special vanguard of the king. The brothers, armed with swords instead of guns, exhibit the courage of the vanguard when they rush in to save their sister.

Moral

Curiosity, in spite of its mirth,
Often costs more than it's worth.
Everywhere and always examples abound.
No offense to the ladies, it's an illusory crutch.
As soon as you seize it, it is nowhere to be found
And it always costs too much.

Another Moral

Even a wit of the dimmest cast,
Who is not so very worldly,[20]
Will discover anon that this story
Is a tale of times long past.
No more the horrible husband of old
Whose demands were impossibly bold.
Though now he be discontent and domineering
Still with his wife he's endearing.[21]
The color of his beard no longer stands
To show among them who wears the pants.

---

[20]*Savoir le grimoire*: literally, to know the book of spells. The sentence here is about not knowing the book of spells "du Monde" (of the world).

[21]The expression here, *filer doux*, means to control yourself in a situation, as though walking on eggshells. The metaphor comes from the verb *filer*, to spin yarn, the action associated with women, like the old woman in "The Beauty in the Slumbering Woodland," and *doux*, quiet, kind, sweet. The expression's roots feminize the submission.

The Master Cat; or, Cat-in-the-Boots

A miller once left as the entire inheritance for the three children he had only his windmill, his mule, and his cat. The portions were quickly divided; neither the notary nor the attorney general was called in—they would have quickly swallowed up the whole piddling[1] legacy. The older one got the mill, the middle one got the mule, and the youngest got only the cat. The latter could take no solace in the piddling lot he got: "My brothers," he said, "can make an honest living if they join forces; as for me, once I've eaten my cat and had a muff made from his fur,[2] I am doomed to die of hunger."

The cat, who understood this statement but pretended not to, told him in a solemn and earnest voice: "Do not be anxious, Master.[3] If you will only give me a sack and have a pair of boots made for walking in brambles, you will see that your lot is not as bad as you think."

While the master of the cat put little stock in what he said, he had seen the cat many times perform such clever maneuvers to catch rats and mice—when he hung by his feet or when he hid himself in the flour and played dead, for example—that he did not give up hope on the cat's ability to relieve his misery.

When the cat got what he had requested, he ably sported his boots.[4] Throwing his sack over his shoulder, he grabbed the pull-strings with his

---

[1] The word behind "piddling," *pauvre*, encourages creative translations besides the simple "poor" as these are instances of penury, small sums, and seemingly inconsequential legacies.

[2] Historically, muffs could be made of several types of fur, among them dog and cat. According to the dictionary, cat and otter skins were used to make equestrian muffs known as *manchon de campagne* in contrast to the more luxurious variety that would have been worn with elegant attire (*Dictionnaire de l'Académie française*). In other words, cat did not make the finest muff.

[3] While the cat addresses the man with the formal *vous*, the man responds to him in the informal *tu*, marking their relationship hierarchically.

[4] The word in the French is the adjective *bravement*, whose first meaning, courageously or valiantly, seems operative here. Equally relevant is the second and more basic meaning for this context, "bien ou comme il faut" (well or as it should be, capably) because it suggests that the cat takes to this new role easily, as though it is second nature to him. The whole phrase, "se botter bravement" can also be read as a poetic way to say "se botter bien," a proverb for "wears well-made boots." In this case, we might say, once he had what he asked for, he looked the part. I chose the verb and adverb combination "to sport ably" in English because it captures both the sense of well made (we "sport" fashions) and the sense of wearing it well, with ease.

front paws and headed to a warren[5] where there were a lot of rabbits. He put bran seed and milkweed[6] in his sack and stretched out like a corpse, waiting for a young rabbit still unwise to the deceptive ways of the world to come poke his nose[7] into the sack to eat what he had put there. No sooner had he lain down than he got satisfaction. A young impulsive rabbit got into the sack and, pulling the strings right away, the master cat[8] caught[9] him and killed him mercilessly.

Triumphant in the capture of his prey, he went to the king's castle and asked to speak with him. He was shown up to His Majesty's apartment and upon entering bowed deeply to the king and said to him, "Sire, I give you this wild rabbit[10] that Monsieur the Marquis of Carabas"[11] (that was the name he resolved to give his master) "ordered me to present to you with his compliments."

"Tell your master,"[12] replied the king, "that I thank him and that I am pleased."

---

[5]A marvelous double-entendre that proves frustrating for translation, Perrault's *garenne* ("une garenne oú il y avoit grand nombre de lapins") means "warren," but also served at the time as a sarcastic term for a tale (*conte*) or learned commentary (*trait d'esprit*) (*Dictionnaire de l'Académie française*). While the second meaning remains implicit in the sentence, mockery of the world's rectitude plays a role in this story. It begins at the cat's first trick, duping a young rabbit that is "unwise to the deceptive ways of the world."

[6]*Laiteron*, milkweed or sow thistle, is known as the "Hare's Palace" (*le Palais au lièvre*) because they graze it and, according to folk wisdom, could also hide under it for protection. The herb Perrault uses here gets its name from the milky liquid in its central stem, a kind of latex. Perrault makes the poetic choice of *lasseron*, a regional word for *laiteron* from the northeast areas of Île de France (which includes Paris), Picardie, and Champagne, which rhymes nicely with *son* (bran). I have added "seed" to bran for the rhyme.

[7]*Se fourrer* means both to get into and to get interested in an affair where you don't belong.

[8]With the success of his first exploit after putting on the footwear, the cat acquires the moniker "Master." These boots offer the cat more than protection or a comfortably long stride; they give him the social clout he will need to pull off his trickery. It is interestingly unclear in the narrative whether he would have achieved this title if he had failed at the first task.

[9]The verb *prendre*, to take, has this particular meaning when it refers to game and fish.

[10]The term is "lapin de garenne," which means it fed and grew in nature.

[11]Marquis ranks immediately below duke, which ranks immediately below king in the hierarchy of French nobility. A number of famous literary marquises of the late seventeenth century, notably in plays by Molière, retained their titles but had squandered their money. On the other hand, a clever unsolvent courtier could earn a title by purchasing it outright or, as in this story, by inviting favor. The name Carabas may be Perrault's invention. Émile Littré lists the fairy tale as the first definition of the word in his *Dictionnaire de la langue française* of 1872. A large carriage eventually takes this name (written in lowercase), but Littré indicates that it probably borrows its name from the story, not the other way around. Another very involved way to look at it is through the word *caraba*, or mahogany oil, which has traditionally been used for medicinal purposes as a vermifuge, or treatment for intestinal worms—an ailment to which cats are especially prone.

[12]Here again, the cat uses *vous* and the king uses *tu*. See footnote 3 above.

Another time, he hid in a field, his sack open again, and when two partridges had gone in, he pulled the strings and caught both of them. He then went and presented them to the king, as he had the wild rabbit. The king again accepted the partridges with pleasure and ordered a drink brought to him. For two or three months, the cat carried on this way, from time to time bringing the king game from his master's hunting expeditions.

One day when he knew the king would be taking a carriage ride along the river with his daughter, the loveliest princess in the world, he said to his master: "If you simply follow my advice, you will strike it rich. All you have to do is bathe in the river at a spot I will show you and then leave it to me."

The Marquis of Carabas did as his cat had advised him without any sense of what good it would do. As he bathed, the king came by and the cat set to screaming at the top of his lungs: "Help! Help! Monsieur the Marquis of Carabas is drowning!"

When he heard the cry, the king stuck his head out of the carriage door and, recognizing the cat who had so many times brought him game, he ordered his guards to go quickly and help Monsieur the Marquis of Carabas. While they extracted the unfortunate marquis from the river, the cat approached the carriage and told the king that as the marquis bathed, thieves had come and stolen his clothes, even as he cried, Thief! at the top of his lungs (the wag had hidden them under a large rock). The king then ordered his wardrobe officers[13] to go fetch one of his most beautiful outfits for Monsieur the Marquis of Carabas. The king showered him with compliments and as the beautiful clothes he had just received brought out his good looks (he was gorgeous and well built), the daughter of the king thought he was just her type; and it did not take more than a few respectful but affectionate glances from the Marquis[14] of Carabas for her to fall madly in love with him. The king asked him into his carriage to take a ride.

Thrilled to see that his plan had begun to succeed, the cat set out ahead of them and when he came upon farmers reaping a field, he said to them: "Good people who reap, if you do not tell the king that the field you reap

---

[13] *Officiers de sa garde-robe*: sovereigns in France had a staff to organize and manage their closets, plan clothing choices for the day, mastermind celebratory costumes, and tend to the acquisition of sumptuous fabrics and accessories. Imagine the finery layered upon bodies to turn them into regal spectacles; many hands were involved in the process under the ancien régime. Perrault may add this detail about his fairy-tale king to give him gravitas and remind the reader of the great social leap the "Marquis de Carabas" could make through this marriage alliance.

[14] An unexpected title change from *marquis* to *comte*, which is also a slight demotion in rank, occurs in this line. Jean-Pierre Collinet considers it a simple mistake in the Barbin edition, one accidentally left in the second state printing (*Perrault, Contes*, 332n16).

belongs to Monsieur the Marquis of Carabas, I will grind you up like flesh for pâté."[15]

The king, of course, asked the reapers to whom the field they were reaping belonged.

"It belongs to Monsieur the Marquis of Carabas," they said in unison, frightened by the cat's threat.

"You have a very nice estate here," said the king to the Marquis of Carabas.

"You know, Sire, it is a field that produces an abundant yield every year."

The master cat, who was still up ahead of them, came upon balers and said to them: "Good people who bale, if you do not say that all this wheat belongs to Monsieur the Marquis of Carabas, I will grind you up like flesh for pâté."

The king, who passed by a moment later, wanted to know to whom all the hay he could see belonged.

"It belongs to Monsieur the Marquis of Carabas," answered the balers, and the king again expressed his pleasure with the marquis.

The cat, who was walking in front of the carriage, continued to say the same thing to everyone he came upon, and the king was amazed by the immense wealth of Monsieur the Marquis of Carabas. The master cat eventually reached a beautiful castle whose master was an ogre, the richest you've ever seen; in fact, all the lands the king had passed were on the grounds of the château. The cat, who had taken the trouble to inquire about this ogre and his skills, asked to speak with him, saying that he did not want to be so close by and not do the honor of paying his respects. The ogre received him as politely as possible for an ogre and let him relax.

"I have it on authority," said the cat, "that you have a talent for transforming yourself into all kinds of animals; that you can, for example, change into a lion or an elephant."

"That's right," said the ogre gruffly, "and to demonstrate, I'll let you watch me become a lion."

The cat was so frightened by the lion in front of him that he jumped up on the gutters—with considerable difficulty and risk, because his boots were useless for walking on rooftops. A short while after, seeing that the

---

[15]The proverbial expression "Hacher menu comme chair à pâté," literally to grind fine like flesh for pâté, means to cut up into pieces. Although "make mincemeat of you" or "tear you to pieces" might do as translations, I've opted to keep the literal meaning for the sake of the cultural reference to pâté, that classically French spreadable meat. See Perrault's other references to food in "The Beauty in the Slumbering Woodland" and "Ashkins."

ogre had shed his animal form, the cat came down and declared that he had been really scared.

"I also have it on authority—but do not believe it," said the cat, "that you also have the power to turn into the smallest animals, for example, to change into a rat or a mouse; I must say that seems utterly impossible to me."

"Impossible?" replied the ogre, "watch this"; and he turned into a mouse that scurried across the floor. As soon as the cat spotted him, he pounced on him and ate him.

Meanwhile, the king had seen the beautiful castle and wanted to go inside. The cat, who heard the sound of the carriage on the drawbridge, ran out and said to the king: "Your Majesty, welcome to the castle of Monsieur the Marquis of Carabas."

"Well, Monsieur the Marquis of Carabas," exclaimed the king, "this castle also belongs to you! This courtyard and the structures that surround it are beautiful beyond compare. I would like to have a look at the inside, if I may."[16] The marquis offered his arm to the young princess,[17] and, following the king's lead, they entered a great room where they discovered a splendid spread that the ogre had prepared for friends who were coming to see him that very day, but who did not dare enter now that the king was there. The king, charmed by the fine qualities of Monsieur the Marquis of Carabas and also by the fact that his daughter was crazy about him, and considering the immense wealth that he possessed and the fact that he had had five or six drinks, said to him: "The decision to become my son-in-law is up to you."

Bowing deeply, the marquis accepted the honor the king was granting him and married the princess that very day. The cat became a great lord and from then on only chased mice for fun.

Moral

However great the opportunity,
Of a wealthy legacy
Passed down from fathers to sons,

---

[16]This request takes a bit of creative license with Perrault's sentence "Voyons les dedans; s'il vous plaît." The combination of the command *voyons* (let's see) and the *s'il vous plaît* (please) rings odd in English. Instead, I've opted to drop the command but to retain the meaning of please, which tempers the command mode in French, permitting the king to recognize the Marquis of Carabas as a man worthy of respect.

[17]In French he gives his hand, probably extending his arm out as a support for the princess, who would lay her hand on top of his and walk with him, their arms perpendicular to the ground.

For the average parvenu[18]
Plain hard work and smart "how-to"
Go farther than inherited sums.

Another Moral

If the son of a miller, with such finesse,
Wins the heart of a young princess,
And finds himself the object of such affection,[19]
It's that the clothes, the face, and the fitness
that inspire fondness
Are not indifferent to love's progression.

---

[18]The idea of the "parvenu" (French for upstart or self-made, but also used in English) does not appear in the French, which simply says *jeunes gens* (young people). I have chosen it for the rhyme and also because it seems a legitimate way to describe the social climb depicted in the story.

[19]The expression in this line is "s'en fait regarder des yeux mourants," to be gazed upon with dying (passionate) eyes. I have folded the idea of her gaze into the word "object."

The Fairies

Once there was a widow who had two daughters. The older one bore such a striking resemblance to her in attitude and appearance that to see her was to see her mother. They were both so despicable and haughty that no one could stand them. The younger one, who was the very image of her father in kindness and manner, was one of the prettiest girls you can imagine. As like attracts like, the mother was crazy about her older daughter and at the same time had a terrible aversion to the younger one. She forced her to eat in the kitchen and work all the time.

The poor thing was charged with, among other things, fetching water miles away[1] at a fountain. Twice a day, she filled a large pitcher and carried it back to the house. One day when she was at the fountain a needy woman came to her and asked for a drink.

"Of course, good mother,"[2] said the girl, quickly rinsing her bucket and filling it from the nicest part of the fountain. She held the bucket out to her so that she could more easily drink from it.

The good mother drank and then said to her: "You are so lovely, so kind, and so well mannered that I feel compelled to endow you with a gift." (She was actually a fairy who had disguised herself as a poor countrywoman to see just how well mannered the girl really was). "I grant you this talent," continued the fairy, "that with every word you say, a flower or precious stone will come out of your mouth."[3]

---

[1] *Une grande demi-lieue*, or long half league, which would correspond to about two miles according to the classic Roman measurement of the league: the distance a man can walk in one hour. See "The Beauty in the Slumbering Woodland," footnote 6.

[2] *Ma bonne mère* has a more literal meaning than the metaphorical language created by adding "good" to a word for woman such as *bonne femme*. *Bonne femme* connotes a woman of a certain age and/or of a lower class. According to eighteenth-century dictionaries and the use Jean-Honoré Fragonard makes of the term in the title of one of his genre paintings depicting a young woman attending to her children, *bonne mère* judges a woman fit to take care of children. In the context of "The Fairies," where the mother does *not* care for the girl, we could argue that she responds to the fairy as a kindred spirit who could be a mother to her and for whom she would like to be a good daughter.

[3] On the use of the word "talent" for the French *don*, see "The Beauty in the Slumbering Woodland," footnote 1.

When the lovely girl finally arrived back at her house, her mother scolded her for returning so late from the fountain. "Please forgive me, Mother, for taking so long!" And as she spoke the words, two roses, two pearls, and two diamonds came out of her mouth.

"What's this?" said her mother in amazement. "I think there are pearls and diamonds coming out of her mouth! What is causing this, Daughter?" (That was the first time she had ever called her "daughter.") The poor thing innocently recounted the whole story to her mother, all the while spitting heaps of diamonds.

"Indeed," said the mother, "I need to send my daughter there. Look, Fanchon, do you see what's coming out of your sister's mouth when she opens it? Wouldn't you like the same thing to happen to you? All you have to do is go fetch water from the fountain and when a beggar woman asks for a drink, kindly offer her some water."

"I would not be caught dead going to the fountain," said the churl.

"I want you to go," said the mother, "and right now."

She went, but moaned about it. She took with her the most beautiful silver bottle she could find at the house. No sooner had she arrived than a sumptuously dressed noblewoman emerged from the trees and asked for a drink. It was the same fairy who had appeared to her sister, but disguised now as a princess to see just how rude this girl really was.

"Did I come all this way to give you a drink?" asked the haughty churl. "I purposely brought a bottle in silver so that I could serve Madame some water? Sure, that's just what I'll do.[4] Drink straight from the fountain if you want to."

"You really are rude," replied the fairy, without getting angry. "So be it. Since you are so disagreeable, I will grant you this talent: that with every word you say, a snake or toad will come out of your mouth."

As soon as her mother spotted her, she cried out, "Well, Daughter?"

"Well, Mother!" said the churl, spitting vipers and toad.

"God in heaven!" cried the mother, "What's this? This is your sister's doing and she will pay for it." And she ran to beat her.

The poor thing fled and escaped into the neighboring forest. The son of the king was on his way back from the hunt, approached her and, seeing how lovely she was, asked what she was doing all alone in these woods and what she had to cry about.

---

[4]This is the same expression used by the stepsister in "Ashkins." See footnote 18 to that tale.

"It's terrible,[5] Monsieur, my mother drove me out of the house."

The son of the king, who watched as five or six pearls and as many diamonds came out of her mouth, asked her to explain how this happened. She told him the whole adventure. The son of the king fell in love with her and, reasoning that such a talent was worth more than anything else one could offer someone in a marriage, brought her to the palace of his father the king and married her.

As for her sister, she proved so detestable that her own mother drove her out of the house, and the miserable wretch, after running around to find someone who would take her in with no success, went off to die, alone and lonely.[6]

Moral

Diamonds and money
Are sweet on the mind
But words of honey
Have even more weight and prove the far greater find.

[5]In lieu of "alas," with its romantic overtones in modern-day North America, I chose the short phrase "It's terrible." Talking out the feeling implicit in "alas" deflates the interjection, but it carries a range of potential meanings from disappointment to shock to outright frustration, depending on intonation, the sag of the shoulders, and the look on the face of the speaker. That ambiguity approximates how seventeenth-century *hélas* expresses pity but has a range of meanings, from a sorrowful cry to a more sober tone, as in Hamlet's "Alas, poore Yoricke, I knew him." The reader can hear in the girl the type of emotion she or he finds appropriate to the scene. What's more, there is poignant humor in this scene because, while she speaks the words "It's terrible," her mouth drips pearls and diamonds—and drips them all over a very interested prince. This modern response to trouble sounds overtly ironic under the circumstances and thus has more potential for humor than the now-romanticized "alas."

[6]Perrault says she died "au coin d'un bois," in a corner or recess of a forest, which is how translators have traditionally rendered it. The expression also has a proverbial meaning that appears in the dictionary of 1762: to die alone, unprotected and without solace (*Dictionnaire de l'Académie française*). While this familiar usage is not offered in the 1694 edition of the dictionary, the idea of the forest as not merely a geography but also an existential state of alienation makes good sense in the context of the sister's loss of community.

Another moral

Civility[7] comes at the cost of great care
And a bit of compliance,
But sooner or later finds recompense
And often at the moment you are least aware.

---

[7]The word in French is *honnêteté*, which may be the most important practice related to sociability at the court of Louis XIV. It means something quite different from what one might assume following its logical translation, honesty. *Honnêtes gens* were successful courtiers, those who had mastered the art of civility and social grace. In other words, they were highly skilled in the performance of sociability, not personal honesty. Such artifice was not necessarily negative; it was a fact of high court life. On the other hand, "wolves" such as the one the little red tippet encounters could also use those skills to prey on the uninitiated. In both cases, civility was a steep learning curve.

Ashkins; or, The Little Slipper of Glass

Once upon a time a nobleman married a second wife, the most conceited and arrogant woman you've ever seen. She had two daughters with the same disposition who were exactly like her. For his part, the husband also had a little girl, but she was sweet and kind beyond compare. She got that from her mother, who had the most charming personality in the world.

Hardly had the marriage ceremony ended than the stepmother let her ugly disposition explode. She could not stand the appealing qualities in this young child, which made her daughters seem even more odious. She gave her the most menial chores in the house: she was the one who cleaned the dishes and put them away; who scrubbed Madame's bedroom, as well as Mademoiselles her daughters'. She slept on the top floor of the house in the attic on a pathetic straw mattress, while her sisters had bedrooms with parquet floors, the most fashionable style of bed, and mirrors in which they could look at themselves from head to toe.[1] The poor thing suffered it all patiently and could not even complain to her father, who was utterly controlled by his wife and would have punished his daughter. When she had finished her chores, she would head to the fireplace hearth and sit in the ashes, which made people call her Ashwipe[2] in the home. The younger sister, who was not as mean as the older one, called her Ashkins.[3] And yet, Ashkins with the ugly clothes managed still to be a thousand times prettier than her sisters, however splendidly dressed.

It happened that the son of the king threw a ball and that he requested the presence of the nobility. Our two demoiselles were also invited thanks

---

[1]See footnote 9 in "The Blue Beard" on the significance of the mirror.

[2]The cruel name Perrault invents for his heroine, Cucendron, is a combination of *cu*, probably from *cul* (ass), and *cendron*, a deformation of *cendre* (ash). The word sounds vulgar and comical in French, as it identifies the girl with her habit of putting her ass in the ashes. My translation aims for similarly crude comedy.

[3]Cinderella, the standard translation of Cendrillon, opts for the homophone cinder instead of ash. Robert Samber's translation of 1729 initiated that tradition with the name Cinder*illa*, which lost the "i" and acquired its now universal "e" in 1804. See the annotated bibliography at the end of this volume. The suffix I use here, *-kin*, creates the diminutive "little ash," a construction parallel to Perrault's Cendrill/on. Using the variant *-kins*, as in the term of affection "babykins," adds a layer of patriarchal affection and contrasts starkly with the crueler sister's choice.

to their considerable celebrity in town. And so they were very pleased and very concentrated on choosing the clothes and hairdos that would best suit the occasion. More hardships for Ashkins, who was of course the one to iron her sisters' lingerie and flute their cuffs.[4] They went on and on about how they would dress. "I," said the older one, "will wear my red velvet ensemble and my English lace."[5]

"I," said the younger one, "will just wear my everyday skirt, but to make up for it, I will wear my brocade bodice with the gold flowers and my diamond festoon,[6] which has a certain charm."

They brought in the best hair designer to create double-rowed hairpieces[7] and commissioned beauty marks from the best craftswoman. The sisters called Ashkins in to ask her opinion. Ashkins gave them the most excellent advice—she had good taste—and even offered to do their coiffures, to which they agreed. While she was doing their hair, they said to her:

---

[4] The expression *godronner les manchettes*, which I have rendered "flute their cuffs," comes from the language of laundering, as it would have been a professional cleaner who performed this operation on collars—*collets,* or ruffs—and *manchettes,* or cuffs. Like ironing, it consisted of pleating starched fabric around a heated metal cone (goffering iron) to give it a scalloped shape that would last through the evening.

[5] A *garniture d'Angleterre* refers to lace made in Belgium and imported through England in the second quarter of the seventeenth century. Because *garniture* refers by the end of the seventeenth century to headpieces and ribbons as well as the traditional lace trim, it could indicate fabric laced through the hair to create one of the elaborate coiffures popular during the period of Louis XIV's trendsetting mistress, Madame de Montespan. These hairdos are discussed below, footnote 7.

[6] *Manteau,* which refers today to a long coat or cloak, designated a belted dress in the vocabulary of seventeenth-century women's fashion: "Women also call 'manteau' a type of pleated dress that they cinch at the waist with a belt" (Les femmes appellent aussi, *Manteau.* Une espèce de robe plissée qu'elles serrent avec une ceinture). *Dictionnaire de l'Académie française.* Diamond festoon is my translation of *"barrière de diamants,"* an expression that no longer exists in French and may not have existed when Perrault wrote it. The historical expression for a bib diamond necklace is *rivière de diamants.* It is interesting to think that Perrault intended this change deliberately to make a statement about what the sisters are wearing. *Barrière*—barricade, fence, barrier—gives a much less romantic sense to the necklace than "river" of diamonds. Perrault may be suggesting that the sister's necklace is excessive and in bad taste, like some kind of body armor. There is a sense that the sisters' accessories are out of fashion in 1697. See footnote 7 below.

[7] *Cornettes,* pleated ribbons, were in high vogue when the king's second mistress, Madame de Montespan, influenced fashion at court (roughly 1670–85). The high hairdos worn by noblewomen had names that reflected their extravagant playfulness, such as *Hurluberlu* (meaning unthinking or scatterbrained). In the later styles, which called for cornettes, the hair was swept up high on the head, done in stacks of curls, and ornamented with cascading pleated or bowed ribbons. These works of art were long out of fashion in 1697. By that time, Louis XIV had taken another mistress whose piety and devotion to the church legislated against excessive body ornament. The sisters, then, are over the top and outdated because they are not ahead of the curve. We will find that Ashkins is beautiful in her relative simplicity, not because the court preferred a natural look (far from it), but rather because she innovates on the reigning style of the day. Naturally, the prince prefers Ashkins.

"Ashkins, wouldn't you just be delighted to go to the ball?"

"Ah, Mademoiselles! You're joking around. I really don't need that."[8]

"It's true. People would have a good laugh if they saw an Ashwipe at the ball."

Someone else would have set their coiffures lopsided, but Ashkins was kind and she set them just right. They went two days without eating in a delirium of pleasure, broke more than a dozen laces tightening their corsets to make their waists look smaller, and they stood all day in front of their mirrors.

When at last the special occasion arrived, they set out and Ashkins followed them with her eyes as long as she could. When she could not see them anymore, she broke down crying. Her godmother, who saw her in tears, asked what was the matter.

"I would really like . . . I would really like . . ." She sobbed so hard that she could not finish.

Her godmother, who was a fairy, said to her: "You would really like to go to the ball, right?"

"Well, yes," said Ashkins, heaving.[9]

"So, then, will you be a good girl?" said the godmother. "I will help you go."

She took her into her bedroom and said, "Go to the garden and find me a pumpkin." Right away Ashkins went to cut the prettiest one she could find and carried it to her godmother, but could not imagine how this pumpkin was going to get her to the ball. Her godmother scraped the inside clean, leaving only the skin, and tapped it with her wand. The pumpkin suddenly turned into a magnificent gilded carriage. Next she went to look in her mousetrap, where she found six mice, all of them alive. She told Ashkins to lift the door of

---

[8]The French of this response, "vous vous moquez de moi, ce n'est pas là ce qu'il me faut," is oddly complex because the second clause has only indeterminate pronouns. "Ce n'est pas là ce que"—translatable as "It is not that which"—is followed by "is necessary for me": It is not that which is necessary for me. But what is not necessary? Modern translators link it to the ball: "that would not befit me" (Zipes, *The Great Fairy Tale Tradition*, 450), "that's no place for me" (Appelbaum, *The Complete Fairy Tales in Verse and Prose*, 167), "that kind of thing is not for me" (Betts, *Charles Perrault: The Complete Fairy Tales*, 131). I opted for phrasing that leaves the question of what Ashkins does not need somewhat ambiguous. On the one hand, *là* could refer to going to the ball; on the other hand, its most recent antecedent is the verb *moquer*, to make fun of / joke about. I have opted for the latter meaning, but the phrasing is ambiguous enough to leave the question open. Literally, the French emphatic cleft *ce n'est pas là ce que* (it is not that which) might be rendered "That is really not what I need," but as the "c'est-cleft" is more commonly used in French than in English, I chose a colloquial phrase conveying similar emphasis.

[9]In this context, where she is having trouble speaking, the verb *soupirer*, which can be translated to sigh, might also suggest heavy sighing or heaving.

the mousetrap and as they scurried out, she tapped each one with her wand, which instantly turned it into a beautiful horse; together they made an impressive team of six horses with coats in dappled mousy gray.

She struggled with what to use for a coachman. "Let me see," said Ashkins, "if by any chance there is a rat in the rattrap. We will make a coachman out of him."[10]

"Good idea," said the godmother. "Go see."

Ashkins brought the rattrap, which held three fat rats. The fairy picked one among them for its commanding facial hair and, tapping it with her wand, turned him into a corpulent coachman with one of the most dashing moustaches you've ever seen.

Next she said: "Go to the garden. You'll find six lizards behind the watering pot.[11] Bring them to me."

No sooner had she delivered them than the godmother turned them into footmen, who climbed on the back of the carriage in their brocade livery and stood at the ready as though they had done this all their lives. Then the fairy said to Ashkins: "And, voila, everything you need to get to the ball. Aren't you just delighted?"

"Yes, but will I go like this, in my ugly clothes?"

Her godmother no more than touched her with the wand and at that moment her clothes turned into an ensemble[12] of gold and silver fabric encrusted with precious gems; next she gave her a pair of glass slippers, the prettiest in the world. Once she was outfitted in finery, she got into the carriage, but her godmother advised her first and foremost not to stay out past midnight,[13] warning that if she stayed at the ball one minute more, her carriage would again turn to a pumpkin, her horses to mice, her footmen

---

[10]Readers may notice here that Ashkins has found her voice—one she did not have just a page earlier when she stuttered through her tears. What's more, she now aids in her own advancement by stepping in when the godmother leaves her a bit of room by "struggling" with what to use for a coachman. Fairies being extraordinarily competent and efficient in matters of transformation, such a glitch in the flow of action must be deliberate. Pedagogically, it serves as a tactical measure to force Ashkins to reason, make decisions, articulate her thoughts, and help herself. By voicing praise—"Good idea" (my translation of "Tu as raison" / You are right)—the fairy confirms the success of this lesson in autonomy. Ashkins will need that self-confidence at the ball.

[11]This portable garden technology was new in Perrault's day.

[12]She wears "un habit de drap," language found in archives that inventory the wardrobes of kings and high nobility and primarily associated with the matching ensembles of the gentleman. The fabric (*drap*) of these ensemble outfits would have been understood to be wool unless otherwise indicated, as here, where it is spun of gold and silver.

[13]Balls at Versailles during the reign of Louis XIV raged long into the night. A curfew of midnight would vex a young woman terribly, forcing her to leave just as the festivities came to life.

to lizards; and that her old clothes would return to their usual state. She promised her godmother that she would absolutely leave the ball before midnight. She leaves, giddy with happiness.

The son of the king, who had been alerted to the arrival of a grand princess that no one recognized, ran to receive her; he extended his hand as she stepped down from the carriage[14] and led her to the room where the guests were gathered. Then there was total silence. They stopped dancing, the violins stopped playing; all attention turned to take in the many glorious splendors of this mystery woman. All that remained was the buzz of voices: "Ah, she is so beautiful!"

Even the king, old as he was, could not stop watching her and telling the queen under his breath that it had been a while since he'd seen someone so attractive and appealing. The ladies turned their attention to studying her hair and clothes so they could look like that the next day—provided they could find fabric beautiful enough and artisans capable enough. The son of the king gave her the most prominent seat at the table and then took her by the hand to lead her in a dance. She danced with such grace that the crowd admired her even more. A very fine meal was served that the young prince did not touch because he was fully occupied with taking her in. She sat down with her sisters and showed them every manner of courtesy. She even gave them some of the oranges and lemons[15] that the prince had given her, which shocked them because they had no idea who she was.

As they chatted away, Ashkins heard the clock strike 11:45. Quickly she bowed to the guests with great ceremony and ran out as fast as she could. As soon as she got home, she went to find her godmother and, thanking her, told her that she hoped very much to go to the ball again the next day because the son of the king had requested her presence. She was caught up in telling her godmother everything that had happened at the ball when the two sisters banged on the door. Ashkins opened it.

"You certainly took your time getting back," she yawned, rubbing her eyes and stretching as though she had only just woken up and even though she had had no desire to sleep since they left.

"If you had been at the ball," one of the sisters told her, "you would never have tired of it. There was the most beautiful princess, the most

---

[14]This is the same gesture the king makes to welcome the fairy in "The Beauty in the Slumbering Woodland."

[15]Expensive and rare, citrus fruits were cultivated at great expense in the gardens of Versailles—the Orangerie, which still bears the name today—to be enjoyed by royalty and the wealthiest courtiers.

beautiful you've ever seen. She was so polite and gracious toward us; she gave us oranges and lemons."

Ashkins was giddy with happiness: she asked the name of the princess, but they answered that no one knew who she was, that the son of the king was just sick about it, and that he would give everything in the world to know who she was. Ashkins smiled and said: "She was really beautiful, then? God, you are so lucky! Could I at least get a glimpse of her? What to do . . ."[16] Mademoiselle Javotte,[17] lend me the yellow ensemble that you wear all the time."

"That's just what I'll do,"[18] said Mademoiselle Javotte. "Honestly. Lend your clothes to a disgusting Ashwipe like that. I would have to be utterly nuts."

Ashkins naturally expected this refusal and was glad for it because she would have been in quite a bind if her sister had agreed to lend her the clothes.

The next day the sisters were at the ball, as was Ashkins, but even more finely dressed than the first time. The son of the king planted himself next to her and showered her nonstop with compliments. The young lady never tired of it and forgot how her godmother had cautioned her—to the point that when she heard the clock strike 12 she thought it had not yet struck 11. She got up and dashed out, lithe as a doe. The prince tracked her but could not catch her. She dropped one of her glass slippers, which the prince picked up gingerly. Ashkins arrived home mightily winded with no carriage, with no footmen, and in her ugly clothes—nothing left of all her splendor but one of her little slippers, the twin of the one she had dropped. People asked the guards at the palace gate if they had possibly seen a princess leave. They said that they had not seen anyone leave except a young girl who was very poorly dressed and looked more like a country girl than a young lady.

---

[16]This is a simple *hélas* (alas) in the French. I opted to draw out the ironic sense of her exclamation in the translation "What to do." She does not despair, but has set up a brief yet highly effective ruse to bait her sister into insulting her just to toy with her emotions, well knowing that she will once again appear at the ball as the mysterious, enviable woman in glass slippers.

[17]Ashkins is the first in the narrative to speak her sister's name, which creates an echo of the scene in which her sisters named her. This gesture attests to a change in her character; she has acquired a certain power over her sisters and over the plot.

[18]Mademoiselle Javotte exclaims idiomatically, "Vraiment, j'en suis de cet avis!" There is no simple equivalent for the idiom "en être de cet avis" because the surface meaning, "I am of this mind about it," means the opposite of what the phrase expresses. To be of the mind in this case is ironic. She absolutely is not of a mind to do it. My translation has her forcefully saying the opposite of what she intends, which becomes clear with the next word, "Honestly." The phrasing occurs again in the toady mouth of the second sister in "The Fairies."

When her two sisters came home from the ball, Ashkins asked them if they had again amused themselves and if the beautiful woman had come. They said yes, but that she ran off when the clock struck midnight and so hastily that she dropped one of her little slippers, the prettiest in the world; that the son of the king had picked it up; that all he did for the rest of the ball was stare at it; and that, for certain, he was deeply in love with the charming someone to whom the slipper belonged.

They were right since a few days later, the son of the king announced by trumpet blast that he would marry the woman whose foot was a perfect match for the slipper. They started trying it on princesses, then duchesses and the rest of the court, but it was futile. They brought it to the sisters, who tried everything in their power to get their foot into the slipper but did not succeed. Ashkins was watching, recognized the slipper, and chuckled,[19] saying, "Maybe I should see if it fits me!"

Her sisters cracked up and made fun of her. The gentleman trying the slipper, who had looked carefully at her and found her very attractive, said that this seemed fair and that he had been ordered to try it on every girl. He directed Ashkins to the seat and, drawing the slipper to her foot, saw that it went in easily and that it fit like a hand in a glove.[20] The sisters' shock was great, but it was greater still when Ashkins took the other little slipper out of her pocket and put it on her foot. Just then the godmother arrived and, giving a little tap of her wand to Ashkins's clothes, made them look even more magnificent than her other outfits. Now the two sisters could see in her the charming someone they had seen at the ball. They threw themselves at her feet, apologizing for all the cruelty they had put her through. Ashkins helped them up, embraced them, told them that she forgave them willingly, and asked them to be her friends forever. They brought her before the young prince dressed in her finery: he thought she looked more beautiful than ever and, just days later, married her. Ashkins, who was as good as she was gorgeous,[21] moved her sisters into the palace and married them that very day to two great lords of the court.

---

[19]The simple French *rire* means to laugh, but in the theatrical awkwardness of this moment, the laugh foreshadows her triumph. If the laugh is strategic, it might be more like a chuckle.

[20]The expression "comme de cire" (like wax) refers to two surfaces that come together equally and with a perfect fit.

[21]I have enhanced the sense of *belle* to create the alliteration Perrault achieves with *bonne* and *belle*.

Moral

In the ladies, beauty is a rare treasure
Its marvelous features we tirelessly praise
But to have what we call good grace
Is priceless and the greater pleasure.
Ashkins's godmother gave her grace on loan.
Dressed her, taught her not to fail,
So much and so well that she grabbed a throne.
(For such is the moral we'll give this tale.)

Beauties, this talent is more precious than your hair's lift
To win his heart, to someday be crowned,
Good grace is the real fairy's gift.
Without it you are lost, with it you are found.

Another Moral

No doubt it gives a girl a strong lead
To have wit, bravery,
Breeding, good sense,
And other similarly fine talents
That the heavens dole out as meed.
But in you they will come to nothing
Bloom in vain, try as you might,
If you have not godfather or godmother
To bring their worth to light.

Riquet the Tufted

There was once a queen who gave birth to a son so unattractive and misshapen that they wondered for a long time if he was human.[1] A fairy present at his birth insisted that he would surely be lovable because he would be extremely intelligent; she even added that by virtue of the talent[2] she had just granted him, he would be able to grant such intelligence to the person he loved most. That was all small consolation to the poor queen, who was terribly distressed about bringing such an ugly urchin[3] into the world. To be sure, as soon as the child started speaking, he said thousands of wonderful things and there was a certain *je ne sais quoi*[4] in everything he did that was so brilliant it charmed everyone. I forgot to say that he was born with a little tuft of hair on his head, which is why he was named Riquet the Tufted, since Riquet was his family name.

Seven or eight years later, the queen of a neighboring kingdom gave birth to two daughters: the firstborn was lovelier than the dawn[5] and the queen was so pleased with her that people thought the excess of delight she felt might do the queen harm. The same fairy who had witnessed little Riquet the Tufted's birth was in attendance and to moderate the queen's delight, she told her that the little princess would have no intellectual capacity at all and that she would be as dumb as she was lovely. The queen was completely devastated by this news, but a few moments later she suffered a far greater devastation when the second daughter she brought into the world turned out to be exceptionally ugly.

---

[1] The words here are "douta s'il avait forme humaine," for which Betts offers "seemed doubtful for a long time that he was of human form" (*Charles Perrault: The Complete Fairy Tales*, 142). I have opted for the properly physiological definition of *forme*, for which one example in the dictionary is "il est si defiguré qu'il n'a presque pas forme humaine" (he is so disfigured that he has almost lost his human form). *Dictionnaire de l'Académie française*. Identifying his physique with lack of humanity repeats but also enhances the idea that being disfigured enough throws into question one's humanity.

[2] On the use of the word "talent," for *don* see "The Beauty in the Slumbering Woodland," footnote 1.

[3] *Marmot* has the primary meaning of small monkey, but is also a pejorative term for child. See also the moral for "Little Thumblette."

[4] The expression *je ne sais quoi* in the French has passed into English to mean a special undefinable quality.

[5] "Plus beau que le jour," more beautiful than the day, is an idiomatic expression for very beautiful.

"Do not be so anxious, Madame," said the fairy, "your daughter will be compensated in other ways and she will be so intelligent that people will hardly notice that she wants for beauty."

"God willing," said the queen, "but is there no way to give the older one, who is so beautiful, a bit of intelligence?"

"I am powerless when it comes to intellect, Madame, but all powerful when it comes to beauty and since there is nothing I would not do to satisfy you, I will grant her a talent, the power to turn anyone she wants into a beauty."

As the princesses grew tall, so their perfections grew proportionately with them, and people spoke everywhere of the beauty of the oldest and the intelligence of the youngest. To be sure, their flaws also intensified a lot with age. The younger grew noticeably uglier and the older grew dumber by the day. Either she did not respond at all to questions, or she said something stupid. It made her so clumsy that she was incapable of putting four porcelain vases on the chimney mantle[6] without breaking one, or drinking a glass of water without spilling half of it on her clothes. Although beauty gives the young a strong advantage, nevertheless the younger one almost always outshone her older sister in public. First they gravitated toward the prettiest to look at and admire her, but soon they made their way toward the one who was more intelligent to hear her say a thousand pleasant things; it shocked people that in under fifteen minutes the older one had no one around her and that everyone had gathered around the younger one. Even though she was very dumb, the older one clearly noticed and she would have gladly given all her beauty to have half the intelligence of her sister. The queen, wise as she was, could not help but reprimand her again and again for her stupidity, which almost caused the poor princess to die of grief.

One day when she had taken refuge in the woods to give vent to her misery, she saw a small, incredibly ugly and incredibly unattractive but most excellently[7] dressed man walking toward her. It was the young prince

---

[6]This detail recalls a particular type of porcelain display popular among the elite at the end of the seventeenth century: a *garniture de porcelaine*. A garniture, or display set, consisted of similarly sized vases and jars that would be arranged on the mantle above a chimney to make that otherwise empty space a point of visual interest in the room. Interestingly, there were typically an odd number of pieces in a garniture (three or five, not four), which means that the set would look complete after she broke one. Her carelessness with porcelain at a time when it had to be imported from China and cost a small fortune helps to reinforce the gravity of her problem.

[7]Perrault uses a compound adjective, *très-magnifique*, which has the effect of being grammatically redundant. In French as in English, "magnificent" connotes a condition that does not require modification; in fact, modification could be considered incorrect except as a poetic flourish.

Riquet the Tufted, who had fallen in love with her from the portraits[8] of her being passed around and left his father's kingdom for the pleasure of seeing her and speaking to her. Thrilled to find her there all alone, he advances toward her with all possible respect and civility. After expressing the basic niceties and noticing that she was extremely melancholy, he said to her: "I don't understand, Madame, how someone as beautiful as you are could be as sad as you seem to be; while I have had the pleasure of seeing dozens and dozens of beautiful people, I can say that I have never seen any whose beauty comes close to yours."

"Whatever you say,[9] Monsieur," the princess responded, and nothing more.

"Beauty," replied Riquet the Tufted, "is such a strong advantage that it supersedes all the others; and when you possess it, I don't see why you would be particularly upset about anything."

"I would rather be as ugly as you and intelligent," said the princess, "than have the good looks I have and be as witless[10] as I am."

"There is no better indication of wit, Madame, than thinking you don't have any, and such is the nature of the thing that the more you have the more you think you lack it."

"I wouldn't know about that," said the princess, "but I do know that I am totally witless, and that's what is killing me with grief."

"If that's all it is, Madame, that upsets you, I can easily put an end to your suffering."

"And how will you do that?" said the princess.

"Madame, I have the power," replied Riquet the Tufted, "to endow the person I am meant to love the most with as much intelligence as anyone could have, and since, Madame, you are that person, it is up to you to decide if you want as much intelligence as anyone could have—provided that you marry me."

---

[8]Portraits figure often in literature of the period because a picture was often the first way a young woman and man of the court would encounter each other before marriage. It could also fill the role, as it does in Madame de Lafayette's *La Princess de Clèves* (1678), of the promise of love. Circulating the portrait of a beautiful princess would draw suitors and allow the family choice among the eligible.

[9]According to the *Dictionnaire de l'Académie française*, you would respond with the expression "Cela vous plaît à dire," as the princess does here, to indicate that you found a compliment too flattering to accept. The English expression used here can have the same effect.

[10]The word *bête*, stupid, in this context serves as the antonym of *esprit*, which in the seventeenth century referred to the kind of social intelligence that made courtiers appear clever and sophisticated. As the English "wit" also refers to a talent related to sociability, I have chosen "witless" as its antonym.

The princess stood there dumfounded and gave no reply.

"I see," replied Riquet the Tufted, "that this proposition confuses you, which does not surprise me; but you have a full year to make up your mind."

The princess had so little mental capacity and at the same time so much desire to have it that she convinced herself the end of the year would never come; so well, in fact, that she accepted his proposal. She no sooner promised to marry Riquet the Tufted on the same day one year later than she felt quite different from how she had felt before; she found herself effortlessly able to express whatever she wanted to say, and saying it in a refined, comfortable, and natural way. Right away she struck up a gallant and sophisticated conversation with Riquet the Tufted, in which she shone with such brilliance that Riquet the Tufted thought he might have given her even more intelligence than he had kept for himself.

When she returned to the palace, her extraordinary transformation surprised everyone at court; for as much as they had heard nothing but nonsense[11] from her before, now what she said sounded very reasonable and thoroughly brilliant. The whole court felt unimaginable delight; only her younger sister was not very pleased, because without the advantage of intelligence over her sister, she was nothing but a really unappealing monkey[12] by comparison. The king managed things according to her advice and sometimes even met with his council members in her apartment.[13]

When word of the transformation spread, all the princes of the neighboring kingdoms did what they could to win her love and nearly all of them asked for her hand in marriage. But she found not a one with enough intelligence, and listened to all of them without promising herself to any of them. That said, one came that was so powerful, so rich, so brilliant, and so good looking that she could not help but be persuaded by him.[14] Her father noticed and told her that the choice of a husband was hers and that she had

---

[11]The word *impertinence*, which passed into modern English as "impertinence" or verbal insubordination, referred in the seventeenth century to discourse or argument that lacks pertinence and relevance. A secondary meaning, speech that offends the rules of sociability or sounds unmannerly, became salient in French and English in the eighteenth century.

[12]The word *Guenon*, designating a type of monkey belonging to the genus *Cercopithecus*, was and can still be used in French to describe a woman considered very unattractive. In English it refers only to the monkey.

[13]In a château or noble household, family members would each have an "apartment," which consisted of several connected rooms, some private and some designed to host visitors.

[14]She had *bonne volonté* (goodwill) for him. In the world of the court, she felt positively disposed toward him.

only to decide.[15] Because the smarter you are, the harder it is to make a final decision in such a case, she thanked her father and requested more time to think about it. She walked by coincidence into the same woods where she had discovered Riquet the Tufted to reflect more comfortably on what she had to do. While she walked, in a deep reverie, she heard a muffled sound coming from under her feet, as though several people were moving around and doing something. Listening more carefully she heard someone say, "Bring me that marmite," another "Give me that cauldron,"[16] and still another, "Put wood on the fire."

Then the earth opened and under her feet she saw a large kitchen full of chefs, busboys, and all sorts of personnel required to host extravagant banquets. A group of twenty or thirty rotisserie masters emerged from the ground and went down a path in the woods to sit around a very long table. Larding needles in hand and hats cocked to the side,[17] they set to work to the beat of a melodic song. Stunned by this spectacle, the princess asked them whom they worked for. "Madame, we work for Riquet the Tufted, who is getting married tomorrow," said the most notable of the group. Even more surprised than she had been and remembering all of a sudden that a year ago that very day she had promised to marry Riquet the Tufted, the princess nearly fell over. What happened to cause her to forget is that when she made this promise, she was an idiot[18] and that

---

[15]She shares with other heroines in the collection a privilege most royal and aristocratic women would not have had in the seventeenth century: the right to choose your mate by inclination rather than political motivation. Women writers of the previous generation, notably Mademoiselle de Scudéry and Madame de Lafayette, took up the problem of arranged and political marriage in their fiction.

[16]Both a *marmite* and a *chaudière*, or cauldron, were and remain essential tools in the French kitchen. Both pots were used for cooking over an open flame, the marmite for boiling meats and vegetables, the larger cauldron for heating liquids. Here, as in "The Beauty in the Slumbering Woodland," Perrault and his well-heeled characters display a certain knowledge of fine cookery.

[17]A *lardoire* is an instrument specific to the task of "larding" a piece of meat by inserting bacon or pork fat deep into the meat before roasting to add flavor. The "queue de renard" (foxtail) that the roasters have "sur l'oreille" (on the ear) has confounded critics because the ready explanation of *queue-de-renard* from the period—a type of amaranth plant used for millet, among other things—does not make sense in the context of "on the ear." Betts references the *Oxford Companion to Food,* which indicates that "queue de renard" refers to a hat with a tassel worn by chefs, which gives him "tassels on their hats over their ears" (*Charles Perrault: The Complete Fairy Tales,* 146). If the expression does suggest a hat of some kind, another way to make sense of the whole phrase, which I have done here, is to interpret the expression "sur l'oreille" idiomatically. Although this meaning is not explicit in the seventeenth century, to have the hat on your ear, "chapeau sur l'oreille," later acquires the sense of being confident. (See "oreille" in the modern *Petit Robert.*) The idea that the cocked hat functions visually to connote conviction makes good sense in the context of the sentence.

[18]Here *bête* is nominative; she is "une bête."

when she accepted the new intellect the prince gave her, she forgot all of her nonsense.

She hadn't gone thirty steps further into her walk when Riquet the Tufted appeared before her, noble, sumptuous, and every bit the prince about to be married.

"As you see, Madame, I am a man of my word and do not doubt but that you have come here to live up to your own and, in giving me your hand, make me the happiest of men."

"I confess in all honesty," responded the princess, "I have not yet made my decision about that and do not think I will ever be capable of making the decision you are hoping for."

"You surprise me, Madame," said Riquet the Tufted.

"I can imagine," said the princess, "and of course if I were dealing with a churl, a witless man, I would find myself in quite a bind. He would tell me that a princess has nothing if not her word and 'You have to marry me since you promised me you would,' but since I am speaking to the man with the most sense in the world, I am sure he will listen to reason. You know that when I was an idiot I could not convince myself to marry you; how can you expect me, with the intellect you gave me, which makes me even pickier than I had been,[19] to make a choice today that I could not make then? If you seriously expected to marry me, you made a big mistake taking away my idiocy and helping me see more clearly than I did before."

"If a witless man would be in a position, as you just suggested, to criticize your failure to keep your word," replied Riquet the Tufted, "why would that not apply to me, Madame, in a case that concerns my lifelong happiness? Is it reasonable to assume that people who are intelligent should be in a worse position than those who are not? Do you really believe that; you, who are so intelligent and who so hoped to be? But let's get back to the real issue, if you don't mind: with the exception of my ugliness, is there something about me that annoys you? Are you unhappy with my status, my mind, my personality, or my manners?"

"Not at all," replied the princess. "I appreciate in you everything you just said."

"If that is the case," continued Riquet the Tufted, "I shall be happy because you can make me the most appealing of men."

---

[19]The line is "difficile en gens," which likely comes from the expression "se connaître en gens," to be discerning of character or, as we might say today, to have good instincts with people. Extrapolating from that, it appears she is saying that she has become more discerning and judgmental of personality than before.

"How can that happen?" the princess said to him.

"That will happen," replied Riquet the Tufted, "if you love me enough to wish that it be; and, Madame, so that you have no doubt, know this: the same fairy who, on the day of my birth, gave me the ability to make a person of my choice brilliant also gave you the ability to make beautiful the person you love and want to grant such a favor."

"If that is the case," said the princess, "I wish with all my heart for you to be the most beautiful and appealing prince in the world; and I give you as much of that talent as is in me."

No sooner had she spoken these words than Riquet the Tufted appeared in her eyes to be the most beautiful, best-looking, and most appealing prince you've ever seen. Some insist that this was not the work of the fairy's charms but that love alone performed this metamorphosis. They say that once she reflected on the perseverance of her lover, on his subtlety, on all the virtues of his soul and his mind, the princess no longer saw the deformity of his body or his face; that his hump now seemed to her to be nothing more than the pose of a man puffed up with pride; and that even though she had up until that point noticed his monstrous limp,[20] she now saw only a certain affectation that she found charming. Furthermore, they say that even though his eyes were crossed, to her they only looked more dazzling, and she took their irregularity as a sign of the violent throes of passion; and that in the end she saw something commanding and heroic in his huge red nose. Whatever the case may be, the princess promised right there and then to marry him, provided that he got permission from her father the king. Knowing that his daughter held Riquet the Tufted in high regard, and that he himself knew him for a very brilliant, very wise prince, the king received him with pleasure as his son-in-law. The very next day, the marriage took place as Riquet the Tufted had planned it and according to the arrangements he had made far in advance.

Moral

These words in black and white
Are less a tall tale than the truth, by Jove;
All is beauty when we love,
Whatever we love is bright.

---

[20]The adverb *effroyablement*, derived from the noun *effroi* (fear), describes something excessive or unusual. In this case he limps *effroyablement*, which adds excessive oddness to an already uncommon walk.

Another Moral

When Nature crafts a creature,
Gives it a healthy glow and fine features
With a tone that art's brush cannot achieve,
All these talents combined cannot stir passion's storm
Like a single hidden charm
That Love helps us perceive.

The Little Thumblette

There was once a man and woman, both woodcutters, who had seven sons, all boys. The oldest was only ten and the youngest only seven. It amazed people that the woodcutter had had so many children in so little time, but it was that his wife rushed through it[1] and made at least two at a time. They were destitute and their seven children were a huge imposition because none of them was old enough yet to make a living. Even more distressing was the fact that the youngest one was very frail and never spoke; they took for stupidity what was really a sign of his good nature. He was extremely small and when he came into the world, he was hardly larger than a thumb, which is why they called him the little Thumblette.[2] The poor thing was the household whipping post and he was always in the wrong. Nevertheless, he was the brightest and sharpest of all the brothers, and if he spoke little, he listened much. There came a very harsh year and the famine was so severe[3] that the miserable couple resolved to give up[4] their children.

---

[1]"Aller vite en besogne" suggests working quickly. Unlike the expression "ne pas être long à sa besogne" in "Beauty in the Slumbering Woodland," which I translated "did not waste time," *aller vite* has the pejorative edge of a job done unthinkingly and in haste.

[2]The *Dictionnaire de l'Académie française* specifies two things about the thumb that are worthy of note: "The largest of the fingers on the hand. The thumb is stronger than all the other fingers" (Le plus gros des doigts de la main. Le pouce est plus fort que les autres doigts). His strength, in spite of looking the smallest, gives Thumblette his unlikely appeal. Perrault coined the diminutive of thumb, *poucet*, whose definition as of the nineteenth century, when it entered the dictionary, refers exclusively to this tale. I have chosen the ending -*ette* to render Perrault's diminutive. Note, too, that the name twice reduces the child's size: once in the diminutive and again in the adjective.

[3]There is immediate historical precedent for this detail. In 1694 France experienced the worst famine of the century. With nearly 2 million dead and rotting corpses in the street causing a typhoid epidemic, 1693–94 became known as "the years of misery." The most extensive study on this deadly period of French history is Marcel Lachiver's *Les Années de misère: La Famine au temps du Grand Roi* (Paris: Fayard, 1991), of which just more than half covers the 1694 famine.

[4]The verb here, *se défaire*, is not quite as pejorative as some translations suggest. Typically, the parents are said to "get rid" of their children (Zipes, *The Great Fairy Tale Tradition*, 705; Betts, *Charles Perrault: The Complete Fairy Tales*, 151; Appelbaum, *The Complete Fairy Tales in Verse and Prose*, 191). But the closest synonym in the *Dictionnaire de l'Académie française* is *s'aliener*, which means to transfer the rights to land or some other possession to another party—not so much to dump as to transfer ownership. Since the context of this passage suggests that the transfer is forced, "give up" captures that urgency.

One evening when the children had gone to sleep and the woodcutter was sitting by the fireplace with his wife, his heart racked with grief, he said to her, "You know very well that we can no longer feed our children. I cannot watch them die of hunger right in front of me and have resolved to leave them behind in the woods tomorrow,[5] which will be very simple: while they are busy bundling twigs,[6] we just need to steal away and not let them see us."

"Augh!" cried the woodcutter-wife.[7] "Could you really leave your own children behind?"

Her husband pointed out[8] the extent of their poverty, but in vain; she could not consent to this plan. She was poor, but she was still their mother. That said, after giving some thought to the pain it would cause her to watch them die, she consented and cried herself to sleep. The little Thumblette picked up everything they said because from his bed he had overheard them talking business and got up quietly and slipped under his father's stool to listen without being seen. He went back to bed and, thinking about what he needed to do, did not sleep a wink the rest of the night. He woke up early the next morning and went down to the banks of a stream where he filled his pockets with little pebbles and then returned to the house. They[9] set out, and the little Thumblette kept what he knew from his brothers. They went into a very dense forest where you could not see someone ten steps away. The woodcutter set to chopping wood and his children to collecting twigs for bundles of kindling.[10] Seeing that the children were occupied with their work, the father and mother moved away from them little by little and then

---

[5]Perrault's *mener perdre*, again of his coinage, became a stock expression that does not translate easily. Others have used cumbersome phrasing to capture the sense of both verbs: "to take them with me into the woods tomorrow and leave them there to get lost" (Betts, *Charles Perrault: The Complete Fairy Tales*, 151). I have attempted here to pare it down to phrasing that sounds like it could be an expression, although no such expression as "lead and lose" exists in English.

[6]The verb in French, *fagoter,* has a straightforward equivalent in English, to fagot or bundle kindling, of which the result is called a fagot of wood. Given the nefarious uses to which its variant "faggot" has been put in English over the past century and its potential confusion with the woodcutting term, I have opted against it.

[7]The feminine *bûcheronne* (female woodcutter) has no simple translation as it also refers to her status as the wife of a woodcutter. As it is her title, I have opted to create a compound word rather than use the possessive "woodcutter's wife."

[8]This usage of *représenter*, to represent, draws on one of its secondary meanings: *remontrer*, or demonstrate, with the specific nuance of demonstrating the negative consequences of an action done or about to be done (*Dictionnaire de l'Académie française*).

[9]Very occasionally, as in this sentence, the third-person plural *ils* (they) is replaced by *on*, which yields "one" or "we" in English. The shift does not follow logically from the context, where the *on* of the present sentence and the *ils* of the next one have the same semantic value and the use of one or we does not make sense.

[10]Instead of "firewood," as is sometimes used, *broutilles*, small branches, or twigs for fagots, suggests very small bundles that would be used as fire starters.

suddenly stole away by a small remote trail. When the children saw that they were alone, they started to scream at the top of their lungs and cry their eyes out.[11] The little Thumblette let them scream, knowing full well how to get to the house, because as he walked he had dropped the little white pebbles he had in his pockets all along the path. Then he told them, "Have no fear, brothers, my father and my mother left us here, but I can bring you safely back home, just follow me."

They followed him and he led them to their house by the same path that had brought them into the forest.[12] At first they were too nervous to enter, but they all pressed against the door to listen to what their father and mother were saying.

As soon as the woodcutter and woodcutter-wife arrived home, the lord of the village sent them ten *écus*,[13] which paid a debt long overdue and which they never thought they would see again. It brought them back to life because the poor were dying of hunger.[14] Right away the wood-cutter sent his wife to the butcher's. Because it was so long since she had eaten, she ordered three times as much meat as she needed to feed two people for dinner.

When they were sated the woodcutter-wife said: "Oh, where are they now, our poor things! They would eat well on these leftovers! And what's more, Guillaume, you are the one who wanted to leave them behind. I *told* you we would regret it. What are they doing now in that forest? Oh, god, the wolves may already have eaten them! You are a monster[15] to have left your children behind like that!"

---

[11]In French the children scream and cry "de toute leur force," with all their might, which I have rendered in English with the idiom appropriate to each type of outburst.

[12]This phrasing is economical to the point of elision: "par le même chemin *qu'ils* étaient venus dans la forêt," by the same path "that" they had come into the forest, rather than "le même chemin d'où ils," the same path by which they had come.

[13]The *écu* circulated in the monetary system in place before the old *franc* and was worth three *livres*, or pounds. In modern terms, the sum of ten is not negligible, perhaps about $200.

[14]The article in this clause implies a population larger than the family: "car les pauvres gens mourraient de faim" (because the poor people were dying of hunger). The definite article *les* (*the* poor people) makes the poor a social category, whereas the demonstrative adjective *ces* (*these* poor people) would more clearly reference the family. As such, the statement becomes a commentary on the problem of an economically unstable nobility incurring debt to its people. Aristocratic ruin was a reality during the luxurious reign of Louis XIV that Molière, for example, spoofed in the comedy *Le Bourgeois gentilhomme* (The Bourgeois Gentleman, 1670). Told from the perspective of the peasants and in light of the 1694 famine, as it appears in this tale, the crisis looks tragic.

[15]She tells him "Tu es bien inhumain"—You are being completely unhuman, or perhaps inhumane. This charge has strong resonance in a collection of stories with child-eating ogres and wolves, some of whom stand in for aristocratic abuse.

The woodcutter finally lost patience after she repeated more than twenty times that they would regret it and that she had told him so. He threatened to hit her so she would shut up. It's not that the woodcutter was not perhaps even angrier than his wife, but it's that she was badgering him;[16] and he was inclined, like many others, to love women who tell you well but find very bothersome women who have always told you so.[17]

The woodcutter-wife sobbed: "Oh, where are my poor things now?"

One time she said it so loudly that the children, who were listening at the door, heard her and all started screaming, We're over here! We're over here![18]

She ran to open the door and hugged them, saying: "I am so pleased to see you again, my darling children, you are so weary and so hungry, and you, Pierrot,[19] look how muddy you are! Come let me clean you up."

Pierrot was her oldest son and she loved him better than all the others because he had a touch of red hair and she had a touch of red hair.[20] The sons sat down to eat and ate hungrily, which pleased the father and mother, as they told them how frightened they had been in the woods, all of them speaking on top of one another. These good people were thrilled to have their children with them; the thrill lasted as long as the ten *écus*.

But when the money was gone, they relapsed[21] into their former melancholia; they resolved to leave them behind again and, to ensure the plan's success, to lead them much farther away than they had the first time. They were unable to speak privately enough to avoid being heard by the little

---

[16]The expression is "lui rompre la tête": literally, she was breaking or shattering his head and figuratively, overwhelming him with noise and arguments.

[17]The sentence plays on the semantic contrast of the expressions *dire bien* (to speak well) and *bien dire* (to be right or convincing): "qui aiment fort les femmes qui disent bien, mais qui trouvent très importunes celles qui ont toujours bien dit." The joke here is that husbands like women who speak well, but not women who are always right.

[18]In two instances, the narrator moves directly from a description of action to reported direct speech, which I have left without quotation marks.

[19]Although translators tend to substitute classic English names (Samber chooses Billy and Betts opts for the more literal Peter), the name Pierrot has a history worth evoking and has passed into English through that history. Pierrot is a character best known for his role opposite Harlequin in the commedia dell'arte Italian performance tradition. Comic playwright Molière, among others, contributed to the immense popularity of the farcical style and main characters of the commedia in French theater of the period directly preceding the publication of the *Histoires ou Contes du temps passé*. That association could suggest an interpretation on the story in which Thumblette plays the part of Harlequin. Critics have also noted its resemblance to Perrault's son's name, Pierre. I have left the father's name, Guillaume (William), in French to serve as a cultural anchor for the story.

[20]They are both "un peu rousseau" (a little bit redheaded).

[21]The verb *retomber* can be physical, to fall again, but also has this standard medical usage in the seventeenth century.

Thumblette, who figured[22] he would get out of it as he had before; but even though he got up bright and early to go collect little pebbles he did not succeed because he found the front door double-locked. He had no idea what to do, but when his mother gave them each a piece of bread for breakfast, he realized he could use the bread in place of the pebbles, throwing crumbs all along the path they would walk; so he shoved it in his pocket.

The father and mother led them to the densest, darkest part of the forest and as soon as they got there, they took a secret footpath[23] and left them there. The little Thumblette did not feel so bad because he thought he could easily find the path with the help of the bread he had scattered everywhere he walked, and he was stunned when he could not find a single crumb. The birds had come and eaten it all. Now they were very vexed, because the more they walked, the more they wandered and wallowed in the woods.[24] Night fell and a strong wind picked up that terrified them. Everywhere they thought they heard the howl of wolves coming to eat them. They were almost too nervous to speak or turn around. A downpour erupted and soaked them to the bone; they slipped with every step and fell in the mud, which left them filthy and with no idea what to do with their hands.[25]

The little Thumblette climbed to the top of a tree to see if he could locate anything. Turning his head all around, he saw a little glimmer, like a candle flame, but it was far off beyond the forest. He came down from the tree and when he was on the ground he could no longer see anything; that troubled him. Nevertheless, after he had walked a while with his brothers in the direction where he had seen the light, he saw it again as they left the forest. Eventually they got to the house with the candlelight, but with frequent

---

[22]To "faire son compte de," literally to make one's account to do or to count on something, has a range of idiomatic meanings from hope (*espérer que*) to expectation (*s'attendre à*). The verb "to figure" in English covers a similar breadth of possibility and has the advantage of mimicking the business metaphor of calculation.

[23]A *faux-fuyant* is an out-of-the-way footpath, one presumably made by and known in this context to people familiar with the terrain of the woods, and taken as a way of exiting or escaping without being seen.

[24]This is one of the more poetically structured lines in the story. In the French, a string of like-sounding verbs keeps the sentence rhythmic and tight: "Les voilà donc bien affli**gés**, car plus ils march**aient** plus ils s'égar**aient**, et s'enfonç**aient** dans la forêt" (my emphasis). I attempt with more textured verbs to capture this rhythm. The simple past and imperfect endings of the verbs also all rhyme with the ending of *forêt*. I have replaced this assonance with alliteration.

[25]This scene has a striking amount of sensual detail in it. Rarely does Perrault describe a character's response to the condition of her or his body. It does not last long. The next sentence cuts back to the narrative. This detail about their hands, which Samber takes as a metaphor for crawling, "forced to go up on all four" (173), does not appear to be a stock metaphor in French and remains enigmatic. It could refer to the fact that their hands, wet and muddy, were useless to them, which left them with no tools.

moments of panic when it disappeared from sight, which happened whenever the land sloped down. They knocked on the door and an old woman came and opened it. She asked what they wanted and the little Thumblette told her that they were poor things who had gotten lost in the forest and who appealed to her sense of charity to request lodging there. The woman thought they were all so cute that she started crying and said to them, "Oh! You poor things, where have you come? Did you know that this house belongs to an ogre that eats small children?"

"Oh, Madame!" responded the little Thumblette, who was trembling all over like his brothers. "What can we do? There's no question the wolves in the forest will definitely eat us tonight if you won't board us here. And in that case, we'd rather it be Monsieur who eats us; maybe he'll have pity on us, if you feel like asking him to."

The ogre's wife thought she could hide them from her husband until the next morning so she let them in and took them to warm themselves near the roaring fire, where a whole sheep turned on a rotisserie for the ogre's dinner. As they started to warm up, they heard three or four loud knocks at the door; it was the ogre returning.[26] Right away, the woman hid them under the bed and went to open the door. First the ogre asked if dinner was ready and if wine had been drawn,[27] and then sat right down at the table. The mutton was still bloody, but that only made it taste better. He scented left and right, saying that he could smell raw meat.[28]

"It must be," said his wife, "this calf I just dressed[29] that you smell."

"For the second time, I smell raw meat," replied the ogre, glaring at his wife, "and something is going on here that I don't like."[30]

---

[26]Note that the ogre knocks to be let in to his own house. Perhaps this detail signals that he lives like an aristocrat and his wife tends to him like a servant.

[27]A good French ogre, this one has his wine in barrels that would be drawn off into a carafe and set out on the table for dinner. Note, too, that he mentions wine immediately after the meat, elevating it to a primary concern of the well-lain table.

[28]The staccato rhythm of this run of sentences makes the scene chaotic. Something about the figure of the ogre brings a mania into the narrative that is reflected in disjointed sequencing. Arguably the choppy movement began when the children were still in the forest and falling in the mud, perhaps a form of foreshadowing.

[29]*Habiller*, to dress meat, involves skinning it and preparing it for cooking.

[30]One of the common meanings of *entendre*, to hear, has to do with comprehension, which is how the word is usually translated. Another connotation has to do with approval: to give one's consent, to consent, to approve ("Donner son consentement, consentir, approuver"). *Dictionnaire de l'Académie française*. The latter meaning appears to me to be operative here, and I have extended the idea of approval to "liking" something in the sense of being comfortable with it.

Saying these words, he got up from the table and went straight to the bed.[31]

"So," he said, "that's how you're going to cheat me, is it, damnable woman! I don't know why I don't just eat you, too; must be because you're an old brute.[32] Now here's some game that has arrived just in time to regale[33] three of my ogre friends who plan to come see me in the next few days."[34]

He pulled them out from under the bed one by one. The poor things got on their knees for mercy, but they were dealing with the cruelest of all ogres who, far from taking pity, was already devouring them with his eyes and telling his wife that they would have themselves some tender morsels once she cooked up a nice sauce. He went to get a large knife and, moving closer to the poor things, he sharpened it on a long stone that he held in his left hand. He had already stabbed one of them when his wife said to him:

"What do you want with them at this hour? Won't you have enough time for this tomorrow morning?"

"Shut up," replied the ogre, "they won't stay tender until then."

"But you still have so much other meat," replied his wife. "There's a calf, two sheep, and half a pig."

"You're right," said the ogre. "Give them plenty to eat so they don't lose weight and put them to bed."

The old woman was overjoyed and brought them plenty to eat, but they could not eat, they were so racked with fear. As for the ogre, he went back to drinking, thrilled to have enough to regale his friends so well. He drank a dozen glasses more than usual, which went a bit to his head and forced him into bed.

The ogre had seven daughters who were still young children. These little ogresses all had beautiful complexions because they ate raw meat like

---

[31]Throughout this scene, the husband speaks to his wife in the informal *tu* while she responds with the formal *vous*. This disparity among married couples in Perrault seems to be associated with suspicion and anger: the Blue Beard uses *vous* with his wife for most of the story but switches to *tu* when he becomes unhinged toward the end. By contrast, the woodcutter and woodcutter-wife both use *tu*.

[32]He says, "bien t'en prend qu'être une vieille bête," an odd turn of phrase. *S'en prendre à quelqu'un* means to attribute a flaw or lay blame on someone for something (*Dictionnaire de l'Académie française*). The conjugation suggests "il t'en prend bien," or it is good you have the flaw of only being an old brute. The expression *vieille bête*, literally old animal, idiomatically insults her intelligence and plays on her age. She is not young fresh meat.

[33]The verb *traiter*, to treat, can also have a very specific meaning: to entertain with a finely prepared meal. Today in France you go to a *traiteur*, delicatessen or caterer, to buy prepared specialty foods.

[34]As the next line suggests, during this monologue, the ogre has already noticed the children under the bed. His "here's some game" refers to them.

their father, but they had small and very round gray eyes, a hooked nose, and a huge mouth with long, razor-sharp teeth that had big spaces between them. They had not yet become vicious, but they had a lot of promise because they were already biting babies to suck their blood. They were put to bed early and all seven of them were in one big bed, each one with a crown on her head. There was another bed of the same size in the room; it was in this bed that the ogre's wife put the seven little boys to sleep; then she went to bed next to her husband.

The little Thumblette noticed that the ogre's daughters wore little crowns of gold on their heads and, fearing that the ogre might have some regret about not slitting their throats that very evening, got up in the middle of the night to take his brothers' caps and his own and put them on the heads of the ogre's daughters after he removed the crowns of gold and put them on his brothers' heads and his own; this way the ogre would take them for his daughters and his daughters for the boys whose throats he wanted to slit.[35] It worked just as he'd thought; the ogre woke up around midnight and regretted putting off until tomorrow what he could have done today; so, leaping headlong out of bed and grabbing his big knife, "Let's go see," he said, "how our little rascals are feeling; do it once, do it right."[36]

He groped his way up to the girls' room and came toward the bed with the little boys in it, all sleeping except the little Thumblette, who was terrified when he felt the ogre's hand grope his head just as he had groped the heads of all his brothers. When the ogre felt the crowns of gold, "Indeed," he said, "that would have been fine work;[37] evidently I drank too much last night."

Next he went to the girls' bed, where he felt the boys' caps: "Aha, here are my boys!" he said. "Let's do this."

With these words and without a second thought, he cut the throats of his seven daughters. Extremely pleased with the results of his mission,[38] he went back to sleep next to his wife.

As soon as the little Thumblette heard the ogre snoring, he woke his brothers up and told them to get dressed quickly and follow him. They

---

[35]This exceptionally long sentence has almost no punctuation in the French besides commas, a rare run-on for Perrault that does not make liberal use of semicolons. I have reproduced its heft here, but conceded to a semicolon toward the end.

[36]See the explanation of this expression in "The Beauty in the Slumbering Woodland," footnote 15.

[37]Perrault uses *un bel ouvrage*, a nice job, ironically here.

[38]The word *expédition* in French can have the sense of a military exploit.

quietly went down into the garden and jumped over the walls. They ran almost all night, trembling, and with no idea where they would end up.[39]

The ogre woke up and said to his wife, go ahead up and dress those little rascals from yesterday evening. The ogress[40] was stunned by her husband's kindness, completely oblivious to what he meant by "dress" and thinking that he was telling her to put clothes on them. She went upstairs, where she got a powerful shock when she noticed her seven daughters, throats slit and swimming in their own blood. First off, she fainted (this is the first solution for nearly all women in similar situations).

Worried that something was keeping his wife too long at the task he'd given her, the ogre went up to help her. His shock was no less than hers when he saw that horrific spectacle.

"Augh! What have I done!" he cried. "They will pay for this, those wretches, and right now."

He threw a bucketful[41] of water in his wife's face and, once he had woken her up, "Get me my seven-league boots,"[42] he said to her, "so I can go catch them." He set out for the countryside and once he had run far and wide, he ended up on the path where the poor things were walking and were within a mere one hundred steps of their father's house. They saw the ogre bounding from mountain to mountain and crossing rivers as easily as he would have crossed the smallest stream. The little Thumblette, who saw a hollowed rock not far from where they were, hid his six brothers in it and also crammed himself in, always watching for the ogre. The ogre found that he was wearied by the long road he had traveled uselessly (seven-league boots just exhaust a man) and wanted to rest; by chance he went to sit down on the rock where the little boys were hiding. Since he was worn out with fatigue, he fell asleep after resting a short while and started snoring a snore so terrifying that the poor things were no less frightened than when he was clutching his huge knife to slit their throats. The little Thumblette was less frightened and told his brothers to steal away promptly to the house while the ogre was sleeping deeply and not to worry themselves one bit about him. They took his advice and made it quickly to the house. The little Thumblette came up to the ogre and took off his boots, which he immediately put on.

---

[39]The pace picks up again in short sentences.

[40]This is the first time Perrault does not refer to her as "the ogre's wife." This scene marks a new role for her in the narrative as well.

[41]Perrault uses *potée*, which refers to the quantity that a jar or pot can hold.

[42]See "The Beauty in the Slumbering Woodland," where the fairy's informant wears the same boots. Master cat's boots are not enchanted in this way, although they afford him intangibles such as a nobler persona.

The boots were extremely long and wide, but because they were enchanted, they had the capacity to grow or shrink according to the legs of the person slipping them on such that they happened to fit his feet and legs as though they had been made for him. He went straight to the ogre's house, where he found his wife crying over her butchered daughters.

"Your husband," the little Thumblette said to her, "is in grave danger. A band of thieves took him and swear they will kill him if he doesn't give them all his gold and silver. At the very moment when they held the knife to his throat, he noticed me and asked me to warn you about his predicament and tell you to give me everything of value in his possession and not hold anything back because otherwise they will kill him mercilessly. Because there is no time to waste, he wanted me to take these seven-league boots to make tracks and also so that you know I am not a fraud."

The terrified old woman immediately gave him everything she had— the ogre still managed to be a good husband even if he did eat babies. Loaded up with the ogre's wealth, the little Thumblette then went back to his father's house, where he was greeted with much delight.

There are many people who disagree on this last incident and who believe that the little Thumblette never stole from the ogre; that in truth he could not conscience stealing seven-league boots that the ogre used exclusively for chasing babies. Those people claim to have credible sources and even to have drunk and eaten in the woodcutter's home. They insist that when the little Thumblette slipped on the ogre's seven-league boots he headed to the court, which he knew was being threatened by an army that was only two hundred leagues away and which was already depleted from a battle they had recently waged. He went, they say, to find the king and tell him that if he so wished, the little Thumblette would bring back intelligence about the army before the end of the day. The king promised him a huge sum of money if he accomplished it. The little Thumblette brought back intelligence that very evening and because this first exploit made his name, he got everything he wanted: the king paid him handsomely to take his orders to the army and dozens and dozens of ladies gave him whatever he wanted for the promise of news from their lovers, which was his most profitable gain. It happened that there were several women who gave him letters for their husbands, but they paid him so badly and it amounted to so little that he didn't even take into consideration what he earned that way.[43]

---

[43]Literally, "mettre en ligne de compte," enter it on a line of an account ledger. The implication here is that court women would not pay much to get news to their husbands, but spent liberally to communicate with their lovers.

After some time as a professional courier, which earned him a small fortune, he returned to his father's home, where the delight they felt seeing him again was unimaginable. He gave the whole family a comfortable life. He bought his father and brothers newly established government posts, both setting them up and masterfully working his way up[44] at the same time.

Moral

No need to trouble if you have a large brood
When they all have beauty, good height, and good mood,
And skin as bright as a lily.
But if one of them is weak or drawn in
We chide him, mock him, punch him silly,[45]
Yet sometimes it's this little urchin
Who will be the pride of the whole family.

---

[44]In the French, *faire sa cour*, literally, make your court, means to fulfill your social obligations. But the word *cour* refers also to the royal court. In this sense, the narrator plays on that double meaning: he purchases court jobs for his family and also "makes his court" to move up in the world.

[45]The verb *piller*, which I rendered "punch him silly," is a synonym of *saccager*, to sack or ransack. The idea of attack in this action along with the need to rhyme "family" led me to this colloquialism.

Annotated Bibliography of the *Histoires ou Contes du temps passé* in French and English

This annotated bibliography is not designed to be exhaustive, for there are numerous collection reprints and single-story prints of Perrault's tales—indeed, too many to be discovered or counted. They are scattered around the world in special collections, children's libraries, collections of book/art/doll dealers, and private collections. To be sure, there are very fine catalogues of editions held by institutions, many of which appear in the source list below, and a few important nineteenth-century bibliographies (of rare books, of children's literature) that offer substantial help. But to date no one has drawn together information from these sources about the various French and English titles by which the collection was known over its first two-hundred-year history. The modest goal of the present bibliography is to begin that process. I have endeavored to gather significant and revelatory editions in French and English (including as well early Dutch examples) that are extant and appear in catalogues. I have not consulted private collections except in the very rare case of a text coming up for auction. While the partial lists below cannot provide a complete picture of the publication history of the Mother Goose tales, they do offer insight into the various ways the book was presented to readers in both French and English before the twentieth century. Because one interest of this book is to document the collection's early reception history, which has not yet been well explored, this bibliography is designed to illuminate trends and rare examples from 1695 to about 1900, with a few important editions extending into the twentieth century. It is annotated to identify the particular interest of each edition and locate it on the world map.

As in the footnotes and image captions in the preceding text, this bibliography retains the original capitalization and orthography of the historical works.

PUBLISHED BIBLIOGRAPHIES

Albers, Neeltje Chiela. *Moeder de Gans in Nederland. Nederlandse Perrault uitgaven; voorlopige bibliografie.* Amsterdam: BDA, 1969.

Bottigheimer, Ruth B. "Misperceived Perceptions: Perrault's Fairy Tales and English Children's Literature." *Children's Literature* 30 (2002): 1–18.

Cohen, Henry. *Guide de l'amateur de livres à gravures du XVIIIe siècle.* 5th ed. Updated by Baron Roger Portalis. Paris: P. Rouquette, 1886.

France, Peter, ed. *Oxford Guide to Literature in English Translation.* Oxford: Oxford University Press, 2000. https://books.google.fr/books?id=pmNoS2d-ndKsC&lpg=PA108&ots=MzRyBRrbUf&dq=guy%20miege%20fairy%20tales&pg=PP1#v=onepage&q=guy%20miege%20fairy%20tales&f=false.

Hahn, Daniel, Humphrey Carpenter, and Mari Prichard, eds. *Oxford Companion to Children's Literature.* 2nd ed. Oxford: Oxford University Press, 2015. https://books.google.fr/books?id=Dt_XCQAAQBAJ&lpg=PA82&ots=au6Vi-jCDXa&dq=newbery%2C%20Tales%20from%20the%20Past%20with%20Morals%2C%201760&pg=PA277#v=onepage&q=mother%20goose&f=false.

Immel, Andrea. "List of Fairy Tale Books in the Opie Collection." Digitized by the Bodleian: www.bodleian.ox.ac.uk/__data/assets/pdf_file/0014/28103/C_Fairy_tales.pdf.

Le Men, Ségolène. "Mother Goose Illustrated: Perrault to Doré." *Poetics Today* 13, no. 1 (1992): 17–39.

Opie, Iona, and Peter Opie. *The Classic Fairy Tales.* London: Oxford University Press, 1974.

St. John, Judith. *Osborne Collection of Early Children's Books, 1476–1910: A Catalogue.* 2 vols. Toronto: Toronto Public Library, 1975.

Tchemerzine, Avenir. *Bibliographie d'éditions originales et rares d'auteurs français des XVe, XVIe, XVIIe et XVIIIe siècles.* Vol. 9. 1928. Reprint, Paris: Hermann, Editeurs des sciences et des arts, 1977.

Watson, George. *The New Cambridge Bibliography of English.* Volume 2, 1660–1800. Cambridge: Cambridge University Press, 1971.

Welch, D'Alté Aldrich. *A Bibliography of American Children's Books Printed Prior to 1821.* Worcester, MA: American Antiquarian Society, 1972.

ABBREVIATIONS USED FOR LIBRARY COLLECTIONS

AAS—American Antiquarian Society, Worcester, MA
Arsenal—Bibliothèque de l'Arsenal, Bibliothèque nationale de France, Paris
Beinecke—Beinecke Rare Books, Yale University, New Haven, CT
BL—British Library, London
BNF—Bibliothèque nationale de France, Paris

Bodleian—Bodleian Library, University of Oxford, Oxford
BRB—Bibliothèque Royale de Belgique, Brussels
Clark—William Andrews Clark Memorial Library, UCLA
Cotsen—Cotsen Children's Library, Princeton University, Princeton, NJ
Grand-Troyes—Médiathèque du Grand-Troyes, Troyes
Houghton—Houghton Library, Harvard University, Cambridge, MA
KB—Koninklijke Bibliotheek, The Hague
Lilly—Lilly Library, Indiana University, Bloomington
Marseille—Bibliothèque de Marseille, Marseille
NLS—National Library of Scotland, Edinburgh
Osborne—Osborne Collection of Early Children's Books, Toronto Public Library, Toronto
PML—Pierpont Morgan Library, New York
Sorbonne—Bibliothèque de la Sorbonne, Paris

EARLY FRANCOPHONE EDITIONS

"Contes de ma Mere Loye." MDCXCV [1695]. Manuscript with dedicatory epistle to Elisabeth-Charlotte d'Orléans.

Contains "La Belle au bois dormant," "Le Petit chaperon rouge," "La Barbe bleue," "Maître chat," and "Les Fées." Handwritten manuscript dedicated to "Mademoiselle," or Elisabeth-Charlotte d'Orléans, from "P.P." (Pierre Darmancour Perrault). The dedicatory epistle has a decorative cartouche with an image of putti holding banners that read in Latin and in French: "Je suis belle et suis née pour être couronnée" (I am beautiful and was born to be crowned). Hand-painted gouache illustrations by Antoine Clouzier, which are printed in black and white in the 1697 edition. Clouzier is not well known today and seems to have left little trace besides the illustrations for Barbin's edition of Perrault. Nonetheless, because they were reprinted hundreds of times, albeit often with considerable alteration in style and tone, throughout the eighteenth and well into the nineteenth century, the scenes he chose for woodcut illustrations in 1695 became some of the most iconic in European popular literature. Ma Mère L'Oye, soon to be known in English as Mother Goose, had a tradition before Perrault and a long legacy visible in this bibliography.[1] [PML]

---

[1] A contemporaneous title from the Théâtre de la foire, or popular theater tradition, bears witness to the linkage of Mother Goose and tales of entertainment for adults, as Perrault used the name in 1695: *Les Fées en contes de ma mère l'oye. Comédie.* Claude-Ignace Brugière de Barante and Charles-Rivière Dufresny d'après Barbier (Paris, 1696). [Arsenal] One of Perrault's prolific contemporaries, Marie-Catherine d'Aulnoy, used the title *Les Contes des fées* (Tales of the Fairies) in 1698 for her collection, christening the genre with the name made famous in English as "fairy tales."

"La Belle au bois dormant, Conte." *Mercure galant, dédié à Monsieur le Dauphin* 2 (February): 74–117. Paris: Michel Brunet, 1696.

> First publication of the "La Belle au bois dormant." Presented anonymously with a short commentary by the editor, the work contains an extended heroic speech by the prince (98–99)—present in the 1695 manuscript—that was removed for the 1697 Barbin publication. Curiously, this speech reappeared in modified form at the end of the eighteenth century. See the 1799 French edition below. As it differs from the version that was printed by Barbin, facsimile pages of the *Mercure*'s "Belle au bois dormant" has been included as figure 11 in the present volume. [BNF]

Pièces curieuses et nouvelles, tant qu'en prose qu'en vers. 30 parts in 5 volumes. The Hague: Adrian Moetjens, 1696–97.

> One of two unofficial Dutch printings of the *Histoires* in 1697. Volume 5 is composed of six parts printed in two bindings: parts 1–3 (1696) and parts 4–6 (1697). "Belle au bois dormant" from the *Mercure* appears in part 2 in the binding printed in 1696 (130–49). The rest of the stories from *Histoires ou Contes du temps passé* appear in part 5 of the second binding, after they were published by Barbin in 1697. The Desbordes family likely produced the other Dutch edition, which appeared with no attribution (see below). [PML, 1697; BNF, 1696]

Histoires ou contes du temps passé avec des Moralitez. Illustrated by Antoine Clouzier. Paris: Claude Barbin, 1697.

> "Avec Privilège de Sa Majesté," January 11, 1697, granted to Sieur P. [Pierre] Darmancour—Charles Perrault's son—for six years and ceded to Claude Barbin. Dedication to Elisabeth-Charlotte d'Orléans signed P. Darmancour. Contains an edited version of the dedication that appeared in the 1695 manuscript and a new version of "Belle au bois dormant" without the prince's speech. Jean-Marc Chatelain, curator of rare books at the BNF, has identified seventeen extant copies of the book produced in Paris in 1697, which represent two different printing runs: a "first state" with mistakes listed on an errata page, of which there are four known copies (two in private collections); and a "second state" with corrections, of which there are thirteen (eight in

private collections). When the fourth copy of the first state came up for auction at Binoche et Gigello in 2013, this edition was publicized as "one of the rarest and most precious of all French literature."[2] [BNF, Sorbonne: first state printing with errata page; Cotsen: second state printing with corrections]

Histoires ou contes du temps passé avec des Moralitez. Trévoux: S. A. Seren. Mon. [Son Altesse Sérénissime Monseigneur] Prince Souverain de Dombes, 1697.

Not listed as unofficial, but technically outside the sphere of the Barbin privilege.[3] Reprinted from Barbin at the press of His Serene Highness, Monsieur the Prince de Dombes. An independent land at the end of the seventeenth century, the principality outside the city of Lyon in southeast France was given by King Louis XIV to Louis-Auguste, the first son he had by his influential mistress, Françoise Athénaïs de Rochechouart de Mortemart, the Marquise de Montespan. Legitimized in 1673, Louis-Auguste de Bourbon became Duc du Maine and later Prince de Dombes, a sovereign in his own right. The prince founded the press in Trévoux, the principality's capital city, and issued books under his own imprimatur. [Marseille]

Histoires ou contes du temps passé avec des Moralitez, par le Fils de Monsieur Perreault de l'Académie François. Suivant la copie, à Paris. 1697.

First Dutch edition, pirated from the second state of the Paris edition (corrected) with Clouzier's illustrations, and presumed to be the first edition in Amsterdam by Jaques Desbordes, although his name does not appear on any extant editions believed to be done by his press.[4] Frontispiece by Clouzier and vignettes are reversed, a habit picked up by Desbordes (below) and Robert Samber ("Early Translations") that will continue in most editions throughout the eighteenth century. First explicit attribution to Pierre Darmancour, Perrault's son. Desbordes's editions became the standard for the eighteenth century in French and then in English when Robert Samber used a Desbordes

---

[2]For a full description of the two printings and their characteristics, see Binoche et Gigello, www.binoche-renaud-giquello.com/html/fiche.jsp?id=3514790.

[3]Tchemerzine, *Bibliographie d'éditions,* identifies it circa 1930 as the rarest edition of 1697 (178).

[4]Ibid. lists a 1698 reprint, but it is not extant in the BNF collection.

copy for his inaugural translation in 1729. See "Early Translations" below. [BNF, PML]

Histoires ou contes du temps passé. Avec des Moralitez. Par le Fils de Monsieur Perreault de l'Académie François. Suivant la Copie, à Paris. 1700.

Reprint of 1697. No publisher listed on this very small, simple volume, which could be Desbordes or pirated from the unofficial 1697 edition attributed to Desbordes. Frontispiece image by Clouzier and vignettes printed in reverse. [Cotsen, PML][5]

Contes de Monsieur Perrault. Avec des moralitez. Paris: la Veuve Barbin, 1707.

"Avec Privilège du Roi," 1706, granted for three years to the Veuve Barbin for unlimited reprinting and sale throughout the kingdom. Illustrations by Clouzier. First edition credited to Charles Perrault rather than his son and the first edition published after the death of Claude Bardin in 1698. Perhaps an attempt to establish the credibility of this edition against the two others (Amsterdam and Trévoux) circulating at the end of the seventeenth century. [BNF]

Histoires ou contes du tems passé. Avec des Moralitez. Par le Fils de Monsieur Perreault de l'Académie François. Suivant la Copie de Paris. Amsterdam: Jaques Desbordes, 1708.

Identical to 1700, but with the publisher's information on the title page. The first edition published under Jaques Desbordes's name. He died in 1716, after which his widow's name graced title pages until 1742 when Jaques, with the same spelling, reappeared (see next entry). [PML]

Histoires ou contes du temps passé avec des Moralitez. Par Mr. Perrault. Nouvelle édition augmentée par une nouvelle à la fin. Amsterdam: la Veuve Desbordes, 1721.

First edition published after Jaques Desbordes's death in 1716. Reorders the table of contents with "Petit chaperon rouge" first and "Belle au bois dormant" in fourth place. Most French and English editions

---

[5]Indiana University's Lilly Library has this edition and a copy dated 1697 as well, but indicates Moetjens as the likely publisher.

printed in the eighteenth century reproduced this order. Also first to include "L'Adroite princesse" by Marie-Jeanne Lhéritier, Perrault's niece, which continues henceforth to appear in editions by Desbordes and others. [Cotsen]

Contes de Monsieur Perrault. Avec des Moralitez. Nouvelle édition. Paris: Nicholas Gosselin, 1724.

Only the third edition to be issued in France "Avec Privilege du Roi," granted for three years. Uses the Veuve Barbin's 1707 title and 1697 table of contents with "Belle au bois" first, rare for the century except in the Troyes chapbook editions (see below). Gosselin removes the illustrations. The privilege, granted in 1723, notes that he also requested permission to print fairy tales by other writers: Charlotte-Rose de Caumont la Force, Henriette Julie de Murat, and Jacques Préchac, all contemporaries of Perrault. Reproduces the dedicatory epistle cartouche, simplified and only with the French: "Je suis belle et suis née pour être couronnée" (I am beautiful and was born to be crowned). [BL, BNF, PML]

Histoires ou contes du tems passé, avec les moralitez par le fils de Monsieur Perrault de l'Académie Françoise. Amsterdam: Estienne Roger, 1725.

Roger was known already to readers as a publisher of Marie-Catherine d'Aulnoy's fairy tales, *Les Contes des fées*, which he began issuing in the Netherlands in 1708. The press reprinted d'Aulnoy's collections four times until 1725, one of them in an eight-volume complete works (1717). This title takes the spelling of *tems* from the Desbordes edition of 1708. [PML]

Histoires ou contes du temps passé avec des Moralitez. Nouvelle édition augmentée par une nouvelle à la fin. Amsterdam: la Veuve Desbordes, 1729.

Reprint of the 1721 edition, published the same year as Robert Samber's first English-language translation. See "Early Translations" below. Appears to be the last printing by Desbordes. Cotsen has a 1771 copy credited to the publisher, but its provenance is suspect. [Cotsen]

Les Contes des fées de Monsieur Perrault.[6] Troyes: Pierre Garnier, 1737.

> Chapbook edition. Reprinted through at least 1760. The Troyes editions by Garnier and Oudot (below) mark the beginning of the chapbook or *bibliothèque bleue* editions of Perrault's tales and the use of the title *Contes des fées*, lifted from Marie-Catherine d'Aulnoy's 1698 volume of tales with that name. While these editions are attested in period catalogues, few are extant. The Troyes chapbooks are the rare eighteenth-century editions that reproduce the 1697 table of contents after the Veuve Desbordes reordered the tales in 1721. [Cotsen, 1760; Grand-Troyes, 1737]

Histoires ou contes du temps passé avec des Moralitez. Par M. Perrault. Nouvelle édition augmentée par une nouvelle à la fin. Drawings by Jacques de Sève, engraved by Simon Fokke. The Hague / Paris: Coustelier, 1742.

> Desbordes's table of contents. Fokke's frontispiece, new in this edition and reprinted with minor alteration throughout the century, changes the ethos of the iconic Mother Goose image. De Sève imitates the older-looking figures—the young woman and seated man—the cat, and the seventeenth-century fashions visible in the Clouzier, now two young children kneel before the teller and one young man stands behind them. They are modestly dressed in the style of the teller. They are also reversed, as in the 1697 Amsterdam, Desbordes, and Samber editions. Fokke's illustrations were reprinted frequently: Neaulme 1745, Bassompierre 1777, Lamy 1781, and Le Francq 1785, and in Van Os's 1754 bilingual editions.[7] [Cotsen]

Histoires ou contes du tems passé avec des Moralitez. Par M. Perrault. Nouvelle édition augmentée par une nouvelle à la fin. Amsterdam: Jaques Desbordes, 1742.

> Title spelled as in 1708. Considered a pirated copy of The Hague 1742 edition.[8] Includes a rare change in the wording of "Petit chaperon rouge,"

---

[6]This title graces a number of volumes listed here and more than thirty-five undated chapbook editions published in Paris, Troyes, Rouen, Lille, Lyon, Toulouse, Avignon, Montbéliard, Montereau, and Douai.

[7]Henry Cohen's collectors' guide to illustrated books attributes all the illustrations to Fokke, linking this edition to the Neaulme bilingual edition of 1745 and the Bassompierre French edition of 1777 (*Guide de l'amateur de livres*, 448–49). Perrault does not appear in the 1870 edition of the guide, Cohen's first edition.

[8]See Christie's auction notes for the 2014 sale of copy of this edition: www.christies.com/lotfinder/books-manuscripts/perrault-charles-histoires-ou-contes-du-5814427-details.aspx.

wherein the little village girl (*petite fille de village*) becomes a little city girl (*petite fille de ville*). Reprinted in 1771. [PML, Cotsen 1771]

Les Contes des fées de Monsieur Perrault. Troyes: Jean Oudot, 1756.[9]

Like Garnier's edition (above), used the 1697 table of contents. According to nineteenth-century bibliographies, this edition was also sold bound with other books and sold by the publisher as a large volume.[10] [PML]

Histoires ou contes du temps passé, avec des moralités, par M. Perrault. Nouvelle édition augmentée d'une nouvelle et d'une fable. Illustrated by Simon Fokke. The Hague / Liège: Jean-François Bassompierre, 1777.

Fine edition with red and black print on the title page. Reproduces the Desbordes 1721 table of contents with illustrations from the 1742 Coustelier edition.[11] First edition to feature both the novella by Lhéritier and a new tale, "La Veuve et ses deux filles" (The Widow and Her Two Daughters), by Jeanne-Marie Leprince de Beaumont. Author of "La Belle et la Bête" (Beauty and the Beast), Leprince de Beaumont wrote a series of didactic tales under the title *Magasin des enfants*, which Bassompierre had published in 1762.[12] Called a "fable" in this volume, the story is attributed to Leprince de Beaumont in a footnote on the tale's title page. In 1777, Bassompierre also published the complete works of Jean-François Marmontel, known as the progenitor of the moral tale. [BNF]

Contes des fées, par Charles Perrault de l'Académie françoise. Nouvelle édition. 3 volumes. Paris: Pierre-Michel Lamy, 1781.

Reproduces the Desbordes 1721 table of contents of the *Histoires ou Contes* with Lhéritier's novella. Includes for the first time Perrault's

---

[9]Appears in Pierre Champion's edition of the *Catalogue de la bibliothèque de Marcel Schwob* with the date 1723 (Paris: Editions Allia, 1993), 87, but I have not seen it attested elsewhere. Welch erroneously lists the publisher as "Veuve de Jean Oudor" (*Bibliography*, 61). The only extant copy at the Pierpont Morgan Library, referenced here, was printed by Oudot in 1756.

[10]A copy bound together with seven other books in a large volume (#257) is mentioned in Léon Techener's *Bibliothèque champenoise* (Paris: L. Techener, 1886), 82. Techener's bibliography of literature of the old province of Champagne, which includes Troyes, covers the sixteenth to the nineteenth centuries. The 1756 Oudot is the only volume of Perrault's tales that appears in it.

[11]Cohen, *Guide de l'amateur de livres,* 448.

[12]Jeanne-Marie Leprince de Beaumont made a living as a governess in England. She published stories for her charges, all elite young women, in the four-volume *Le Magasin des enfants ou Dialogues entre une sage gouvernante et plusieurs de ses élèves de grande distinction* (London: J. Haberkorn, 1756), which included both "La Veuve et ses deux filles" and "La Belle et la Bête." That edition does not appear to be extant, which makes Basssompierre's the oldest surviving French versions.

verse tales—"Grisélidis," "Peau d'âne," and "Les Souhaits ridicules"—
for a total of twelve texts. Frontispiece and woodcuts after Fokke and
identified as "original" by Lamy. Very luxurious edition on velum
with gilded pages and silk moiré lining on the inside covers. "Peau
d'âne" has been done in French prose. Tale vignettes adapted from
the Coustelier 1742 Fokke plates, with verse illustrations done by
Didot after Fournier and Martinet.[13] Lamy takes this title from the
chapbook tradition, drops the formality of M. or Monsieur, and dedicates it to "Son Altesse Sérénissime Mgr. le Duc de Montpensier," or
Louis Philippe Joseph d'Orléans. His Most Serene Highness Monsei-
gneur le Duc supported the French Revolution, changing his family
name to Equality and going by Citizen Equality (Citoyen Égalité),
but fell by guillotine under the Reign of Terror. In the dedication,
which follows Pierre Darmancour's style, Lamy invites the duc, "Allow yourself a smile, Monsieur, for the measures truth took years
ago to instruct and please."[14] The texts are preceded by a "Précis"
that gives the reader background on Perrault, the collection, and a
summary of each story's plot and meaning. Lamy printed a single
copy of this edition on velum for Madame royale, Marie Thérèse
Charlotte, oldest child of Louis XVI and Marie Antoinette and first
princess of France, according to the publisher's note on the back of
its title page.[15] [BNF, velum and first edition; Lilly, first and second
edition (1782)]

Contes des fées. Par Charles Perrault de l'Académie française. Paris: André, An
huitième [1799].

Produced in the eighth year of the First French Republic after the
Revolution (founded in 1792). Rare edition that includes the verse
tale "Peau d'âne" and Lhéritier's tale "L'Adroite princesse." Illustrated
with richly colored plates of scenes not often depicted in the eigh-

---

[13]Perhaps because of its dedicatee, this edition was already listed as rare and highly collectible
in the nineteenth century. According to period catalogues, it was worth far more to collectors
circa 1880 than contemporaneous editions—Bassompierre 1777 and Le Francq 1785, for example—with finely bound copies fetching astronomical sums above 4,000 francs (Cohen, *Guide
de l'amateur de livres*, 449). The listings attest to the recognition of Perrault as a collector's item
in the second half of the nineteenth century.

[14]"Daignez sourire, Monsieur, aux moyens que la vérité prenoit autrefois pour instruire et
plaire." Dedicatory epistle, "A Monsieur le Duc de Montpensier," signed by Lamy. The English
translation is mine.

[15]The Arsenal has an earlier printing (not on velum) under the title *Histoires ou contes du temps
passé, avec des moralités, par M. Perrault. Nouvelle édition.* The Hague / Paris: Lamy, 1778.

teenth century, such as Petit chaperon rouge talking to the wolf in the forest instead of being eaten by him in bed, and Cendrillon putting on the slipper at the end of the tale instead of losing it at the ball. That image of Petit chaperon rouge replaces the image of the old woman teller to serve as the frontispiece. Includes the speech given by the prince in the 1696 *Mercure galant* version of "La Belle au bois dormant" that had not been seen for a century. The volume's publication under the Republican flag seems to have inspired a return to the earliest editions of Perrault's tales, though it follows the Desbordes table of contents.[16] In "An IX" (1800), H. Tardieu reprinted the volume in Paris with the truncated title *Contes des fées*. As a testament to the rapidly evolving political landscape at the turn of the century, an 1815 edition with the same title published in Paris by Salmon returned to the earlier frontispiece and dressed the figures in empire fashion.[17] [Osborne]

Contes des fées. Par Perrault. Nouvelle édition ornée de cent trente vignettes, Dessinées par MM. Tony Johannot, A. Devéria, [Jean] Gigoux, Thomas, Célestin Nanteuil, etc., et gravées par Lacoste jeune. Brussels: Méline, Cans, et cie, 1837.

Published in the Bibliothèque des familles series. Late example of the Troyes title still attached to Perrault. Identifies itself as the first volume for children with "worthy" illustrations, done by major French artist-illustrators of the period.[18] Beginning of the period in which Perrault comes to be identified only by his last name. Following Jacob and Wilhelm Grimm, the introduction to this volume presents him as "The author, or rather the collector of these simple narratives" (L'auteur ou plutôt le collecteur de ces narrations naïves) from what the press calls the old Breton traditions. The editor demonstrates the immense celebrity of the book in France, noting that "50,000

---

[16]Catherine Velay-Vallantin has discussed a Port-Malo edition of 1799 held in a private collection whose frontispiece depicts both the teller and the listeners in Republican clothing. Catherine Velay-Vallantin, "Charles Perrault, la conteuse et la fabuliste: 'L'Image dans le tapis,'" *Féeries* 7 (2010), feeries.revues.org/759.

[17]Reprinted in Le Men, "Mother Goose Illustrated," 30. She rightly notes that as of the period of this edition, the spindle of the earlier illustrations is replaced by a book from which the woman reads (35). She also wears spectacles, which reappear in Doré's illustrations.

[18]They include giants of literary illustration Johannot (Rousseau, Alfred de Vigny, Hugo) and Gigoux (*Gil Blas*, 1836), and the odd choice of Devéria, known for his explicitly sexual lithographs.

copies of this little book are printed each year in Tours and Limoges" (cinquante mille exemplaires de ce petit livre sortent, chaque année, des imprimeries de Tours et de Limoges) for children. The exaggeration notwithstanding, this characterization of Perrault's popularity with a young audience in the second quarter of the century is worthy of note. [Held at a variety of libraries, including Houghton][19]

Ulliac-Trémadeure, Sophie. *Contes de ma mère l'oie dédiés aux grands et aux petits enfans*. Illustrated by Charles Chandellier. Paris: J. Bréauté, 1842. 12 plates.

Rare collection of stories from the period published with a Mother Goose title formally associated with Perrault but containing entirely original tales by Sophie Ulliac-Trémadeure. Later in the century, the name's history was recovered, partially thanks to folklorist Charles Deulin and the celebrity of the Mother Goose rhymes.[20] See "Early Collections" below. [BNF]

Les Contes de Perrault. Illustrated by Gustave Doré. Paris: J. Hetzel, 1862.

The most iconic edition of the *Contes* ever produced. Doré's illustrations have, more than those of the 1697 edition, come to characterize the ethos of Perrault's fairy tales for modern readers. Although the text marks the apotheosis of Perrault in French print history, crediting him with "incomparable" talent and making folktales "immortal," the table of contents is not based on that of 1697. Instead P. J. Stahl's introduction links French literary genius to brevity: "Indeed, all intellectual works should be brief."[21] The idea takes concrete form in Hetzel's volume, which opens with the "little" tales: "Petit chaperon rouge" followed by "Petit poucet." "Barbe bleue," the most vicious tale, replaces "Petit poucet" in last place. The unusual inclusion of "Peau d'âne," (Donkey Skin), no doubt a pleasure to illustrate, gives the volume nine tales. [BNF]

---

[19]The Houghton copy has been digitized: hdl.handle.net/2027/hvd.hwtq3w.

[20]See Charles Deulin, *Les Contes de ma mère l'oye avant Perrault* (Paris: E. Dentu, 1878). In his introduction, Deulin addresses the preoccupation of folklorists of the period with tales, and with Perrault's in particular: "a subject that is fashionable to treat today from a philosophical and ethnographic perspective" (un sujet qu'il est de mode aujourd'hui de traiter au point de vue philologique et ethnographique) (1). The English translation is mine.

[21]"Toute œuvre d'esprit doit être courte, en effet" (xxiv). The English translation is mine.

EARLY TRANSLATIONS

Histories, or tales of past times: viz. I. The Little Red Riding-Hood. II. The Fairy. III. The Blue Beard. IV. The Sleeping Beauty in the Wood. V. The Master Cat, or Puss in Boots. VI. Cinderilla, or the Little Glass Slipper. VII. Riquet a la houpe. VIII. Little Poucet, and his Brothers. IX. The Discreet Princess, or the Adventures of Finetta. With morals. By M. Perrault. Translated into English. Translated by Robert Samber. London: J. Pote and R. Montagu, 1729.

The first translation of Perrault's tales, based on the Desbordes 1721 edition. Printed with Clouzier's 1697 woodcuts from the Desbordes. As in the simple French edition of 1700, the frontispiece image is printed in reverse. Follows the table of contents in Desbordes after 1721, with "Petit chaperon rouge" first. Robert Samber (1682–c.1745) was a writer and translator of eclectic texts, including a Dutch treatise on midwifery (1716) and *Venus in the Cloister* (1724), an erotic satire against the Catholic Church first published in France in the 1680s.[22] Samber's translation of "Cendrillon" is "Cinderilla," which endures until the beginning of the nineteenth century (see Tabart 1804 below). He did not translate the French dedication and instead wrote his own to the Countess of Granville. This edition also contains the first translation of Lhéritier's "L'Adroite princesse," printed in the 1721 Debordes, dedicated to "the Right Honorable Lady Mary Wortley Montagu."[23] Subsequent English-language editions until the early nineteenth century nearly all reproduce Samber's translations with minor alterations, even those credited to "Guy Miège" (see below). Finally, Samber called the wolf "wicked" (for *méchant*), that legendary fearsome identity by which he was henceforth known. [Houghton, PML]

Histories or tales of passed times. With Morals . . . By M. Perrault. Englished by R.S. Gent. The Second Edition, Corrected. With Cuts to Every Tale. Translated by Robert Samber. 2nd edition. London: R. Montagu / Eton: J. Pote, 1737.

---

[22]On Samber's writings and political connections, particularly to Freemasonry, see Paul Kléber Monod, *Solomon's Secret Arts: The Occult in the Age of Enlightenment* (New Haven: Yale University Press, 2013), 182–87.
[23]Samber's translation of Lhéritier's tale was also published in a single-story edition: *The Discreet Princess, or the Adventures of Finetta. A Novel* (London, 1755). [BL]

From the second edition on, errata printed in the previous edition were corrected with some rewriting. This volume is bilingual, the sole printing of the Montagu and Pote edition with the French on facing pages. The French is identified on the title page as "Troisième Edition," or 1721, thus of the Desbordes. Pote and Montagu put out a third edition of the English in 1741,[24] then from the fourth on they were issued by other publishers, whose editions are numbered descending from this one and credited to Samber until the nineteenth century. The *London Magazine* advertised its publication by Montagu under the title *Mother Goose's Tales* in July 1737 for the price of 1 shilling, 6 pence.[25] The 1741 edition identifies the author as "Mr. Perrault of the French Academy of Sciences" and was sold for the same price. [Bodleian, 1737; Cotsen, 1737 and 1741]

Contes de ma mère l'Oye. Mother Goose's Tales. Illustrated by Simon Fokke. The Hague: Neaulme, 1745.

First bilingual edition published in Holland. First use of the name of Perrault's 1695 manuscript and repeats Desbordes's table of contents. New translation of several titles: Le Petit chaperon rouge / Pretty Miss Red-Cap; La Belle au bois dormant / The fair sleeper in the wood; Le Maitre chat, ou, Le Chat botté / The witty cat, or, The cat in boots; Cendrillon, ou, La Petite pantoufle de verre / The Ash-maid, or, The glass slipper; Riquet à la houpe / Sir Ugly Tufted. Fokke illustrations from Coustelier 1742. Does not seem to have been impactful on the translation tradition. [Cotsen, Houghton]

Contes de ma mère l'Oye en français et en hollandais. The Hague, 1747.

Perhaps the first bilingual French/Dutch edition, but not listed in Dutch bibliographies. Translator unknown. [Arsenal]

Contes de ma mère l'Oye. Vertellingen van moeder de gans. Met negen keurlyke koopere plaatjes: zeer dienstig voor de jeugdt om haar zelve in het Fransch

---

[24]The third edition appears to be the first to contain an illustrated "Discreet Princess." See the Cotsen catalogue entry.

[25]The *London Magazine: and Monthly Chronologer 1737*, vol. 6 (London: Cox, Clarke, & Astley, 1737). This volume contains the full year of the monthly for 1737, which corresponds to its sixth year of publication. Available as an ebook: play.google.com/store/books.

en Hollands te oeffenen. Seevende druk. Illustrated by Simon Fokke. The Hague: Pierre van Os, 1754.

Considered the first bilingual Dutch edition and explicit in the title about its linguistic applications: "Very helpful to children for practicing French and Dutch" (my translation). To that end, some outdated language and spelling was changed.[26] Includes nine illustrations by Simon Fokke from the Coustelier 1742 edition. Translator unknown. Van Os reprinted the French/Dutch in 1759 and issued the sixth edition in 1765, then also published a bilingual French/English edition (below). [KB]

Contes de ma mere L'Oye. Vertellingen van moeder de gans. Met negen keurlyke koopere plaatjes: zeer dienstig voor de jeugdt om haar zelve in het Fransch en Hollands te oeffenen. Seevende druk. Illustrated by Simon Fokke. Frontispiece by Hendrik Immink. The Hague: Pierre van Os, 1759.

Reprinted from the 1754 edition with a new frontispiece and illustrations after Fokke by Immink, not all signed. Immink chooses different moments to illustrate for several tales and has the prince in "Belle au bois dormant" enter what looks like a harem with the princess's entourage sleeping at the side and base of the bed in loose fabrics draped to expose one breast. [KB 1759 and Cotsen 1765]

Histories or Tales of Passed Times, Told by Mother Goose. Englished by G.M. Gent. Third edition, corrected. Salisbury: Benjamin C. Collins / London: William Bristow / Devizes: Mrs. Maynard, 1763.

Identifies itself as the third edition, perhaps since the Pote/Montagu Samber translation of 1729 (a spot also occupied by the Pote/Montagu 1741 edition), as there are no earlier Collins printings attested in catalogues. An advert for the volume in the August 22, 1763, issue of the *Salisbury and Winchester Journal* indicates in a nota bene that "short extracts have been published of some of the above Tales in various Books, but here they are altogether and complete" (4), suggesting that this is the first complete Collins edition. The same advert appeared again in 1766.

---

[26]On ways in which Van Os updated the French, see Daphne M. Hoogenboezem, "Du salon littéraire à la chambre d'enfant: Réécritures des contes de fées français aux Pays-Bas," *Féeries* 8 (2011): 102, feeries.revues.org/799.

Collins made two lasting changes to the Samber legacy. First, he translated *coutelas* in "The Blue Beard" (rendered as "cutlass" by Samber) as "scimitar." This detail initiates a practice of identifying the main character of the tale as Middle Eastern that thrives in the English print tradition with later versions actually setting the tale in Arabia.[27] Second, he wrote footnotes for two terms in "Sleeping Beauty," presumably construed as too culturally French to be understood by English readers: an ogre "is a giant, with long teeth and claws, with a raw head and bloody bones, who runs away with naughty little boys and girls, and eats them up," and *sauce Robert* "is a *French* sauce, made with onions shred and boiled tender in butter, to which is added vinegar, mustard, pepper, and a little wine." These notes are reprinted in several later editions including Le Francq 1785. Collins also credited the translation to one G.M. Gent. [gentleman], who henceforth shared the limelight with Samber as English translator of Perrault. Later editors identified the initials with Guy Miège, although his full name never appears in a period title.[28] Miège was a Swiss lexicographer of some repute (1644–1718?), who made his career in England and produced a series of dictionaries and a grammar in French for language learners: *A New Dictionary French and English* (1677) and *The Great French Dictionary* (1688). While the *Oxford Guide to Literature in English Translation* recently identified Miège as the author of the posthumous translation and Samber as the pseudonym, the Opies argued convincingly in 1974 that incorrect dating of the first G.M. edition led to this misconception.[29] Indeed, the translations in this edition are not substantially different from Samber's, as the numbering of the edition implies, and include his 1729 spelling of "Cinderilla" and his translation of "Discreet Princess" by Marie-Jeanne Lhéritier de Villandon, which remained the only translation of this tale printed in the eighteenth century. Fairy-tale scholars today accept Samber as the translator, but the initials G.M., if not the name Miège, appear on every reprint of Collins (under his name and others) through the early nineteenth

---

[27]On the Orientalizing of the tale of "Blue Beard" over the eighteenth and nineteenth centuries, see Casie E. Hermansson, *Bluebeard: A Reader's Guide to the English Tradition* (Jackson: University Press of Mississippi, 2009).

[28]For more on Miège, see "Portrait d'un dictionnaire révolutionnaire: Le *New Dictionary French and English* de Guy Miège," *Seventeenth-Century French Studies* 30, no. 2 (2008): 154–69. Samber had also been associated with licentious literature and perhaps considered a less interesting source to publicize than Guy Miège (see above).

[29]France, *Oxford Guide to Literature in English Translation,* 108; Opie and Opie, *The Classic Fairy Tales,* 24n1.

century.[30] Collins reprinted this edition at least twelve times up to 1802.[31] The earliest extant reprint appears to be 1769. [BL, 1802; BNF, 1780; Cotsen, 1769; Lilly, 1777–99]

Contes du tems passé de Ma Mère l'Oye. Avec des Moralités. Augmentée d'une nouvelle, viz. L'adroite princesse / Tales of passed times by Mother Goose with morals, Englished by R.S. London: S. van den Berg, 1764.

Bilingual edition that borrows and alters Desbordes's title, also truncating the English, which influenced later editions, as several feature this title. In spite of the "R.S." [Robert Samber] in the title, the catalogue of the British Library credits the translation of the tales (but not Lhéritier's novella) to Guy Miège. [BL]

Tales of Passed Times by Mother Goose. Englished by R.S. To which is added a new one, viz. The Discreet Princess / Contes du Tems passé de ma mere l'Oye. Avec des Morales. Augmentée d'une nouvelle, viz. L'adroite princesse. 6th edition. London: J. Melvil, 1764.

Also uses the altered Desbordes's title. Counts itself as sixth edition since 1729. [Cotsen]

Mother Goose's tales in French and English: with morals, written by M. Perrault and Englished by R.S. 6th edition. The Hague: Pierre van Os, sold by J. Pridden, London, 1765.

Bilingual edition by the same publisher that issued a French/Dutch translation in 1754. [Cotsen, PML]

Histories, or, Tales of past times told by Mother Goose: with morals / written in French by M. Perrault, and Englished by G.M. gent. Fifth edition, corrected. Salisbury: Benjamin Collins / John Newbery and Charles Carnan, 1769.

Fifth edition counting from the 1763 Collins third edition and the first extant of the series.[32] Newbery's name, which appears alongside Col-

---

[30] If G.M. is indeed a reference to Guy Miège, we might speculate that the midcentury impulse to invoke his authority was part of Collins's marketing scheme. The initials G.M. are also a reversal of those of Mother Goose.

[31] The Opie bibliography lists an eleventh edition in 1799.

[32] Editions of 1777, 1780, 1783, 1791, and 1799 held at the Lilly Library of Indiana University are identified as the seventh through eleventh under the G.M. attribution published by Collins et al.

lins here, figures prominently in the history of literature marketed to a young readership. As a young bookseller, John Newbery launched the Juvenile Library series: small books for young readers in bound, attractive editions more durable than those issued as chapbooks.[33] Benjamin Collins and John Newbery collaborated on a series of intellectual books for children with the title the Circle of the Sciences (1745).[34] Newbery also famously published *The Original Mother Goose's Melody* along with *Short Stories for the Improvement of the Mind* circa 1760 (see below, 1892). Editions that reprint the Collins/Newbery title through the early nineteenth century attribute the translation to "G.M."[35] [Costen]

Mother Goose's Histories or Tales of Times Past. Containing I. The little red riding-hood. II. The fairy. III. Blue beard. London: C. Sympson, 1775.

Title unique in its pairing of Mother Goose and "histories." Features only three of Perrault's eight tales, chosen perhaps because they are the shortest. Possibly the chapbook edition of the Le Francq that Cotsen has bound with other titles. See 1785 below. [BL, NLS]

Histories, or, Tales of past times told by Mother Goose: with morals. Written in French by M. Perrault, and Englished by G.M. gent. Eighth edition. Salisbury: Benjamin Collins, Johnson, and S. Crowder, 1780.

Tiny embossed example of the Collins edition with multicolored cover. Features very primitive woodcuts based on Clouzier (not Fokke), with the young woman in seventeenth-century dress. Images are reversed, as in Desbordes/Samber, and footnotes are present. An advertisement for a conduct book on the back page gives insight into the audience

---

[33] As an innovative marketing venture, the Juvenile Library series has been widely credited with inspiring the reading and book-purchasing habits of children and their parents in the eighteenth century. See the introduction to John Thomas Gillespie and Corinne J. Naden's *The Newbery Companion: Booktalk and Related Materials for Newbery Medal and Honor Books* (Greenwood Village, CO: Libraries Unlimited / Greenwood, 2001), xiv.

[34] On this collaboration, see Christine Y. Ferdinand, *Benjamin Collins and the Provincial Newspaper Trade in the Eighteenth Century* (Oxford: Oxford University Press, 1997), 39–42.

[35] A 1763 issue of the *Salisbury Journal* advertised the first English-language edition of *Mother Goose's Tales* credited to G.M. Gent. It listed Perrault as author and promoted the volume as "the cheapest as well as most entertaining story book ever yet published." *Salisbury and Winchester Journal*, August 22, 1763, 4. The British Newspaper Archive, in partnership with the British Library: www.britishnewspaperarchive.co.uk/. Sources attest to an earlier advert in the *Public Ledger* (1756), but I have not been able to verify it.

addressed by this volume: *The Polite Academy, or, Social Behavior for Young Gentlemen and Ladies. Intended as a Foundation of Good Manner and Polite Address* (London: Baldwin, Crowder; Salisbury: Collins, 1780). [BNF, Lilly]

The histories of passed times or The Tales of Mother Goose. With morals, by M. Perrault. A new edition, to which are added two novels, viz. The discreet princess, and the Widow and her two daughters / Histoires du temps passé, ou les Contes de Ma Mère l'Oye avec des Moralités, par M. Perrault. Nouvelle édition augmentée de deux nouvelles, savoir: de l'Adroite princesse, et la Veuve et ses deux filles. Illustrated with footnotes. London, sold in Brussels: Benoît Le Francq, 1785. 2 vols. 9 plates.

Published as early as 1775 as a chapbook bound with other miscellany [Cotsen]. Illustrator unknown. Reproduces Samber's translations, including "Cinderilla," with certain changes. Includes Collins's translation of scimitar for "coutelas," spelled "scimetar." Reprints Fokke illustrations, linking this edition back to the Coustelier. First edition to feature a translation of Leprince de Beaumont's "La Veuve et ses deux filles" (The Widow and Her Two Daughters), credited in catalogues to Miège.[36] Le Francq, like Collins, includes footnotes. Le Francq translates Lhéritier's dedication of "L'Adroite princesse" to the Comtesse de Murat. Earlier editions reproduced Samber's dedication, which was not a translation of the one that appeared in French but a new one addressed to Lady Mary Montagu. [BL, BRB, Lilly and Osborne]

Tales of Past Times, by Old Mother Goose. With morals. Gainsbrough/London: W. Osborne, J. Griffin, and J. Mozley, 1786.

Claims to be the 22nd edition of this translation, which attests to the widespread acknowledgement and continual reprinting of the Samber translation as the source text in English. The appearance of the word "scimitar" also links it to the Collins edition. [Cotsen]

Fairy Tales, or Histories of Past Times. With Morals. Haverhill, MA: Peter Edes, 1794.

---

[36] Leprince de Beaumont also did her own translation of *Le Magasin des enfants* in 1759 under the title *The Young Misses Magazine, Containing Dialogues between a Governess and Several Young Ladies of Quality, Her Scholars.*

Chapbook based on Samber, with "Cinderilla." Perhaps the first trans-lation published in the United States[37] and an early use in English of Marie-Catherine d'Aulnoy's title *Contes des fées*, popularized by the Troyes chapbook editions: "fairy tales." [AAS]

Tales of Past Times, by Mother Goose, with Morals, written in French by M. Perrault, and Englished by R.S. Gent. Illustrated by Alexander Anderson. 7th edition. New York: J. Rivington, 1795.

Perhaps the first bilingual edition published in the United States, and a reprint of a British or Dutch edition (possibly Melvil, 1764). In 1890, William Whitmore (see footnote 55 below) identified it as the sev-enth edition of a London publication and the first in the United States. Barchilon and Flinders identify it as a "luxuriously illustrated edi-tion."[38] This is presumably the edition owned by Andrew Lang, which he mentions in his introduction to *Perrault's Tales* and which helped him reconstruct the early translation history of the volume, and it is the one that appears in the 1892 *Original Mother Goose's Melody*. See "Early Collections" below. [AAS, Houghton]

Tales of passed times by Mother Goose with morals. Written in French by M. Perrault, and Englished by R.S. gent. To which is added a new one, viz. The discreet princess. London: T. Boosey, 1796.

Bilingual edition, listed by Cotsen as seventh edition, but may be the eighth after the Rivington. Credited in the British Library catalogue to Guy Miège. [BL, Cotsen]

Fairy Tales, or Histories of Past Times. Containing The little Red Riding Hood. The fairy. Blue Beard. The sleeping beauty of the wood. The master cat, or Puss in boots. Cinderilla, or The little glass-slipper. Riquet with the tuft. Little Thumb (Price Twelve Cents). New York: John Harrison, 1798.

Listed by Cotsen as the third American edition. The edition cost roughly one-third to one-half a day's wage for Northeast mill or shoe factory workers.[39] [Bodleian, Cotsen]

---

[37]Cotsen gives a date of 1793 for the chapbook edition published at Haverhill. Welch lists it as the first edition (*Bibliography*, 321).

[38]Barchilon and Flinders, *Charles Perrault*, 91.

[39]See Stanley Lebergott, "Wage Trends, 1800–1900," in *Trends in the American Economy in the Nineteenth Century*, Conference on Research in Income and Wealth (Princeton: Princeton Uni-versity), 451, www.nber.org/chapters/c2486.

Mother Goose's Fairy Tales. Edinburgh: J. Morren, c. 1800.

The first use of this title, which takes its cue from Newbery's 1760 *Mother Goose's Melody.* May have been reprinted in 1817 by R. Hutchison in Glasgow at the time when Lumsden & Son published chapbooks of the collection (see below).[40] [BL]

Tales of Passed Times: by Mother Goose. Written in French by M. Perrault. To which is added, The Discreet Princess. Edinburgh: John Moir for S. Cheyne, 1800.

Picks up Melvil's 1764 English title, also used by Boosey 1796. Reproduces Samber's edition without the woodcuts.[41] [BL, Cotsen]

Histories, or, Tales of past times: told by Mother Goose: with morals / written in French by M. Perrault and Englished by G.M. Gent. London: John Harris, c. 1803.

Harris was successor to Elizabeth Newbery at John Newbery's Juvenile Library and would go on to reprint the whole collection and then issue many of Perrault's tales in single-story editions (see below). This version of Samber's title had been modified only slightly for the Newbery 1769 edition (*Histories, or, Tales of past times told by Mother Goose*). Illustrations attributed to Isaac Cruikshank, satirist/illustrator and the father of George Cruikshank, the famed caricaturist/illustrator of Dickens and translator/illustrator of Perrault (see "Early Collections" below). [Lilly]

Histories, or Tales of past times: told by Mother Goose, with morals. Written in French by M. Perrault and Englished by G.M. Gent. London: John Harris, c. 1810.

A reprint of the circa 1803 edition, perhaps produced less expensively, and a late appearance of "G.M." still associated with translations of Perrault's fairy tales. No frontispiece and simple woodcut illustrations that showcase the period clothing, notably an empire waist, worn by female characters since Tabart's 1804 editions for the Juvenile Library. [Osborne]

---

[40]Welch, *Bibliography,* 62.
[41]The Cotsen catalogue identifies it with the Newbery/Harris edition.

Fairy tales of past times from Mother Goose. Glasgow: J. Lumsden & Son, 1814.

> First use of this title, a combination of the Edinburgh editions by Cheyne and Morren. Lumsden & Son produced chapbooks and higher-priced editions. Perrault's collection was published as a tiny inexpensive chapbook with woodcut vignettes in the Ross's Juvenile Library series. Contains only "Little Red Riding Hood," "Blue Beard," "The Fairy," and "Cinderilla." The press reproduces Samber's translation with "Cinderilla," but credits neither Perrault nor Samber on the title page. The frontispiece credits instead "Old Mother Goose," who delights "good boys and girls." [Osborne]

The entertaining tales of Mother Goose: for the amusement of youth: embelished with elegant engravings. Glasgow: J. Lumsden & Son, c. 1815.

> A larger and finer chapbook edition than the 1814, this includes "Riquet with the Tuft." The same year, the firm issued an adapted version of Swift's satire under the title *The adventures of Captain Gulliver in a voyage to Lilliput*, and in 1818 a single-story edition of Leprince de Beaumont's "Beauty and the Beast." [Osborne]

The Celebrated Tales of Mother Goose. London: John Harris, 1817.

> This series of titles characterizing Mother Goose as entertaining and celebrated emphasizes the legendary quality of this figure—along with the allegory for Marie-Catherine d'Aulnoy, Mother Bunch—in publishing by the early nineteenth century. Appropriately, it is bound together with *The Celebrated fairy tales of Mother Bunch, now republished with appropriate engravings, for the amusement of those little masters and misses, who, by duty to their parents, and obedience to their superiors, are likely to become great lords and ladies*. [Iona and Peter Opie Collection]

The Renowned Tales of Mother Goose: as originally related. London: John Harris, 1829.

> New title at a veteran press, attesting to the popularity of the collection at the quarter century. Harris's press produced single-tale editions of Perrault's tales as well. See also Harris's use of the Mother Goose figure in 1823 in "Early Collections." [Osborne]

The Good child's fairy gift: with numerous illustrations. Boston: Phillips, Sampson & Company, 1852.

Three tales by Perrault—"Cinderella, or the Little Glass Slipper," "Blue Beard," and "Little Red Riding Hood"—printed together as part of the Nursery Fairy Books series, numbers 1–3. Phillips, Sampson & Co. published Shakespeare's drama and poetry in 1846 (reprinting the work in 1850–51), published Harriet Beecher Stowe from 1854 to 1858, and launched the *Atlantic Monthly* (now the *Atlantic*) in 1857. [Houghton]

Perrault's Popular Tales. Translated by Henry Frowde. Illustrated by Adolphe Lalauze. Introduction by Andrew Lang. Oxford: Clarendon Press, 1888.

Andrew Lang's introduction to this edition served as a source for late-century information about the print history of Perrault's volume in English. Samber had yet to be formally identified as the first translator at this time. Lang's argument for a translation as early as 1729 rests on two pieces of evidence: (1) a comment to him by one Austin Dobson, who himself references only a note in the March 1729 issue of the *Monthly Chronicle*[42] advertising a translation by "Mr. Samber" published for J. Pote: and (2) his own copy of the 1795 Rivington edition, which lists "R. S. Gent." as the translator. Lang's reconstruction efforts offer humbling insight into the painstaking recovery of early print history in the nineteenth century. [Osborne]

The Tales of Mother Goose, as first collected by Charles Perrault in 1696. Translated by Charles Welsh. Illustrated by D. J. Munro after Doré. Boston / New York / Chicago: D.C. Heath and Co., 1901.[43]

The title comes from the version included in the Damrell/Thomas/Newbery edition of *The Original Mother Goose's Melody* published with Perrault's tales (see "Early Collections" below). In his intro-

---

[42] Perhaps the *Monthly Catalogue*, an eighteenth-century magazine that published new titles for the London market. Issues from 1723 to 1730 are now bound together in one volume that has been digitized. March 1729 does not contain the notice mentioned by Lang. *Monthly Catalogue, being a general register of books, sermons, plays, poetry and pamphlets, printed and published in London, or the universities*, vols. 3–4, 1727–30, facsimile (London: Printed for John Wilford, 1964), babel.hathitrust.org/cgi/pt?id=chi.78599965;view=1up;seq=381.

[43] www.gutenberg.org/files/17208/17208-h/17208-h.htm.

duction, Michael Vincent (M.V.) O'Shea pitches these fairy tales as "concrete living examples" of "supreme worth in individual and social life" for the young. A scholar of childhood development at the University of Wisconsin, he describes Welsh's style as close to "the style of the early chap-book versions" without the "the pompous, stilted language and Johnsonian phraseology so fashionable when they were first translated." [Held at a variety of libraries, including the Houghton and Osborne]

Old-Time Stories Told by Master Charles Perrault. Translated by Alfred Edwin Johnson. Illustrated by William Heath Robinson. New York: Dodd, Mead, & Co., 1921.

A prefatory note situates "Master" Perrault as an intellectual involved in the great Quarrel of the Ancients and Moderns who will be familiar to students of French literature. Fashionable illustrations, the matter-of-fact tone of the translation, and the artful layout of the book suggest at least a young adult readership. Includes Perrault's eight tales, "Beauty and the Beast" by Leprince de Beaumont, and "Princess Rosette" and "The friendly frog" by d'Aulnoy. [Held at various libraries, including the Beinecke, Cotsen, and Osborne]

The Fairy Tales of Charles Perrault. Illustrated by Harry Clarke with an introduction by Thomas Bodkin. Translated by Robert Samber. Translation revised and corrected by J. E. Mansion. London: George G. Harrap and Company, 1922.

A late edition formally credited to Robert Samber and "corrected" by Mansion. Correction in this sense means overlaying the 1729 translation with early modern English ("'tis" and "thee") that rings older than Samber's. Here again the wolf is called "wicked," an identity he will retain throughout the twentieth century. The long introduction by Bodkin (discussed in my introduction) provides a biography of Perrault's life. Clarke's black-and-white couples are drawn in the lanky lines of art nouveau and ballet. A striking vignette ushers in the list of illustrations with a couple doing a pas de deux. This edition is available online as an ebook through Google Books and in a 2012 reedition. [BL]

EARLY COLLECTIONS FEATURING PERRAULT'S FAIRY TALES

The history of the tales of the fairies. Newly done from the French. Translated from the French of the Countess d'Aulnoy. Dublin: R. Cross, 1785.

> Contains "Blue Beard," "Little Red Riding-Hood," and "Master Cat, or Puss in Boots." This was an early appearance of Perrault's tales alongside those of Marie-Catherine d'Aulnoy's under the translation of her title, "contes des fées," which was first used for Perrault's collection in the Troyes bibliothèque bleue editions of the 1730s. See "Early Francophone Editions" above. Multiauthor editions credited to Perrault or d'Aulnoy would serve to confuse the authorship of some tales during the nineteenth century. [Bodleian]

Précis de la vie des ouvrages de Ch. Perrault. Les Contes de fées par Charles Perrault. Vol. 1 of *Le cabinet des fées; ou Collection choisie des contes des fées et autres contes merveilleux.* Edited by Charles-Joseph, Chevalier de Mayer and Charles Georges Thomas Garnier. Amsterdam, 1785.

> This forty-one-volume work (1785–89) is considered the first major collection of fairy tales written in French dating from the 1690s to the moment of its publication. Shortly after this period, the heyday of the tale was said to decline in France, making the *Cabinet* its apogee, but English publishers renewed interest in tales by identifying them as vintage and selling their antiquity as an asset (see especially Tabart 1804 and later). The *Cabinet* contains all of Perrault's tales in prose and verse, as well as those of his contemporaries and Jeanne-Marie Leprince de Beaumont. A resource in the nineteenth century for such translators as J. R. Planché (see below).[44] [BNF]

Old Mother Goose's Interesting Stories of Past Times. Being a Collection of the best Fairy Tales; some of them related by eminent princes and princesses, Who, By the Gifts of Fairies, have risen from Obscurity and Oppression to the Highest Pitch of Grandeur: as reward either for their Good-nature, Fortitude, Virtuous Inclination, or Docility of Disposition. London: S. Fisher and T. Hurst, 1803.

---

[44]See Paul James Buczkowski, "Le Cabinet des fées," in *The Greenwood Encyclopedia of Folktales and Fairy Tales*, ed. Donald Haase and Anne Duggan (Westport, CT: Greenwood, 2016), 1:164–65.

Perhaps a reprint of Collins's version of Samber—the character's name is "Cinderilla" and Blue Beard's cutlass is a scimitar—without illustrations or morals. Omits "Little Red Riding Hood" and "Puss in Boots," and places d'Aulnoy and Leprince de Beaumont's stories first, followed by "Sleeping Beauty in the Wood." Title is evidence of a shifting perception of the stories, notably reading them as a celebration of virtue and "docility," and their past as a golden age. Images of the period also age Mother Goose, who goes from being a strong young maternal figure in the Clouzier, reprinted for much of the century, to a very old woman. A rare translation that returns to the 1697 order of the stories after the Desbordes/Samber reordering. [Osborne]

Winter Avond Vertillingen van Grootmoeder de Gans. Amsterdam: G. Roos, 1803.

Dutch edition of adaptations listed here for the rare change in title from Mother to "Grandmother" Goose,[45] which is not unlike the addition of "Old" in the Fisher edition above. The introduction, registering concern about the violence in traditional tales, encourages parents to read them aloud to their children and explain that they are make-believe.[46] [private collection]

Tabart's Collection of Popular Stories for the Nursery: Newly Translated and Revised from the French, Italian, and Old English Writers. 3 vols. London: Tabart & Co., 1804.

Perrault's tales appear in part 2 of the volume, along with "Beauty and the Beast" by Leprince de Beaumont and "Fortunio," published by Marie-Catherine d'Aulnoy in her collection *Contes des fées* (1698). Here is the first translation of "Les Fées" as "Diamonds and Toads," the name by which the tale type is commonly known today. All parts are bound together with a single table of contents. [Clark]

---

[45]The title page has been reprinted and can be viewed in P. J. Buijnsters, "Nederlandse kinderboeken uit de achttiende eeuw," in *De hele Bibelebontse berg: De geschiedenis van het kinderboek in Nederland & Vlaanderen van de middeleeuwen tot heden,* ed. Harry Bekkering (Amsterdam: Em. Querido's Uitgeverij, 1989), 226, www.dbnl.org/tekst/buij001nede02_01/buij001nede02_01_0001.php#2.

[46]The editor's introduction is discussed in the recent MA thesis on Perrault and Dutch Romanticism by Dan Doedens, "La Traduction des contes de Charles Perrault, l'influence du Romantisme" (MA thesis, Utrecht University, 2012), 23–24, dspace.library.uu.nl/handle/1874/252603.

The court of Oberon, or, Temple of the fairies: a collection of tales of past times originally told by Mother Goose, Mother Bunch, and others. Adapted to the Language and Manners of the Present Period. London: John Harris and Son, 1823.

The title references the allegorizing habit of the period, during which Mother Goose begins to stand in for Perrault and Mother Bunch for Marie-Catherine d'Aulnoy, whose tales achieve widespread celebrity under these monikers. These are Samber's translations from Collins (e.g., "scimitar") without the morals. Lhéritier's "Discreet Princess" is printed with Perrault's eight tales, as in Samber, and thus credited to Mother Goose. After Mother Bunch's tales (all d'Aulnoy's) appear "Popular Tales," among them "Beauty and the Beast." [Osborne][47]

The Book of Nursery Tales. A Keepsake for the young. London: James Burns, 1845.

Ornately illustrated in the Arts and Crafts style. Cinderella is depicted in the frontispiece and appears first in this volume, which describes its contents as "a series of old favourites, in a somewhat new, and it is hoped, agreeable dress." Published in three series of single-story prints, each of which included adapted versions of tales first published by Perrault: series 1, *Cinderella*; series 2, *The Sleeping Beauty*; series 3, *The Story of the Little Red Cap*[48] and *The Story of Blue Beard.* The preface goes on to explain that the uniqueness of the volume consists in the fact that "no particular traditional version of any of [the tales] has been adhered to." Instead, the editors explain, they took many versions and from them formed "one which should embrace what is most pleasing to all." The preface ends with "The Adventures of Fairy-Tale," a story of how the genre was threatened by science but survived to become a "keepsake." In the wake of the Grimms' *Kinder- und Hausmärch*en, published in seven editions from 1812 to 1857, Perrault's tales were slowly absorbed into what was construed as a popular well of story plots. While many editions still appeared under his name and the names his English translator, Robert Samber, gave to characters, the folkloristic idea that the stories themselves were timeless and organic

---

[47]The Osborne copy has been digitized: archive.org/details/courtofoberonort00perriala.
[48]"Little Red Cap" became the standard translation of the Grimm's "Rotkäppchen." Note that this title had already appeared as the English translation of Perrault's "Petit chaperon rouge" in Neaulme, 1745.

exerted increasing influence on how tales were packaged and pitched to readers. [Osborne]

The Traditional faëry tales: of Little Red Riding Hood, Beauty and the beast, & Jack and the beanstalk. Illustrated by Eminent Modern Artists. Edited by Felix Summerly. London (Old Bond Street): Joseph Cundall, 1845.

Summerly is the pen name of Sir Henry Cole. One of two collections of "faëry tales" published by Cundall in the 1840s. Three of Perrualt's tales are distributed between them (see below). The Clark has two copies, one with the illustrations in black and white and another with them hand-colored. [Clark]

The Popular faëry tales of Jack the Giant Killer, Cinderella, and Sleeping Beauty. Illustrated by Eminent Modern Artists. Edited by Felix Summerly. London (Old Bond Street): Joseph Cundall, 1846.

Finely designed pages with black and red lettering in the title, ornate borders of drawn flora and fauna, and Summerly's initials in a crest. Illustrated by popular Victorian illustrators Henry James Townsend ("Jack the Giant Killer") and John Absolon ("Cinderella" and "Sleeping Beauty").[49] Townsend was a member of the Etching Club group of artists, which over its forty-year existence put out illustrated editions of such early modern authors as Milton and Goldsmith. Absolon was a watercolor artist and secretary of the New Society of Painters in Water Colour who painted scenery for royal productions of Shakespeare. Cinderella's crueler sister calls her "Cinder-wench," the translation that Andrew Lang chose later in the century. [Osborne]

George Cruikshank's fairy library: Hop O' My Thumb (1853), Jack and the Bean Stalk (1854), Cinderella (1854), and Puss in Boots (1864). Translated and Illustrated by George Cruikshank. 4 vols. London: Bell and Daldy, 1853–64.

As the dates in the title suggest, each tale had been published separately as elements of the collection, printed over ten years. Cinderella has no nasty name in this version and instead of a fairy has a dwarf godmother, described as a "little old lady." The godmother refers to

---

[49]The Osborne catalogue notes that this attribution appears in Ruari MacLean's *Joseph Cundall, a Victorian Publisher* (Pinner, UK: Private Libraries Association, 1976), 83.

her charge as "Cindy, my darling." Numerous extant copies, some catalogued with graphic arts or sketches. The Osborne has digitized the 1870 edition.[50] [BL]

Four and Twenty Fairy Tales. Selected from Perrault and Other Popular Writers. Translated by James Robinson Planché. London / New York: Routledge & Co., 1858.

Large volume that begins with six of Perrault's tales: "Blue Beard," "The Sleeping Beauty in the Wood," "Master Cat; Or, Puss in Boots," "Cinderella; Or, The Little Glass Slipper," "Riquet with the Tuft," and "Little Thumbling." In addition to translation, James Robinson Planché was known for staging fairy tales as extravaganzas. He adapted tales by Perrault and Marie-Catherine d'Aulnoy for the musical burlesque. In the earlier part of his career, he staged *Riquet with the Tuft* as a "grand, comical, allegorical, magical, musical burlesque burletta."[51] Such burlesques have roots in street theater, especially the Théâtre de la foire, popular theater performed during the annual Easter fairs in France, of which the main center in Paris was Saint-Germain (now Saint-Germain-des-Prés).[52] At the turn of the nineteenth century, fairy-tale characters danced and sang in vaudeville follies and *opéra-féeries* (fairy operas) at indoor venues, notably the Opéra-Comique and Théâtre des Variétés in Paris.[53]

Planché had previously published a translation of Marie-Catherine d'Aulnoy's tales, *Fairy Tales of the Countess d'Aulnoy* (London: Routledge, 1855). Because his annotated translations of d'Aulnoy met with success, he explains in the preface to *Four and Twenty Fairy Tales*, he wanted to try his hand at others, beginning with the "earliest" and

---

[50]The British Library has digitized an illustration from "Jack" and the "Cinderella" frontispiece: www.bl.uk/collection-items/george-cruikshanks-fairy-library.

[51]J. R. Planché and Charles Dance, *Riquet with the Tuft: A grand comical, allegorical, magical, musical burlesque burletta in 1 act* [performed at London's Royal Olympic Theatre, December 26, 1836] (London: Chapman and Hall, circa 1837).

[52]See footnote 1 above. By the mid-eighteenth century, Perrault's characters were appearing by name alongside traditional commedia dell'arte characters such as Pierrot in librettos for comic opera; see Louis Anseaume, *Cendrillon, opéra-comique de M. Anseaume* [performed in Paris, Saint-Germain, February 20, 1759] (Paris: N.-B. Duchesne, 1759). [BNF]

[53]See Marc-Antoine Désaugiers and Michel-Joseph Gentil de Chavagnac, *La petite Cendrillon ou La chatte merveilleuse: folie vaudeville en 1 acte* [Performed in Paris, Théâtre des Variétés, November 22, 1810]. According to the notice at the Bibliothèque nationale de France [FRBNF39499023], the part of Cendrillon was played by an actor, Brunet, who was also artistic director at the Théâtre des Variétés. The part was cross-dressed, a feature of vaudeville in France and panto in Britain.

"latest" of the celebrated French authors in the *Cabinet des fées*, to wit, Perrault and Leprince de Beaumont. Taking issue with the century of Samber and, we come to understand, the infantilizing tendencies of the early nineteenth century, he argues that none of the authors of the period save Leprince de Beaumont (who did her own translations) has been "placed in their integrity before the English reader" until now. The tales have been chosen—the shortest tales are gone—and ordered, with "Blue Beard" first, to appeal to "children of a larger growth." This translation returns to the word *cutlass* in "Blue Beard" and adds historical footnotes for items such as fashion and food, e.g., a description of the *collet-monté* (high collar) in Cinderella and that the name *sauce Robert* was coined by Tallevent, chef to Charles VII in 1456 (that is, Guillaume Tiral, known as Taillevent, chef to Charles V and VI). It ends with a lengthy appendix that presents each author's biography and a discussion of each tale in the volume. [Clark]

Fairy Realm. A Collection of the Favourite Old Tales. Illustrated by the Pencil of Gustave Doré. Told in Verse by Tom Hood. London: Ward, Lock, & Tyler, 1866.

Includes "Sleeping Beauty," "Little Red Riding Hood," "Puss in Boots," "Cinderella," and "Hop O' My Thumb" in verse translations. The tales are called "fairy legends" in the short preface by Hood. Title attests to the century's desire to give fairy tales a patina, associating them both with the faraway past and with popular culture. Language like "original" and "the history of" becomes common in this period, especially attached to Mother Goose. See "Early Translations" above. [UCLA and numerous others]

Old Nursery Tales and Popular Stories. With eight coloured pictures and numerous other illustrations. London: Ward, Lock, & Tyler, 1869.

Same publisher as the *Fairy Realm,* with the same reference to age in the title. Tales are not in verse. Includes "Little Red Riding Hood" from Perrault alongside "Jack in the Beanstalk" and "Beauty and the Beast," as in the Summerly 1845. [Osborne]

The Original Mother Goose's Melody, as issued by John Newbery, London, circa 1760; Isaiah Thomas of Worcester, circa 1785, and Monroe & Francis, circa 1825. Reproduced in fac-simile from the first Worcester edition. With Introductory notes by William H. Whitmore. To which are added The Fairy

Tales of Mother Goose, first collected by Perrault in 1696, reprinted from the original translation into English by R. Samber in 1729. Boston: Damrell & Upham / New York: Griffith, Farran, & Co., Limited / London: Newbery House, 1892.[54]

The tales reprinted here are taken from a 1795 edition of Samber's translation.[55] Nineteenth-century editors promoted the idea of Perrault as a collector rather than author of fairy tales, as well as the conjunction of fairy tales and nursery melodies under the figure of Mother Goose. Jacob and Wilhelm Grimm had popularized this image of Perrault in the 1812 introduction to their *Kinder- und Hausmärchen*, when they cited him as a source for their nationalist project of folktale recovery within the Germanic states. With the rise of folklore and ethnography as disciplines, it became convenient for some—such as Andrew Lang—to consider Perrault a collector and disseminator of popular lore and for others—folklorists such as Vladimir Propp—to identify him with authorship and literary history, distancing Perrault from what they defined as folktales.[56] A review of the book in the *Nation*, March 10, 1892, notes, "This entertaining monograph . . . is of course mainly for adult readers." [Cotsen; a dozen copies worldwide]

The Sleeping Beauty and other Fairy Tales. Translations by Sir Arthur Quiller-Couch (1863–1944). Illustrations by Edmund Dulac. New York: George H. Doran, 1910.

In an editorial gesture that is rare for books on this list, Quiller-Couch explains his motivations as a translator in the preface. He admits that the choice "to omit Perrault's conclusion of *La Belle au Bois Dormant*" was bold. "To my amazement the editor of the *Cabinet des Fées* selects this lame sequel—it is no better than a sequel—of a lovely tale, and assigns to it the credit of having established 'la véritable fortune de ce

---

[54]Welch lists 1786 as the first print of the Isaiah Thomas edition (*Bibliography,* 295).

[55]William Whitmore's introduction, dated 1890, first appeared in a reprint of the Isaiah Thomas edition. In it, he clarified for the first time the relationship of Perrault to Mother Goose and Mother Goose to nursery rhymes, *The Original Mother Goose's Melody* (Albany: J. Munsell's Sons, 1889). The problem with the dates suggests that the Munsell edition must have been released in 1890. Whitmore became an authoritative source on the subject, as evinced here. In his introduction, Whitmore registers confusion about the first date of an English publication of Perrault's stories. He takes as proof the mention by Andrew Lang of a 1729 translation that no one, to date, had seen. babel.hathitrust.org/cgi/pt?id=mdp.39015013339307;view=1up;seq=10.

[56]See the discussion of Mother Goose in the introduction and Maria Tatar's genealogy of the term in *The Hard Facts of the Grimms' Fairy Tales*, 106–14.

genre' [the great success of this genre]. Frankly, I cannot believe him." Although this is not the first edition to significantly edit the tales, it is the first one that provides an explanation related to the genre. The lengthy tale construed by the 1785 *Cabinet* editors as formative of the genre no longer corresponds to what the early twentieth-century identifies as a fairy tale. Quiller-Couch's explanation thus provides a litmus test for the sensibilities of his age. That "lame sequel" was the story of married life, here removed to bring Sleeping Beauty in line with the stereotype that tales should tell the story of courtship and end in marriage. [BL, Lilly, and various other libraries]

EARLY SINGLE-TALE TRANSLATIONS IN CHAPBOOK EDITIONS

A series of early single-tale editions at the Bodleian attest to the popularity of inexpensive, small-format books for a wider and increasingly younger audience at the end of the eighteenth century. Once Perrault's plots began to appear individually in chapbooks, often with condensed or adapted story lines and rarely attributed to him, "Sleeping Beauty," "Cinderella," and a highly Orientalized "Bluebeard" emerged as the most popular, as far as extant editions would suggest. After Jacob and Wilhelm Grimm published the *Kinder- und Hausmärchen* (first edition 1812), "Little Red Riding Hood" gained in popularity, and finally so did "Puss in Boots." Other media, such as pantomimes and extravaganzas, helped promote particular story lines as well.

The sleeping beauty in the wood. London: Aldermary Church Yard, c. 1775.[57]

> The Bodleian has a series of chapbooks under this title: Derby 1787 and 1790, and possibly Nottigham 1796 (illustrated with woodcuts). Also, *The Master cat; or, Puss in boots. Whereunto is added, The story of a man with a blue beard*, published at Aldermary c. 1740–70. [Bodleian]

The sleeping beauty in the wood: an oriental tale. Nottingham: Burbage & Co., c. 1790–1800.

> Simple edition with a single woodcut on the title page, which includes a "New song call'd poor Davy and Molly." This title heralds the Romantic "Orientalizing" of many classical fairy tales in the nineteenth

---

[57] The Opies, *The Classic Fairy Tales,* mention a copy as early as 1764, but do not identify its location (perhaps a private collection).

century. Perrault's "Barbe bleue" became one of the most consistently Orientalized tales of the collection. [Osborne]

The History of Blue Beard or, The fatal effects of curiosity & disobedience. London: John Evans, c. 1792–1812.

Evidence of another nineteenth-century habit of making explicit in the title or language of an edition a moral interpretation of the "Blue Beard" tale, rendering it a cautionary lesson for women. In point of fact, curiosity and disobedience are fatal not to the heroine who perpetrates them but to Blue Beard. [Bodleian]

The Sleeping Beauty in the Wood. A Tale. 1796.

A basic edition that was never prepared for reading, it consists of a large piece of square paper folded up to the size of a small card. Pages remain uncut, but unfolded it contains twenty-six frames. The title and back page both have a bulky woodcut of unclear relationship to the text. It is a slightly modified reprint of the Collins edition with footnotes. (See "Early Translations" above). [Osborne]

Little Red Riding Hood, The Fairy, and Blue Beard. Philadelphia: John M'Culloch, 1797.

Selective collection of Perrault's shortest tales, with the rare addition of "The Fairy." [AAS]

Blue-beard; or, Female curiosity!: a dramatick romance; first represented at the Theatre Royal Drury-Lane, on Tuesday, January 16th, 1798. Written by George Colman. London: T. Woodfall for Cadell and Davies, 1798.

Several of Perrault's stories were adapted to the stage at the turn of the nineteenth century. This one offers the title "Female Curiosity," which will become the hallmark theme associated with the tale for the rest of its print history. [Bodleian]

Cinderilla, or, The little glass slipper. Litchfield, CT: Printed by T. Collier, c. 1800.

Early U.S. single-story reprint of the Samber translation with his spelling, "Cinderilla," which persists until about 1825.[58] [Beinecke]

---

[58]Ibid., 326–27.

The History of Blue Beard: an entertaining story for children. c. 1800.

> Curiously titled chapbook that explicitly targets child readers for the lessons of "Blue Beard," undoubtedly Perrault's most macabre tale. [Bodleian]

A new history of Blue Beard. Written by Gaffer Black Beard, for the amusement of Little Lack Beard, and his pretty sisters. Adorned with cuts. Hartford, CT: John Babcock / Philadelphia: John Adams, 1800.

> A fully Orientalized story of a man named Abomelique, known as "Blue Beard," and his daughters Fatima and Irene. Fatima is married off to a nobleman named Selim who forbids her to go into one chamber of his home. When she does, she finds the bodies of his former wives and a belated warning written in blood upon the wall, "*The punishment of curiosity.*" In the period, according to the *OED*, "gaffer" referred to a man below the rank of those addressed as "Master." Typically classified among the stories of Perrault, who is credited as the source.[59] [Beinecke, Bodleian, Osborne]

Cinderella, or, The little glass slipper: a tale for the nursery. From the French of C. Perrault. With three copper plates. 16th edition. London: Tabart and Co. at the Juvenile and School Library, 1804.

> Identified on the cover as an "updated" new edition. Hand-colored plates. Tabart's version of the story may be the first appearance of the current spelling of Cinderella, though he places it in the genealogy of Samber reprints as the sixteenth edition. Explicitly identifies the story with young children. A host of theatricalized versions of the story of Cinderella, under this title, were performed and printed at the time. See the Toronto Public Library Catalogue. All single-story prints issued by Tabart in 1804 are hand colored and part of the Tabart's Collection of Popular Stories for the Nursery series edited by William Godwin.[60] [Osborne]

The Sleeping Beauty in the Wood. London: Laurie & Whittle, 1804.

> Published November 9, after Tabart's edition published in July, the date on the frontispiece (below). Perhaps a pirated edition. [Osborne]

---

[59]See Welch's list of American editions (*Bibliography*, 323–25).
[60]The Osborne catalogue indicates that Godwin may also have translated them (vol. 1, 24).

The Sleeping Beauty in the Wood. With Three Copperplates. A New Edition. London: Tabart and Co. at the Juvenile and School Library, 1804.

This version ends the story when the princess wakes and marries the prince, omitting about the last third of Perrault's tale, a feature that becomes standard in editions meant for all ages over the century. New in Tabart's frontispiece and illustrations are the Orientalized costumes of the prince and princess. [Osborne]

Blue Beard, or, Female curiosity; and, Little Red Riding-Hood. Tales for the nursery from the French of C. Perrault. With copperplates. London: Tabart and Co. at the Juvenile and School Library, 1806.

Listed as the tenth edition in Lilly's catalogue and testimony to the widespread interpretation of "Blue Beard" as a cautionary tale about female curiosity, paired here with the ultimate cautionary tale about a girl who perishes. Part of the series Tabart's Popular Tales, edited by William Godwin. [Lilly]

Blue Beard, or, The fatal effects of curiosity and disobedience, illustrated with elegant and appropriate engravings. London: John Harris, 1808.

Marks the beginning of two decades of single-story prints from Harris, who issued Perrault's whole collection in 1804. A rare verse edition of "Blue Beard" with attendant illustrations that claim explicitly to serve the didactic purpose to which the otherwise macabre story is put. [Lilly]

Cinderella, or the Little Glass Slipper. London: John Harris, 1808.

Rhymed version of the tale, thus adapted for very young readers/listeners. Republished in 1825 in Cambridge bound with other stories under the title *A New Year's gift for little masters and misses.* [Osborne]

The curious adventures of Cinderilla, or, The history of a glass slipper. Price three-pence. London: R. Harrild, 20 Great Eastcheap, c. 1809–21.

Eastcheap is a marketplace in east Cheap, a ward in London. Cheap takes its name from the Old English *ceapan*, "to buy," which is also the root of *chapbook*. It was an important market area from the Middle Ages on. The price and location of sale of this edition suggest that it was produced very inexpensively—even among chapbooks—for the mass market. As a point of comparison, Tabart sold the 1804 *Sleeping Beauty* for six pence. [Clark]

Riquet with the tuft: a tale for the nursery. London: Printed for Tabart and Co. at the Juvenile and School Library, 1809.

One of Perrault's less commonly printed tales, except in the Juvenile Libraries series. This nonviolent story of beauty and intelligence is a logical choice for a children's adaptation. This edition borrows from Catherine Bernard's 1698 version and makes Riquet the "King of the Gnomes." Part of the series Tabart's Popular Tales, edited by William Godwin. [Lilly]

The Adventures of Cinderella. London: G. Martin, Cheapside, 1810.

Cheapside was the district on the west side of London formerly known as Westcheap, in contrast to the Eastcheap market area. [Clark]

Blue Beard or, The fatal effects of curiosity & disobedience. Philadelphia: William Charles, 1810.

The American edition of the 1808 Harris title above, which brings to the U.S. market the now widespread habit of associating curiosity in this tale with a type of disobedience that warrants punishment. Published again in 1815. [Beinecke]

Cinderella, or the Little Glass Slipper; versified and beautifully Illustrated with Figures. London: S. and J. Fuller, 1814.

A paper doll book printed in 1814 and reissued in 1819 in England; published in the United States in 1815 (see next entry). Fuller began issuing books with cutout paper doll characters in 1810. This book comes with seven hand-painted figures, five bodies with moveable heads (including Cinderella), and a fold-up coach. Its pages feature costumes as headless images onto which the cutout of Cinderella's head can be placed as she moves through the various scenes of her adventure.[61]

---

[61]The Opies reproduced a few pages from it in color, including the floating head to show how the book worked (*The Classic Fairy Tales*, 118–19). A more extensive series of photos from the Morgan edition have been scanned and are described on the *Jane Austen's World* blog, especially for their historical relevance to the culture of Regency England. janeaustensworld. wordpress.com/2011/05/29/1814-and-1819-edition-of-the-childrens-book-cinderella-or-the-little-glass-slipper/.

The costumes are a hybrid of period and Renaissance style, attesting to playful innovation that comes of preserving and also updating a tale from the past. Versification was an opportunity to turn a tale into an extended nursery rhyme designed for children old enough to be able to read it while playing with the cutout scenes. The figures further provide an opportunity for embellishment of the scenario by the reader. [Osborne, 1814; PML, 1819]

Cinderella, or the Little Glass Slipper. Beautifully versified. Illustrated with Elegant Figures to Dress and Undress. Philadelphia: William Charles, 1815.

Another William Charles reprint of a British edition of a Perrault adaptation, this one of the Fuller 1814 paper doll book. [AAS—missing the figures]

Blue Beard, and The Little Red Riding Hood; Tales for the Nursery. With Three Copper Plates. A New Edition. New York: L. & F. Lockwood, 1818.

"Tales for the Nursery" may refer to Tabart's 1806 edition, especially as it features the same pairing of cautionary tales about girls issued for young children. [AAS]

The Entertaining Story of Little Red Riding Hood. To which is added, Tom Thumb's Story. Adorned with cuts. York: J. Kendrew, c. 1820.

A penny chapbook in prose. Pairing of the two tales in the collection that feature protagonists identified with being little. [Osborne]

The History of Cinderella, or, The glass slipper. London: R. Miller, 1820.

This edition features a new practice of using "the history" for *histoires*, usually translated "histories" or "stories." In this period, too, the age of the stories adds to their charm and becomes a way of offering them as lessons from the past. [Osborne]

The History of Little Red Riding Hood; or, The Deceitful Wolf. Plymouth: Bird and Ackland. Sold in Devonport by W. Pollard and J. Mudge, 1820.

Bound with "The Entertaining History of little Goody Two-Shoes," a well-known tale, and "The holiday queen" by Mrs. L. L. B. Cameron. There appear to be no single-print editions of "Little Red Riding

Hood" from the nineteenth century, no doubt owing to its brevity. Here, Bird and Ackland give the wolf equal billing in the title and highlight the quality that comes to define the popular moral of the story. [Osborne]

Mother Hubbard: The Adventures of the beautiful little maid Cinderilla, or, The history of a glass slipper. York: J. Kendrew, 1822.

Late occurrence of Samber's spelling of "Cinderilla"; the name stabilized as Cinderella in England and the United States circa 1820. The Osborne copy has a rhyme on the cover, suggestive of its intended youthful audience: "Now for rabbits, a shilling a piece / Pray will you buy a couple? / Or, if you choose to buy a leash / I'd not quite charge you double." [Clark, Osborne]

Adventures of the beautiful little maid Cinderilla, or, The history of a glass slipper: to which is added, An historical description of the cat. York: J. Kendrew, c. 1825.

Reprint of the 1822 edition followed by a cautionary description of the domestic short-haired cat, its descent from wild cats, and its "thieving propensity," "uncommonly rough" tongue, and "exceedingly sharp" claws. [Clark, Osborne]

The history of Cinderella; or, The little glass slipper. Otley: William Walker, 1825.

Printed as part of the Walker Juvenile Library series, which includes twenty-five other titles. Editors tell readers in the preface, "The story of Cinderella has generally been allowed to be pleasing and interesting to the youthful mind. We are not, however, about to assert the truth of what is here related." These stories were once believed, they relate, but can no longer be regarded as true. While youthful minds may be astonished by the tale, they can also learn something from it. Already in the first quarter of the century, editors became interested in emphasizing the antique, fantastical quality of classic fairy tales. Disclaimers about the tales' fictional nature also justified accommodating plots to current cultural norms; here, the editors add a sequence to the beginning so that readers witness Cinderella's father wooing his second bride. The rise of folkloristic methods in the second quarter of the century intensified these editorial practices. See Ward, Lock, & Tyler, 1869 in "Early Collections" above. [Osborne]

The surprising adventures of Puss in Boots, or, The master-cat. Printed by S. and R. Bentley. London: John Harris, c. 1827.

A verse translation of the tale with hand-colored plates. Harris published many editions of the collection and other stories in prose, and also issued a rhymed version of Cinderella in 1808 (see above). [Clark]

Blue Beard; or, Female Curiosity. An Eastern Tale. London: Orlando Hodgson, c. 1835.

Female Curiosity is a common subtitle of this tale by the beginning of the nineteenth century and appears to work in tandem with the Orientalizing fashions of the day. The tale's heroine, Fatima, finds a clear and frightening message when she enters the former wives' death chamber; "The Reward of Disobedience and impudent Curiosity." See Adams edition of 1800 above. [Osborne]

Twenty seven Devonport chapbooks. Devonport: Printed by Samuel & John Keys, c. 1835.

Samuel and John Keys published a series of twenty-seven chapbooks, each one numbered, of which four are tales by Perrault: "The History of Cinderella," "The History of Little Red Riding Hood, "The History of Tom Thumb," and "The History of Blue Beard." No. 1 in the series, "The Child's gift," seems to have lent its name to a new edition printed in Boston in 1852, *Good child's fairy gift*, with the three tales numbered as in the Keys edition. Much later in the century, the Keys continued to publish these single-story editions of Perrault. "The History of Blue Beard" and "The Surprising Adventures of Puss in Boots" are listed in the Opie Collection. No. 26 in the series is entitled "The amusing history of Mother Goose." [Clark]

Little Red Riding Hood: An entirely new edition. Edited by Felix Summerly. Illustrated by Thomas Webster. London: Joseph Cundall, 1843.

Sir Henry Cole's edition from Cundall's press, with which he also worked to put out a collection in 1846 featuring "Cinderella" and "Sleeping Beauty." See "Early Collections" above. The preface indicates that the British Museum owns a 1698 copy of Perrault's French text under the title *Contes de Ma Mère L'Oye,* but that Cole does not know when it was first translated into English. He notes, too, that he has "not less than five *penny* editions of a primitive sort" that do not look more than fifty years old. The "new" edition transforms the story into a culturally relevant moral tale, about fifteen pages in length. Little Red Riding Hood lives in a thatched cottage in Hampshire, the daughter of a faggot maker and a spinner whose grandmother teaches her to knit and pray. [Clark, Osborne][62]

Little Red Riding Hood. Derby and London: John and Charles Mozley, c. 1845.

Mozley issued *Blue Beard, or, Fatal Curiosity* the same year. Identified as "half-penny" and "two-penny" editions, respectively, they are thus inexpensive. Both are illustrated with woodcuts.

The History of Cinderella. Printed for the booksellers. Otley: Yorkshire J. S. publishing co., limited, c. 1850.

Otley issued *Little Red Riding Hood* the same year. Rhymed versions of the tales with plain, colored woodcuts and printed, as the title suggests, for wide distribution. Poems wittily sum up whole scenes in just a line or two, such as this couplet on the book's last page: "Her foot slipp'd in with ease—the girls looked blue, / When from her pocket she its fellow drew" (8). [Osborne]

The History of the Sleeping Beauty. A fairy tale play together with two Christmas stories. London: W. S. Johnson, 1850.

Perrault's and d'Aulnoy's tales were adapted by the early nineteenth century to be performed as pantomimes, or "panto." These extravagant stage shows were based on traditional fairy tales done into song, dance, and slapstick physical comedy with stock characters that encouraged audience interaction, of which the main performances, such as Principal Boy and Dame, were cross-dressed roles. They were (and still are) traditionally performed around Christmas. [Osborne]

Little Red Riding Hood, illuminated with ten pictures. Illustrated by W. H. Thwaites. New York: H. W. Hewet, c. 1855.

Produced in the Hewet's Illuminated Household Stories for Little Folks series. At twenty-eight pages, this edition of the tale is longer than the

---

[62]The Osborne copy has been digitized: archive.org/details/littleredridingh00summiala.

already greatly expanded Summerly edition above. In most editions in French and English, the tale does not exceed three to five pages in length. Thwaites was a prolific "penny dreadful" illustrator. The same year he illustrated "Puss in Boots" to be published in the Hewet's series through D. Appleton & Company of New York and "Beauty and the Beast" through Loomis & Co., New York. [Clark]

Puss in Boots. Illustrated by Otto Speckter. New Edition. London: John Murray, 1856.

In this version, the ogre is a "wicked Magician" who has "carried science to such a pitch" that he can shape-shift. Speckter's plate shows him wearing Merlin's hat and robes in a room of curiosities with a telescope and large books.[63] [Houghton]

The Marquis of Carabas, picture book. Illustrated by Walter Crane. London: George Routledge and Sons, 1874.

A versified version of "Puss in Boots" named instead for the fictitious title and kingdom given to the poor protagonist by his cat. Done by the printer Edmund Evans, who pioneered color woodblock printing (chromoxylography) in the 1850s, which permitted long runs at a low cost, ideal for books designed for children. Taking advantage of the decreasing cost of printing in color, Routledge commissioned a series of "picture books" from Crane. Illustrations cover the page, often printed across two (verso and recto), and the text appears in a simple rectangular cartouche off the side or bottom of the image. Today Evans's picture books are considered the first type of reading materials designed expressly for child readers to make sense of the story through images—what we know today as a children's book. [BL]

---

[63] Appears between pp. 16 and 17: babel.hathitrust.org/cgi/pt?id=hvd.hn2gk7;view=1up;seq=39.

Index

CPSIA information can be obtained
at www.ICGtesting.com
Printed in the USA
LVOW01s0818121016

508382LV00003B/3/P